FATAL BLADE

Decker's War — Book 3

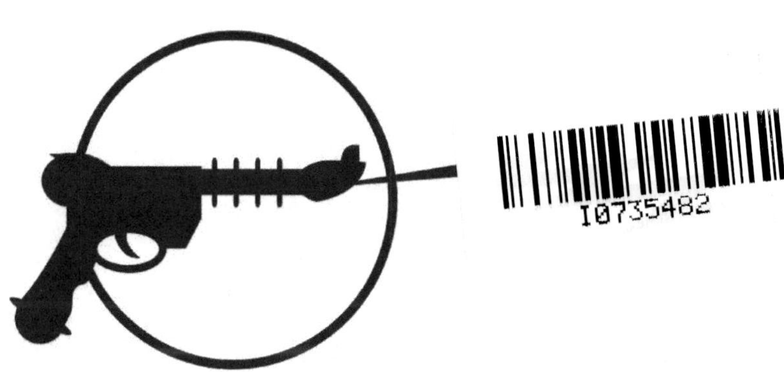

ERIC THOMSON

Fatal Blade
Copyright 2016 Eric Thomson
This paperback edition February 2019

Published in Canada
By Sanddiver Books
ISBN: 978-1-989314-10-4

— ONE —

"I have a lock on the beacon, Major." *Mikado*'s chief signalman glanced up at the tall officer standing behind him. "But it's broadcasting something strange."

"Why am I not surprised?" The Marine asked. "After all, we're dealing with some of the weirder folks from naval intelligence."

"Did we get the bugger yet, sir?" A gravelly voice asked from the door to the bridge. "The guys are loading up."

"If the message '*try to remember north is at the top of the compass*' means our drop zone party is in place, then yes."

A sound very much like a volcano about to erupt rumbled deep within the newcomer's barrel chest.

"I'm going to guess," Sergeant-Major Augustus Vanleith said, "that Decker is sitting comfortably under a tree, making bets with his partner over how many of us are going to miss the tiny clearing he's marked."

"You may laugh all you want, sarn't-major, just as long it's secure, and he's scouted out the target area properly," Major Kal Ryent, commanding officer of the 251st, replied.

"I doubt spending time with intelligence has rotted Zack's brains to the extent of forgetting where he came from, sir. He'll have us in the stockade and out again before dawn, with the Garonne rebels and the Navy's undercover guy."

Vanleith fell into step beside his CO as they headed for the starboard hangar deck to join the assault group.

"Although," he continued, "promotion to chief warrant officer sometimes does screw with an old command sergeant's brains, I'll grant you that."

"Not for you then, that kind of promotion?"

"And do what? I'm not a specialist, and I don't want to become one."

"Decker's a grunt and still got a warrant," Ryent pointed out.

They climbed down a circular staircase and stepped into a cavernous hold where troops in battle armor were boarding black stealth shuttles.

The compartment, configured as a flight deck, took up half of the extra space in *Mikado*'s belly. Although at its core a fully armed frigate wrapped in a large freighter's hull, the special operations Q-ship looked like nothing more than an innocuous merchantman.

"Scuttlebutt says he wasn't given a choice," the sergeant-major pointed out. "Not for the warrant nor the detail to intelligence, and considering the route he took to get there, via the bottom of an endless whiskey bottle, early retirement and all, no thanks. I'm just glad he's back in the Corps and doing something he's good at."

"So I shouldn't be worried about the drop zone or the target recon?"

"Not even for a second and if it makes you feel any better, remember that he's got adult supervision with him."

"Seeing as how I know Decker's NILO personally, I'm not sure you're giving me much comfort."

**

The Naval Intelligence Liaison Officer in question checked their perimeter sensors one last time, to make sure none of them had decided to grow legs and walk away, or gone on strike; of course, sensors weren't unionized, but one never knew with intelligent technology.

Satisfied, she glanced at her partner, who seemed comfortably ensconced between the gnarled roots of a tall tree, faced lifted towards the night sky, a satisfied smile on his hard face.

"You look uncommonly pleased with yourself, Zack."

"It's good to be on the ground for once and watch intrepid pathfinders fly down, trying hard not to crash into trees or other painfully solid terrain features."

"Bullcrap." She smiled indulgently at him. "You miss jumping out of perfectly good shuttles."

"True, true." He nodded happily. "But I can get sufficient gratification in other ways."

She narrowed her eyes in suspicion at his pleasant smile. Though a commander outranked a mere chief warrant officer like Zack, Hera Talyn knew better than to take control of an operation involving his beloved pathfinders.

Decker had laid out the drop zone markers himself which meant he'd probably done or would be doing something to amuse himself at the jumpers' expense if the message he'd attached to the beacon's carrier wave was any indication.

"What are you up to?"

"Nothing, sweetie." He smirked at her. "Just keep your eyes and ears on the perimeter and I'll look up at the stars."

"Don't fall asleep while you're waiting. You seem awfully snug."

"No fear. We got a ping from *Mikado*. They have our signal locked in, and the drop ships are launching as we speak."

"You were going to share this with me when exactly?"

"The ping came in two heartbeats before I told you. If you weren't so busy clucking over my comfort, you'd have heard it."

Talyn glared at him.

"You're an ass, Decker."

"So you keep saying and yet we've been traipsing across the stars together for almost two years, knocking off the odd menace to the Commonwealth. You want to change partners, I'm sure Captain Ulrich will be happy to oblige."

"You think? You're my rescue project. I'm responsible for you and likely will be until the day you screw up again and go for retirement part two or until one of us swallows a shot of plasma."

"And I'm ever so grateful, commander, sir."

She gave him the rigid digit salute and for some reason, that seemed to amuse him more than it should have, but he settled back into his carefully smoothed out hollow and dropped the eyepiece of his night vision sensor down in front of his eyes. Then, he leaned his head against the rough bark of the exposed root at just the right angle to catch the pathfinders when they'd be on final approach. Decker had learned long ago that any idiot could be uncomfortable.

******

Mikado ejected its stealth shuttles moments after it was hidden from the orbital station by the bulk of Marengo, a minor and not very profitable colony near the Shrehari frontier. With the geosynchronous habitat out of sight, the assault force had little to fear from the civilian-grade satellites that encircled the planet's equator.

The craft sped downwards on a shallow approach, cutting through the upper atmosphere without leaving a trace. No light reflected off their black skins, no sensor wave bounced back to betray them. They made a full orbit around Marengo before reaching the planned jump altitude, some fifty kilometers southwest of Decker's position, at an altitude of twenty thousand meters, in a zone of rarefied air and intense cold.

Three pathfinder troops spilled into the night air, quickly pulling into a tight formation that would allow them to land near each other. Wind howled over their helmeted heads, but their battle armor sealed them off from both noise and chill.

Decker heard brief clicks from the lead shuttle over his receiver, signaling they'd dropped their load, and he began scanning the sky in earnest. Though only the pathfinders should be able to see the drop zone markers, it wouldn't do to turn them on too soon.

"We've got a flock of birdies in the sky, Hera."

Though his words were light-hearted, his tone had become deadly serious. She could never tell when Decker would act the consummate professional Marine or when he'd be the sarcastic, if not cynical warrior who'd long since grown weary of the Fleet's chickenshit. Evidently, manning a drop zone warranted the former.

"Yeah, I heard *that* signal. All is quiet on the perimeter."

Finally, after a long period of silence, the short-range link came to life with a human voice.

"Rookie Trooper, this is Grey Goose. I need a compass."

Zack glanced at Hera.

"This is it. Light up the markers and keep your eyes glued on the sensors. If the opposition got wise and made us, now would be the moment to attack."

Talyn touched her control pad and nodded.

"Done."

She could have sworn she heard Decker laugh softly in the darkness.

**

The kite parachutes opened at one thousand meters out and up from the drop zone just as the markers came on. When the command push crackled in Augustus Vanleith's ears, he knew exactly what his commanding officer's words would be.

"Please tell me I've had a stroke, sarn't-major."

"Sorry, sir. You're no more confused than the joker who set those markers. If it's any consolation, there's no doubt now that Decker's in charge of the DZ."

"Who in his right mind programs them to transmit a profoundly obscene sexual invitation in gutter Shrehari?"

"Decker?"

"He's not in his right mind." Ryent sounded resigned.

"Zack would be the first to admit it. Intelligence work isn't going to improve his sanity either. I just hope he didn't extend the prank to having us land in a fragrant cattle pasture or some reeking swamp."

"You'd think his NILO would be able to stop him from going that far, but I'm not sure I trust her any more than I trust him."

**

"Jumpers inbound." Decker climbed out of the comfortable hollow and grabbed his weapon. "Turn off the markers when I give you a shout, then make them vanish. I'll go greet my little airborne buddies."

"Zack?"

"Yeah?"

"You look much too pleased with yourself. What didn't you tell me?"

"Look at your controls."

He grinned at her, teeth shining white in the shadows.

"Really?" She said, shaking her head in disgust after scanning the readout. "The day you decide to grow up, let me know. I'll have the Fleet Times there to record the blessed event."

"It'll never happen, sweetheart. I may not be able to stay young, but I'll always remain immature. Besides, practical jokes are a tradition in the pathfinders."

He blew her a wet kiss and then vanished between the shrubs at the edge of the wood line.

Moments later, she heard the soft rustle of kite parachutes and then the equally muffled sound of feet touching the ground. Decker uttered a single word: off.

Talyn swiped the pad's screen, ordering the marker array to self-destruct and leave nothing behind but mounds of dust that would disperse on the morning breeze.

Ryent saw a dark silhouette with the correct IFF patch emerge from the gloom. By the size and the way the shape moved, it had to be Decker. That was soon confirmed when he dropped into a crouch and whispered a few nonsense words – the pre-arranged recognition code.

"It's Grey Goose, I assume?" Decker asked. "If it isn't, you've got the wrong DZ and are going to have to move along. I'm waiting for some sex tourists."

"Rookie Trooper, eh? Still a dumb name," Ryent replied, grasping Zack's hand, "but I suppose intelligence pukes need something to make themselves feel better about their sorry business. By the way, don't ever set the markers in a non-standard way for my outfit again."

Zack chuckled.

"Doctrine says the DZ master can arrange them to transmit anything he wants, provided they mark the area correctly."

"He's got you there," Vanleith said, going down on one knee beside his commanding officer. "The markers outlined the DZ magnificently. How's it going, Zack? One still hanging lower than the other?"

"You know it, Gus." Decker thumped his old buddy's shoulder.

"*Et tu*, sarn't-major?" Ryent shook his head. "Okay, I get it: non-com mafia. Subject closed and yes, it was funny in a stupid kind of way. Continuing the theme, therefore, what flesh pots do you have on offer, Mister Decker, and why are you wearing the local militia uniform rather than something more appropriate to a Fleet spook?"

Talyn joined their little cluster before Zack could answer, while around them, pathfinders packed their chutes and spread out to cover the perimeter.

"Our esteemed NILO I presume?" Ryent turned towards her. "How are you coping with your rescue project, commander?"

"He has his moments, Kal, but he's actually pretty good at it when he stops horsing around."

"Glad to hear. Perhaps one day, he'll grow up and become an entirely reasonable adult."

"I am here, you know," Zack said in a mock wounded tone.

"So you are." Ryent's mouth twitched. "You were about to tell me how we're going to liberate your colleague and his freedom fighter buddies, and also why you're looking like rejects from the Marengo militia. We thought of bringing you some armor, but the mission parameters were pretty clear."

"That's because we're going to waltz right through the main gate and take it from the inside."

"This, I've got to hear," Vanleith said, snorting.

"You're going to love my plan, Gus."

"The last time you said that we had to run for cover, but I'm willing to listen if the major is."

"The major would like to listen." Ryent's tone signaled that the time for banter was over.

"Yes, sir. Here's how I see it going..."

Decker went on to explain how he wanted to tackle the assault and when he fell silent, Ryent had to admit the plan seemed sound and unlikely to leave traces the local authorities could follow back to the Fleet. Plausible deniability was one of the pathfinders' unofficial principles of war. It was a way of life for Naval intelligence operatives.

"You're sure the sensor grid won't trip?" He asked, trying to poke holes in Decker's scheme.

"We found a way to spoof them. I won't guarantee we found every single one, but the necklace close to the fence is definitely ours. You can move up the squadron through the woods and no one the wiser."

"Comms?"

"We've got a cutter charge on the landline and a jammer ready to turn the airways into white noise on command."

"How about the relief force?"

"Ten klicks on the other side of the pass. They come in at first light every morning to change the guard detail and always by road. The militia has aircraft, but they're back at the main base outside Treves. We get in and out before sunrise, and they'll be looking at an empty camp."

Decker's jaw tightened.

"I mean, empty except for the militia pukes who'll get a taste of what they've been inflicting on the prisoners. There's just one wrinkle to work through. Four out of the five, including Badhorn — that would be our guy - are on the wrong side of walking wounded."

Ryent grimaced.

"And the orders say we need to keep Badhorn's cover intact. That means we need a pick-up on site. I had hoped we could hoof it out far enough that the dropships didn't have to come within sight of the prison. If we were only extracting him, that would still be an option, but I don't want to try carrying four of them through the jungle."

"As it happens, the central courtyard is big enough for your four birds. Where are they now?"

"Their glide path should have taken them to the off-shore island you designated." Ryent turned to his commo tech. "Deran, get a link with *Mikado*. Have them warn the shuttles that the pick-up will be inside the target perimeter."

"It'll take us about an hour to get there," Decker said, "and maybe another half hour to finish the operation. If your transport can loiter around the area starting in about ninety minutes from now, that'll keep your time on the ground at a minimum."

"*Your* time? Aren't you coming back with us?"

"Two off-worlders arrived on Marengo to conduct legitimate business. Those same two will leave Marengo via Valeux spaceport, their business concluded. The bastards might get wise to our involvement if we simply disappear with you and maybe then they'll start thinking it was a Fleet op and not a mercenary raid on behalf of the Garonne rebellion."

"Sensible precaution from your point of view, I suppose. If you change your mind, there's always room for two more." Ryent rose to his full height. "Let me brief my troops and we can be on our way. Deran, you heard the chief. Tell the Navy ninety minutes for the dropships."

— TWO —

"Where the hell did you get that thing?" Ryent watched Decker and Talyn dig a battered military skimmer with Marengo militia markings out of the undergrowth.

"There's not a quartermaster sergeant in the galaxy who doesn't have a price. This one came cheaper than I expected."

Decker tossed a branch aside and heaved the vehicle around.

"Mind you, the kind of entertainment he likes is pretty cheap on Marengo, especially for a militia puke."

"What kind of entertainment is that?" Vanleith asked.

"Trust me, Gus, you don't want to know. This shithole is one self-immolation away from turning into a three-dee copy of Garonne, and then we'll be pulling Marengo freedom fighters from someone else's stockade, just to balance things out. Fucking Senate might want to keep a closer eye on colonial matters so we don't have to yank their dicks out of the grinder all the time."

The bitterness in Decker's tone didn't surprise anyone within earshot. They'd all felt the same way at one time or another.

"And we're here to help keep the crap from spreading," Ryent said, "so let's get going, folks. Marengo isn't going to slow down its rotation to accommodate us, and the shuttles are going to be inbound on schedule. Decker, it's your show."

"Roger that, Major. We're ready." Zack jumped into the driver's seat and switched on the power plant. He grinned at Talyn and patted the passenger seat.

"If you're ready for a little fun, hop in. Otherwise, I'll do it by myself, and you'll miss out on what promises to be a wonderful session of militia bashing."

When she'd settled in beside him, Decker gave the major an ironic wave and set off towards the stockade on a narrow road hemmed in by thick vegetation on either side.

He knew there was a squadron of the toughest Marines in the galaxy behind him, waiting for his signal, but damned if he could pick up the slightest trace of their presence, be it through his night vision gear or the sensor he'd propped up on the dashboard. He felt unaccountably proud of that. The bastards wouldn't know what hit them.

"Is the IFF working okay?"

"It's working, though I can't guarantee that we're sending the right codes," Talyn replied.

"If that quartermaster dipshit sold us the wrong ones, I'm going back to rip his guts out and turn them into guitar strings, while they're still attached to his stomach and asshole."

They emerged from the forest into a wide glade, and there it sat, brooding under the starlit, moonless sky. The stockade might have been primitive by most standards, but it had one redeeming feature: it was well hidden from the few Commonwealth officials who roamed Marengo.

"Nothing stirring," Decker whispered. "It's quiet. Almost quiet enough to give me a bad feeling about this."

"Stop the dramatics and remember to brake before we slam into the main gate. Unless they've been tipped off, and that's pretty unlikely, the guard shift is half-asleep, happy they don't have to patrol the jungle at oh-dark-thirty."

Zack brought their skimmer to a halt a bare meter from the main entrance to the enclosed compound. On either side, a compacted earth berm topped by opaque fencing faded into the darkness. They knew from their earlier recon that a double barrier system encircled the camp, with some nasty automatic devices between the inner and outer fence. Sensors festooned the perimeter, but these were now in thrall to Talyn's spoofer.

"I hope you remembered to power up the jammer, because we're on."

"No worries." She glanced down at the pad in her lap and tapped its screen. "And the land line's now cut."

A querulous voice rang out.

"Who are you?"

"I guess someone's awake in the guard hut," Zack said loud enough to be heard by whatever microphones were pointed at them. "A good start."

"Major Yang and Warrant Officer Klebs from the Inspector General's office."

"Inspector General? At this hour?" Outrage mixed with incredulity.

"You know what they say: no one ever expects the IG." Decker let out an evil laugh. "We do our best business when folks don't think we'll show up."

After a moment's silence, a different voice came on.

"I'm Captain Beore, officer of the watch. May I ask for your ID and orders?"

At least he had the presence of mind to be polite. It was the same everywhere in the galaxy, no matter the organization. Never piss off the IG.

Decker and Talyn held out small data wafers and waited for the unseen guards to scan their fake IDs.

"Here you go, Captain. Take your time and match them with our ugly mugs; security's always the first thing we check whenever we visit our victims – sorry, I mean the unit we've been detailed to inspect."

As he spoke, Decker felt the tiny hairs on the back of his neck prickle, and he knew that the pathfinders were creeping up to the stockade, unseen by either the spoofed sensors or what few eyes looked outwards.

He had to fight the urge to turn his head and scan the low brush on either side of the road. Talyn, who'd also felt the presence of the assault force, did her best to look like a bored and increasingly irritated field grade officer.

The IDs must have passed muster because the gate slid aside with a tired rasp, revealing an inner barrier, also opening wide. They now had a direct route into the darkened camp. A few shadowy figures stood to either side of the entrance, weapons slung over their shoulders.

Decker gunned the skimmer's fans, and a horrible screeching noise erupted, followed by the sound of blades disintegrating. The vehicle lurched forward, almost throwing both operatives through the windshield and came to rest across both gates, effectively jamming them open.

He jumped out, cursing loudly in the local patois at the infernal gods that had made the motor pool give him a defective piece of crap. Three guards rushed up to take a closer look at the scene.

"Can you believe it?" Decker shouted angrily. "Why does the militia always get crap the National Guard doesn't want any more? Now we're stuck here until the bastards in Larolle can send up a mobile repair team and you know how lazy they are."

Talyn climbed out of the grounded skimmer and calmly walked up to the cluster of guards surrounding an increasingly unhappy Decker.

"Perhaps," her voice cut through his rant, "we should move this wreck out of the way so the gates can close. We'll investigate the motor pool soon enough, Mister Klebs."

Zack snapped to attention.

"As you wish, Major."

He turned to the guards.

"You heard her — let's get your camp secure again."

Pointing at the surprised men, he barked, "You three, on that side, you three on the other and get ready to heave."

They were anxious to comply and didn't notice Talyn stroking the screen of her small pad. It would take a few minutes for the watch in the control room to figure out all comms were jammed, but they'd not need much longer than that.

Nightmarish shapes emerged from the brush on either side of the road and silently ran towards the open gates. Further shadows came out of the wood line to join them.

Without warning, Talyn and Decker each struck a guard hard in the midriff and then on the back of the head. They fell down, out for the count, with no more than a brief grunt of pain. That sudden, unexpected attack was just enough to ensure the remainder didn't hear the pathfinders behind them. Seconds later, they'd joined their comrades in unconsciousness while Marines flowed through the gateway and spread out across the compound.

"The ops center is over there," Decker pointed at a small building when Ryent stopped beside him to get his bearings, "and the guard barracks is the one beside it. The other two huts are for the prisoners."

Captain Beore must finally have figured out something was wrong because a siren rang out over the stockade, but the garrison never stood a chance. The Marines quickly rounded the militia troopers up, disarmed them and shoved the disoriented men into small boxes reserved for prisoner punishment.

Decker and Talyn entered the ops center after the pathfinders had secured it, to find Beore sitting on the ground, hands bound behind his back, a mixture of shock and anger twisting his face.

Zack squatted down beside him and grinned.

"No one ever expects the IG to not be the IG, eh?"

"Who the fuck are you?" Beore demanded.

"How cute." Zack patted him on the head. "It still growls even though it's totally screwed. We're just some private contractors hired by concerned families to liberate folks held illegally by your government, son."

He rose to his full height again and waved at the Marine sergeant by the door.

"Make sure he's in the nastiest box they have. If he stumbles a bit along the way, I won't be overly sad. I watched him use prisoners as practice dummies for what he thinks is proper aikido."

"Will do, chief." The pathfinder grabbed Beore by the arm and hauled him to his feet.

Talyn pointed at a bank of expensive consoles against the far wall.

"Shall we cost the militia a bit of money?"

"You have some explosives hidden away in that ugly uniform?"

"Always." She held up a small device. "Don't you know it's a court-martial offense to go on a mission without a little something to turn big stuff into small stuff?"

"Good. I didn't think my stash of detcord would be enough."

Something caught Talyn's attention, and her head snapped around to stare at one of the screens.

"Shit." She studied the readout. "We have company coming. They just tripped the sensors covering the pass."

"Militia?"

"No – pizza delivery." She made a face at him. "Of course, the militia."

"It's too early for a watch change."

"Five points for stating the obvious, Zack. They might have picked up *Mikado* or the shuttles, or maybe the battalion commander had a pricking in his thumbs." Talyn tapped her communicator. "Grey Goose, we need to get out in the next couple of minutes, or we'll have to expend some ammo."

"Shuttles are about to land. We've got the detainees ready to load."

Decker stuck his head through the open doorway and listened.

"Yep, they're right above us. Ryent and his boys will be okay, but we won't have time to blow this place up and still get out from under the relief column's nose."

"I think that we might have to reconsider the plan and hitch a ride with your buddies. Ulrich won't be happy, but it beats spending a few weeks dodging patrols in the jungle only to show up at the spaceport looking like we were raised by wolves."

Zack shrugged.

"I never pass on the chance to avoid walking. C'mon. They're loading. If we don't want to get left behind, we have to move now."

She nodded, then quickly armed the explosive package and tossed it over her shoulder at the consoles.

"Ten-second detonator. Time to go."

Once out in the open, they ran towards the shuttles, two of which were already in the air while the other two were preparing to raise their ramps.

"Hang on," Decker shouted, "we changed our minds about leaving with you."

They scrambled into the last shuttle and realized there was nowhere left to sit but on the floor. A stocky figure removed his helmet and laughed.

"Can't stay away, can you, Zack?"

"It's your charm that keeps me coming back, Gus."

"Strap yourselves in." The sergeant major nodded towards restraints hanging off the forward bulkhead. "We'll be flying hard, and you're not exactly dressed to bounce around."

"Considering the renegades you have driving your crates, I'm going to agree just this once." Decker staggered when the craft lifted and banked hard to follow its companions on a steep path towards orbit and the waiting Q-ship.

He grabbed hold of a jump strap and wrapped his other arm around Talyn's waist to keep her from sliding towards the rear.

"Or you could stand there for the entire flight, looking like a caveman ravishing his intended." Vanleith shrugged. "Your call."

"I'll just wait until the cowboy in the cockpit finishes learning how to drive this thing before I move."

— THREE —

"Your rescuees are housed in a segregated passenger pod. They haven't had a chance to see much of *Mikado* during the transfer, so I think it's safe to say they have no idea the Fleet rescued them."

Captain Stodola pointed at the image on the conference room's main screen.

"As you can see," he continued, "we've got them in separate cabins, each tended by one of my medical staff. You agent is in my real sickbay where my surgeon will give him his full attention. He's in pretty bad shape, but you'll be able to speak with him shortly. No one, present company excepted, knows who he really is, so I'd say his cover is still intact."

"Thank you, Tom." Talyn patted his arm. "It's always a pleasure working with you. At this point, other than the relief column showing up a few hours early for some reason, I'd say it was a successful operation."

"Do you have any idea why one of your spooks was in a prison camp with a bunch of freedom fighters from a backwater colony on the edge of sweet fuck all, sir?" Vanlieth asked. "And why we took all of them with us and not just him?"

"Command chose not to tell us, sarn't-major," Talyn lied, "though I'm sure we can all speculate until the heat death of the universe. It's best not to dwell on it. If we aren't going to be involved in whatever's going on, then it becomes none of our business."

Decker grunted.

"Buddy down in sickbay is one of ours, and he was playing footsie with the rebels. Beaten up as he is, the boss will be looking for fresh meat to take over the mission. Somehow I think we'll end up in the Garonne mess, you and me, Hera. I'm willing to bet a month's danger pay on it."

"Fancy-pants spies get danger pay?" Vanleith sounded incredulous. "All you do is live in the best hotels, sipping cocktails at all hours and shagging each other non-stop."

"You know how it is, Gus." A broad smile split Zack's face. "The amount of shagging we have to do has been determined by the Navy's surgeon general to be a severe health risk."

"Only if you catch the Halterian clap, my overeager friend. Full spectrum immunization doesn't cover that one yet."

"I think we should move to the saloon," Talyn made a helpless face at *Mikado*'s captain, "and leave those two to argue who has the tougher job. I have a feeling it'll go downhill faster than any of us wants to witness."

She tapped Decker's shoulder.

"Don't forget we need to debrief Badhorn the moment *Mikado*'s sawbones gives us the all-clear, so don't go on an all day trip down memory lane."

******

"How are you, Josh?" Talyn smiled at the battered face framed by a large white pillow.

The agent tried to smile back, but his contorted face mostly showed pain.

"I've been better, and I've been worse." His vocal cords sounded raw, abused. "Doc tells me I'll mend."

Decker ran his eyes over the regen sleeves covering Badhorn's arms and legs.

"Sure, but will you ever be able to swing a golf club again?"

"Never was able to break a hundred, so I don't think it'll make much of a difference."

"Do you feel ready to talk?" Talyn pulled up a chair and sat down by the bed. "I've made sure no one can listen in on us."

"No, but I doubt Captain Ulrich would care about my feelings. He'll expect my preliminary report on his desk before we leave this system. Go ahead."

"Alright, then. Tell me how you ended up in a stockade on Marengo."

"We left Garonne on the *Tigris Maru*, captain and sole crew by the name of Hasaka. I was traveling with four of the rebellion's top specialists, all ex-military, all highly experienced in guerilla warfare. We were on a mission to procure advanced weaponry and other supplies, and had traveled about three parsecs when a pair of needle ships appeared out of nowhere while we were sublight, spooling up for the next jump."

Badhorn paused to catch his breath.

"Hasaka locked up the passenger deck, and before we knew what was going on, we were fighting off a boarding party that had found its way in with the bastard's connivance. That's how we got most of our injuries."

"Any idea who the attackers were?"

The agent tried to laugh but coughed painfully instead.

"You'll never believe me."

"Try."

"The Confederacy of the Howling Stars."

"What?" Decker's eyebrows shot up. "Since when are the Jackals playing pirate? I thought they made sure to stay on the clean side of organized crime laws."

"If Hasaka let them come on board, and then they let him go unharmed, it wouldn't be piracy, strictly speaking, just unlawful detention of Josh and the rebels," Talyn pointed out. "The Jackals have been known to dabble in kidnapping for hire, among other things."

"It was for hire," Badhorn confirmed. "They didn't mistreat us, even though we gave them a lot of black eyes. After five days, we were transferred to another ship. It looked civilian from what I could see, but I'd swear it was an Avalon Corporation sloop in disguise. They brought us to Marengo where the militia took over."

"Any attempts at interrogation?"

"Plenty," the agent confirmed. "That's when we got beat up all over again. They didn't dare try mind probes for fear that we'd been conditioned and die on them. I'm sure someone well above the Marengo militia commander's pay grade was pulling the strings, and they didn't dare disappoint whoever that was."

"Sounds likely. Getting the Confederacy to openly kidnap folks off a starship either takes a lot of juice or a lot of money."

"Or both," Decker added, "and it takes someone to finger this *Tigris Maru* as your transport."

"Did you at least get a chance to pick up the trail on Garonne?" Talyn asked.

"No. The only good news is that no one's found out we're interested in what's happening."

Zack snorted.

"I'll bet you I know who's going to be thrown into that mess next."

"Doubtful." Talyn shook her head. "I'm sure the boss already has another operative making his way into the rebellion. *We* are under orders to return home with Josh."

— FOUR —

Decker stepped through the open door and met a wall of stagnant hot air that nearly took his breath away.

This deep inside a box canyon in the middle of an endless desert, the slightest breeze would have been a miracle.

Two months had passed since the rescue on Marengo and their return to Caledonia. Captain Ulrich had immediately given them the Garonne mission, as Decker expected, but with a twist neither of them had anticipated.

Turning to look back the way they'd come, he felt a stab of regret for the enticing coolness of the underground naval station. They'd arrived on this minor colony world only two days earlier, but he'd developed a fondness for the quirky and very secret installation, suspecting that he'd soon come to miss its clean, wholesome atmosphere. The engineers who maintained and refurbished ships for naval intelligence had turned out to be his kind of people.

"I should have forced you to take the bet," he grumbled, sizing up their new home.

"So you keep saying," Talyn replied, sounding distracted, her attention on the worn, shabby-looking spaceship squatting beneath a shimmering camouflage net. Its sleek lines seemed eerily familiar though she couldn't quite figure why.

"Getting involved in a rebellion never turns out well for anyone, mark my words," Decker continued. "We're going to regret poking our noses into the Garonne business."

"So you keep saying," she repeated. "Zack, does this tub remind you of anything?"

"What?" Decker frowned while he ran his eyes over the pitted and blackened hull. "It's an old sloop. Something the Navy took from your standard down-market pirate and kept for spook work. I'm more worried about you flying the thing out of here. Unless I'm mistaken, you don't have much time at the controls of a starship, especially a lander."

The big Marine ran a calloused hand through the mop of sandy hair covering his skull, wishing his current cover identity didn't require him to wear it so long.

"Why do you think I spent so much time in the simulation tank after coming home from Marengo?"

She turned to look at him with a raised eyebrow. Talyn, in contrast to Zack, wore her hair short, and that gave her a harder, leaner appearance than usual.

"You were bored enough to play first person shooter games?" He shrugged. "I was too busy to pay attention."

Talyn snorted.

"I'm sure your companion of the moment found you busy alright. Come on, let's climb aboard and fire her up. Neither of us is getting any younger just standing here."

Duffle bags slung over leather-clad shoulders, they walked up the ramp into the belly of the beast, inhaling the sharp tang of metal, lubricants and all the other familiar scents of a starship.

"You know," Zack said, looking around at the bare corridors, "now that I think about it, this tub does feel familiar, but there's something missing."

He stopped by a closed door.

"I'm going to venture that this is the main cabin." It slid aside at his touch, revealing a plain compartment but one that was, by the standards of a small ship, rather spacious. "We can leave our gear here unless you want to take separate quarters."

"And miss hearing you whine about the mission in your sleep?" She chuckled, then tossed her bag inside. "I'll decide once we're under way."

The bridge had that same aura of familiarity, though it seemed as well used and strictly functional as the rest of the vessel. Talyn sat down at the helm console and touched its screen, sending power through dormant systems. Within moments, they came to life, and she scanned the data on the readout before looking at her surroundings again.

"Zack."

"Hmm?" Decker, at the tactical console, was busy running through pre-flight checks and didn't raise his head.

"We're on *Syrah*."

"Amali's yacht? The one we stole at Nabhka? I thought the Navy planned on returning it to his heirs and successors. How do you figure?"

"She has the right feel. I sailed her long enough to remember."

"Well, if it is the bastard's ship, the Navy's given her a serious upgrade. Remember the mercenary sloop that ran us down by the Talkin array after we stole this thing?"

"Sure."

"Next time, we'll be the ones chasing the mercs away. It'll make up for the engineers taking out all the beautiful luxury fittings it used to have."

"I would have been difficult pretending to be rogues if our ship looked like a high-class brothel."

"The old *Syrah* was comfortable, though." Decker sounded wistful for a moment, eyes raised to the deck head. He sighed theatrically. "But I'll grant you that I wouldn't be able to pass for a pimp and you sure as heck wouldn't pass for a working lady."

"Why would I be the entertainer? I'm willing to bet I could pimp you out easily enough, big boy." She smirked at him over her shoulder.

"I'm willing to try if you are."

"No doubt. Now how about you get your mind out of the gutter and earn your pay?"

"All systems are up and running," he replied without missing a beat. "The Navy did a good enough job that I might just stop complaining."

"That'll be the day. Give me some time to sort myself out. It's not like we have much leeway getting out of this slot and I'd rather not scrape our nacelles on the way up."

"It'll add character." He touched his screen. "Incoming from the station, they're ready to withdraw the cammo net."

"How kind. Tell them I'd like a few more minutes."

"Sure. Just don't let us get too old sitting here, will you?"

Talyn mumbled something that might or might not have been obscene, and he smiled fondly at her back.

"I'm ready to go," she finally announced, flexing her fingers. "They've put a good AI aboard, so I'll not be flying her alone."

"Glad to hear that." He touched his screen again. "Control, this is *Chimera*. We're ready."

"Overhead retracted," a voice replied moments later. "There's no traffic in any direction for a thousand kilometers and nothing in orbit above this location. Godspeed and good hunting, *Chimera*. Try not to damage her too much. We put a lot of hours into the conversion."

"No promises," Talyn replied absently, her attention on the controls.

Though she seemed calm, Decker could read the tension in the set of her shoulders and the hard lines marking her face. There was nothing he could do to help, so he simply sat back and tried not to think of all the things that could go wrong lifting out of a tight space in a large thing with the flight characteristics of a slab of granite.

"I hope you're strapped in, Zack."

"Why? Are you going to perform aerobatics to amuse the folks on the ground?"

"Strap in, Zack."

"Yes, ma'am. You concentrate on flying. I'd like to keep the nice engineers who gave us this toy happy, so don't dent it."

She briefly scowled at him over her shoulder, then pushed the thrusters to full strength. *Chimera*'s lift-off rumble echoed through the canyon, and the rock walls began to drop away. The little ship felt steady to a degree that surprised both operatives and within seconds, it was free of the mesa and gaining altitude fast.

"Remember to retract the landing gear," Decker said. "We might need it some other time."

"Done. The AI in this thing is impressive. I thought we'd sway like a boat in a storm until we were out of the canyon."

"Thank you." A disembodied voice startled the two agents. They looked at each other, then Decker shook his head.

"Oh no. Not happening. I'm not having it speak to us, especially in that voice." He called up the relevant subroutine and entered a command string. "That should do it."

This time, a soft chime sounded.

"Much better." Zack smiled at his partner.

******

Gradually, the blue of the sky faded to purple and then to black when they passed through the upper atmosphere and into the vacuum of space. Talyn chose not to spend any time in orbit and broke out immediately, headed for the hyperlimit. With nothing else to do, Decker spent his time productively by compiling a detailed inventory of the ship's systems while happily humming a marching song.

They'd almost reached the point where they could go FTL when his tactical screen flashed an insistent warning.

"A Navy sloop just lit up, and it's targeting us." Pause. "We've been ordered to heave-to and prepare to be boarded."

"No reply," Talyn said, shaking her head. "We can outrun her."

"Can I ping her with my targeting sensors, just for shits and giggles?"

"That's probably not a very good idea. We might show that we're stronger than we look." She glanced at her screen. "Besides, we'll be jumping out sooner than you might think."

"Aren't we still twenty or thirty minutes away from the hyperlimit, even in this little tub?"

"Only if we follow Navy rules. You can jump a lot closer to a gravity well than is generally assumed but it'll take years of usable service off a ship's lifespan if you do it too often. We don't have to follow those rules. The sloop behind us does, and only a life or death situation would warrant breaking them."

"They're becoming insistent," he said, "but I get the feeling they're not really trying hard to catch us. Their rate of acceleration is pretty anemic."

"Ah." Her face lit up with understanding. "A little misdirection then: anyone watching will assume we're not exactly honest if the Navy takes too great an interest."

"I hope that you're right." His jaw clenched. "They just fired two rounds, and they'll graze us enough to feel real."

Bright balls of plasma streaked by on the starboard side and a voice on the radio warned them that the next shots would be aimed at their engines.

"A few more seconds," Talyn said, "though we're still a tad closer than I like."

"In that case, keep your hand right on the controls, ready to punch it in. The moment I see their gun barrels begin to glow again, we need to be out of here."

"You sound a little stressed, Zack."

"I have a healthy dose of paranoia to work with, and I don't like being shot at, sham or no sham. The last time I was on the receiving end of a few salvos, my life went to hell."

"Understood," she replied, remembering the chain of events that had brought Decker back into the Corps as an intelligence operative. "But the Navy won't sell you into slavery, you know."

"I'm already in a state of servitude, thanks to you, what with my involuntary recall to active duty."

"And here I thought you were happy. Goes to show you how ungrateful some folks are, eh, chief warrant officer?"

"Was I complaining, commander, sir? No. I was merely stating a fact. And they just fired again."

Talyn's hand came down, and the universe went sideways, forcing Decker's stomach in the opposite direction.

"Tell me I didn't just break something," she said once the jump nausea had passed.

"Nope," he said a few moments later. "Everything seems to be working the way it should. How long are we on this leg?"

"I figured we'd do about ten hours, to see how she handles. I don't want to find out that they forgot to tighten a widget when we're five light-years from the nearest left-handed spanner."

"Lunch?" He asked, putting the systems console on automatic before rising to stretch his massive frame. "And then a game of strip poker?"

"Lunch and no strip poker. We need to spend some time crawling through the ship so we can memorize where everything is. Studying schematics and fooling around in the simulation tank for two days just doesn't cut it. We can play grab-ass when that's done."

He gave her a mock salute.

"Aye, aye, Captain Bligh."

"You can have a drink with lunch. One bottle only, though."

"Do you really think they were kind enough to stock the booze locker with good stuff?" Decker rubbed his hands in anticipation.

"You do know that you've developed quite a reputation in the intelligence branch, right?"

"You make it sound like that's a bad thing." He put on a mock-wounded face at her acerbic tone.

"Perhaps not for you but for me, seeing as how I'm your partner and the one who brought you in."

She led the way aft to the small saloon, which now looked nothing like the luxurious salon it had been when *Chimera* still sailed under the name *Syrah*.

"See, that's the problem when you're working in black ops. We can't boast about the stuff we do to the same extent as the rest of the branch, so they figure all we do is screw and drink our way through a mission."

He opened one of the cabinets and grinned broadly.

"This is one of those times where I'm glad my reputation precedes me."

Decker held up a purplish bottle with a label inscribed in alien runes.

"*T'Klach* vintage at that, top shelf Shrehari ale. They must have found a few cases on one of the prize ships brought in to be reconfigured. No one in their right mind would pay the freight to bring this nectar all the way to the ass-end of the Commonwealth."

"Enjoy the good stuff while it lasts. The whiskey is so-so and the gin not much better than rotgut."

She closed the bar cabinet and winced.

"Wine?"

"Dordogne mass-produced plonk." She shook her head in amazement while she watched Decker enjoy his first sip of the potent brew. "Either you have fans among the station's engineering crew, or you're the luckiest bastard alive. You get good stuff while I have to make do with booze I wouldn't buy for myself."

"I'll quickly point out that it's free, so that should add a few points to the quality score," he replied, mischief dancing in his deep blue eyes.

"Food seems to be prepared trays," she said, ignoring his comment, "civilian versions of the standard navy rations; not gourmet, but tolerable."

"Provided we don't have to eat rat-bars, I'm happy."

"We seem to have a supply of those as well if ever you get nostalgic for your pathfinder days."

She shoved two slim packs into the autochef and touched a screen.

"What's on the menu?"

"I don't know. I just pulled two trays out from the lunch stack at random."

"So it might be mystery meat on a shingle with hot sauce."

"Or it could be duck à l'orange."

The autochef chimed softly and spat out the trays.

They sat down and peeled back the lids covering their now hot meals.

"Chicken product with green stuff on noodles," Decker said, examining his food with a jaundiced eye, "or more likely, some product not containing meat made to look like chicken."

"Why should you care what it is if it feels and tastes like chicken?" She took a tentative bite of her fish and smiled. "I don't care if this is cleverly disguised tofu. It tastes pretty good."

Zack shoved a morsel into his mouth and chewed slowly, his facial expression on the wrong side of skeptical.

"Okay," he finally said, after swallowing, "it's not nearly as bad as I feared, but I'll tell you what. If we get the chance to buy some fresh food, I'll cook."

She considered him for a moment and then chuckled. "I do believe that's something I'd like to witness."

**

"Okay," Decker said, wiping his hands on a rag, "those spanner monkeys knew what they were doing. This ship is in perfect condition under a believable veneer of hard use and abuse. I'm impressed with how they managed to fit full-sized anti-ship missile launchers in there. We might not have much of a magazine, but it'll be enough for any asshole wanting to do us grief. And the guns - much better than what she originally carried."

"We should still be wary of who we let aboard." Talyn stripped off the coveralls she'd found hanging in the engineering compartment. "The wrong person with the right knowledge of starships might see there's more than advertised."

"True, especially if it's someone who knew her when she was called *Syrah*. You got the vibes, and we only spent a few days in her a year ago so you can imagine a long-term crew member."

"Another five hours until we emerge," she said looking the nearest screen. "Supper?"

He was about to reply when his stomach rumbled loudly.

"Traitor," he muttered at the offending organ.

"Supper it is." She laughed, knowing exactly what Zack would have proposed they do instead of eating right away.

**

"So," Decker asked, slumped back in his seat now that his appetite was sated, "what do you think Ulrich is going to do with the guys we pulled off Marengo? I mean the real rebels, not our guy. He won't be in any shape to go back out for a while yet."

"No idea, but if I had to bet, I'd say he'll keep them out of circulation until we find something. Letting them go back to Garonne now would just make our job harder. Our boss likes to be in control of as many variables as possible." She picked up the empty trays and tossed them in the recycler. "Coffee?"

"Sure, though I should probably stay off the hooch until we've gone through the emergence cycle."

She snorted.

"The way you metabolize alcohol? I'm touched at your considerate attempt to deprive yourself in the name of safety, but if you want a dram with the coffee, be my guest. We've got a little over three hours left. That's plenty of time."

"In that case, sure, don't mind if I do." He was about to get up, but she waved him down. "Thanks. You're a peach, and with that haircut, you've got the fuzz to prove it."

"I know that Ulrich is convinced the Coalition's somehow behind the doings on Garonne," she said after sitting down again, "even though our man and his traveling companions were taken by the Confederacy of the Howling Stars. It's a shame he couldn't find any evidence."

"What interest would the Coalition have in fomenting unrest on a colony owned by Celeste? I thought its government was thoroughly infested by assholes wanting a return to the glory days from before the last Migration War."

"Or maybe assholes who want to bring about an Empire that'll make the Shrehari look like amateurs, but I take your meaning." Talyn took a sip of the bitter brew and scrunched up her face. "I'm going to guess this isn't one of the top shelf brands."

"Ulrich is the last of the big paranoids," she continued, "I think you got that from the few times you met him; that's why he lasted so long in this business and got black ops to himself, but his instincts are uncanny. If someone could distil them and create a vaccine, we'd all get a dose."

"True. The good captain is one of the few officers who actually scares me, and that's saying a lot, but it baffles the brain to think about buddies of the Amali clan *supporting* rebel movements against colonial governments owned by their political allies."

"And yet, the boss thinks that's the case, which is why we're on this ex-Amali yacht." She pushed her cup away in disgust. "He was one of my instructors when I got recruited into the intelligence branch, by the way; he was an uncanny bastard then and still is one now."

"You know," Decker said, washing the lousy coffee taste from his mouth with a shot of cheap whiskey, "I think it's not the grounds but the machine. Let me take a look. They might have forgotten to clean it properly before they installed it."

"You mean we've been drinking lubricants and the like?"

"Yep." He downed his glass. "You should take a shot; it cleans the palate and your ability to metabolize booze isn't bad either, so you'll be completely sober when we drop out of hyperspace."

He shook his head.

"The damn Coalition again. Well, maybe it'll give me a chance to take down the rest of the Amalis and then get a head start on the second and third cousins."

"Watching Harmon Amali get eaten by sand sharks on Nabhka wasn't enough for you?"

Decker shrugged.

"I'm two for two with both him and his cousin Walker. Why stop now?"

"You know Ulrich won't sanction a hit without a good reason," she warned.

"It doesn't mean I can't kill any in the heat of the action. A little double tap to the head and no regen tank's going to save them."

"Plenty more of their kind out there, Zack. You can't get them all."

"So long as I make a dent in their numbers, I'll die happy."

"The only way you'll die happy is in the middle of a hot session with a young lady."

"Yep." He smiled contentedly at the thought. "Though I'll take a hot session with an older woman too. I have very flexible standards."

"Don't I know it? Well, come on, Marine Boy. We do have three hours to kill."

— FIVE —

"Does the Fleet know the station exists, officially I mean?" Zack stared at his sensor readout. "They've done a good job at hiding the place, but it's not like Tortuga, stashed away inside a nebula."

"A private colony like this on the Rim has its uses," Talyn replied, her eyes glued to the navigation screen. "We ignore them provided they don't cause trouble. Collecting taxes isn't the Navy's business. Mind you, they start to dabble in things we don't like, and a visit by your friendly neighborhood frigate soon sets them right. The folks operating this place know that and tend to police themselves pretty well, better than some officially acknowledged colonies of your acquaintance."

"Nice. It sounds like a great spot for subversives to plan and prepare for the revolution." Decker scowled at the station's image.

"If they're not subverting the Commonwealth itself, we don't care." She shrugged. "The Fleet might even nudge a few useful idiots in the right direction if it'll help keep the peace within our sphere."

"They're hailing us."

"By all means, feel free to reply," she said with a touch of asperity. "Try to remember that I'm Dynes, and you're Gant."

When he'd done so and listened to the reply, he frowned.

"The docking fees they just quoted are on the wrong side of extortionate. I'm assuming those were taken into consideration when the boss handed out our covert funding."

"They were. Look at it this way: they can keep out the riff-raff by charging a lot for one of their slips. Only those who have profitable business on Kilia or have money to spare are going to bother docking. Anyone else either buggers off or keeps at a distance and shuttles in; though I have no doubt the hangar fees are equally eye-watering."

"Makes sense. I'm glad we're spending the taxpayer's money and not our own. Back when I was sailing aboard *Demetria*, we wouldn't have been able to afford it. Margins were much too thin."

The memory of life before his return to active duty didn't hurt quite like it used to, but he nonetheless felt a brief stab of pain in his gut.

"There," he said a few minutes later, "we're being welcomed by the Kilia Station cooperative. I hope the AI has been programmed for funky docking maneuvers. We've been assigned an outside docking arm and that thing is using spin for gravity."

"No fears. I ran simulations to train for a situation like this."

"That makes me feel so much better."

"Why don't you take the controls then, Mister Sarcasm?"

"I'm a Marine. We don't sully ourselves by driving vulgar starships."

She snorted with suppressed laughter.

"More like driving a starship is beyond a Marine's limited abilities."

Decker was about to utter a few pungent words in reply when the sensor readout drew his attention again.

"I think it might take a bit more than a frigate to scare these guys into obedience, Hera. That's some heavy ordnance they've got pointing at us."

"It wouldn't do them any good against a volley of missiles. The station's a sitting duck. A few kinetic strikes from a stand-off position and they'll be singing the Commonwealth anthem with feeling."

"True." He nodded. "But I don't see our chances as being good if they decide they don't like the cut of our hull."

"We're not a frigate. Now, kindly keep any fantastic observations to yourself and let me dock, so we can get some fresh food. Then you can demonstrate that you're good for more than just fighting and fucking."

"Aye, aye, Captain Dynes, sir." He tossed off a mock salute and went back to his detailed scan of Kilia.

A hollowed-out asteroid with a spin to approximate one standard gravity, the station blended in with the other remains of what had once been a major planet, destroyed in a cataclysm hundreds of millions of years earlier. Only close up did the marks of human habitation become evident.

Chimera's naval grade sensors were able to pick the details out from a decent range but most civilian vessels passing through the system without knowing that Kilia existed would remain in blissful ignorance. Of course, if one didn't know about the station, there'd be little incentive to visit this particular system since it had no habitable planets.

"Oh goodie," he muttered when he finally got a clear look at the other ships docked along the asteroid's rim.

"What?"

"I thought you told me to keep any observations to myself."

"I know that tone, Zack. It means you've seen something I might wish to know about before we dock."

"There's a Shrehari trader in the slip next to the one we've been assigned and in these parts, it's a given that he's doing some commerce raiding on the sly."

"If they're docked, they have money and aren't causing problems. If we run across any Shrehari on the station, we'll give them our best snarl and go about our business. The war ended seventy years ago. Now hush. I need to make sure we line up with a thin docking arm stuck into a big rotating rock."

**

"I'm pretty sure the last fifteen minutes took a few years off my life," Decker commented, switching *Chimera*'s systems to standby mode, now that they were securely attached to Kilia Station.

"Everyone's a critic. Tell you what: you can dock us the next time. I'll bet you're going to make way more adjustments than I had to."

"Like I said, Marines don't lower themselves to driving the damn things. There," he stood, "we're all set. Shall we sample the local wildlife?"

"The only sampling on the menu is fresh food and of course finding out whether or not this is the right place to start snooping."

The airlock shut behind them with a finality that pleased Zack. Short of using high explosives, no one would be able to break in, and if they did manage to overwhelm his security measures, they wouldn't make it through the inner hatch in one piece.

He sniffed the air cautiously as they climbed up a spiral staircase inside of the docking arm.

"Not rancid like the last unregistered station I visited."

"That's probably because Kilia is trying to stay on the lighter side of the gray zone."

A barrier at the end of the slip slid aside after its sensor had determined they were who they said they were and carried nothing more worrisome than personal side arms. They passed through several additional airlocks before emerging into the natural cavern that had been enlarged and sealed to create the small colony.

"Not bad," Zack stepped to one side and stopped to get his bearings. "I hate places that have been set up like a spinning cylinder. Looking up at the other side's down always makes me feel queasy."

"Give it time," she replied. "It'll eventually get big enough to build entirely around the axis."

A trio of Shrehari, looking every millimeter the pirates they probably were, walked around the corner of a nearby building, apparently headed for their ship.

Although not military, they had the bearing and arrogance of warriors, right down to the crest of stiff hair on their bony, ridged skulls. They examined the two humans, and the nearest one said something to his companions that caused visible mirth.

"My understanding of their damned tongue might not be the greatest, but I get the feeling I've just been insulted," he muttered in an aside to Talyn.

"He wondered whether a weak human like you was warrior enough to handle that stolen Imperial Armaments blaster on your hip."

"Figures."

Zack turned his head to look over his shoulder and shouted an imprecation in broken Shrehari at them. One of the humanoids made an obscene gesture at the Marine before they vanished through the open airlock.

"I wish you hadn't done that," Talyn said, amusement dancing in her dark eyes.

"Why? Some of the bastards never got over the fact that they didn't win the war, even if it was seventy years ago."

"Problem is, you told them to have sexual relations with their fusion reactors. I'm afraid they're laughing even harder right now."

"Meh," he shrugged, "fusion reactor, mother, they both sound like a constipated raptor giving birth. Bloody barbaric language, that. Speaking through the business end of my gun used to get the point across just fine."

"Brush up on your Shrehari if you're not going to ignore them. Shouting out an invitation to commit acts of fornication with a power source won't get you any respect."

"Although it might be fun to witness the buggers do it. Crispy Shrehari. Sounds just about right." He scanned the immense cavern again. "Where to?"

"The bazaar. It's in the middle of the cavern."

She stepped off so suddenly that he had to take long strides to catch up. They made their way between low buildings painted in a bewildering array of colors, dodging humanoids from a dozen species.

Decker's eyes kept scanning his surroundings for threats, something that had long since become second nature for the Pathfinder. A quickly glimpsed face caught his attention before it disappeared again into the crowd.

He grunted softly.

"What?" She didn't slow down but glanced sideways at him.

"I'm sure I just saw one of the sector's head Jackals, the man our analysts figure was behind the little hijacking that had our guy and his rebel buddies end up in the Marengo stockade."

"One of them on a semi-legal Rim station? Shocking." She nudged him. "Next thing you'll tell me is that they have their thumb on the local government. By the way, do try not calling the Confederacy of the Howling Stars by that name in public, okay. It's not worth the trouble that'll ensue."

"I sure won't call them Star Wolves. That would be giving the bastards a compliment they don't deserve."

"Then don't mention them at all. It'll be better that way, for us and the mission."

She slowed her pace when they emerged from the side street into a large plaza dominated by a tall, central pyramid. The construct's top tier seemed to merge with the cavern ceiling as if it were supporting the weight of the spinning asteroid.

"I think we're here."

"Your bazaar reminds me of the underground Casbah in Hadley," Zack said, a sad smile twisting his lips, "except cleaner and less aromatic."

"And safer." She pulled him out of the way while she scanned the perimeter. "Or to be more accurate, it's safer if you stick to the station's rules. The policing here tends to be a bit harsher than elsewhere."

"Personal experience?"

"I try to learn from the experience of others. You should try it someday."

"Where's the fun in that?"

"To each his own I suppose." She nodded towards the left side of the plaza. "Let's try over there."

"Any reason why there and not in the other direction?"

"Was that an idle question or do you want a lesson in field craft?"

"Both." He matched his stride to hers, heedless of people stepping out of their way to avoid being run down.

"Then pay attention, Ser Gant. I'll explain this only once. See the rather subdued sign for a ship chandlery over there?"

"Sure."

"That's where we'll order the fresh foodstuff you'll need to cook me some gourmet meals."

"Thanks for that completely unneeded reminder, funny lady."

"And it's bound to be the place most starship officers visit when they touch port, so the owner likely knows more of what's going on along this part of the Rim - at least when it comes to dodgy business - than the average tavern proprietor."

"I see," Decker nodded, "a local and very informal intelligence hub. That does make sense for once."

"Careful, big boy."

"I am that."

"Careful?"

"No, big."

She jabbed him in the ribs with her elbow by way of reply.

They were halfway to their destination when a uniformed security officer stepped across their path. He wasn't particularly menacing, but he did have a holstered blaster and a shock stick hanging from his belt.

"You are Dyne and Gant of *Chimera*?" He asked, looking from Talyn to Decker.

"We are," Hera replied pleasantly, smiling. "I'm Captain Dyne and the big boy here is Gant, my first mate."

"The port controller has asked to see you. If you'll follow me." He gestured towards the pyramid.

Hera looked at Zack, eyebrows raised, then she shrugged before nodding.

"I'd ask you what this is about, but I'll bet your answer is going to be that you don't know."

"Correct." The man replied, deadpan, and set off without looking back, confident that the two newcomers would follow him.

**

The port controller's office turned out to be a relatively austere thing: a few pieces of furniture, the expected terminal, large view screens and not much more. The woman behind the desk seemed to be cut from the core of the asteroid itself: hard, craggy, and topped by hair that bristled like a steel brush.

She didn't waste any time on niceties, merely waving towards two hard chairs in front of her desk by way of greeting.

"You're Dyne and Gant of *Chimera*." It wasn't a question. She glanced at her terminal and back at the two operatives.

"We are," Talyn confirmed.

"And you own *Chimera*? Or is it owned by a third party?" Her tone was matter-of-fact, emotionless. It matched her expression.

"We own it."

"You have the appropriate documentation to prove ownership?"

"Indeed." Talyn nodded. "May I ask what this is about?"

"As a law-abiding entity, we keep a lookout for vessels reported to have been taken through illegal means. *Chimera* is of a tonnage and configuration that approximates a ship called *Syrah*, stolen in the Nabhka system approximately one year ago."

She paused, looking for some sort of reaction, but if she had hopes of witnessing a guilty glance between the two spacers, these were immediately dashed.

"We've owned *Chimera* for over five years," Talyn replied.

"You'll understand that I have to verify your claim of ownership."

"It's hardly a claim," Decker said, shrugging. "More like a fact."

Talyn fished a data wafer from her breast pocket and slid it across the desk.

"Proof of ownership," she said.

"Thank you." Eyes locked on her screen, the port controller downloaded a copy of the relevant documentation before returning the chip.

"Your proof seems to be in order, but of course, those things can be faked. I'll still need to have your ship inspected."

Again, the search for a reaction.

"We have nothing to hide."

"And we'll establish that quickly enough, Captain Dyne. The owners of *Syrah* have provided us with detailed specs to use as a baseline for comparison."

"Who would these owners be? Or is that confidential?" Decker asked.

"The request was made via the Avalon Corporation on behalf of the conglomerate that owns both. Are you familiar with Avalon?"

"Private Military Corporation." Decker shrugged again. "One of the bigger operations. Checkered reputation, but compared to some of the others, not all bad."

The woman stared at him for a few seconds, then glanced back at her screen.

"My people are waiting by your airlock. I presume that you've rigged your ship to prevent unauthorized entry. Therefore, I'll ask you to return to the docking slip and cooperate with the inspector."

"Of course." Talyn inclined her head politely. "I assume that we may go?"

"Correct."

As they were about to leave the office, she spoke again.

"Be advised that if you've lied and are indeed operating a ship reported taken from its rightful owners, we will hand you over to said owners for disposition. Out here on the Rim, people don't always involve Commonwealth authorities, especially when it comes to pirates."

"As a ship owner myself, I wouldn't wish it any other way," Talyn smoothly replied, giving the port controller a quick smile. "Come now, Ser Gant, let's not keep the inspectors in suspense."

**

"Why wait until we'd disembarked?" Decker asked once they were back outside and headed for the docking ring. "They could have greeted us at the airlock with this little spiel."

"It's likely that they tried to get into the ship with us absent to conduct their inspection and found your little enhancements to our security. If we'd passed muster, we'd have been no wiser, and if they determined it was stolen, they'd have picked us up on the station with minimal fuss."

"Smart." Decker nodded. "Much easier than to come on like a herd of elephants with plasma carbines."

"Something to remember, eh?" Talyn chuckled.

"I can be as subtle as the best of them. Except when it comes to my sense of humor, I suppose," he added after a moment's thought.

"Correct," she replied, imitating the port controller's tone. "There's nothing discrete about that. The next time we have to set up a drop zone, I'll program the markers."

"And I'll just reprogram them at leisure."

They walked in silence for a while before he asked, "Is this kind of procedure normal? Checking out ships that look like others who've vanished?"

"Yes and no. The Navy and Constabulary issue be on the lookout for bulletins every time a starship is declared overdue and presumed lost by its owners. Actually inspecting a ship on suspicion of being stolen is a bit unusual, even on the Rim."

"The long arm of the Coalition?"

"Perhaps. We've got the only recording of Amali's execution, and the desert nomads are the only other eyewitnesses. Considering that they're more likely to offer the same end to any *Sécurité Spéciale* goon than testify, Amali's friends in high places are probably still trying to find out what happened, if only to make sure they don't suffer the same fate."

******

Six humans wearing station security uniforms waited for them at the bottom of the docking arm. There was nothing subtle about the weapons they carried.

Dyne and Gant were to be considered dangerous until the authorities established to their satisfaction that *Chimera* was not the ship that had belonged to Harmon Amali, a man last seen at his oasis hideout in the Nabhkan desert, said hideout now lying in ruins, its waters back under the control of nomad clans.

"Captain Dyne," the team leader politely nodded at her the moment they stepped off the spiral staircase. "If you'd please disarm your systems so we can conduct our inspection?"

Talyn glanced at Decker and jerked her head towards the airlock.

"Open her up, Ser Gant."

When Zack's had rendered his booby traps safe, the inspector motioned him to stand aside and let his men step aboard. Though Decker remained expressionless, he was surprised that they didn't send him in first.

Someday the station's rent-a-cops would come across folks who forgot to either disarm all of the security measures or leave some active on purpose and then where would they be? With a shrug, he complied.

The search took hours. Four members of the security team were equipped with detailed specs of *Syrah,* and they consulted them frequently, measuring compartments, verifying component serial numbers, and their unique manufacturing tags, measuring power emission curves and much more.

Decker followed one pair around while Talyn followed the other, answering questions clearly designed to test their knowledge of the ship. Zack was glad Hera had made them crawl through every tube, examine every nook and cranny, and memorize every detail of the layout during their passage to Kilia.

It proved impossible for either agent to determine whether or not the inspectors found anything suspicious and at the end of it, the team departed without saying a word, pausing only to collect the duo they'd left guarding the airlock.

"So?" He asked once the armored hatch shut them off from the docking arm.

She reached out and brushed his hand with dancing fingertips, spelling out a message in the tactile code used by naval intelligence agents.

They probably bugged us.

Zack nodded his agreement. Their hands reversed position so he could signal.

If the engineers forgot to hide something that could link us back, they'll wait until we're both off the ship to take it and us.

It was her turn to nod.

"It's been a long day, Zack," she said aloud. "Why don't you go get us stocked up with fresh food while I put the ship to rights. Our friendly inspectors weren't exactly subtle."

Her fingers signaled *although we shouldn't stick around longer than necessary, if we leave right away, it'll look suspicious.*

"Good idea," he replied. "Any special requests?"

"Stick to fruit and veggies. I doubt their protein vats grow anything better than the rations we've got."

"I'll see. A good vat steak is pretty much indistinguishable from what passes for beef in most outer systems."

"At your discretion, then. Just don't overspend. Until we get a contract, we're living off savings," she added, for any hidden listening devices.

Her fingers danced one last time. *While you're out, I'll see if they left anything nasty behind.*

If you find something, don't touch it until I'm back, he replied, blowing her a kiss before opening the hatch again.

— SIX —

"So?" Talyn looked up from her scanner when Decker stepped through the airlock, burdened with what seemed like an entire food locker's worth of victuals.

"I got plenty of fruit, veggies and meat – vat meat, but it looks good." He dropped his bags and reached out to touch the back of her hand.

We need to talk. Did you find anything?

She nodded, but said, "Go stow the stuff. I'll look at it later."

"Aye, aye, Captain." He winked.

"Once that's done, you and I are going to take a close look at the inside of your forward launcher. Something needs to be adjusted, but I'm damned if I can figure out what that is."

"That's why you hired me."

He vanished down the passageway, whistling an out of tune ditty.

**

As an improvised conference room, the missile compartment left a lot to be desired. Once Talyn shut the hatch behind her, they were more intimate than if they'd just hopped into a one-person bunk.

"This is one of the few places they didn't seed with microscopic bugs," she said after Decker finished snuggling up to her. "The rest of the ship is lousy with them. You told me you needed to talk?"

"We have to leave this place quickly and quietly. There are a few too many folks distinctly interested in us, or rather our ship, more so than just a harbor master doing due diligence with the BOLO list."

"Explain."

"Item one: the man running the chandlery acted like a terrified rabbit the moment I walked in; he couldn't throw me

45

out, but I've never been served so quickly anywhere. Of course, the goon in station security get-up hiding in the backroom probably had something to do with it. We won't get anything out of him short of a mind probe."

"Damn."

"Item two: the Confederacy of the Howling Stars definitely has a chapter on this station, and they're well connected. I saw two of them having a quiet chat with the guy who inspected our ship. No mistaking the affiliation – they wore gang tattoos. I'd say there's a good chance the Jackals are interested in us."

"And the organized crime section is pretty sure they're in deep with the *Sécurité Spéciale*." Talyn nodded.

"Yup. Item three: I was tailed by more of the Jackals from the moment I left the docking arm to the moment I returned, and they weren't too subtle about it."

"Item four: I saw a military-looking type with an Avalon corporate pin on his suit having a drink with the head Jackal I spotted when we first went ashore. Both took a good long look at me, like they'd seen pictures of Zack Decker and figured I could be related to him. Somehow, the idea that one of the biggest private military corporations is in cahoots with mobsters doesn't give me the warm and fuzzies."

"Either Captain Ulrich didn't find whoever was leaking information to the *Sécurité Spéciale*," Talyn replied after digesting Zack's report, "or they have a new source in place, or it could just be coincidence related to the search for the late Harmon Amali and his yacht."

"Occam's Razor, honey." Decker tried to shrug in the confined space. "Our mission was tightly compartmentalized. I doubt the bastards know we're Fleet. Chances are good there's a substantial bounty on *Syrah*, enough to get the Jackals interested, and because of that, every ship within the right tonnage range and of similar configuration is under the microscope. Avalon involvement is a no-brainer. They almost caught us right after we stole the ship and their management will have had its collective butt kicked for not closing the deal."

"Most likely," she conceded. "My paranoia does have me jump to the worst case scenario all too often. Considering the Amali family has enough money to make it interesting, the possibility of a bounty seems pretty good, now that I think of it, especially if the rest of the Coalition inner circle kicks in a few million creds of their own."

"What do we do?"

"We leave. There's no way we'll pick up a trace on Kilia now. The station's management has apparently been co-opted by *Sécurité Spéciale* goons via their Jackal puppets."

"So much for this place staying on the straight and narrow."

"When the choice is between keeping gangsters with a gun at your head happy and keeping the Fleet happy when it only sends a frigate through the system four times a year, it's no contest."

Zack grunted. After a moment, he said, "I can wipe out all of the bugs at once the moment you want me to. A small electromagnetic pulse will do it. They can't put enough shielding on things that tiny. It won't do squat to our systems, though we should make sure all of our loose items are stored in a shielded box. Of course, the moment I do that, they'll know we're on to them. A few devices failing would be normal. All of them at once, no."

"The bigger question is undocking and getting away if they're inclined to keep us put until they can get confirmation. Unless we're willing to tear off part of the airlock and brave their guns, they can keep us here at will, and I'm not ready to risk damaging the ship."

Zack's mouth curved into a smile.

"Leave it to me."

"Why do I have a bad feeling about this?"

"Because I never bluff unless I have something up my sleeve?"

"No, that's not it. Perhaps because you have the habit of doing unexpected things that both frighten and irritate those of us doomed to work with you."

"And yet you and I are still an item in the wonderful world of black ops."

"Should I ask, or should I just play along while you invent a way out, probably making it up on the spot?"

"What would be your preference?"

"Tell me."

He did, and when he was done, she nodded slowly, evaluating their chances.

"It's stupid enough that it just might work, though I shudder to think what could happen if your plan goes sideways."

"Not a chance." His grin turned predatory. "They won't want to risk their precious station."

"True, but it still sounds amazingly stupid to a naval officer's ears."

"That's why it took a Marine to figure it out. Anyway, as a wise man once said, if it's stupid and it works, it's not stupid. You might wish to record that somewhere for future reference."

She gave him a playful tap.

"Smart ass. Give me an hour or so to prepare the systems, then you can play dumb Marine with the station's controllers. Just make sure you win."

**

"Kilia control, this is *Chimera*."

Zack's voice held a hint of panic, but he had a twinkle in his eyes when he winked at Talyn.

A bored voice came on.

"Yes, *Chimera*, what can we do for you today?"

"Well, we – um – have us a bit of a situation here, control."

"Oh?" The voice didn't lose an iota of its disinterest.

"Um, our magnetic bottles – how shall I put this? They seem to have developed a bit of instability. Nothing much, mind you, but we're thinking..."

"What do you mean, instability?" The boredom suddenly vanished. "Don't you have fail-safes?"

"Well, it seems the fail-safes have...well, um, they failed, and we haven't had a chance to replace them."

"I'm scanning you now *Chimera*, stand by."

Decker nodded at Talyn. She touched the helm station's screen.

"Holy crap, *Chimera*!" The controller's voice had gone up by two octaves. "You just burped some anti-matter."

"Yeah, yeah, we felt that," Zack replied, full-blown terror in his tone. "Can we like evacuate to the station and you guys kick the ship off."

"Ah, wait."

The radio went silent for almost twenty seconds during which Talyn vented a further spurt of anti-matter, creating a tiny, very bright sun aft of *Chimera*. Then, a new voice came on.

"*Chimera*, I'm cutting you loose and pushing you away with my tractor beams. Get yourself out of range pronto. Your presence is no longer welcome here. Any ship dumb enough to sail without working fail-safes on their magnetic bottles is barred from Kilia."

The words were accompanied by a loud mechanical sound as the controller unlatched both grappling arms holding the ship to the docking tower. Then, they were pushed out far enough to engage the sublight drives.

"Now get out of here, *Chimera*."

"Yes, sir. Thank you, sir." Decker replied before cutting the transmission. "We're free and clear, Hera."

"And we're on our way," she replied, stroking the drive controls. The small ship accelerated with all she had, leaving the asteroid field far behind.

**

"Did you run the EMP yet?" Talyn asked once she'd turned the helm over to the AI.

"No, but those things have a pretty short range, so they're nothing more than electronic dust right now, for all they're worth." He touched his console. "Done."

"You know this kind of stunt could get us thrown in jail for reckless endangerment of a spaceport," she remarked, stretching her slender frame to release the tension. "But I'll grant you: it worked, so by definition it wasn't stupid."

"Told you. Now what?"

"We find a quiet spot away from any watchers, switch out the transponder, change names, and try our luck further along the rim."

"Dump the *Chimera* identity so quickly?"

"The Jackals will make sure their *Sécurité Spéciale* sponsors take an interest in our ship."

"Seems like a waste."

She shrugged.

"At least we found out that someone is still looking for *Syrah,* and that means they don't know what happened to Amali, which is all to the good."

"Confusion to the enemy." Decker mimicked raising a glass. "My favorite toast."

"I don't like that the *Sécurité Spéciale* is using gangsters as enforcers."

"With us breathing down their necks at every turn, it was inevitable. I wouldn't be surprised to find full-fledged agents among the tattooed goons."

"It's a shitty universe when the military and civilian arms of government are waging a secret war against each other."

"Imagine how much fun it would be if Admiral Kowalski hadn't rammed through her reforms and insulated the Fleet from Earth's dirty politics."

"And yet, here we are, still playing intramural games at the retail level some forty years later."

"It's still more fun than the alternative," she replied. "I've read the top secret, never to be revealed archives. The SecGen had drafted up orders placing political officers in every regiment and on every ship when Kowalski carried out her forcible reforms and wiped out the old Special Security Bureau."

"Blessed be her name, in that case. Considering I barely survived dealing with the regular sort of useless officers, imagine me and a political in the same unit." He nodded aft towards the passageway. "Buy you a coffee?"

Zack's console suddenly chimed with an agitated rhythm that augured nothing but grief. He turned back and stared at the readout.

"We've been hit by a targeting sensor."

"Shit." Talyn dropped back into her chair.

"I'll assume that's spook speak for battle stations," Decker said, turning on the ship's defensive suite. "Shields are up, weapon systems are powering."

"Where and what?"

"Give me a moment." Then, "it's coming from ahead, range unknown, but the signature is Shrehari. They have a fix on us."

"The ones who made fun of your blaster?"

"Probably." He scrolled back through the sensor log. "They left the station six hours ago. I told you their traders were part-time marauders."

"Maybe they're just screwing with us."

"I doubt it," he replied after a lengthy pause, "and I found them. They're sitting athwart our course in a perfect position to run us down, and their emcon is not bad. If this tub still carried civilian electronics, we'd have been a sitting duck, which is what they're expecting us to be."

"How so?"

"The buggers are good fighters, but they're not very imaginative. For example, the ones out there can't imagine that we might actually be a Q-ship. They figure we're easy pickings."

"We'll blow our cover if we go all out, Zack," she warned.

"Not if we make sure to leave nothing but debris behind." He sounded unconcerned. "What worries me more is why they thought they'd be good for a little piracy almost within sight of Kilia Station."

"What does Kilia care about ships like ours? They're too busy playing best pals with the Confederacy. That, or I'm back to the idea the Shrehari are having some fun."

"If it doesn't involve killing, drinking or singing dirty songs, it doesn't qualify as fun for a Shrehari. Trust me on this. I've taken down enough of them in my time. These guys are looking for a little action."

"We're almost at the hyperlimit anyhow." She glanced at her readout.

"They'll pursue." His console chimed urgently. "I guess we'll have to fight before we can run. Ready to take maneuvering orders?"

She settled back in her seat. "Ready."

"I think we should strap in. They knock out the artificial gravity, and we're floating."

"Done," she replied a moment later.

"Unless they can defeat our emcon, they have no idea yet that we've spotted them and are ready to rumble, so stay on course until they unmask. Let 'em believe we're fat, happy, and stupid until it's too late. I'd like to try out my new toys and pay the buggers back for all the years I spent hunting guys like them in the back of beyond."

"Try not to enjoy yourself too much," she replied in a dry tone.

"No promises."

Decker went through the checklist again, more to kill time than because of any fear that one of the systems might not perform properly.

When the Shrehari finally lit up to intercept *Chimera*, it almost came as a surprise.

"Game on, baby." A manic grin spread across Decker's face. "Change course thirty-five degrees to starboard and zee minus fifteen degrees."

"Thirty-five degrees starboard, zee minus fifteen, aye," Talyn replied, entering the corrections. Thrusters fired almost immediately, sending the ship on an arc away from the oncoming Shrehari ship.

"A stern chase, Zack?"

"Yup. We have the legs on them, for sure. They're bigger than we are and chock-a-block full of second rate Shrehari technology. They do maintenance when something breaks and not before. Also," he chuckled, an evil sound that matched the light in his deep blue eyes, "we have as much ordnance facing aft as forward. I guess the engineers who reworked this tub are fans of running away to fight another day."

"Why not just escape?" She asked, amused by his enthusiasm.

"And let them try a do-over on a ship that doesn't have our hidden charms? Not likely, commander."

"Just don't shoot first, Zack. I mean it. There could still be a chance the bastards are screwing with us."

"I know the rules of engagement. Just you wait. They'll start with a few warning shots; then if we don't decelerate and let them board us, they'll try some trick shooting on our hyperdrive nacelles. After that, they'll do the same to our sublight drive."

"Is that what happened to *Demetria*?"

"Yeah." He shrugged irritably, annoyed that he could still feel the sting of Avril's death after so long.

"Would your enthusiasm at taking on these Shrehari instead of running be a form of payback?" Her tone was even, and her eyes remained glued to the tactical display.

"Why not? Turning marauders into a cloud of atoms is payback for everything done by every scumbag cruising the star lanes." The sarcasm was heavier than usual, and she turned to glance at him.

"Just make sure you have the right motives for this, Zack. An agent can't afford to indulge in personal vengeance during a mission unless it's been sanctioned."

"Like I said, we're going to do local shipping a solid by taking these guys out. I seem to recall that we're both part of the Fleet, and this ship is an armed Navy sloop, be it ever so small and well camouflaged."

"Q-ship tactics now?" She snorted. "You read up on those?"

"No, though it can't be too hard. I'll make up the rules as I go along."

"For someone who has a saying for every occasion and can reach back into history on command, I'm surprised that you're not quoting Admiral Dunmoore at me. She wrote the book on modern Q-ship tactics during the last war. Maybe you'd like to tell her about your innovations in person the next time we're on Caledonia. She still lectures at the Naval War College from time to time."

"Really? She's got to be what? A hundred and ten?"

"A spry hundred and ten, by all accounts."

Zack's console beeped at him.

"Ah. They're powering up weapons. They might have had good emcon when they were lying doggo, but now that they've lit up, my sensors can make out every last fuel cell."

"Remember, let them fire first."

"And they've fired." Decker sounded strangely satisfied.

Two streaks of plasma grazed the port shield, briefly lighting it up like an aurora borealis.

"Those were warning shots." He touched his controls, chortling under his breath. "And we're unmasking."

The rumbling sound of hull panels moving aside made a counter-point to the sharper noise of the aft launcher pumping out a brace of anti-ship missiles.

The main turrets, one on each beam, rose from hidden recesses and swiveled to point their twin barrels aft, joined simultaneously by small multi-barrel guns emerging from the top and keel of the ship, just forward of the sublight drive nozzles.

"I wish I could see the look on the Shrehari captain's face right now. Thought we were harmless, did he? How about a taste of our plasma to wash down those birds?"

He felt rather than heard autoloaders feed pure copper discs to the guns, ready to be turned into plasma by a power spike from loaded capacitors.

"Give us zee plus twenty, Hera." He shouted excitedly, watching the Shrehari open fire on the oncoming missiles. One vanished in a bright flash but the second exploded against the marauder's shields, giving birth to a bluish-green flare as the energy of the warhead fought that of the force field surrounding the ship.

"Yee haw! A hit on the first try."

He stroked his controls again, and a stream of plasma erupted from *Chimera*, aimed straight at the enemy's weakened shields. The one-two punch proved enough to collapse them entirely, and the next salvo landed on the ship itself, eating through the tough metal armor. Decker kept firing until he saw streams of rapidly freezing gasses escape from the blackened holes he'd ripped into the hull.

"Kick it, Hera. We need to get out of here."

She lit the sublight drives without argument, then glanced over her shoulder at Zack.

"Why?"

"That thing's done for. The buggers are going to self-destruct and hope they take us with them."

"Experience talking?"

"Yup. Shrehari don't let themselves be taken prisoner. It violates their honor code." He slumped back in his seat and wiped a few beads of sweat from his brow. "Space battles are short but intense, aren't they?"

"They get more intense when the enemy actually has a chance to fire back."

"I'll pass on that. Surprise is my favorite principle of war and this little beauty is tailor-made for it." He patted his console like a proud papa.

A bright spark suddenly lit up the view screen.

"Hang on. We might still be a little close."

An energy wave washed over *Chimera* moments later, buffeting the small ship, then their little corner of the galaxy was quiet again, save for an expanding cloud of debris, destined to float through space until the heat death of the universe.

"One less to worry about." Decker rubbed his hands with glee. "That was fun."

"Remember to turn us back into a harmless trader again before you go sleep off your gunnery orgasm. We can jump any time now."

He touched his screen, triggering the faint noise of the turrets slipping into their recesses followed by the slightly louder sound of the hull plates settling back into place, hiding all evidence that *Chimera* was, in fact, a well-camouflaged, pocket-sized man-of-war.

"Done. Now I have to see to my missiles and make sure they're ready the moment we need them."

Talyn cocked a quizzical eyebrow at him.

"We have to manually load the launchers," he explained, undoing his seat restraints. "An autoloader would be too big for this tub. We get a single shot from each before one of us has to go down into the hold and reload. I'm kind of surprised they actually managed to fit those full-sized tubes into that tiny space, but as I like saying if it works..."

"I guess caressing those birds is as close to a wet dream come true as a Marine master gunner will ever have, eh?" She chuckled at his beatific smile.

"You said it, sister."

—SEVEN—

"Fighting usually gives me an appetite, but this is ridiculous for the amount I actually did. No wonder you swabbies get fat in shipboard billets," Decker commented around a mouthful of vat-grown beef. "What now?"

"I have us programmed to emerge in interstellar space. When we get there, and the coast is clear, I'll reprogram the identification beacon. While I do that, you get to go outside and shift some of the hull panels to change our silhouette."

"And change the markings," he added before shoving another forkful into his mouth. "Great times will be had by all."

"Then I've got to think of our next steps. I was hoping someone on Kilia might help us trace the Garonne rebels' suppliers, so we could work our way to whoever's behind the funding, but that's no longer an option."

"We might find it just as challenging wherever we go. Considering they had goons breathing down the chandler's neck, I'm not sure we'll get lucky anywhere else along the Rim."

"That leaves me wondering whether there's still a leak at HQ or whether some people are just extra paranoid, and I don't necessarily mean about the things we're after. The Jackals might be in the *Sécurité Spéciale*'s pockets, but that doesn't mean they're not running their own operations. I can't see government work, even if it's for the SecGen's pet spies, paying enough."

"What kind of a universe is this anyways," he replied, picking a strand of meat from his teeth, "when honest gangsters get in bed with the secret police? At least the Shrehari have enough honor to blow themselves up. I'll take boneheads over mobsters any day."

"You mean take on, don't you?"

"That too." He burped contentedly. "How long is this leg?"

"About ten hours."

"That means I have time for a nice cold one."

"I'll join you. It might help me figure out our next move."

"Good plan. It always helps with my moves." He leered at her, then he reached into the cold box and grabbed two bottles.

"I'll bet, you incorrigible lecher."

"Ever heard the one about the hooker and the Marine?"

"Yes, and I don't want to hear it again. Thanks," she said accepting a bottle. "Hanging around with you is giving me some atrocious habits. I used to hate this stuff."

"Honey, hang around with me long enough, and I'll make you love just about anything."

"That's what I'm afraid of." She raised her bottle. "Congratulations, Zack. That was a half-decent Q-ship surprise you pulled on the Shrehari, for a Marine, I mean."

"I'll let Admiral Dunmoore know next time we're on Caledonia. Mud in your eye, swabbie." He took a healthy swig and sighed. "The water of life, this stuff."

**

"Fun, fun, fun," Decker muttered under his breath, shuffling out the aft airlock. Magnetic soles under his pressure suit boots made the spacewalk feel like a slog through a thick mire.

"What was that?" The radio crackled in his ears.

"Nothing you need to worry about. Just make sure you don't accidentally go FTL while I'm outside."

"If I go FTL while you're outside, it won't be by accident."

"Nice to know you've got my back." He crept up the hull towards the superstructure where shifting a few panels would make a noticeable change to the ship's silhouette.

"Why is it me who gets to do the hard work anyway?" He asked, contemplating the first piece of the camouflage puzzle.

"Remember when this ship was still a floating brothel? Remember the mirror on the deckhead in the main stateroom?"

"Yeah."

"Remember seeing us side by side in bed, in our birthday suits?"

"Of course. Good times."

"Then I'm sure you didn't fail to notice the size and musculature differences between us. Big boys get to do big boy jobs."

"Sexist."

"I also outrank you."

"Hierarchist."

He attached a handling frame to the first panel and released the clamps holding it to the hull.

"That's not actually a word," she replied.

"It is now." He shifted the panel and re-attached it to the hull. "One down."

"Ah yes, the famous Decker dictionary. In case you care, we're no longer transmitting an ID beacon."

"Lovely." He wrestled with the second panel. "It's a fine thing we're doing this out here in space and not on anything with a gravity pull."

"I'm sure you'd have been able to manage."

"Maybe, but I'd have added a few new swear words to the Decker dictionary."

"Don't hold back now on my account."

"When I feel the need to curse, you'll be the first to know. Two down."

He shuffled backward and stared at the star-filled darkness above the curvature of the hull, feeling unaccountably drawn in by the abyss.

"Zack," Hera's voice snapped him out of his contemplation, "is everything alright? You went strangely silent there for a moment."

"Yeah." He shook his head. "I'm all right, but I think the universe just reminded me how small and petty my life actually is."

"EVA has that effect on a lot of people."

He attached the handling frame to the third panel and continued working in silence until *Chimera* looked just different enough to fool most people, if not all algorithms.

"Done with the hull plates," he announced, wishing he could wipe his brow. And scratch his nose. He suddenly had an urgent need to scratch his nose.

"Got the new marking overlays ready?"

"Sitting in the airlock," she replied.

"Fun, fun, fun," he muttered again, making his way back down the hull to the open hatch, where he found several large self-adhering carbon fiber sheets, rolled up and tucked into a bag. He stowed the now folded handling frame in the airlock and clipped the bag to his utility belt before shuffling out onto the hull again, this time across a short pylon to the starboard hyperdrive nacelle.

He carefully unrolled the first of the sheets and aligned it to the marks on the side of the housing. Taking a rod from the bag, he ran it over the edge, activating nanites that bonded the new nameplate and registration number over the old one.

After a long, slow walk back onto the hull, over it and out on the port hyperdrive nacelle, he had the markings in place.

"Done. You want to send out a drone to check that it looks right?"

The itch on the tip of his nose was back with a vengeance.

"Sure. Give me a second."

Decker returned to the airlock where he found a small basketball-sized spacecraft waiting. He picked it up and pushed it out into space, where its tiny thrusters kicked in under Talyn's control from the bridge. It vanished from his sight for a few minutes, then hovered just outside the airlock again, waiting for him to reach out and grab it.

"The markings look good, Zack. Well done."

"Let's just get this airlock cycled so I can get out of the suit."

"Nose itching?" She asked, sounding deliberately mischievous.

"Like a son of a bitch. And I desperately need a shower too."

The outer hatch slammed shut, air hissed into the tiny compartment, and soon enough, the inner hatch swung open to Talyn's ironic grin.

"Welcome aboard *Phoenix*, Ser Whate. I'm Captain Pasek. Have you ever sailed with us before?"

"More often than I care to remember," he replied, lifting the suit's helmet over his head and handing it to her.

Scratching his nose had never felt so good.

"Come on, big boy. We need to give ourselves a makeover. The folks on Kilia Station might not circulate our portraits to the rest of the sketchy frontier tribes, but why take a chance?"

"Can I not have long hair this time? Feeling it on my ears bugs the crap out of me."

"Sorry. The ID experts have decreed that long hair does a better job of turning you into not-Decker than short hair."

**

He took a healthy swig from his bottle and sighed contentedly.

"So, now that I'm partially refueled, would you care to tell me what our next stop is going to be?"

"Andoth."

She pulled two warmed up trays from the autochef and placed them on the table.

"Andoth?" Decker searched his memory for the vaguely familiar name. "Isn't that the place they tried to turn into a prison colony after the war? Lasted maybe thirty years. All settlements are at the bottom of deep chasms because the air pressure at the surface is too weak. Lots of volcanic activity, etcetera, etcetera?"

"Got it in one. It's a fairly nasty environment, with a single industry and no homesteading. Other than taxing the export of rare ores and gemstones, the central government doesn't have much interest in the place. A miners' consortium runs it with a passel of mercenaries for law and order."

"About as frontier as it gets and still be within Commonwealth borders, eh?" Zack cocked a sardonic eyebrow. "We should fit right in."

"A damn sight more dangerous than Kilia though, which may actually help." She took a bite of her food and chewed slowly, eyes unfocused while she thought about their destination.

"The shipping brokers in a place like that are bound to be dabbling on the dark side, where organizations like rebel movements would look to hire. That being said, we might be better off to leave the ship in orbit and shuttle down to the surface when we get there."

"Scared of flying down one of their chasms?"

"I'm more worried that I won't be able to lift *Phoenix* out of there if things go sideways again."

"Ah." He nodded knowingly. "It would be pretty hard to scam our way into open space from ten kilometers below the surface."

"Give yourself another drink, Marine Boy. You're getting smart."

"Must be the company I keep."

"Flattery will get you everywhere, once you've showered."

"Promises, promises." He drained his bottle and reached into the cooler for its successor. "I could really enjoy this lifestyle, you know."

"Wait until we get to Andoth."

"You going to let Ulrich know?" Decker took a sip and smacked his lips with pleasure.

"Can't. No subspace array we can tap into within light-years. I'd rather not send anything via a commercial relay. Even if we encode it, someone could get the idea that we're not cuddly space rogues."

"Yup. Got to keep our street cred intact." He burped loudly and smiled. "Almost as good coming up as it was going down."

"You're a pig, you know that?"

Decker's sole reply was to blow his partner a big wet kiss.

**

"Cripes, and here I thought Nabhka looked depressing." He shook his head in amazement. "Why do people insist on living in places that defy common sense?"

"The usual reasons," Talyn replied, gently nudging *Phoenix* into a stable orbit, "greed, desire to get away from authority, looking for adventure."

"Looking for insanity, more likely. I'm going to guess there's no orbital control. The sensors aren't picking up anything bigger than unmanned satellites, and precious few of those. No other ships in orbit either."

"There's not much for off-world visitors to see."

"You're still determined to leave the ship in orbit and shuttle down?"

"Sure." She touched the controls one last time. "There. The AI has its instructions. *Phoenix* will be fine up here."

"What if someone comes along, sees a nice oversized space yacht or undersized sloop, depending on how you look at it, and decides it would make a beautiful addition to their stable."

"The AI will make sure no one can do that."

"Seriously?" Decker didn't hide his disbelief. "You're supposed to be the professional paranoid, Hera. A ship without a crew can be taken, given enough time. The AI might be able to navigate hyperspace, keep a stable orbit, and do almost anything related to moving the thing, but it can't fight properly. I can think of three dozen ways to take it in my sleep."

"You can, but then you've trained for it and done it for real often enough. The average pirate isn't quite as skilled, and he sure doesn't have a Marine's patience. I'd rather take my chances up here, where the AI can at least sail the ship out of harm's way if needed than ten kilometers down a rift valley with only one way out."

She stood, rotating her shoulders to loosen the muscles.

"Then I'll make sure to add some refinements of my own to the security system. Anyone tries to board without permission is going to end up missing a limb or two at the very least."

"Knock yourself out, Zack." She smiled briefly. "And make sure the emcon is perfect. The ship can't be boarded in the first place if it can't be found. I'll do the pre-flight check on the shuttle."

"Aye, aye, Captain, sir." He tossed off a mock salute. "I'll head to the armory for a few bits and pieces I can use to thoroughly booby trap *Phoenix*. This might actually get entertaining."

Whistling tunelessly, he left the bridge on his quest, already mentally building the contraptions he'd attach on the various airlocks. This was the kind of work he enjoyed.

Talyn shook her head, then headed aft to the small hangar deck. Decker had the strangest notions when it came to fun.

**

The hangar deck hatch slammed shut behind Zack, cutting them off from the ship's interior, and he felt unaccountably cheerless at the thought of leaving *Phoenix* unattended. He'd become rather fond of the little ship.

Talyn's voice rang out from the ancient-looking shuttle.

"Ready?"

"As ready as she'll ever be. No one's getting on board without finding at least one nasty little Easter egg. The systems are down to minimal, and the non-essentials are in hibernation. We can bring them up from the shuttle on the way back so she'll be ready to go. You had your long commune with the AI?"

"It's been thoroughly briefed."

"Then I guess we can head out to the enchanted land of Andoth."

Decker climbed aboard and strapped himself into the right-hand seat beside Talyn, examining the cockpit while he did so.

"Looks well aged. I hope that's only on the surface. Oh well, off we go then, driver."

"Would you like to 'drive' instead?"

"No, no." He waved his hands at the controls. "I believe we've already had this discussion. Driving is for swabbies."

"I suppose you could always put on a pressure suit and spacewalk your way to the surface."

"Only if I'm on jump pay, which I'm not."

The shuttle's rear ramp closed up, sealing the agents inside. At Talyn's command, the hangar deck depressurized to the flashing of a red warning light. When the strobe stopped, the main doors opened, exposing a broad swath of stars.

Talyn gently nudged the small craft free of the sloop using only maneuvering thrusters, then turned on the main drives.

"Hangar door's closed again," Decker reported, glancing at the visual of a rapidly receding *Phoenix* and then at the tactical readout. "Her emcon's tight and her albedo is almost zero."

"Told you. Absent naval grade sensors, a ship thief would have to be very lucky if he comes near enough to find her."

"Don't underestimate the power of corruption. Naval-grade gear goes walkabout all the time. Some of it ends up on ships with bad intentions. Then, guys like me have to go sort them out; a good time will be had by all; the end."

She looked at him quizzically.

"Did you just have a stroke or something?"

"No. I'm not comfortable leaving the ship with no one aboard. It's a Marine thing. We like to know our ride will still be there, ready to extract us after a drop."

"There's the AI."

"It's a computer code, not a someone."

"Don't tell it that. You might hurt its feelings."

"Now who's being strange? Caring about a machine just because someone programmed it to sound like you? Pay attention to your driving instead; if we land anywhere other than at the bottom of the equatorial chasm, we won't have a fun time. You need enough air pressure to have a fun time."

"Right, so why don't you do your job as second fiddle and give the Yavan spaceport a call?"

"Second fiddling for the mistress, aye." Decker scanned for the expected beacon, and when he found it, he locked in.

"We have a positive link with the relay at the surface. They're transmitting approach and landing instructions automatically."

"How nice: no inconvenient questions from a bored controller. My kind of place."

They flew in silence for almost an hour, the dun-colored, desolate looking planet growing rapidly on the main screen. Decker pointed at a dark slash near the equator.

"That's where we want to go, in case you forgot. Yavan is somewhere at the bottom of it."

"To quote a Marine of my acquaintance, it looks like fun, fun, fun."

"Everyone's a comedian," he grumbled. "Try not to add to the collection of dents on the hull and I'll be happy."

Talyn brought the shuttle to a hover just above the fissure, and they got their first glimpse of Andoth's settled area. They expected the darkness, but not the thousands and thousands of distant lights scattered along the bottom for hundreds of kilometers in either direction.

"It's almost ten klicks down, Hera." A touch of awe escaped his normal self-control.

"Does it make you feel small, big boy?"

"Nah, but I can see why you wanted to leave *Phoenix* in orbit. Trying to fly a sloop out of there when someone's on your ass wouldn't be ideal, not least for my nerves."

"No, it wouldn't." She shook her head at the thought. "They mustn't get much sunlight down there."

"Probably none at all. Artificial light twenty-four seven. Shall we?"

"Have you locked in the actual spaceport beacon, not the surface relay?"

"Do I love Shrehari ale?"

Without answering, she banked the shuttle towards the source of the transmission and began shedding altitude. Soon, they dropped below the rim of the chasm and began descending into eternal darkness, passing helpful, brightly lit markers set on the walls at regular intervals.

The lights on the bottom grew in size and began to separate into individual sources, revealing a broken, nightmarish landscape that somehow had sprouted a carpet of human structures.

"Not exactly pretty, is it?" He grunted. "It must be profitable, though; Yavan doesn't look like just a two-bit mining town. That spaceport tarmac can probably take half a dozen standard transports with room to spare for nervous helmsmen."

Decker switched a side screen to the overhead view and was rewarded by the sight of a thin thread of lavender sky high above them.

"It would definitely have been a bitch to lift off in *Phoenix* if someone wanted to keep us down there," he said.

Talyn brought the shuttle down in an increasingly shallow glide, aiming the nose at a yellow circle outlined by flashing lights near a single story building at the edge of the tarmac. When they were directly above the landing spot, she killed all forward momentum and gently touched down. The markers immediately stopped flashing.

"We're here," she announced, unfastening her seat restraints.

"So I noticed, but thanks for making sure. I suppose we should visit the port master first and pay our fees. This doesn't look like the kind of place that'll open a tab."

"Indeed." She rose and stretched to the extent possible in the confines of the cockpit. "Lock and load?"

Decker pulled out his blaster and fed a copper disc into the ignition chamber, checking the battery's charge at the same time.

"Lock and load."

— EIGHT —

The air was cold and thin and tasted like a mixture of flint, metal, and old lubricants. Sounds, continually amplified by echoing back and forth across the chasm, fed an insistent hum of human activity under the harsh glare of a thousand different lights. Yavan lived in an eternal night, yet the only stars in its sky were the flashing beacons rising up on either side of the rift.

"Charming," Decker murmured, scanning his surroundings while Talyn sealed up the shuttle. "Exactly the kind of place I wouldn't choose for shore leave. Your brain thinks it's past midnight, and yet it's what? Late afternoon, local time?"

He jerked his chin at the hubbub around one of the large transports loading battered containers.

"I bet we'll want to be inside something soundproofed when that thing takes off."

"No doubt," Talyn agreed. Looking upwards, she shivered slightly. "Boy am I ever glad we left *Phoenix* in orbit."

"At this point, I'm with you one hundred percent." He jerked a thumb at the single story building. "Shall we go see how extortionate their landing fees are before they send a couple of goons after us?"

From somewhere several kilometers southwest of Yavan, a dull roar reverberated and they saw a streak of light climb upwards.

"Headed for another settlement? There's no ship in orbit other than ours." They began walking towards the larger of two doors opening out onto a cracked concrete path. "Did you bring some money? I think I forgot my wallet on the ship."

"Then you'll have to watch me drink once we hit the local saloon."

"Evil woman."

"You know, that could also have been an unmanned pod hauling refined ore into orbit for a ship that's on its way."

"Makes sense." He pulled the scarred door open and stepped into a dingy waiting room.

Devoid of life but filled with tired looking chairs and benches that appeared to have been scrounged from a crashed starship, it suffered under anemic lighting and walls shaded a lovely institutional green.

"Over there, I'd say." Decker pointed at a faded sign directing visitors to the port administrator.

They entered an office overgrown with computer consoles, data tablets and other bureaucratic junk Zack couldn't be bothered to identify. Its sole inhabitant, an overweight woman wearing creased gray coveralls glanced up at them with a sad, bulldog face. Her skin beneath an unruly mop of red-tinted hair had the pallor of someone who regularly skipped her turn under the solar lamps, a necessity when you lived in perpetual gloom.

"You the shuttle on pad four?" She had the voice of a drinker and smoker, two of the four recreational activities usually favored on places like Andoth, the others being gambling and whoring.

"That's our shuttle, yes," Talyn replied.

"One thousand a day, no discount for partial days. How long are you staying?"

"Three, four days maybe. Perhaps less."

"Okay," the woman nodded, "I'll put you down for three days. If you leave earlier, I'll refund you for any full thirty hour period not taken."

"Thirty hours?"

"Standard Andoth day, not that we notice it much down here. That'll be three thousand — cash. For an extra two hundred a day, you can buy enhanced security services."

Decker tilted his head to the side, crossed his arms, and studied the woman quizzically.

"What happens if we don't buy enhanced security?"

She shrugged.

"Then I can't guarantee that nothing whatsoever will happen to your shuttle. This is a rough place."

"So you're offering a protection racket, is that it?"

"Just looking out for visitors to our beautiful spaceport, sir."

"I'll bet." He nodded at Talyn, signaling that she should add an extra two hundred a day to their landing fees.

A malicious look of triumph in the woman's piggish eyes confirmed Decker's guess that it was a racket. If they hadn't paid up, they might have found all sorts of problems when they returned to the spaceport. When she put the three thousand in a lock box and pocketed the other six hundred, he locked eyes with her.

"I expect to find not so much as a strange fingerprint on our shuttle."

"Come on, Ser Whate," his companion said, turning to leave, "we have a contract to hunt up."

Zack, still looking at the woman, saw a flash of interest replace the malice in her eyes.

"Let me guess," he said, "for a fee, you can hook us up with folks looking to shift cargo, no questions asked."

"Maybe." She began fiddling with a stylus, flipping it between her thick fingers. "Tell me what you offer and I can pass the word."

Decker looked over his shoulder at Talyn, eyebrows raised in question. She gave him a quick nod.

"Free-trader, five thousand tons; we look at cash, not bills of lading and we land wherever there's a flat piece of ground big enough for our ship. We can take care of ourselves and keep under the Navy's sensors."

"Five hundred up front and a thousand when I have a contact for you." When she saw his hesitation, she chuckled. "If you're the kind who runs high-value cargo, no questions asked, it'll be money well spent."

Talyn handed over another five hundred creds, glad that the black ops fund was paying for all this, with no questions asked.

"I'm Triane Lyde, by the way," she said, pocketing the money with practiced ease.

"Pasek," Talyn replied, then pointed at her companion, "and he's Whate. Our ship is *Phoenix*. Got any recommendations for a place to stay?"

"Sure." Lyde's smile perked up enough to warn both agents they were about to be directed to an establishment that gave her generous kickbacks. "The Andoth Paradise is the best place in Yavan. Got all the amenities: food, clean beds, casino, and brothel. You name it, they offer it."

Her wink made it clear the Andoth Paradise was prepared to offer more than what it advertised openly, provided the payment was right.

"Sure." Decker shrugged. "Provided they have Shrehari ale, I'm happy."

"Then the Paradise is your place, Ser Whate. When you leave here, turn right, and head towards downtown. It's about a kilometer away. You can't miss it."

"Thanks." Zack nodded. "We'll see you tomorrow then."

After they'd gone, Triane Lyde touched her console and called up one of her contacts. Spacers trolling for cargo who were that free with bribes and didn't bother haggling were unusual enough to warrant attention.

**

"You know what I like most about this job?" Decker glanced at his partner, walking beside him along the dusty road. "It's all the lovely, hard-working, honest folks you meet along the way."

"Cynic." She jabbed her elbow into his rock-hard side.

"Just a student of human nature, Sera Pasek," he replied with an affected air of innocence, "alternating between amazement and despair. Mostly despair."

"Feeling the years creeping up on you, Zack?"

"No, but I see that we're creeping up on one of the more garish displays of frontier tastelessness I've seen in a long time."

They had come around a bend in the road that skirted a warehouse complex and got their first glimpse of Yavan's outskirts which, being close to the spaceport, aimed to provide any and all entertainment money could buy.

"Garishness to make up for the scarcity of decent offerings?" Talyn grimaced. "I confess to being both underwhelmed and a little nauseous, especially considering that without daylight, this little display is on continuously."

"Welcome to Andoth. You chose the destination, remember?"

"If we're going to trace the Garonne rebels' supply chain, it's only second to Kilia in this sector."

"And last in sanitation." He sniffed the air, a disgusted expression twisting his features. "I'm going to guess they didn't spend a lot of time and money putting in a modern sewage system."

"Not much air movement at the bottom of a rift this deep, I suppose."

"Open air septic dumps don't help." He pointed at a large, circular vat by the side of the road with biohazard signs on it.

"You signed up for the Corps. Don't complain when you're sent to exotic places."

"I only signed up once, and they kicked me out after my twenty. The second time I re-upped it wasn't voluntary. You shanghaied me, sweetheart, remember?"

******

The Andoth Paradise, three tiers of mismatched, stacked containers unified by a paint scheme that offended even Decker's plebian tastes, gradually emerged from behind pulsating lights.

"I think we're here," Decker remarked, staring at the building. "Frontier recycling at its best. If this is the finest Yavan has to offer, I'd hate to see the lesser places."

"It's the best that pays our spaceport friend backhanders, not necessarily the local equivalent of a five-star hotel." Talyn shook her head. "If we wanted to live in the lap of luxury, we wouldn't be in this line of business."

"As I keep reminding you, I'm not exactly in this line of business by choice."

He stepped onto the wide veranda and pushed the swinging doors aside, allowing a blast of music spiced by the tang of fried food to assault his senses.

They entered what seemed to be a combination of main lobby, eatery, and bar. To one side, men and women, under the influence of who knew what spirits or pharmaceuticals danced to an irregular rhythm beneath lights pulsating at a frequency almost purposely designed to trigger fits.

Decker blinked a few times, trying to chase afterimages from his protesting retinas.

"Charming." He turned towards the other end of the vast room and homed in on a corner well equipped with individual booths and seemingly beyond the typhoon of light and noise devastating the dance floor.

"This way, I think."

A few meters from the first table, he felt a soft tingle on his exposed skin and the noise level suddenly dropped to no more than a soft background murmur.

"Sound curtain." Zack nodded with approval. "This layout's not as dumb as it looks. It might be tolerable after all."

"Let's sample the food before we declare the place tolerable, shall we?"

"Ale, then food." Decker slid into a booth built to cut off the worst of the flashing lights. Moments later, a tiny holographic waiter emerged from the tabletop and smiled at him ingratiatingly.

"What may I offer?" It asked in a squeaky voice.

"Shrehari Ale," he glanced at Talyn, who nodded, "twice. What's the special of the day?"

"Our famous Paradise stew made with the finest vat-grown beef on the planet."

Zack snorted.

"Doesn't sound like much of a stretch."

"I can assure the good sir that we do not stretch our stew with non-meat ingredients." The hologram sounded hilariously prim. "This is the finest eating establishment in Yavan."

"Two servings of your stew then," Talyn quickly said, afraid Decker might engage in a lengthy discussion with a computer program just to see how far he could take things before it broke down into an endless loop.

The hologram bowed and vanished, leaving the two operatives to study their surroundings in silence. Discussing the mission at a table that could sprout an AI waiter on its own wasn't a good idea.

"You think we might find a profitable run?" He finally asked, figuring that it couldn't hurt to play his role to the hilt.

"Stuff the Navy doesn't like to see shipped comes through here for a reason," Talyn replied, "and that's where the money is. We need a few good contracts. Otherwise, we won't be able to pay off the mortgage on the ship and when that happens..."

"Yeah, we get the kind of financial counseling that usually ends up being fatal."

A human waiter who, by his looks, wouldn't have been out of place among the Confederacy of the Howling Stars, appeared with a tray holding two mugs of frothy purplish liquid and two steaming bowls of a chunky, brown substance, along with several slices of dark bread.

"Ten for the drinks, another twenty for the stews." He said by way of greeting after placing the tray carefully on the table.

Decker pulled three ten cred chips from his jacket's inner pocket and dropped them into the man's open palm.

"Any chance of getting a room?"

"Sure. Fifty a night. See Wim over by the bar when you're ready." With a last nod, he left them to their meal.

Decker took a tentative sip and swished it over his taste buds before swallowing.

"Not the worst I've ever had, but far from the best," he concluded. "At least they have the stuff, and it's genuine from over the border, not imitation."

"Maybe this place has direct or semi-direct links with the Empire, even if it's just importing booze."

"Most places along the Rim do." He took a healthier swig. "There's money in some of the stuff the Imperials make. Why do you think I carry a Shrehari blaster?"

"To tenderize the meat in this stew?" She began chewing on a hunk of vat-grown beef. "I'm glad we're having the best Andoth can offer."

"It's not so bad," he replied after taking his first bite. "I've had stuff massacred by autochefs that you could use as armor after rinsing off the gravy."

He chewed contemplatively, washing each bite down with a sip.

"I wonder if we could get a hook into some of the Shrehari trade," Talyn said after wiping the bottom of her bowl with a bit of bread.

"I hope you don't mean the leg from the Empire to this place. Shrehari traders who work those routes won't like competition and I don't particularly feel like visiting the Empire. You break one of their taboos, they can get medieval on your ass to the point where your family will wonder years later why you stopped calling at Christmas."

"Not a problem for us, then. Neither you nor I have any family worth mentioning." She smirked. "No, I was thinking about the shipping between here and the final destination. There's got to be real money in carrying Imp wares."

"Probably." He looked over his shoulder at the dance floor. "What do you say we get a room and do the horizontal samba?"

"What if I'm more in the mood for a slow dance?" She stood, eyes on automatic scan, like any good agent.

"You're in luck; the next dance is ladies' choice." He gave her his best leer.

"That sounded plural to me," she replied looking at him with suspicion. "Are you implying that you'll be inviting someone to join us?"

"If you insist." He managed to look so perfectly innocent that she had no choice but to smile.

The waiter must have warned Wim that the newcomers were looking for a room because he waved them over to the side of the bar where the crush of patrons wasn't so dense. Decker handed over fifty creds and got a key chip in return.

"You room is on the second floor. The stairs are in the back." Wim gestured over his shoulder. "You want anything special, you let me know."

"I think he offered to arrange a third party for our dance," Decker whispered in Talyn's ear.

"No doubt he would arrange it if asked," she replied. "But he probably meant something more in the line of stuff you shove up your nose."

"That, he can shove up his ass."

"I hear it gives you a quicker high that way."

"Pretty shitty addiction, if you ask me," he replied, deadpan, getting the expected groan in return.

Mercifully, the sounds of the eternal party faded quickly once they reached their floor.

The second floor corridor consisted of painted metal walls and a hard, plasticized floor designed for an easy clean up after the night's drunks had tossed their cookies on the way to bed. However, the room they'd been given was much different.

"Basic brothel chic," Decker said looking at the red wall hangings, velvet bed cover and plush chairs. "And there's even the obligatory mirror on the ceiling. I guess these rooms do double duty as hot sheet screwbicles. Hopefully the linen's fresh."

"Just a suggestion, Zack, don't run a sensor scan over the room. You might not be able to fall asleep after that."

He tossed his small bag on a side table while Talyn visited the washroom.

"No windows," he said after checking behind the fabric curtains.

"Thank God. There's nothing to see outside except constant night and the damn lights," she called out through the half-open door.

"It does mean there's only one way in and out of this room. I'll just have to make sure no one gets in that we don't want in."

"Try not to maim the housekeeping staff. Toilet's clean," she said, coming out of the washroom, "though if your plan is to shower with me later on, be warned that there's not enough room to play hide the soap."

"Shower sex is overrated anyway," he replied, pulling off his boots, "unless you're on a starship about to go FTL. Then it's just plain freaky. We going to play for a bit and then go looking, or are we in for the night?"

"In for the night, I think," she replied, shrugging off her jacket and pulling her shirt over her head. "Between the piggy bank at the spaceport and the folks who run this listening post, we might just wait and see if we get any takers before we start to solicit."

"Good," Decker grinned, stepping out of his trousers. "That stew seems to have put a spring in my step, so to speak."

"Something's on a spring alright," she replied, glancing down at his groin area. "Good thing I know a cure."

"So do I. Want to play doctor?"

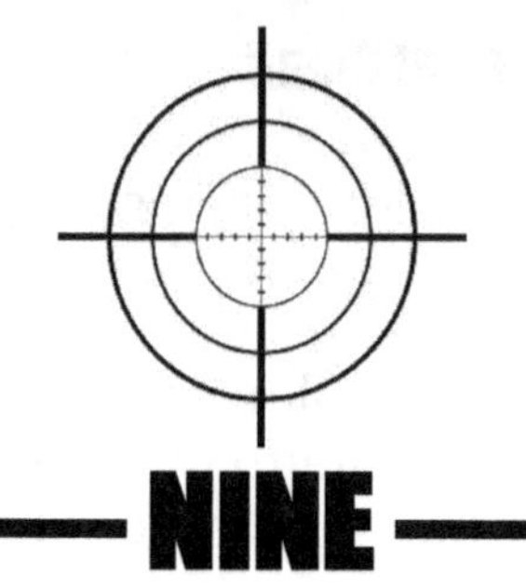

— NINE —

The next morning, while Talyn watched Decker devour a huge breakfast, a ponytailed man in a business suit approached their table.

His pockmarked face creased into a smile when he saw Zack's appetite.

"Hard night?"

"You have no idea," Zack replied between two mouthfuls. He nodded towards Talyn. "Women of her age have cravings that would leave the fittest Marine in the dust."

The man chuckled briefly, then his smile vanished. He pulled up a chair and sat at their table without waiting for an invitation.

"I hear you have a fast ship and empty cargo holds. Maybe I can help you with that. I'm Pavel Krig, by the way."

"Captain Pru Pasek." Talyn shook Krig's hand. "The competitive eater there is First Mate Bill Whate."

Zack nodded wordlessly but kept his attention on the rapidly diminishing pile of hash. Krig could damn well wait until he'd finished his meal.

After a contented belch, washed away with a gulp of coffee, he finally acknowledged the newcomer.

"Did the spaceport bribe queen tell you about us?" Decker asked.

"No. How much did dear Triane Lyde charge you to 'help out'?"

"Five hundred up front, a thousand if we get a contract."

The man's smile returned, this time with a hardness that matched his dark eyes.

"I bet she sold you enhanced security too, right?"

"Yup. She saw us coming a parsec away." Decker shrugged.

"Throwing bribe money around like that could get you some attention you don't want, Ser Whate. Folk here are a suspicious lot."

"You mean the authorities?"   He smirked dismissively. "They haven't pinned anything on us yet."

"Andoth is, shall we say, self-governing in pretty much all things.   Provided we pay a reasonable amount of taxes, the Commonwealth leaves us alone." His smooth tone spoke of the seasoned negotiator or the expert con man. "We have varying interests who aren't always necessarily in agreement when it comes to dealing with outsiders, especially those looking for work."

"Meaning?"

"Come now, Ser Whate, surely a citizen of the galaxy like you can appreciate how unknown spacers who land here and declare they're ready to haul any cargo – wink, wink – provided it pays, might raise suspicions. Especially when they're free with creds."

"True. And I suppose you can smooth over said suspicions, for a fee." Decker made it a statement rather than a question.

"The people I represent wish to diversify their shipping channels. We have nothing resembling regular service this far from the regular star lanes, and so many of the smaller shippers aren't as reliable as some business interests might wish."

Decker's fingers began to dance slowly by his now empty plate.

Do we see what this guy has to offer? He asked.

Turning him down might look suspicious. Talyn replied.

He nodded at her and gave Krig his best Decker grin.

"We're – ah – open to suggestions." Zack then proceeded to pick at a strand of vat pork stuck between his teeth, knowing that the gesture made him look like an uncouth and hopefully clueless hick.

"Perhaps you'd be open to meeting the interests I represent?" Still smooth like a frigate in hyperspace.

"Sure. We're here for business, after all."

Krig's eyes flicked between Talyn and Decker, evidently uncertain which of the two was the real leader.

"Would now be convenient?"

**

"Your employers hang out in a mine shaft, Ser Krig?"

They were headed towards a well-guarded, well-lit opening at the base of the ten-kilometer tall cliff.

"In a played-out section that's been improved, yes. It has its advantages. With the constant darkness down here, one doesn't yearn for offices with windows and there's no rent to pay."

"Good security too, I'll bet," Talyn said, "with limited ways in and out."

Krig nodded warily.

"That as well, yes. As I mentioned, business on Andoth is controlled by varying interests who don't always agree. Sometimes, it's best to appear well protected. It helps calm hotter tempers until negotiations can be completed."

Zack guffawed. "This place sounds like a lot of fun."

"If you enjoy profit, then yes, it is fun," Krig replied, deadpan.

The two guards framing the entrance could have come from the same mold. They both had that aging athlete build where a massive musculature had slowly turned to fat. Bullet-shaped, shaven heads, a standard issue scowl, and impressive looking side arms completed the picture. They gave Decker such a thorough, unfriendly visual once-over that he blew the older of the two a kiss, just out of sheer devilment. To his credit, the man didn't react.

"No weapons check?" Decker asked once they had passed the sentry post and in what could easily pass for an office hallway rather than a horizontal mine shaft.

"We wouldn't wish to insult you and Captain Pasek, Ser Whate. Many on Andoth are armed; it's more or less expected."

"An armed society is a polite society?"

"As you say." Krig inclined his head.

"So you're carrying?"

"Of course." He lifted the side of his jacket to reveal a small but nasty looking needle gun.

Leading the way through a warren of passages, Krig kept speaking of inconsequential matters, as if trying to distract them so they'd have difficulty memorizing the way out, but it was in vain.

Both Decker and Talyn had quickly shut him out to examine their surroundings with the kind of intense focus that comes from long experience.

They eventually entered a larger area with a few tastefully arranged settee groupings. Two men, quasi-clones of the guards outside, were the only occupants, and they studied the two agents with the same dispassion.

"Ser Syko is expecting us," Krig informed them.

The guard on the right nodded once while the other reached out to open a padded door.

"Please go ahead," Krig told Decker and Talyn. "I have other duties I must now attend to."

He turned on his heel and left without waiting for an acknowledgment. The guard by the door made an impatient motion.

"Ser Syko isn't used to waiting."

They entered a large, well-appointed office where a balding older man, sitting behind a large marble-topped table, examined them with obvious interest. Though not another copy of the guards, he apparently came from the same background though with a more advanced case of obesity.

Two tough guys stood against the far wall, arms crossed, faces as if carved from stone. They, on the other hand, were still in the prime of physical fitness.

Syko gestured towards the chairs in front of the table.

"Please sit." When they'd done so, warily but by all outward appearances relaxed, he continued. "Pavel tells me you own a fast, well-armed free-trader and are looking to break into the transport business in this area of the Rim."

"Indeed," Talyn said. "We can guarantee that we'll never be intercepted by the Navy, the Constabulary or marauders."

"That's a big claim to make, Sera Pasek." Syko sounded amused rather than skeptical.

"Perhaps," she replied, unconcerned. "I'd offer to prove it, but I can't call on the Navy to witness the claim. They've never caught us. Any marauders who've tried didn't survive the encounter."

Syko chuckled. "I admire your self-confidence."

Then, he leaned forwards and placed his forearms on the marble tabletop, all pretense at pleasantness erased from his soft features.

"On the other hand, I have a few problems with your story. Your ship, though registered, doesn't have much of a verifiable history and neither do the two of you. Yes, I checked and yes, we have a subspace relay in this system, in case you didn't know."

When neither reacted, Syko snorted and sat back in his chair.

"I'm pretty sure that when the feelers I've put out come back, I won't find anyone in the sector who'll acknowledge knowing you."

"That's because we used to operate in the Yotai area before we had a bit of a quandary with an ungrateful client." Talyn smiled briefly. "A change in name and registry, and we're working again, a few hundred light years away, free and clear of trouble."

"Possibly." Syko looked down at his fingers before staring up at them again with small, deep-set eyes. "If you were Constabulary or Navy operatives trying to infiltrate what the authorities deem illegal trade, your background would be much less sparse and more convincing. Still..."

"The other problem I have is this," he continued after a brief pause, "my folks have scanned for your ship in orbit and have come up with nothing. I know it's there. Yavan Control has a record of your arrival in this system."

"Make that three more problems, actually," Syko corrected himself. "First, not being able to see your ship, I can't figure whether you're bullshitting me or not. Second, I'm having a hard time figuring out why you're hiding it, and finally, there's the fact that you're doing it well enough to fool every sensor my people have used."

A hard, almost mocking smile spread across Decker's face.

"It's amazing what a bit of anti-reflective paint and serious emissions control can do to hide a ship, if you know how, Ser Syko." He fished a data wafer from his shirt pocket and tossed it on the table. "Here are *Phoenix*'s specs and some recent imagery."

Syko snapped his fingers and one of the goons handed him a thin tablet. He took the wafer, tapped it against the reader, and waited for data to appear.

"Nice ship," he commented, eyes focused on the screen. "Right size, right build. Very marketable. Well done."

He looked up at them with a thin smile.

"I could definitely use a ship like yours to expand my business opportunities. That is, of course, if you're not feeding me some sales brochure."

"We came here on something," Decker replied, "and we're not offering our services unless we can deliver. Disappointing potential clients is bad for business."

"True," Syko nodded agreeably. "Your ship interests me, Ser Whate."

"I hear a 'but' in your voice," Talyn said.

"Very perspicacious, Sera Pasek. Very perspicacious indeed. You see, I need a ship. I don't particularly need a crew."

"We're not interested in selling," Decker replied with affected nonchalance.

"Oh, I understand that, Ser Whate. I really do." Syko's smile turned ugly. "What I think I'd like to do is simply take it. From a business point of view, it makes the most sense to me. Surely you can see that. No initial outlay, my own loyal crew and," he snapped his fingers, "I have my own means of shipping whatever I want, wherever I want."

"What makes you think we'd go along with that?" Talyn asked. Her fingers brushed the back of Zack's hand.

Stand by to bust some heads.

"You have to understand the position you're in," Syko sat back, looking self-satisfied. "Here, I have you deep inside my territory, with only one way out. My men are natural killers, in my service of course, and I'm one of the most powerful bosses on Andoth, so if I just take your ship, no one 'll object."

"There's us for starters, and I see a few problems with your idea, Syko," Decker said, leaning forward and adjusting his posture. "First, you'll have to find the ship. The other problem you have, sorry make that two problems you have, is getting on board without wrecking it and then getting the systems to cooperate with you."

"Surely you don't think we left *Phoenix* undefended," Talyn added, also shifting her body.

Syko shook his head.

"Lock-out codes can be defeated, AIs can be co-opted. Just because I used to be a miner doesn't mean I'm ignorant about starships. But you'll be giving me the proper codes soon enough. I won't need to use any force to take your *Phoenix*. Not a name I like, by the way. I'll have to think about what to call her. Any suggestions?"

"Give you the codes?" Decker snorted. "Good luck with that, rock mole."

"What did you call me?" Syko's back was instantly up.

"Isn't that the right term for people like you: rock moles? Scurrying little creatures with small brains and an instinct to burrow?"

"Take care, Ser Whate, take care. We don't like that term on Andoth."

"So?" Decker shrugged. "You're about to kill us anyway."

"If you cooperate, perhaps I'll let you live. There's always room for indentured labor in some of the deeper shafts."

"But we won't cooperate in letting you steal our ship," Talyn said, a hand creeping slowly towards her concealed gun. "You can hire us at a fair price, or you can let us walk out. There's no other option."

"Ah, but a mind probe is such a useful thing," Syko replied. "With a few chemicals thrown into the mix, your cooperation is practically guaranteed. Perhaps you'll even survive the experience."

Decker started laughing.

"You find me amusing, Ser Whate?" The mobster seemed momentarily nonplussed by Zack's reaction.

"Try that and we'll die. You won't get anything. Like my partner here said, we won't cooperate. The way I see it, someone's going to die today. It's pretty much up to you who that is."

Syko's eyes narrowed with suspicion.

"Are you trying to tell me you've been conditioned against interrogation?"

Decker tapped the side of his nose with a thick forefinger and winked.

"Got it in one."

"I should have known that you're Navy plants, damn it," Syko roared.

"How about you cut it out with the insults, fatso?" Decker slammed his fist on the marble top. "I belong to the animal kingdom even though I've been accused of coming from a different branch than the rest of you pink apes. Your goons, on the other hand, look suspiciously like stalks of broccoli. They have that vacant stare in their eyes. I'd say if anyone was a plant here, they are."

Neither Syko nor his guards knew what to make of Zack's nonsensical declaration, and they stared at him as if he'd sprouted a second head that had immediately begun to sing Shrehari opera. Then, Syko laughed.

"Very good, Ser Whate, very good. I like a man who keeps his sense of humor in the face of adversity. You're almost making me reconsider my decision to simply take your ship. Almost..." He smiled again briefly, then touched something on his side of the table and almost immediately, the door opened to reveal the other two guards. "Take this comedian and his friend to the interrogation room."

The goons behind Syko raised their weapons menacingly while the new arrivals pulled out restraints. Decker glanced at Talyn and nodded.

"Now."

The Marine's right leg shot up, and he caught the edge of the table with his heel, giving it a mighty heave so that it toppled over Syko, pinning the man to the floor. At the same time, Talyn rose from her chair in a fluid motion, pivoted to face the door and pulled out her gun.

One of the guards facing Zack prepared to fire, his facial expression telegraphing his intent. The Marine pulled his pathfinder dagger from its forearm sheath and sent it flying straight into the goon's throat. Blood spurted and the man collapsed. Decker then drew his blaster and shot the other goon without missing a beat.

Two double-tap coughs beside him, with no follow-on shots, proved that Talyn hadn't missed her targets either.

It had taken only a few seconds, but in that brief time, barely long enough to take three deep breaths, four men lay dead and their boss was caught beneath his desk, helplessly pinned down by the marble slab.

"Wonderful," Zack said, walking around the upturned table to retrieve his dagger. "Wherever we go, it ends up with a trail of bodies."

"Can we help it if we're the designated clean-up crew?" Talyn pulled the door shut before someone noticed that their boss' office had been replaced by a charnel house. "I hope you waited until they shot first."

"Sure. Goon on the right had one up the spout and almost out the muzzle."

"Good enough for me." She looked down at Syko. "My partner did tell you someone would die today. You should have listened to him."

"You'll never get out of here," the man whispered, struggling to master his shock at the lethal turn of events. "I have fifty men guarding me, and there are only two of you."

"Fifty?" Decker chuckled. "Those are twenty-five to one odds. I don't think your men are going to make it, do you, Sera Pasek?"

"Nope." She shook her head. "What do we do with this piece of crap?"

"He was going to steal our ship, which makes him guilty of attempted piracy. That's still a death penalty offense, and I'm sure he's made people disappear into his rabbit warren before. So we can also get him for multiple counts of enslavement if not first-degree murder. In most jurisdictions, those can bring down a death sentence too, especially slavery, and I do hate slavers."

"Legally, summary execution isn't an option at this point, you know that, right?" Talyn asked.

"Oh, I don't know." Zack looked down at Syko again. "Maybe fatso will try to shoot me first; then I can kill him. Want to shoot me? You're not getting out of here alive."

Anger warred with terror in the mobster's eyes.

"Who are you?" He asked, hoping against all hope to distract the big man while he struggled to pull his weapon out.

"Just some honest, God-fearing spacers looking for work. Sadly, you picked on folks who don't like to be played for idiots. I wish I could say that you should remember so you don't do it again, but I figure you won't have the chance to be a good boy."

Syko's pistol snapped up, the stubby barrel aimed at Decker's chest, but Zack was faster. His Imperial Armaments blaster coughed once, drilling a neat hole in the mobster's forehead.

"Navy plants indeed. I'm a bloody Marine, you dumb fuck." He looked up at Talyn. "He was about to shoot, so it doesn't count as summary execution."

"Sure. We won't mention that he would have had an entirely good self-defense argument if it had ever come to trial."

"Whatever." Decker shrugged and holstered his gun. He was about to turn away when he noticed something on Syko's neck that had become visible after he'd slumped backward in death.

"Wonderful. Our man here has a Jackal tattoo, which might explain why he was so keen on stealing *Phoenix*. Maybe his buddies on Kilia Station put out a BOLO."

"And that makes a difference to our current situation how, exactly?"

"Other than having the whole pack on our asses once they find out we scragged the local boss? Can't think of a single thing. Not that I have any remorse. I'm just trying to think ahead of trouble."

"Good for you. I doubt all of his goons are part of the pack, though. They've been known to take control of local gangs through one or two members. Anyway, that's for a later conversation. I'd say now would be a good time to see if we remember the way out."

Talyn opened the office door cautiously and looked out into the antechamber.

"Clear."

Decker passed through and took up position by the opening to the passageway. When he glanced back, he saw her pull a dark, nut-sized nugget from her pocket, thumb off the top, and toss it into the office before pulling the door shut.

Expecting a loud bang, he was disappointed at the dull thud he heard seconds later.

"And here I thought you'd joined me in believing there's nothing that can't be solved with a few high explosives. You did a great job in the Marengo stockade."

"Thermal grenade," she replied. "In about thirty seconds, there won't be anything left to identify except that ugly marble slab."

"I guess I'll have to be satisfied with the intent."

He glanced into the passageway again, but before he could move to the next intersection, an alarm began to peal.

"Your little nugget seems to have triggered the fire detectors. Let's hope the rest of Syko's crew is as sluggish as his late bodyguards. Come on."

— TEN —

"Does it actually bother you that we seem to leave a trail of bodies wherever we go or was that a rhetorical statement?" Talyn asked in a conversational tone.

"We don't always. Marengo had a pretty low death count. So did the two missions before that. Mind you, there was that Shrehari marauder, but they don't actually count."

He glanced around the next blind corner.

"This place needed a good cleaning anyway; the next free traders that got conned by Pavel Krig into meeting Ser Syko wouldn't have made it out alive. We did our duty by the spirit of our oath. What really bothers me is that we walked into this one like bloody amateurs."

"Why would you expect us to know that the local Jackal capo felt like expanding his horizons? How many starship hijackings occur planet-side?"

They jogged to the next intersection.

"Shit happens," she continued. "This was one of those times. Mind you, I'll agree that we may have been a teensy bit too easy with bribes. That might have had something to do with Syko's unhealthy interest, even if he got a tip-off from his friends on Kilia."

"Noted for the next time," he replied, eyes scanning the shafts on either side.

She slipped past him to the next intersection, looked around the corner and pulled back almost immediately.

"I think we're about to meet Syko's goons, and they look kind of pissed."

"You think they know we turned their dear leader into a pile of ashes?"

"Probably not, but since we don't wear the right colors, we're prey."

"And the body trail is about to lengthen," he pointed ahead, where a knot of miners blocked the way.

"Only if they have the brains God gave broccoli, to use a Deckerism."

"Which they obviously do." Zack took the lead, leaving Talyn to turn and cover their backs. "Incidentally, those fine specimens *are* blocking the way out. Since we can't go over, under or around, it'll have to be through, unless you want to go spelunking without a map."

"I like easy problems," she replied, eyes on the men filling the passage behind them. "I guess you're rubbing off on me again."

"Nothing wrong with that — the rubbing, I mean."

One of the miners, easily Zack's size, stepped out in front of the rest and twirled a length of metal. It began to glow on one end.

"Oh come on!" Decker groaned. "A vibra-pick? Don't these bozos know you bring a gun to a gunfight?"

"He may be doing that alpha male thing guys sometimes do, you know, a challenge." She drew her blaster. "Or they're under orders to take us alive."

"I don't have time for this." Decker pulled out his gun and shot the twirler, grazing his arm. The pick fell to the ground with a clatter, but instead of deterring the others, a low growl erupted from a dozen throats.

"I think I just made them mad."

"That's what you get when you don't aim for the center of mass," she replied.

"A moment ago, you were the one making sure we didn't cross the line between self-defense and murder."

"So I was too bureaucratic. Sue me."

One of the miners following them sped up and raised a needler. Her gun coughed once, hitting him in the leg. The man's friends, smarter than the miners facing Zack, thought twice and backed off. Between angry shouts and howls of outraged pain, the decibels had reached an uncomfortable level.

"Shit." Decker shot several times, rapid fire, over the miners' heads to check their advance and yelled out, "Syko's dead, you dumb fucks. He stepped in front of my gun. Don't make the same mistake."

A sudden silence fell over the corridor, underscored only by the distant peal of the alarm bell. The group in front of Zack split apart to reveal a man dressed like the rest of Syko's security guards.

"What did you say?" His tone was almost a savage snarl.

"Your boss is dead. He tried to screw over the wrong people. It didn't work. The end. Let us go and no one else has to die."

The goon glanced at Zack's blaster and then back at his face, apparently calculating how many of them would eat plasma before they could take down the stranger and his partner.

"Don't do it," Decker warned. "Four of your buddies died with Syko. We don't have a beef with anyone else here, but if you force the issue, we will shoot to kill."

"You only managed to wing two guys and that at close range. I'm not impressed." A grin spread across the guard's face. "I don't think you bozos can shoot worth crap."

Decker chuckled.

"Warning shots aren't meant to kill, dumbass."

He snapped up his blaster and fired at an encased ceiling light above the miners, destroying it in a shower of sparks with a direct hit.

"How hard to you think it would be for me to drill all of you a third eye in the middle of the forehead? Let us go and no one else gets hurt."

Syko's men slowly backed off, leaving the guard alone in the middle of the corridor. A newcomer forced his way through them.

"Let it be, Dan," he shouted. "We just got word the boss' office is burnt out, with him and your four buddies inside, just like he said. Whatever's going on is no longer our business. You know how it goes: the moment word gets out Syko's dead, the vultures are going to come down on us, and you don't want to be around when that happens. It's time to find another boss."

"Wise advice, Dan," Decker said with a sardonic smile. "Live to fight another day, that's what I always say."

The goon made an obscene gesture, but turned on his heel and followed the miners to the entrance.

"See, I can negotiate us out of another gun fight." He winked at Talyn.

"I'll be sure to note that on your next performance evaluation," she replied, shaking her head. "What a mess."

The guards at the entrance to Syko's lair had left by the time the two operatives stepped out of the maze.

"I guess Dan picked up his buddies on the way out. Smarter than he looked, that one."

Decker holstered his blaster, making sure he could draw it quickly again when the need arose.

"You're probably right," he continued. "Syko and maybe one or two we didn't see are Jackals. The rest are local talent. I doubt full pack members would have let us out of there alive. It would have been bad for their reputation, even worse if they're in cahoots with the *Sécurité Spéciale*. Now what?"

"Now, we get away from here and pretend we never visited Ser Syko."

She waved at the bright lights blow them, and they began walking back to Yavan and the Paradise hotel.

"You know word will get around about us," Decker remarked. "Some of Syko's rivals in the thieves' guild that runs Andoth are bound to get curious; worried even, especially if they knew he had the tattoo. That could be an advantage."

"Or someone with more brains and brawn than Syko could try to eliminate us before we do unto him. In the meantime, we're no further ahead finding the pipeline that's shipping supplies to the Garonne resistance."

"Sucks to be us," he replied with good humor, "but I'll live, though I might have a few words with the analysts who told us Kilia Station and Andoth were good places to pick up the scent."

**

"Do you think Syko went off script or was he acting under orders?"

"I'll tell you once I know how all the parts are supposed to go together," she said dropping into their usual booth. "I assume you're going to have second breakfast?"

He looked at his timepiece.

"More like elevenses by now. Fighting always gets my appetite going. Don't tell me you're not ravenous."

"Okay, I won't, but I'll pass on the pile of *stuff* you shoveled down your throat this morning. Maybe they'll serve us something more civilized."

"A vat steak or three, with plenty of fries?"

"You can have the 'or three,' I'll stick with one, big boy. And we still have to find a contract," she added for the benefit of any hidden listeners.

"I get the feeling we'll be approached soon enough." He rubbed his hands gleefully. "Here's our holographic waiter. Now, what can your kitchen give us that isn't breakfast?"

An hour later, Decker slumped back against the bench with a hearty belch.

"That filled the old ammo locker very nicely. I give this place at least three novae, if not for taste then at least for quantity."

"Look sharp," Talyn whispered, "there's a thin guy at the bar talking to Wim, and they're both looking in our direction."

He turned to glance over his shoulder, then slowly swiveled back to meet her eyes. She reached out and touched the back of his hand with her fingertips.

Someone you know?

Decker nodded.

This could get strange, he signaled back.

The man approached their booth, eyes flicking between Decker and Talyn before finally settling on the latter.

"Captain Pasek of *Phoenix*?" He stopped at a respectful distance and briefly dipped his head.

"Perhaps."

"My name is Tran Kidder. I understand from Sera Lyde at the spaceport that you're looking for a contract."

Though the man, like Decker, no longer bore any sign that he had once been slave soldier in the Trans-Coalsack Sector, there was no mistaking him for anyone other than his old comrade in arms.

So far, Kidder had not recognized the Marine, but even the best disguise can't hide some of the fundamentals and in due time, he'd begin to get the feeling that Ser Whate reminded him of someone. Fooling the human mind was harder than fooling facial recognition software.

"We are," Talyn nodded, "though you'll excuse us if we're a bit less enthusiastic than you might expect. We had a bit of a run-in with a potential client whose ideas were somewhat different from ours."

"Might I join you?" Kidder motioned towards the chair at the end of the table.

"Sure." She shrugged with seeming indifference.

"Information moves fast on Andoth, though its accuracy is always open to question. The word is that off-worlders did a number on one of the local bosses by the name of Syko. I've had some dealings with him in recent days and can fully understand how you might have found your encounter unpleasant."

Decker snorted.

"A number? Is that what they call it around here? Yeah. He won't be flirting with piracy ever again."

"You are aware that he might have had some dangerous affiliations?" Kidder asked, eyes searching Decker's face as if to discover why it seemed vaguely familiar.

"Sure. Didn't do him much good."

The Marine had to repress an overwhelming urge to thump Kidder on the shoulder and ask him what he'd been doing since the day Zack had traded command of Decker's Demons for an intelligence operative's billet. Tran had been a solid platoon leader back then, dependable, honest, and willing.

"Pardon me, Ser Whate, but have me met before?" Kidder frowned, apparently searching through the furthest recesses of his memory.

Decker shook his head. "Nope."

"You said you wanted to hire some transport?" Talyn asked, to derail the man's train of thought.

"Indeed." Another polite nod. "The information provided by Sera Lyde about your ship would indicate that it might meet the requirements of the interests I represent."

"Cripes, another Pavel Krig with his bloody *interests*." Decker made a disgusted face. "We're not following you anywhere, just so you know. We keep our meetings with scumbags to one a day. More would be gluttony."

A faint smile appeared on Kidder's solemn face.

"I can assure you that I'm nothing like Ser Krig, and the interests I represent aren't on Andoth, nor do they bear any sort of resemblance to Krig's. In any case, his business should dry up once word gets around that he's responsible for introducing you to the late Ser Syko and his associates."

"Serves the traitorous little snake right." Decker flexed a ham-sized fist. "Though I wouldn't mind giving him a token of my appreciation."

Only too late did Zack realize that he'd been speaking like the man Kidder remembered, and a brief flash of interest appeared in the latter's eyes.

"Mister Kidder," Talyn said, "what exactly is it that you're looking for?"

Before he could answer, the main door swung open with a crash to reveal a trio of heavily armed men in black uniforms.

"Perhaps I could tell you somewhere else," he replied, suddenly sounding very anxious. "The gentlemen who are now taking a good look around the Paradise belong to what passes for law and order in Yavan. Considering they're in the pockets of virtually everyone with extra-legal interests, I'm going to surmise they're after you two."

"Did you leave anything in the room you feel sentimental about?" Decker asked his partner.

"Negative."

"Then perhaps we should skedaddle to our shuttle and lift off. I'd rather not mix it up with corrupt cops in full public view." He turned to Kidder. "If you have nothing to keep you in Yavan, I can offer a ride out of here while we talk business; otherwise, this conversation is over."

"I think I'll go with you, Ser Whate."

They slipped out of the booth without hurrying and headed for the back door behind the bar, trying to look entirely innocent. It almost worked.

"Hey you!" One of the cops shouted. "Stop right there."

Decker resisted the temptation to raise a rigid digit salute and simply followed his companions down the narrow passage and out into the Paradise Hotel's junk-filled backyard.

"Not the brightest cops, are they?" He asked, scanning his surroundings while they jogged between piles of rusting metal and discarded plastic containers, trying to find their way to the street. "If you're going to take someone in, you cover all the exits."

"If they were smart, Ser Whate, they wouldn't be taking bribes from everyone," Kidder replied, "thereby making themselves unable to go after anyone but off-worlders, and then only those not under the protection of locals."

"Like us. I suppose we could always wave a stack of cred chips under their noses, but since we're headed back to the ship, it would probably be a waste."

They slowed their pace once they reached the main road, to avoid attracting attention.

"Did I understand that you're offering me passage on your ship?" Kidder eyed the big man by his side with undisguised suspicion.

"I'm going to guess that you've come up empty for whatever job you have here because it sounds like you've been in Yavan for a while. That means you were probably close to leaving anyway. Now that the cops have seen you with us, it makes sense that you move up your timetable. If we don't conclude a contract, you can pay us the price of your passage to our next stop. If we do, we'll add it to our fee. Deal?"

"It seems I have little choice, Ser Whate. Thank you."

Talyn glanced back over her shoulder.

"It may not be quite as easy as we'd like," she said. "There's a ground car with nice blue emergency flashers turning away from the Paradise."

"Over here," Decker pointed at the huge septic disposal vat they'd passed the previous day. "A good stench tends to keep dirty cops away. They don't like the competition."

"I hope you're proposing we hide behind it and not inside."

"Considering how many good leather jackets I've lost over the last few years, I'm going to make sure this one lasts, so yeah, we're hiding behind it. If they have sensors, the organic stew in the vat will hide our signature."

"Aren't you worried that they'll seize your shuttle, Ser Whate?" Kidder asked once they were ensconced in the shadows, watching the reflection of the lights grow on the neighboring storage tank.

Decker chuckled grimly.

"Not a chance. That thing is almost impregnable and if they try to cut in, the self-destruct mechanism is going to give them one chance to stop and back away before the entire spaceport vanishes in a bright flash."

"Radical, but practical, I suppose." A pause. "Would you really blow up the spaceport if they try to take your shuttle?"

"Technically, they'd be blowing themselves up, but yeah. Wouldn't you?" Zack grinned at Kidder, knowing that he'd be eroding his disguise even further, but if they were going to take him aboard *Phoenix*, the truth would have to come out at some point.

The man shook his head briefly then turned his eyes back towards the road, just in time to see a police car speed by.

"Let's hope that once they see we're not at the spaceport, they go off on a wild goose chase all over town," Talyn said. "I suggest we wait here until we see them come back."

"I hope that won't take all day." Decker sniffed the air. "If we stay here too long, the stench might become impregnated in our clothes, and I'll lose another good jacket."

"Don't worry, Ser Kidder, he's not like this all the time."

"Like what?" Decker demanded, half-indignantly.

"Whiny." She winked at Tran.

The flashing lights took almost an hour to reappear, this time, headed back into Yavan proper.

"Let's hope they didn't leave someone behind," Talyn said, leading the way out of their hiding spot.

"More likely they told the administrator to keep a lookout and report when we show up. Not that it'll do them any good." Decker banished the lingering smell of decay with a shake of the head.

Talyn pulled out a small pad and stroked it a few times with her fingertips.

"There. The shuttle's going live and warming up. It'll be ready to lift by the time we get there. Since I doubt they'll try to shoot us down if we take off without permission, we shouldn't have any more problems."

******

"We have a problem," Decker said ten minutes later, peering over the perimeter fence at their boxy little spacecraft. "Two cops standing guard."

"I suppose we could just walk up to them and offer a little help with their insomnia," Talyn replied.

"Maybe, but I wouldn't be surprised if they start shooting and we don't want to go there. I think we might get the bribe queen to help us out if we make enough creds stick to her fingers. After all, she pointed friend Kidder in our direction, so she can't be all bad."

"It's worth a try."

Triane Lyde looked up from her cluttered desk when the trio walked in, the expression on her face changing from annoyance to alarm.

"I see you found them, Ser Kidder," she said, quickly recovering her composure.

"Indeed." Tran inclined his head in thanks. "I'll be departing with them, but we appear to have an infestation of sorts on the tarmac."

"Yeah." She raised her chin towards Decker and Talyn. "Damn cops seem to have a bone to pick with you two. I'm to keep you here and call them right away."

Decker pulled out a few cred chips and tossed one on her desk

"I'm sure you'll find our offer to not call them much better."

A second chip joined the first.

"Same with our offer to not keep us here."

Chip number three sailed through the air.

"I'm sure the two goons guarding our shuttle would accept one or two of these to come inside and warm up with a cup of coffee."

Three more chips joined the rest on the growing pile in front of Lyde.

"Your commission to offer the goons their inducement to take a nice coffee break."

Lyde looked at Decker with narrowed eyes, then down at the money, calculating the risk-reward ratio.

"And a performance bonus – payable in advance," she finally said, scooping up the pile.

Two more chips flew towards her and this time, she caught them before they landed.

"The office beside mine is empty." She pointed at the connecting door. "Wait there. When the cops are inside, you can scoot out and take off. The moment you're in your shuttle, there's nothing anyone can do to keep you here."

When they were alone in the neighboring room, Kidder asked, "Do you think she'll stay bought, or bring the police down on us anyway, in the hope of taking what's left in your pockets?"

"Wouldn't do much for her. She's got everything I had and even if she didn't, the cops would steal what was left, then demand she bribe them over and above what I gave her to lure them in. No, I think Sera Lyde is the kind who stays bought where the so-called law is concerned."

Talyn glanced through the grimy window.

"She's got them walking back into the building with her."

"I guess we're about to find out if she stayed bought." Zack checked to make sure he could draw his blaster smoothly.

A sharp rap rang out from the door leading to the waiting room and then, soon after, they heard animated voices in Lyde's office.

"I guess that was our signal." Decker pulled the outside door open with a mighty heave, dislodging years of encrusted dust and grime. "No running, please, just in case there are hostile eyes on us. Amble along casually."

The shuttle's rear ramp came down at their approach and, with a last look around, Decker shepherded his companions aboard. Talyn dropped into the pilot's seat and sealed the craft up again.

"Sera Lyde's a sly little creature," she said, scanning the sensor log. "She tried to break in. I guess that's how she figured we would be safe once we were aboard. So much for her extra security fees."

"Just once, I'd like us to work on a planet where the people are honest, there's no war and everyone's smiling," Zack grumbled from the passenger compartment while he checked Tran Kidder's seat restraints. "You just stay right like you are until we're on our ship, buddy."

"If there is such a thing as a happy, safe, and honest place," Talyn said while Zack strapped himself into the co-pilot's seat, "it wouldn't have any work for people like us, but if you'd like to retire to a planet with those utopian features, be my guest. You'll be starting bar fights within a week just to have some fun."

"Oops."　Decker pointed at the console's tactical screen. "There's a lot of blue light coming up the drive from the main road."

"I guess she hedged her bets."　Talyn gunned the thrusters, and the shuttle lifted off in a cloud of dust, heading for the ribbon of indigo sky ten kilometers above Yavan.

"Or the guys guarding the shuttle smelled a rat and called in before taking the bribe."　He shook his head.　"That's is what I hate about corruption.　You can never tell who's doing what to whom without a program."

He turned his head towards the passenger compartment.

"You all right in there, Tran?"

"Never been better."

— ELEVEN —

Kidder let out a low whistle once he'd stepped off the shuttle.

"Nice. And there's only the two of you to crew a ship big enough for a hangar deck this size?"

"It's a wonder what modern AIs can do," Decker replied, locking the small craft to the deck. "Plus, my partner's a pretty good pilot, and I'm a wizard when it comes to gunnery. You could say that I've mastered it."

"He's a master at something alright, but I'm still trying to figure out what that is," Talyn said, ushering Kidder into the corridor. "I'm going to ask you to stay in your cabin until we're on our way. We have a lot to do before we break orbit."

"Of course."

They stopped in front of an unmarked door which opened at Talyn's touch, revealing a sparse compartment with two sets of stacked bunks, a row of lockers and a table with chairs.

"Just to make sure you don't inadvertently wander around, we'll lock you in. I hope that doesn't present any issues."

Kidder nodded once, "No problem. I understand."

Then he stepped into his quarters.

"Thanks again for taking me with you. Andoth would have become pretty uncomfortable after the cops saw me talking to you."

"We'll discuss business later, Ser Kidder."

She shut the door and nodded towards the bridge.

"Time to get going, master of gunnery and other fun activities."

"You think Kidder's decided that I have more than a passing resemblance to his former commanding officer?" Decker asked, taking his seat at the tactical station.

"I'd say so. The people you brought back probably have your ugly mug permanently engraved in their memory and while your disguise might fool the opposition, it won't fool your friends all the time. Anyway, mannerisms will give anyone away to folks who've known them well, and you have some pretty distinctive ones."

"Tran's smart enough to go along with whatever story I feed him. He'll figure I have my reasons, and he knows I'd never screw him over, not after what we went through together."

"Loyalty is a commendable sentiment," she retorted with a sharp tone. "Don't let it get in the way of the mission."

"I think this time it might coincide with the mission, little Miss Sociopath. Are you going to get us away from here or are you waiting for something magical to happen?"

"Sublight drives need time to spool up, buddy. You'd know that if you truly were a master of anything other than shooting off your big gun." She turned to face him. "What makes you think Kidder might be involved with the Garonne rebellion?"

"Let me see." He began ticking off the items one by one on his fingers. "He's a former soldier and a good one, with no known ties anywhere in the Commonwealth. He's looking for a shipper willing to take risks in one of the places the analysts figured might be connected to the supply pipeline. We know the rebels have been recruiting former soldiers suffering from an excess of idealism and last but not least, I don't believe in coincidences."

"That was my take as well." She nodded. "I'll add that he was quick to take you up on the offer to hitch a ride, meaning whatever he's doing isn't something he wants to advertise."

"Sure." Zack nodded. "That one was so obvious, I didn't think it needed saying."

She made an obscene gesture, but before he could retort, the AI chimed softly, drawing her attention back to the helm console.

"We're ready," she announced.

"And we're going where exactly?"

"Right now, I figure we'd lose ourselves in the outer system, just to make sure we don't get unwanted company, like those Shrehari marauders who mistook us for a yacht. Then, we'll have a nice long chat with your friend Tran."

"I recognize that tone, Hera. You're not interrogating him. If Kidder's involved with the Garonne bunch, we'll have a better chance of tracking down who's behind it by becoming part of their supply pipeline."

"And I recognize that look in your eyes, Chief Warrant Officer Decker. We are not going to get involved in the rebellion, no matter how noble the rebels and how nasty the colonial administration. If the central government decides to intervene, it'll send the next available Marine Regiment."

"Aye, aye, Commander Talyn, sir." Decker tossed off a mock salute. "But my idea is still a good one, so we'll go with it."

"For now," she conceded.

"If the Coalition is trying stir up something that'll further destabilize the sector, then it's our job to sort it out. Just keep in mind what we saw on Marengo. They'll be going down the same path as Garonne if we don't find out what's really going on. And after Marengo? Heck, Cimmeria could be next and wouldn't that make the Shrehari howl with joy."

Talyn sighed.

"I get the picture, Zack. I'm just afraid that your sense of honor, duty, and doing the right thing will make you lose sight of what our job really is."

"Defending the Commonwealth and its citizens?"

"Making sure sweethearts like the Coalition don't undermine the system to the point where we find ourselves fighting a third migration war."

"Yeah." He nodded. "And that would tempt the Shrehari into trying a do-over of their last invasion. Enough talking, Captain Pasek. Let's get *Phoenix* away from this damned place so we can let Tran out of the brig."

"It's a cabin, Zack."

"Does he have access to a bar? No? Then it's a brig."

**

"Please sit, Ser Kidder," Talyn gestured towards the table in the ship's saloon. "Can we offer you some refreshments?"

"Coffee would be nice."

"Bill?" She glanced at Decker. "Could you whip up some of your good stuff?"

"Sure. Give me a moment. Want a splash of something in it. We have a palatable rotgut that won't make your hair fall out."

Kidder instinctively touched his head, now covered in a thick shock of black and Decker smiled.

"I'm glad to hear that, Ser Whate. I've grown rather fond of my mop. Yes, a small splash would be welcome."

After he'd served the coffee, Zack's and Kidder's redolent of whiskey, Talyn broached the subject that sat heavily in everyone's mind.

"At present, we're headed outwards, but with no particular destination in mind - just trying to get some distance from Andoth. I think there are a few things you need to know before we discuss what you're looking for. We're essentially mercenaries, Bill Whate and I. *Phoenix* carries more firepower than you'd expect, which is handy when we're carrying stuff that attracts greedy eyes. We've got plenty of cargo space for a ship this size, but less than most of comparable tonnage because we traded it for weaponry."

Kidder nodded. "That actually makes hiring you more attractive than less."

"Okay, so far, so good." Talyn nodded before taking a sip. "We don't come cheap, but we're willing to go further than most free traders. We can actually outfight what we can't outrun."

"A Shrehari trader tried his marauding sideline on us near Kilia Station recently," Decker said. "The atoms that used to make up its crew might get back to the Empire in a few million years. We can be good friends with the right people and dangerous enemies to those who try to fuck us over."

"I was getting that impression, Ser Whate, after what you did to Syko and his crew." Kidder nodded solemnly. "The people I represent can also be very good friends or very deadly enemies, though we like to think of ourselves as being on the side of freedom."

Talyn and Decker exchanged quick glances. Perhaps Zack's old comrade and fellow former slave soldier had become involved in the Garonne rebellion.

"You'll have to excuse me," Kidder continued, "if I'm a bit scarce on details. I'm sure you can understand the need for operational security."

Decker nodded.

"Sure. We can do business without knowing everything, but if we come up against something you didn't mention, and it puts us at unacceptable risk, the contract is either renegotiated or terminated."

"Understood. I'd feel the same in your place, Ser Whate." He took a long sip of coffee, evidently framing his next words carefully.

"When I first approached you, I was looking for a fast transport that could land on a standard planet with an atmosphere and without needing a spaceport."

"Smuggling?" Talyn raised a questioning eyebrow.

"Yes and no, Captain."

"Let the man continue," Decker growled, "otherwise we'll be in interstellar space before we figure out where we're going next."

"Sorry. Please go ahead, Ser Kidder."

"Now that I've seen your ship, and you've informed me of your status as mercenaries, I've been thinking about the possibility of hiring you not only to transport a few things but to escort the other ships we've hired. Your experience with the Shrehari marauder wasn't an isolated bit of piracy. We lost one of our contracted freighters a few months ago."

"Marauders?"

"We don't know." Kidder seemed pained. "The ship carried some people I worked with. Losing them set us back quite a bit. They were some of the most experienced folks we had."

"We can fight off single ships or even a pair if they're not too big, but we won't fight the Navy, ever," Decker said. "And we're not getting involved in anything that'll have the Commonwealth authorities looking for the nearest tree to hang us."

"You needn't worry on that account, Ser Whate. The Navy has no interest in what we do and the freight we're looking to ship doesn't involve drugs or slavery."

"Then why not hire a regular shipping line?"

"As I mentioned, we need ships that can land just about anywhere." He bit his lower lip, carefully mulling over his next words. "You should know that some planetary governments consider what we ship illegal or borderline illegal, and that's about as much as I can tell you right now."

"So you're saying that provided we keep away from those governments, our risk is just regular piracy and the like?"

"Pretty much."　He seemed relieved that Decker didn't pressure him for more details on the contraband.

"Sounds like something we can handle," Talyn said.

She quoted a fee that might have seemed outrageous, but Kidder didn't even flinch, possibly evidence that someone with deep pockets was financing his organization.

"I'll have to get my superiors' confirmation, of course, but we'll hire you under those terms."　He examined Zack's face again, frowning.　"Ser Whate, you really do remind me of someone I once knew, a man who saved my life; an excellent soldier."

"They say we each have a doppelganger somewhere in the universe."　Zack shrugged.　"The only life I've ever saved is my own and maybe, if she's not too nasty, I might save my partner's.　I'm not what you would call a generous man."

"I can vouch for that," Talyn added.　"I'm sure the day I kick him out of my bunk is the day he won't save my life for love or money."

Kidder looked at the two operatives in turn, and then nodded.

"Understood."

"And where do we go from here, Ser Kidder?"　Talyn asked.

**

"I'm not feeling the warm and fuzzies right now."　Decker stared glumly at his readout.

They had made a long passage out of Commonwealth space and now orbited what he'd charitably described as a useless hunk of rock.

"If there were any way to get out of landing, it would have my vote."

"Your buddy Kidder isn't worried.　Why should you be?"

"You can stop rubbing it in any time now, Hera."

"I'm a sociopath, as you keep pointing out.　I have no empathy for your feelings."

"Bull. You were feeling things just fine last night."

"Sex and emotions are two different things, lover boy."　She turned and blew him a kiss.

"Maybe in your twisted world."

"You're living in that same twisted world now."

"Sadly." He nodded at the main screen, which showed their destination on the planet's surface. "The term hive of scum and villainy comes to mind, though I'll be damned if I can remember where I picked up that expression."

"In the last hive of scum and villainy you visited?"

"That would be Tortuga Station, of ill fame." He snorted. "Though I'm sure the folks there remember my visit with a lot less fondness than I do."

"You have that effect on a lot of people."

"Those two ships with the sleek look aren't honest. I'm sure we outgun them once I drop the camouflage plates, but that's not going to do us much good on the ground."

"Maybe we should do a strafing run before landing, you know, to clear the way."

"Don't tempt me, woman."

"And that's another thing you didn't mind about me last night. I'm sure we'll be okay. These places can only exist because they keep the various parties from killing each other when they're in port."

"The Navy ought to run a clean-up sweep one of these days."

"Why? It's a great place to get intel, run covert ops, and generally put stuff into circulation that makes the bad guys' lives miserable. If it didn't exist, naval intelligence would have to invent it."

"And there's that twisted world again." He rubbed his chin, looking at the image with narrowed eyes. "You know, it wouldn't even have to be much. A couple of the close in defense missiles, no warhead, coming in at hypersonic speed and we're done. Kinetic strikes are a lot of fun if you do them right."

"No." Talyn shook her head emphatically.

"In that case, I'll deploy the calliope turrets once we're on final approach. That ought to keep most semi-functional morons from trying something stupid, unless of course, this is the place where the universe invents better idiots."

"It might be, but let's stick to the plan. You can show some of our muscle, but try not to let your fingers slip and turn large objects into smaller ones."

"I am a master gunner, my dear."

"That's what I'm afraid of." She touched the helm controls, sending *Phoenix* into a controlled descent towards Rakka, a self-proclaimed free port in the heart of the Protectorate zone wedged between the Commonwealth and the Shrehari Empire.

Zack reached for the intercom.

"Tran, time to strap yourself into your bunk. We're heading down."

"Roger. I'll try to enjoy the ride."

"Good man." He cut the transmission and pulled out his own seat restraints.

Kidder had been diffident to the point of self-effacement during the passage from Andoth. He'd used the ship's entertainment library extensively; he'd also joined Zack and Hera on the hangar deck for daily physical training, but had so far refrained from exploring any touchy subjects.

"Why is it that every planet we visit on this mission is pretty much useless for sentient life?" He asked, eyes on his sensor readout. "The atmosphere is breathable, but that's the only positive thing I can say about the place. It's dusty enough to make Nabhka look like one great oasis, where it isn't frozen over, that is."

"If it were a paradise, it would have been overrun with colonists by now. The people who founded Rakka wanted to stay far from honest sentient beings. Now do me a favor and chat with the AI if you feel the need to complain. I've got to land us without breaking anything."

**

"That was fun," Decker said an hour later, removing his seat restraints. "The calliopes are out, and you'll be glad to know they're not quite pointing at the reivers parked on the other side of the tarmac."

"Be thankful the AI was quick enough to stabilize us when that damned wind shear hit. Otherwise, we might have seriously dented the landing gear." She stood and stretched, loosening her tense shoulder muscles. "You may wish to let Tran know he can get out of his bunk now."

"Right."

They met Kidder in the corridor moments later.

"Where do we find this colleague of yours and the contraband she's supposed to have bought?"

"I tried calling her." He pulled out a compact commo device. "Your ship's hull is not bad at blocking my transmission so I'll have to make another attempt once we're ashore."

"Are you carrying?" Decker patted the Imperial Armaments blaster at his hip.

Kidder lifted the side of his jacket.

"Needler."

"Good. I've set a hard security lockdown on the ship, some of it really nasty if you don't have the magic password, so don't ever try to get aboard without us once we button her up, okay?"

"Understood."

Talyn touched a control panel and part of the keel dropped slowly to form a ramp. A swirl of dust rose up through the opening and enveloped them. Decker sneezed heartily, and then cursed with equal enthusiasm.

"And we've found another excellent place for a very brief visit. Let's get this show going so we can be off before my nostrils are terminally gummed up."

Once on the ground, Talyn pulled out her small tablet and, with a single touch, sent the ramp back up into the hull, sealing *Phoenix*.

"Security is on," she confirmed.

"Time to make that call, Tran." Decker tapped him on the shoulder.

Movement on the other side of the spaceport caught his eye and he slowly swiveled his head.

"Seems like some folks are interested in us. I might get to see the security system do its magic up close."

He nodded towards a trio of humans emerging from one of the reiver ships.

"Neutral ground, Zack. We're here for a job. They can look at *Phoenix* all they want, provided they don't touch."

"Give it enough time. One of them is going to force us to clean up this place before we leave."

"Hah!" He barked out a laugh when he saw the reivers stop and change course.

"I forgot to tell you that I put the calliopes under the AI's control to track any bastards who come too close. Looks like it scared the living crap out of them."

She shook her head with a small snort of laughter.

"My one-man wrecking crew."

"Okay, thanks." Kidder pocketed the communicator. "She's waiting for us in town. I got directions."

"And the merchandise?"

"She didn't want to say over the communicator, just in case someone was listening in."

Decker stared at the cluster of dun-colored, low-rise buildings in the distance and sighed theatrically.

"We traveled God knows how many light years in an FTL-capable starship, a marvel of modern technology, only to end up walking the last bit like our Stone Age ancestors. Isn't life full of wonderful ironies?"

With a final glance backward at the quickly departing reivers, he trudged off towards the town, Talyn and Kidder on his heels.

— TWELVE —

An aroma of ripe bodies, stale booze, and bad food washed over them when they entered the tavern. Half buried in the ground, the dome-shaped structure reminded Decker of an abandoned ammunition bunker from the First Migration War.

He sniffed the air and grimaced.

"My memories of Andoth are getting better by the second."

"For once, I agree with you," Talyn replied, following Kidder down the half-dozen steps from the street.

They shoved their way through a mass of bodies, many of whom protested loudly until they got a glimpse of Decker's angry stare. Ignoring his companions, who had found an alcove with empty seats, he wedged himself between an ursine Darsivian and a shorthaired, muscular human at the bar. The woman, of indistinct heritage, had a long scar down her cheek and a cynical smile affixed to her lips. The Darsivian growled something at Zack in his language that made her laugh.

"He thinks you're too cute for this place," she said in a raspy voice.

"Coming from a rug with legs, I'll take it as a compliment."

"I'll take a pass on translating that. You might not be too pretty after he's done."

Decker snorted derisively.

"They're big, but they're slow and not just up here." He tapped the side of his head. "Bill Whate, by the way."

"Miko Steiger," she replied with a nod. "You a merc?"

"Do I look like one?"

"You've got the vibe and this joint is pretty much the Rakka clearing house for mercs between contracts."

"I'm just a free trader with a decent right hook." He caught the attention of the bartender and pointed at a twisted green bottle. "You?"

"Merc through and through." She indicated her scar. "I didn't get this from a haircut gone wrong. You looking for cargo?"

"Nope." Decker took the mug and tossed a few cred chips on the bar. "Skoal."

As he drank a healthy swig, he glanced at Talyn and Kidder on the far side of the room.

"Friends of yours?" She asked, following the direction of his gaze.

"Business associates." He wiped his lips with the back of his hand. "Who'd have figured this place serves decent Shrehari ale."

"The Shrehari who ship it in?" Steiger's sardonic tone made him look at her more closely.

"What?" She continued, chuckling. "We're in Rakka. Anything ever produced in this part of the galaxy eventually finds its way here, legal, illegal, and anything in between."

Then, surprising him, she nodded towards the alcove.

"I guess Kidder's waiting for me. I should probably go say hi." She laughed at his startled expression. "I guess you're half of the crew that's here for my toys."

He followed Steiger over to the others, their approach watched intently by Talyn, whose hand never strayed far from her holstered blaster. She slid into the booth beside Tran and blew him a kiss while Zack took a seat at the end of the table.

"I'm Miko Steiger," she nodded at Talyn, "Kidder's contact here. You must be Pasek."

"I guess I am. The first name's Pru."

"How are you, Miko?" Tran asked, visibly relaxing.

"Still one ovary missing and the other firing blanks." She winked at Decker. "Battle damage. Good thing I don't like kids. Big boys on the other hand..."

"We provide the shipping, not the entertainment," Talyn said with a faint smile.

"You're kind of cute too," Steiger replied, grinning briefly before her face lost any hint of merriment.

"All kidding aside, I have two containers filled with the kind of kitchen implements that'll let our friends whip up a storm and I need to get them out of Rakka yesterday."

"Why the hurry?" Talyn asked.

"You noticed those needle ships on the tarmac? Some of their crew got wind of my merchandise and have been sniffing around the warehouse district to see if they can't lighten my load."

"How did they find out?"

"The man who sold me the merchandise has a drinking problem; had a drinking problem, to be precise. When he drank, he talked too much, and places like this have ears growing out of the walls. Sadly for him, a few days ago he decided to get in a Shrehari trader's face after one too many; a losing proposition as it turned out, but by then, the damage had been done."

Decker barked out a laugh.

"Nice place."

"Stupid gets you killed pretty much anywhere. The threshold is just somewhat lower around here." Steiger shrugged. "I'm thinking my snooping reivers might wait until I try moving the merchandise to the spaceport before playing their hand."

"Makes sense," Zack said. "They got interested in our ship when we landed, but my calliopes seem to have discouraged them."

"Calliopes?" Steiger asked.

"Close-in defense guns, eight barrels per mount. Chew up a grounded reiver in no time."

"Too bad we can't put your ship down by the warehouse."

"There are four of us. If we need something heavier than the weapons we're carrying, I'll fix that. Your merchandise can be aboard *Phoenix* whenever you want it to." Decker downed the rest of his drink. "I'm ready to move. What are you packing, Miko?"

She moved her jacket aside and smiled broadly, revealing sharp, white teeth.

"Nice," he said, admiring a nearly identical copy of his own Imperial Armaments blaster. "Chambered for our rounds?"

"Of course – fifteen millimeters."

"Good. I can provide reloads if the bastards get too busy."

"Before the gun love-fest gets into full swing," Talyn said, rising from her seat, "we should probably see what we need to shift and then figure out how to do it. I'm going to hope that you have access to some haulers, Sera Steiger."

"Of course, Captain Pasek. I'd be of little use if I couldn't rustle up the necessaries."

"Glad to hear it. Shall we?"

They headed for the door, eyes carefully searching for anyone paying them more attention than they warranted. If there were such beings, they kept their interest carefully hidden.

**

Steiger led them to a semi-decrepit warehouse on the outskirts of Rakka, halfway between town and spaceport. One of many in the area, it bore no signs that it was any different from the others.

"Cheerful," Decker said, looking around when they came to a stop in front of an unmarked entrance. "Another perfect place to spend an hour or so of shore leave."

"If we don't have to do our annual qualification shoot on the run, I'll take it," Talyn replied.

"Cheap date."

"Sure. And you're complaining?"

Steiger and Kidder exchanged looks.

"You get used to it," he murmured.

The mercenary touched a panel, and they heard several loud clicks as massive locks released the door.

"You know, if those reivers who were sniffing around had more energy and brains, they'd just burn through the walls," Decker said after they'd entered the building.

"True." She stopped and held up her hand. "Tell me if they'd have come close to those containers without losing a limb or three."

Zack pulled out his souped-up sensor and scanned the area.

"Nice." He nodded. "I can barely pick up your little traps. You'll forgive me if I stay right here until you disarm them."

"What did you find?" Talyn asked.

"Improvised security. Very nicely done. Very professional. Lasers covering the area; a few IEDs, that kind of stuff. I think I'm in lust."

"Getting amorous with a high-powered automatic laser isn't going to help your love life." Talyn's tone was bone dry.

Steiger pulled out a small tablet and stroked its screen.

"There. My playpen is deactivated. No more danger of Ser Whate losing parts he'd rather keep."

"If you don't mind," Decker said, "I'd like to look at what's in your containers. Since they're coming aboard *Phoenix*, the good captain and I need to be happy it won't either blow us up when we go FTL or get us thrown into a naval brig if we're ever inspected."

Steiger locked eyes with Kidder and nodded towards the far corner of the warehouse. When they were out of earshot, she glanced back at Decker and Talyn.

"Are you sure we can trust them?"

"As sure as anyone can be under the circumstances, Miko. Whate reminds me of an old comrade, a hell of a soldier. He saved my life and that of two hundred others who were left to die on a planet in the ass end of the universe."

"That doesn't mean he's trustworthy like your 'hell of a soldier,' now does it?" The mercenary's eyes shone with open skepticism.

"I'm going with my gut on this one. You didn't get to meet the other candidates I spoke with. Whate and Pasek are the cleanest of the bunch and quite frankly, *Phoenix* is exactly what we need. She's heavily armed and could be our own one ship navy if we can convince them to fight for us."

She stared at Kidder for a long time in silence, and then nodded decisively.

"If they play us false, I can always shoot them, the big guy first."

"Don't think Pasek's a pushover, Miko. I get the sense that she's as dangerous as a Shrehari assassin and not nearly as scrupulous, and that's when she smiles at me."

When they'd rejoined Talyn and Decker, the mercenary jerked her chin at the containers.

"Feel free to inspect, Ser Whate. Which one would you like to look at?"

"Both," Decker replied, holding up a hand-held sensor. "I gave them a quick once over while Tran was bending your ear. You did a good job masking the content."

"Why thank you, kind sir." Steiger sketched a brief bow. "This isn't my first rodeo."

She undid the locks securing the nearest container's door and pulled it open before stepping aside.

"You might have some problems getting in. If you want to haul out some crates, be my guest, but try to resist the urge to empty the whole damn thing."

"No. This is fine," he replied, looking at his sensor's readout. "With the door open, I can see what's in the boxes. Fascinating. Can I infer that the ammunition and power packs are in the other container?"

"Yep." Steiger nodded. "Mighty good piece of gear you have there. The crates are supposed to be shielded."

"I have this talent when it comes to making things work better."

He turned back to look at her.

"A lot of your ordnance seems to be Shrehari-made. Did you get it re-chambered for standard ammo?"

"Definitely. There's an armorer in Rakka who's a wizard at it."

"I hope you test-fired a sample of his work."

"What I did and didn't do is my business, Ser Whate," she replied with an edge to her voice.

"Meaning you didn't." He nodded knowingly. "If you want, I can check them out for you once we're in space. It'll cost extra, of course, but I'm the best small arms expert you'll find within thirty parsecs. You can close this one up. I'll look inside the other container now."

"As you wish."

A sharp beep broke the ensuing silence and Steiger looked towards the door with alarm.

"Someone's skulking around close enough to trigger my detectors."

Decker pocketed the sensor and drew his blaster.

"Your overly curious reivers?"

"Maybe." Steiger pulled out her tablet and glanced at the screen. "Yup, reivers all right. Fifteen that I can see. Must have followed us back from the bar. Shit, some of them look like Rakka city guards. I always knew the bastards were bent."

"Bent security in a free port? Truly shocking." Decker chuckled softly. "Still, at only four to one odds, the bastards are about to find out life sucks. Where are the other entrances?"

"For all intents and purposes, there aren't any. I blocked them tight. The only way in is through the main door."

"Or by cutting through a wall," Decker pointed out. "They aren't exactly built like a warship's hull."

"That might attract attention they don't want," Talyn suggested.

"True." Steiger locked the container shut. "On the other hand, our only way out is precisely through that door."

"You mentioned a hauler. I trust it's stashed away somewhere in here?" Decker asked.

"Are you thinking of plowing through them?" The mercenary sounded doubtful.

"I don't like sitting around waiting for the bad guys to come after me. This place isn't exactly overflowing with good fighting positions."

"The hauler is in the corner over there, under a tarp. It's pretty old and probably won't make more than one trip to the spaceport before it gives out."

"If it can carry both containers, it won't need to make more than one trip." Decker went over to where the ground-effect vehicle sat and ripped the plastic sheeting off.

"It'll take both. Decide who between you and Tran will drive. We'll ride shotgun up top and keep them running in the other direction."

"I'll drive," Tran said. "I'm the one with the least amount of firepower and Miko needs to trigger the automatic door opener just right. If someone would get the loading gantry going, I'll shift the beast under it."

"Just a thought," Decker turned towards Steiger. "Do you have any Shrehari analogs for detcord, preferably with detonators?"

"What are you thinking?" Talyn asked.

"Shock and awe, for one thing; a way to get out of this place by inventing a new doorway for another."

"I have something that might do the trick, but Shrehari explosives aren't like ours." Steiger sounded dubious.

"If they go bang and destroy what we want destroyed, they're like ours. Show me." Decker headed for the second container.

"I might have to take the cost of expended munitions out of your fee, Ser Whate," Steiger said, jogging to catch up with the Marine.

"Our price just went up because you need my skills with explosives to get your merchandise out from under the reivers. It's a zero sum game. Now open the damn container and point me at the goods before they get the same idea and do unto us before we can do unto them."

"Is he always like this?" The mercenary asked Talyn over her shoulder.

"Most of the time. But then, he's mostly right when it comes to weapons and things that go bang, so it evens out. In this case, I'd do as he asks."

Steiger opened the container and slipped down an aisle too narrow for Zack's wide frame. She re-appeared with a metallic box.

"Standard Shrehari ground forces demolition package. Still factory sealed." She tossed the box at Decker, who caught it handily.

"You can say what you like about the boneheads but they make decent military kit," he said, smiling with glee once he'd opened the package. "This can blow a hole big enough for *Phoenix* with some left over to make the buggers outside dance for their lives."

"Just don't drop the whole damn building on our heads," Talyn warned.

"Not a chance." He turned to Steiger. "Show me a schematic of the place, with the position of the bad guys on it."

"Pissing off local security isn't going to help us, you know that, right?" She replied, pulling out her tablet.

"That's why I'd like to make us a new exit far from our friends outside." He held out his hand for the tablet. "Contrary to popular opinion, I like to avoid fighting as much as the next person if there's a good way out."

He studied the schematic, then oriented himself.

"There." Picking up the demolitions kit, he went to a blank wall to one side of the containers and studied it for a few moments, glancing back at the hauler, now creeping into place beneath the loading gantry.

Quickly, he unraveled a long cord filled with a stable, plasticized explosive and outlined an opening on the concrete big enough for the flatbed truck and its load. Stepping back, he studied the entire wall to make sure his demolition charge wouldn't feed any fundamental weaknesses and bring the roof down. Then he carefully placed a kicker charge and armed the detonator.

The door they'd come through began to rattle with the sound of impatient scavengers smelling a rotting corpse. Then, a faint glow appeared around the locking mechanism.

"We're about to have unwanted company, folks." Decker quickly walked back to the loading area. Steiger and Kidder had just finished securing the first container and Talyn was almost done placing the second one on the hauler.

Once she'd released the container, she joined Decker, gun drawn. He handed her a small lump with a detonator sticking out of the smooth surface.

"How's your throwing arm?"

"Fair. I'm going to guess you'd like me to toss this little gem through the door the moment they push it open."

"Yep. I'll cover you. Try not to miss. It's a four-second fuse."

He knelt on the floor to make himself a smaller target while Talyn took a position against the wall to the left of the opening.

The lock suddenly turned into a blob of molten metal and dissolved. A booted foot smashed the red-hot panel inwards, revealing the rough-hewn shape of a Kardati raider.

Decker shot the humanoid twice, then Talyn armed her improvised grenade and tossed it out over the smoking corpse and into the mass of marauders getting ready to rush them. Four seconds later, the device exploded, scattering the would-be invaders.

"We're ready," Kidder shouted, gunning the hauler's fans. Steiger already perched on top of the containers, had drawn her blaster.

"Go join her," Decker shouted at his partner.

He pulled out the remote control for the breaching charge.

"Fire in the hole, fire in the hole, fire in the hole," he yelled, running to take cover in the lee of the truck while Steiger shot over his head at the open door to keep the marauders out.

A dull thump momentarily drowned out the cough of firing blasters, and a neatly outlined section of concrete wall fell outwards into the alley at the back of the warehouse.

"Hit it, Tran," Decker shouted, jumping on the back of the flatbed.

— THIRTEEN —

The wheezing hauler careened around a corner and almost knocked over half-a-dozen raiders, some wearing Rakka security uniforms.

The would-be thieves jumped out of the way at the last moment, when it was evident Tran would run them down without remorse.

"Did you tell the AI to warm up the drives?" He shouted at his partner over the noise of badly aligned fans. "I don't think they're going to let go so we need to lift the moment this thing is in the hold."

"Already taken care of," she yelled back, peering down at him from her perch on top of the containers. "Good thing you had the calliopes out and ready. They're going to be useful in a few minutes. Just try not to damage anything belonging to the spaceport. We might have to come back here some day."

They emerged from the narrow alley and turned onto the main road, accelerating now that they had a straight run at the landing strip.

"I hope Tran remembers to brake before going up the ramp. Otherwise the hard stop against the forward bulkhead is going to hurt."

Movement on the outskirts of Rakka caught Decker's eye.

"Crap. They're sending ground vehicles after us. I'll bet they have some heavy barrels mounted on them too. If this goes the way I think it'll go, *Phoenix* won't be coming back here."

"Just as long as we get away. I'll warn the others." Talyn's head disappeared.

They crested the last rise before the tarmac and were gratified to see *Phoenix*'s belly ramp slowly dropping while the calliopes turned towards them ready to provide covering fire.

"Bad guys emerging from the needle ships," Talyn shouted.

Before Decker could react, Kidder slewed the hauler around and slowed to a walking pace. The Marine jumped off and pointed his blaster at the newcomers, ready to cover their retreat.

The instant the truck and its cargo were safely inside *Phoenix*, he jogged up the rapidly retracting ramp.

He could feel the vibration of thrusters spooling up but had to check his impatience at getting to the bridge. They had to tie the hauler down properly; otherwise, any maneuvering might send it careening around the hold, causing untold damage, not least to the cargo itself.

When that was done to his satisfaction, he slapped the nearest intercom panel.

"Clear to lift." Then he pointed at Kidder. "Take your friend to your cabin. Make sure you both assume the horizontal position. Same bunk, separate bunk, I don't care. This might get funky real fast."

"Wilco." Tran nodded, then took Steiger by the arm and guided her down the passageway. Decker was already gone, the sound of his running feet echoing in the distance.

"Three technicals coming down the main drag," Talyn announced when he strapped himself in. "Looks like someone bolted twin twenties on the bed of an ore skimmer."

"I'm pretty sure I can peel those open like steamed crayfish," he replied, studying the video feed.

"Those twenties can do us a lot of damage too."

"Right." He aimed the topside calliope at a spot a few hundred meters in front of the lead technical and fired a burst that ate up the rammed earth road.

"I hope they'll take my suggestion to stay clear."

The commo panel began to beep insistently. Decker checked the incoming message stack and started to laugh.

"What passes for a harbor master around here is ordering us to stay where we are and prepare to be boarded by the authorities. We're detained on suspicion of causing the death of several sentient beings in the warehouse district."

"You can't accuse them of lacking a sense of humor," Talyn said through clenched teeth. "Another minute or two and we're off."

"Not only did they not take my suggestion to heart, but the lead technical is also powering up his guns. At least the idiots from the needle ships are smart enough to back off. They know I can turn their tubs into salvage if they get cute. May I assume I'm now weapons-free, oh great commander and *chef de mission?*"

"Indulge yourself."

The ship began to vibrate in earnest as the thrusters pushed against the tarmac.

"Indulging myself, aye."

"We have liftoff," Talyn announced, moments after Decker opened fire on the lead technical.

"And one flaming mess of wreckage blocking the road," he replied. "Sadly, its crew perished at their posts."

"You don't sound sad."

"Meh." He shrugged. "The universe is full of stupid. I consider what I've just done to be a service to sentients everywhere." A pause. "Oh no, you don't."

He fired again.

"More stupid?"

"For a very brief and inglorious moment. You'd think they would have taken the fate of their buddies as a warning. Thankfully, the third and last technical just turned tail. He must be the smart one of the bunch. Always put the smart one in the lead, folks, it saves lives."

Decker chuckled.

"The harbor master is having a spastic fit. He says that if we ever try landing at Rakka again, he'll have the ship seized and us shot. Good luck with that."

"Passing ten thousand meters."

"That puts us out of range of those twin twenties they seem to love. I've retracted the calliopes. We have a smooth-bottomed hull again."

The AI chimed to get his attention and he cursed.

"It might not be for long. One of the needle ships just lifted. I'm going to go out on a limb here and guess they want to keep in touch with us."

"How nice of them. I hope they remember that a stern chase isn't in their favor."

"Trying us on with twin twenties from two klicks didn't turn out in their favor and yet..."

"Passing through twenty thousand. You made sure our guests know they need to stay in their bunks?"

"Yep. Steiger strikes me as an old hand, so no worries."

"Okay."

She touched her controls, firing the aft thrusters and the ship's nose began angling upwards, to where the blue sky turned indigo and then black. Pressure increased on Zack's shoulders until he thought he was going to become one with his chair. It eased when the artificial gravity generators kicked in, just before they began the slide into weightlessness.

"I'm going to assume we're headed for Garonne, even if Tran has been cagey about the final destination of our cargo. We don't have time to dicker, not with a reiver on our tail."

"Two reivers. The second one lifted shortly after his buddy." Decker held up his index and middle fingers.

"You'd think the weapons we're carrying are made of precious metals, the way they're sticking to us."

"Maybe the Empire has been clamping down on the illegal weapons trade. They do make stuff that's so straightforward and sturdy it can be used even by the dumbest semi-sentient numbskull, so it's worth real money out here."

"Maybe." She released her seat restraints. "We're going to have a long talk with Sera Steiger once we're FTL."

"She'll likely want one with us as well. Those anti-ship missile launchers in the cargo hold aren't exactly inconspicuous. Like I said, she strikes me as an old hand at the art of war."

"And you're burning to come clean with your old buddy Tran."

"It's inevitable. We don't have to tell them exactly who we are. Steiger has me down for a merc anyway. For Tran, the story will simply be that I didn't go back into the Corps but signed on with you instead."

"Me being the wealthy, eccentric owner of *Phoenix* who has a bee in her bonnet about sailing the star lanes looking for trouble?"

"Sure. Sounds about right, bonnets and all." His mouth twitched briefly. "Anyway, I'd like to show off some of our toys so we can use the extra manpower to help us sail and fight the ship. If we're going where we think we're going, things might get hairy."

"Let me give it some thought," she replied in a tone that brooked no arguments.

"You're the boss," he glanced at his console, "and boss, it's time to do your astrogation duties. The first reiver just broke out of the atmosphere and is hot on our trail. I don't mind another fight, but at some point we'll need an ammo resupply, so if you want to hold off on that, we'd better run. I don't think it's a good idea for Tran and Steiger to witness us snuggling up to a Navy replenishment ship."

"We can always feed them knock-out gas during the procedure, but I get your meaning, though we may not have a choice when it comes to fighting. The bastard's acceleration curve is steeper than ours. He's got a good chance of catching up before we can jump."

The door to the bridge opened unexpectedly.

"Just so you know," Steiger said, standing at the threshold, unwilling to enter the bridge without permission. "I wasn't exactly planning on leaving Rakka."

"Old hand?" Talyn muttered for Decker's ears only. Then, more loudly, "We're not going back, so if you left anything of sentimental value, your options are to forget about it or take a step through the airlock and hitchhike back."

"Do us a favor, Miko," Decker smiled briefly, "stay in the cabin with Tran. We're not out of this yet. Passengers don't get the run of the ship, let alone show up on the bridge without invitation, capisce?"

The mercenary raised her hands in surrender.

"Capisce, Ser Whate."

"Bill, just to make sure," Talyn said, "why don't you accompany Sera Steiger back to her quarters and see that she and Ser Kidder enjoy the high life while we get this crapshoot into FTL?"

Zack sketched a salute.

"Consider it done."

He took Steiger's arm at the elbow and forced her to turn around.

"Don't make this unpleasant, sweetheart. Captain Pasek doesn't look like it, but she's a titanium bitch if you don't obey orders. It's kept us alive up to now, and I'm not about to jinx things."

"And of course, you go along with her."

"Since we have two reiver needle ships on our ass, I've got more important things to do than flirt with you."

They stopped in front of the cabin door, which opened at Decker's touch. Kidder, sitting on a lower bunk, made a contrite grimace when he saw the Marine's hard face.

"Keep your friend under wraps until we call the all-clear, okay, Tran. We don't have time for distractions."

"It would help if you locked us up, Ser Whate."

"Done." He shoved Steiger inside and then slapped the control panel. The door slid shut with a loud snick, locked into place until either Decker or Talyn released them.

"What is it with mercs and their attitude problems?" He muttered, jogging back the way he'd come.

"Time to go to Q-ship mode, Zack," Talyn said when he re-entered the bridge. "They're almost within range."

"You want me to go all out?"

"Just try to keep them away until I can spool up the hyperdrives and jump out. No need for registered kills to boost your ego."

"Bite my ego," he replied, sliding into his seat. "How soon until we go FTL?"

"Will fifteen minutes strain your ammo reserves?"

"Make it ten and our shot lockers will stay a lot fuller."

"Why do I think we'll need to get cozy with a replenishment ship before this is out?"

"Because you're a realist?"

He dialed in the targeting sensors and fired the first salvo.

"Maybe I should send out a call anyway. It'll take a while to divert one of them."

"In that case, find a spot for a rendezvous along the course I've plotted, send it in, and feel free to expend missiles at will."

"Your command fulfills my wish."

Phoenix vibrated with energy feedback when a reiver salvo splashed against her shields.

"Top marks for aim. Let's see if they're as good on close-in defense."

Decker emptied both aft missile launchers, firing a full salvo from the guns for good measure.

The commo stack beeped for attention.

"We're summoned to heave to and prepare to be boarded. Are these guys for real?"

"They're only for real if they can enforce those orders," Talyn replied, "otherwise, a fart in an ion storm would carry more weight."

"Birds away and that took care of the aft launchers. Deploying all turrets."

Another salvo lit up the shields with a blue-green aurora, and the AI bleeped a warning.

"Their close-in guns are firing but no dice." Moments later, Decker whooped. "Hit. We got a damned hit. His bow shields just collapsed."

The lead reiver, stitched by several hundred rounds from *Phoenix*'s main guns began to split apart in a shower of sparks and ejected gasses. Then, in a flash of escaping antimatter fuel, the disintegrating hull turned into a ball of rapidly expanding debris.

"Chock one up for my ego," Decker snarled, retargeting his guns on the second reiver. "For what they're about to receive..."

Broadside after broadside hammered at the marauder, plasma rounds streaming out until the AI warned Zack to slack off and spare the capacitors from premature burnout.

"Tell me we're going to FTL soon. I'm..."

The second reiver, mortally wounded, exploded, giving birth to a minor nova.

Talyn touched the controls, and Decker felt his stomach shoot up through his throat. A fraction of a second later, the shock wave sped through empty space, *Phoenix* already far away, in her own bubble universe, crossing the void at many times the speed of light.

**

"It almost seems unfair," Kidder said after watching a replay of the reivers' destruction.

"As a wise man once said, if you're in a fair fight you screwed up somewhere along the line." Decker took a long pull at his bottle and sighed contentedly. "I'm glad we were able to give you a taste of what we can do and clean up a part of the Protectorate, be it ever so tiny, at the same time."

"Your ship has impressive weaponry, Ser Whate, and I'm equally impressed that you're carrying Shrehari ale of this vintage." Steiger raised her drink in salute. "A man after my own tastes. And you said you didn't provide entertainment, Captain Pasek. Consider me satisfied."

"Glad to hear it," Talyn replied with an ironic smile. "You realize that we'll be tacking the cost of the expended munitions and the booze to your final bill, right? And we'll need to discuss where you want us to take you, preferably now. I put us on a general course back to the Rim, but when we come out of FTL at the end of this jump, I'll need a destination."

Steiger and Kidder glanced at each other, and the latter nodded once.

"We need to meet up with others like me who bought merchandise in various places and hired ships to carry it before we head to our final destination," Steiger said. "The plan is to travel in a convoy for mutual defense."

"Your final destination is perilous?" Talyn asked with a raised eyebrow. "Depending on the risk, we may have to charge a danger premium."

"Let's just say some parties might try to prevent us from handing the merchandise over to its new owners. You'll get paid what you're owed once that's done."

"Glad to hear it. People who short us when it comes to payment, find their lives considerably shortened." An evil grin briefly lit up Decker's hard features. "Always keep that little video of the unlucky reivers in mind. It'll help you make the right choices."

"Our destination, Sera Steiger?" Talyn asked again.

"It's in interstellar space, far from any of the usual star lanes." The mercenary fished a data wafer from her breast pocket. "The coordinates are encoded. I'll have to feed them to your AI myself."

"What makes you think I'll let you anywhere near my ship's systems?"

"He who pays the piper calls the tune, Captain Pasek." A grin to match Decker's appeared. "And we'll be paying you very handsomely indeed."

"Touché." Talyn inclined her head. "If you'll follow me to the bridge, we'll get this sorted out. Perhaps Ser Whate can tend to his ordnance in the meantime."

"Sure." Decker drained his bottle and tossed it in the recycler. "Tran, I could use another pair of arms down below."

**

Later that evening, Decker was checking the forward missile launchers when he heard footsteps on the other side of the open hatch. He closed the panel that covered the manual controls and turned around.

"Not tired enough to rack out?"

"A good fight always gets me so revved up I'm restless for a while," Miko Steiger replied. "You?"

"Same here," he said, leaning against the smooth housing. She had a predatory gleam in her eyes that reminded him of a hungry Shrehari.

"Since Tran's fast asleep, I figured I'd roam the ship for a while so I don't disturb him."

"And you ended up here," his mouth curved into a smile, "figuring that I might be a kindred spirit in need of coming down from a combat high."

"Sure." She approached him until they were only a few centimeters apart. An exciting, earthy female scent tickled his nostrils. "The best thing to get nice and tired in our condition is a horizontal tango. Fighting makes me so horny I can barely stand it."

When she reached down to touch him an equally predatory smile joined the gleam in her dark brown eyes.

"Are you and Pasek a thing?" She asked, closing the remaining distance between them. "Or do you play the field?"

"We're just business associates." He put his arms around her, cupping her buttocks in his large hands.

"Good. I wouldn't want our good captain to get jealous, and I really have to scratch this itch now." Steiger's mouth closed on Decker's.

**

"You might want to shower," Talyn said when he entered their cabin. "I can smell the two of you from here. Was it fun at least?"

"It scratched an itch," he replied, stripping off his clothes.

"Yours or hers?"

"Hers, mostly. On top of a launcher housing isn't the most comfortable place."

"But it is original." She chuckled. "When was the last time you had sex that close to your beloved ordnance?"

He considered the question for a moment.

"It's a first when it comes to missiles. I've had my fun inside a gun turret before, though."

"I know. I was there."

"That was you? Wow. You sure have changed."

She threw a pillow at his head.

"Wash, mister. We have a busy day ahead tomorrow."

"Yes, sir, Captain, sir." He tossed off a mock salute, did a perfect about face, and stepped into the heads.

"Smart-ass." Talyn smiled at his naked back and settled down into her bunk again. "At least she's not a scratcher."

—FOURTEEN—

"I'm glad they decided to use *Mikado* instead of a regular supply ship. That way we have a better chance of keeping up the pretense."

"True," Talyn nodded, her eyes on the navigation readout, waiting for the Q-ship's appearance. "But it'll make the transfer a much bigger pain in the ass. They don't have all the fancy systems the big boys use to toss missile packs at your cargo hatch without missing."

"I'm sure they thought of that," he replied with the tone of an indulgent uncle. "Are we a tad nervous, Commander Talyn?"

"*We* haven't performed replenishment underway in more than twenty years, and back then I did it under the steely gaze of my captain who'd flawlessly accomplished said feat countless times."

"Again, I'm sure they thought of that. We're not the only spy ship in the Navy, so this is hardly a one-off event. Someone aboard *Mikado* must know how this is supposed to work."

"Changing the subject slightly, how did our passengers react to the cloak and dagger announcement that they were to be locked in and deprived of anything more sophisticated than a deck of cards?"

"Tran took it in stride, but Steiger wasn't happy at all."

"That's what happens when you scratch someone's itch, Zack. They start expecting special treatment."

"Present company excepted, of course."

"Of course."

The AI's chime drew Decker's attention back to his console.

"We have an emergence signature approximately one hundred thousand klicks aft. No IFF beacon."

"*Mikado?*"

"If it isn't, I'm going to end up firing whatever ammo we have left. After that, we'll be tossing empty bottles with the tractor beam." Another chime. "We're being hailed."

"Put it on."

"Hello, *Phoenix*," a cheerful voice rang out from the speakers. "We got your grocery list and are here to deliver."

"Tell me you have Shrehari ale," Decker replied.

"*T'Klach* vintage no less. Is the disreputable lady you work with on board, Rookie Trooper?"

"Hi Tom," Talyn said, smiling when the video feed finally locked in. "Since when am I disreputable?"

"Since you started working with that big lug of a Marine." He grinned at Decker. "No offense. She was respectable not too many years ago, but that changed when you joined the black gang."

"Offense is taken, Captain, but since you're offering me some *T'Klach* vintage, I'll hold off on exacting my revenge."

"Every man has his price, I suppose." The opening pleasantries over with, he became all business. "We'd like to do this on the run so I have to ask, when's the last time you did a replenishment underway?"

"When you were still in high school, Tom," Talyn replied.

"I figured as much. They put a replenishment pod in my port cargo hold. It has all the appendages of the big boys, but I'm going to guess you don't have a force net to catch anything I'll toss out."

"No, and I'm not sure I'd be much help even if we did have one."

He nodded.

"To repeat myself, I figured as much, so here's how we'll do this. I'm going to come up on your starboard side at about a hundred meters, give or take, and grab you with my tractor beams. Once we're locked tighter than a pair of love-sick wrestlers, I'll have you open your cargo hold doors and then I'll very gently push the containers into it."

"Okay. So far, so good."

"I'm hoping you have an exoskeleton frame, because the boxes, especially the missile packs, are big and hard to shift."

"Yes and that would be Zack's gig." She glanced over her shoulder at Decker, who gave her a thumbs up.

"What I'll need you to do, Hera, is keep your ship on the current vector and follow the orders of my ship handler. From the moment we're within ten thousand kilometers until we accelerate away again, I own your helm."

"Understood."

"We're going to get close enough that at this speed, any deviation will end in the kind of disaster that won't even see us face a court-martial because we'll be mixed in with the wreckage. We don't normally like to get so close, but since we have to spoon feed you in the absence of a jackstay, there's not much choice."

"I get that."

For the first time since he met her a few years back, Decker heard real strain in Talyn's voice, and he realized that her nervousness was getting to him.

"Good. Get your end ready and Zack, don't try to play catch with the containers. They're bigger than you, and they weigh a lot more than you'd expect. Let us do the work of getting them down on your deck. You can shift them out of the way once we release the beam, and don't worry, my folks have done this before. They have an artist's touch."

"I guess I'm off then," Decker waved at the video pickup before heading aft to don his pressure suit.

"Your chain of command must be a few atoms short of an antimatter load," Tom said once Zack had gone. "The idea of putting a naval officer who hasn't stood watch aboard a warship in twenty years and a Marine with a gunnery fetish in charge of a miniature Q-ship strikes me as very strange."

"I won't argue the point." She chuckled mirthlessly. "But since we've sailed her before, out of necessity more than anything else, it isn't as much of a stretch as you might think. I could ask you the same sort of question: since when did you start doing grocery runs?"

"Since they told me to." He shrugged, unwilling to elaborate. "As they say, orders are orders. You're not our only customer, so don't be flattered by the impeccable service."

"I'll complete the satisfaction survey once we finish inventorying the goods."

"As if I would short-change my favorite spy."

"In a Shrehari second. You Q-ship yahoos are all pirates at heart."

"I'm reminded of something involving pots, kettles, and the color black. *Phoenix* is *Mikado*'s little sibling beneath the fancy camouflage, don't ever forget that."

He suddenly held up his hand to forestall her reply and turned his head to the left.

"My ship handler tells me we're about to enter the controlled zone," he said looking at her again, "so we'll have to shelve the witty repartee. Prepare to take helm orders. Make sure Zack reports when he's ready to receive."

"Acknowledged." Talyn's earlier nervousness returned.

A few minutes later, the intercom came to life.

"I'm suited up and in the hold. You can depressurize and open the space doors."

"The exoskeleton's working?" Talyn asked.

"Yup. I've got it on, and it'll do just fine."

Talyn looked up at the main screen.

"He's ready. I'm depressurizing the hold now."

"Acknowledged, *Phoenix*," Tom said. "Keep the channel with Zack open. My cargo handler will want to speak with him directly."

Soon, a new voice, a feminine alto, came over the open frequency.

"*Phoenix* cargo, this is *Mikado*, I'm transmitting a list of the containers we have for you. You'll have to figure out in which order I should send them. I understand that your space is limited, and we need to make sure everything will fit the first time around."

Decker examined the familiar compartment with an unfamiliar feeling of anxiety. He'd read the relevant protocols the night before, but faced with the reality of a replenishment operation, he felt well out of his depth.

The hauler with the two containers took up a healthy amount of real estate, as did the missile launchers.

"You should have the list now, *Phoenix*." The alto voice cut through his brief disorientation, and he pulled out his tablet.

"This can't be any harder than combat loading a pathfinder troop for an extended operation," he muttered to himself reading the specifications of each container. "Just on a different scale."

"What was that, *Phoenix*?"

"I was saying that I got your transmission, and am figuring the sequence out now."

"Good. For a moment there, I thought I heard something about pathfinders lost on operations, and we know that never happens." The alto voice held a hint of laughter.

"It must be due to the poor quality of the Navy's commo gear," he replied. "We don't have hearing problems in the Corps."

This time, she laughed outright.

"They warned me about you," the unknown woman said.

"Did they also tell you I make a mean duck à l'orange?"

"No, but I'll have to pass if that was an invitation. We're expected elsewhere after this."

"Okay," he said making up his mind. "Container one five five comes first."

"The one with food and drink? That would have been my call as well. No point in burying the good stuff under a pile of ammunition."

"Glad to hear I got it right," he replied with an edge of sarcasm. "After that, well go in the following order..."

When he finished, there was a moment of silence, then she said, "Sounds like a plan. I can't fault the sequence from my end. You, on the other hand, still have to figure out a way to stack them, but I can't help you with that."

"You'd be surprised at how much time I spent on civilian freighters."

"Probably not. Like I said, they warned me about you." That laughing lilt again.

Talyn's voice overrode Decker's reply.

"Time to stop flirting, Zack; I'm about to open the space doors. *Mikado*'s on final approach."

"Acknowledged."

He studied his pad for a few more seconds, memorizing the order, and then looked around at the hold one last time to sear the planned placement of the containers in his mind.

A red light began flashing, and the wide doors opened to reveal the Milky Way in all its glory. Zack felt irresistibly drawn into the abyss-like void and was startled when a large, dark mass slowly pulled level with *Phoenix*, occluding the stars.

Mikado seemed close enough to touch, so close that Zack could see the details of some very hard service etched into her skin. The radio came to life again.

"*Phoenix* cargo, a word of advice. If you're watching the containers come across head-on, you're standing in the wrong spot."

Decker blinked a few times and then noticed a large, lit rectangle had formed on the side of the Q-ship's matte hull. A small figure in a pressure suit waved enthusiastically at him. He returned the wave and then, feeling slightly sheepish, he moved to one side.

"We have positive tractor beam lock on you, *Phoenix*. Stand-by for the first transfer."

"*Phoenix* helm confirms."

"*Phoenix* cargo confirms."

"Number one away," the alto voice announced.

A standard container emerged from the opening in *Mikado*'s flank and slowly crossed the chasm between both vessels. The Q-ship's cargo handler had a sure touch: it came through the space doors dead center and gently dropped to the deck.

"Clear," the alto said. "I'll let you get this one out of the way before I send the next one over."

"Acknowledged."

Using the powerful arms of his exoskeleton frame, Decker picked up the massive case and shifted it to the spot he'd chosen next to the inner hatch, where it could be unloaded quickly.

"Ready for the next one."

"Number two away."

And so it went until the only thing left was the missile pack.

"This is going to be a bit trickier," the *Mikado*'s cargo handler said. "We don't have much room for error due to the size. What I'm going to do is bring the pack to your doorstep, then have you grab the side and guide it in. I'll keep the tractor beam on until you're happy to have me drop it."

"Okay." Decker took a last look at the remaining space on the deck and hoped that he hadn't made a calculation error. "Send her over."

The missile pack was flatter but much longer than the standard containers, and when it got close to the space doors,

Decker had a moment of panic wondering whether it would actually fit through. When it stopped, he extended his exoskeleton's arms as far out as they would go and took hold of a handling bar welded to the side of the case.

"I have it." He felt a thin bead of sweat run down his forehead. "Slowly now. There's not much room to spare on either side."

His heart almost stopped when he felt the vibration of a hard contact between pack and ship run through his exoskeleton. A quick glance showed him that he'd shifted too far left. Careful not to overcompensate, he pulled it to the right and took a step backward. This time, it cleared the opening.

"We're aligned," he said. "A few more meters...Okay, I'm letting go now. You can drop it."

"Replenishment complete," the alto announced a moment later. "If I can make a last suggestion – secure everything to the deck now. It'll avoid problems later."

"Will do, and thanks."

"My pleasure. I'll buy you a coffee next time you're aboard *Mikado*. Cargo, out."

The Q-ship captain's voice came on again.

"Keep your heading and speed until we're clear. Good hunting, *Phoenix*."

The dark mass blocking the stars slowly moved away on a diverging course and Decker just had time to see massive sublight drives glow bright yellow before the space doors closed.

He removed the exoskeleton and secured it against the bulkhead before locking the containers down so they wouldn't shift. Unpacking would be a bitch, but he'd make sure to conscript Steiger and Kidder. None of the containers bore naval markings so they wouldn't see anything they shouldn't, though there might be questions about the provenance.

Talyn had re-pressurized the hold by the time he secured the last one and he removed his helmet with a sigh of relief.

"All good down there?" She asked over the intercom.

"Yep. You can point us at the next stop. I'll get this suit off and release our guests from the brig."

"From their cabin."

"Locked in with no bar, no food, and no entertainment other than a deck of cards, it's a brig."

**

"We decided to return you to your natural habitat," Decker said, opening the cabin door. "It's done, and you're free to roam again."

"Did your mystery supplier bring anything interesting or was it just more of the same old boring stuff?" Steiger asked in a sarcastic tone.

"Are a few cases of *T'Klach* vintage interesting enough?"

Her eyes lit up at his words.

"In that case, I forgive you for your lack of trust and for locking us up like vulgar defaulters."

"Be happy I didn't get my way. I wanted to blow knock-out gas into your cabin to make sure you couldn't see or hear anything, but the boss nixed that idea."

"Nasty man. And here I thought we were buddies." Steiger glared at him.

"Our supplier doesn't care about who scratches whose itch. The deal is no outsiders can witness who they are and how they operate."

"Now I really want to know who you guys are and who you hang out with," she replied. "Pretty posh operation for a pair of mercs nobody's ever heard of."

"It's a big galaxy." Decker shrugged. "We keep a low profile and stick to jobs the big guys like Avalon won't touch. As long as the pay's good..."

"Tran told me you have a doppelganger somewhere out in that big galaxy," she said, following Zack and Kidder to the saloon, "a big bad former soldier who's quick on the trigger and a whiz with weapons. Care to comment?"

"Nope. I'll stick with the theory is that each of us has a double somewhere. Considering the endless billions of human beings out there, I'm a believer."

He pointed at the table.

"Sit. I'm going to heat us up some meals. We eat and then we go into the cargo hold and start unpacking. When that's done, I'll crack open a few bottles of the good stuff. Deal?"

"And what if we decline to help?" She asked.

"I add the extra hours I spend unpacking to your final bill, and I keep the *T'Klach* to myself. When what we have now runs out, you can drink that Pacifica horse piss which, for some unaccountable reason, takes up space in the cooler."

"You *are* a nasty man, Ser Whate."

He grinned at her.

"I thought the itch scratching session had made that abundantly clear."

"Made what clear?" Talyn asked, entering the compartment.

"That I'm a nasty man."

She sniffed the air around him and made a face.

"Considering how badly you need a shower, I'd say nasty's an understatement."

"Go ahead and play stevedore in a pressure suit for a few hours and see how sweet you smell afterward, darling."

"I have no need to. Fetching and carrying is your job — darling."

She blew Decker a kiss and then winked at Kidder, who quietly shook his head in mock despair.

**

"I'd hate to see your statement of operating costs," Steiger said, hauling another case of ammo from a container and putting it on a grav sled for the move to the magazine.

"Why?" Decker collapsed the container that had held the provisions.

"Because I wonder how you can afford this, especially since some of it looks like it fell off the back of a Navy warship, even though it has no markings. That kind of merchandise doesn't come cheap on the black market."

"Yours is not to wonder how," Zack sonorously intoned, "yours is just to help me shift the stuff so we can make sure we're able to take *your* merchandise to its destination. Besides, since you're all secretive about the where and why of your what, you can't expect me to tell you all of my secrets. We're not really that close, the other night notwithstanding. As a matter of fact, I have no idea who Miko Steiger is apart from her appetites."

She made an obscene gesture.

"Screw you, Bill Whate."

"No play until we finish. Ammo doesn't do us much good sitting here if we run out of what's in the magazines before we run out of targets."

"Sure." She nodded. "If you'll point me at the nearest shot locker, I'll shift this pallet over."

He pulled out his tablet and tossed it at her. She snatched it out of the air with practiced ease.

"Follow the directions. A pro like you shouldn't have problems."

"Combat load?"

"Yes." Decker's face twisted into a mask of disappointment. "You needed to ask?"

"Touchy, touchy."

**

"Steiger smells a rat," Decker said after the cabin door closed behind him.

"Did you forget to run the vermin control protocols after we left Rakka?" Talyn asked, mischief dancing in her eyes.

"She's got time in the Armed Services for sure. When we unpacked the missiles, she wondered out loud what we were doing with Mark Twenty-Threes that weren't, under any circumstances, allowed to end up in civilian hands."

"Too smart for comfort?"

"Yeah. She loaded the magazine for the main guns without calling for help. I checked afterward. Flawless."

"Coming from you, that says something."

"Sure, but what does it say?"

"That we need to tighten our game and maybe give up a few hints to gain her confidence. The question is how much?"

"I'm thinking more and more that if I drop the Ser Whate act and scrub this disguise to become Ser Decker, interstellar mercenary, we might get further. If we're going to be under contract to the Garonne rebels for more than just cargo haulage, Tran will be the first to recommend they take advantage of a former Marine master gunner's expertise, and that gives us a way inside."

"And if the Coalition is behind the rebellion, for whatever Machiavellian reasons, the game's up. You're a known quantity after the affair on Pacifica and that little trick you pulled, returning from the dead."

"Not if the analysts at HQ are right, and Amali's vendetta against me was personal rather than Coalition business, which makes more sense than my being their number one bugaboo. I'm just a small irritant in the grand scheme of things and quickly forgotten."

He stripped off his coveralls.

"Since my personal file is buried so deep the Grand Admiral can't read it without special permission, there's nothing to say I'm back in the Corps. Even better, seeing as I've got no public record since I supposedly retired, I can say whatever I want."

"I'd still like to err on the side of caution. The Coalition has had its tentacles deep inside naval intelligence before. Let's see what happens at this gathering of transports before we make any hasty decisions. Steiger can stew in her suspicions until then. Right now I'm not sure I either like her or trust her and not only because she was a little too quick to scratch her itch with you."

"Jealousy is such an ugly thing," he replied, quickly ducking into the heads before he became the target of a well-aimed pillow.

— FIFTEEN —

"You're not locking us in again?" Steiger asked, twirling a half-empty bottle between her fingers.

Several days had passed since the covert resupply operation, and relations between the mercenary and Zack had remained somewhat strained.

"I can, if that turns your crank," Decker replied with an indifferent shrug. "But this is your tribe, and there's no magic to our approach."

"As opposed to the magic that makes this ship a pocket frigate? I suppose you have a jolly roger in your flag locker somewhere."

"Probably." He finished his drink. "You can join us on the bridge if you like your boredom in generous servings."

"Not very trusting are you?"

"Approaching an unknown rendezvous with colors aloft and the band playing is not really a good strategy for long-term survival. We'd rather know what things look like before we blunder into them."

"At the risk of sounding churlish," Kidder interjected, "that didn't work out too well with the late Ser Syko."

"And yet, he's the *late* Ser Syko, and we're taking a pleasure cruise along the Rim, Tran. I think that worked out splendidly for everyone, Syko and his goons excepted, and that's a blessing for Andoth and the galaxy at large."

"As you say." The former silahdar inclined his head.

Talyn stuck her head into the saloon.

"I've decided to drop out of FTL some distance away from the given coordinates. That means we're going silent in eight hours. I suggest you all take whatever rest, recreation, and sanitation you need. Once we're at sublight, I'm shutting the ship down except for the essentials."

She looked at Decker and jerked her head towards the passageway.

"I'd like a final check on our emcon condition before then. If you haven't had too much of that Shrehari swill, we might want to do it now rather than later, just in case we've had a degradation in some of the shielding."

"Roger that." Decker tossed his bottle into the recycler and rose. "Duty calls. Feel free to enjoy the amenities for as long as you want. Like the boss lady said, we're going to full emcon in eight, so plan accordingly."

Steiger got up too.

"Mind if I tag along?"

"Why?" Decker asked the mercenary.

"Curiosity. Your ship is fascinating; quite unlike any I've seen."

"And your curiosity doesn't become a passenger who's hired us to transport contraband," Talyn said, her tone distinctly unpleasant. "Engineering and combat spaces are out of bounds to passengers."

"And yet I've seen the inside of your magazine after seeing the inside of your distinctly non-standard supply containers."

"A one-off for the sake of expediency. You're restricted to this deck now."

Steiger made a vaguely mocking hand gesture, imitating a salute.

"Aye, aye, Captain."

"You know she's trying to get under your skin, right?" Zack murmured once they were out of earshot.

"Under my skin and into your pants, which she's thankfully managed only once." Talyn gestured at the ladder, inviting him to go down first. "Try to keep it that way, Zack. I hope we can off-load her when we meet the rest of them. If she's ex-Fleet as you suspect, she must have been in the security branch. They irritate the heck out of me every time I get near one. You're sure you secured all the hatches leading off the passenger deck?"

"They aren't going anywhere other than the saloon or their cabins, and if Steiger decides to try overriding the locks, the AI will let everyone know — loudly."

"Doing things with the ship's systems again that the designers never thought of?"

"Got to keep busy during a long crossing. Sex, booze and sleep will only get me so far." They stepped into a tight maintenance passage.

"Maybe studying for a commission might occupy your time."

"Huh." He grunted, dropping into a crouch to check the keel junction box. "Why the heck should I go for a commission? My warrant pays me a major's rates, I get saluted by the enlisted ranks when I'm in uniform, but I don't have to put up with all the officer crap. The way I see it, I'm sitting in the sweetest spot of all."

"The way I see it if you intend to have a long career, your next promotion *is* to major. Might as well get prepared."

"Nope. Not in the middle of a mission." He shut the panel and stood up. "This one's good."

Talyn pulled out a hand-held sensor and began walking aft, looking for emission leaks near the power conduits.

"Anyway," he continued, following his partner down the narrow corridor, "I've got enough time in command of a company group, even if it was made up of Trans-Coalsack slave-soldiers, that I'm eligible for a direct commission without sitting for any exams."

"I didn't know that."

"You're not a Marine, darling." He blew her a mocking kiss. "I just have to apply and get the career management trolls to validate my field experience. After that, it's the Commandant's call whether I skip over the promotion list or get slotted for a career board."

"So prepare your application." She squatted by the aft junction box, opened the panel, and checked her sensor. "Clear. We can do the engine spaces now."

"And we're back to why should I bother?"

"Because you can go a lot further than chief warrant officer."

"I never figured to become a command sergeant, so I'd say my career aspirations have been more than surpassed. Why are you so interested in pushing me up the greasy pole?"

"Because I care?" She looked over her shoulder and gave him a disingenuous smile.

"That's the most insincere thing I've heard all day." Decker's roar of laughter echoed off the bare metal bulkheads. "You're just trying to get me to a rank where I can shoulder some of the officer-type responsibilities for our team.”

“Guilty. Trying to explain your operational decisions to the brass is becoming a full-time chore after every mission.”

“I’m a big boy. I can stand at attention in front of Captain Ulrich’s desk and take my medicine.”

“No doubt.” She opened the hatch to the fusion reactor compartment. “But I’m the commanding officer, so I get to wear the nincompoopery of my staff.”

“May I add nincompoopery to the Decker dictionary?”

“Of course. You caused it to be expelled from my over-tired brain; but enough persiflage, *mon ami*. Let’s pick up the pace so we can get a decent night’s sleep.”

**

“You’re sure we can join you on the bridge?” Steiger wore an entirely feigned look of innocence. “You haven’t changed your mind about locking us up?”

“If you keep up the sarcastic warrior princess act, I will change my mind,” Decker growled, but he waved her and Kidder over the coaming anyway. “You can take the two empty stations over there. I’ve disconnected them.”

“Sixty seconds to emergence,” Talyn announced, cutting off the mercenary’s reply. “You’d better be sitting when the countdown hits zero. I’m not picking you up if you face plant.”

This time, Steiger had the grace to obey without a further word.

The universe shifted, making Decker feel like his guts were about to take a fast trip up his throat. He swallowed hard and then touched his screen.

“We’re systems down.”

“And now the boredom begins, Ser Kidder, Sera Steiger,” Talyn said, rising from the helm console. “The AI will digest and collate anything worthy of our attention. You can stay here and watch the readout. I’m grabbing a coffee. You want one, lover boy?” She asked Zack.

“My usual – black as your soul.”

“I don’t have a soul,” she shot back before disappearing down the passageway.

"So we're going to sit here and wait to see what happens?" Kidder asked.

"We're not exactly sitting, Tran," Decker replied. "When our hyperspace bubble collapsed, it left us sailing along at a good clip on the same course at a non-relativistic velocity. Mind you, considering the distances involved, it feels like we're sitting still, though I wouldn't recommend taking a giant leap off the ship right now."

"Of course." He dipped his head once. "I'm a ground pounder so you'll forgive my less than stellar knowledge of space travel mechanics."

"But to answer your question, we want to see what's happening at the coordinates you gave us before committing and since we're not talking about the place next door, we'll have to wait until useful energy waves reach us. That can take some time, especially if your friends are late."

"You are careful, aren't you, Ser Whate?" If Steiger's crooked smile was meant to be disarming, it didn't work.

"We're alive. People who tried to screw us over aren't. I like to keep the odds in my favor."

Talyn re-appeared with two mugs and handed one to Zack.

"If the coffee is soulless, don't blame me. You ordered it that way."

She took her seat at the helm again and turned to face their passengers.

"There's plenty left for you, but it's self-service. I recommend having some as a way to pass the next few hours without falling asleep. Silent running is about as boring as it gets aboard a starship."

"That's very naval of you, Captain Pasek." Steiger stood up and nodded towards the door. "C'mon Tran, let's sample her brew."

"Anything on the sensors?" Talyn asked once they were alone.

"Plenty but none of it concerns us unless you've suddenly developed a deep and abiding interest in astrophysics."

"Pass. It was my worst subject at the Academy."

"And what was your best?"

"Keeping my mouth shut," she replied nodding towards the sound of footsteps in the passageway.

"I think you coffee has plenty of soul," Steiger said, smiling at Talyn. "Anything yet?"

"You're kidding right?" Decker shook his head. "According to your timetable, we're ahead of schedule."

"So, how long does this go on for?"

"Until I'm happy we won't stumble into something we won't like. I did warn you that running silent can add years to your life if you enjoy boredom." He took a sip of his brew and winced. "Plenty of spirit in this one. You may not be the dark, empty vessel you pretend to be, *mon capitaine.*"

"Perhaps we should head back to our quarters where you can probe my dark empty corners," Talyn replied, watching for Steiger's reaction. When she came up empty, the spy shrugged. "Or not."

Decker stretched his legs out and slumped back, balancing the mug on his stomach.

"This is nice. No one shooting at us, no systems screaming for attention; just four friends enjoying a little coffee break."

"Maybe we could tell each other war stories," Steiger suggested. "I've got a special request because my friend Tran here doesn't want to ask."

"Oh?" Zack's eyebrows shot up, and a sly smile crossed his lips. He knew what was coming.

"Your little legend about doppelgangers is cute. But since we're betting our lives on you two, perhaps it might be the right time to tell the tale of why Zack Decker, the last commander of the Fifth Orta, or what remained of it after the Garada fiasco, is pretending to be Bill Whate, first mate and gunner of a mercenary Q-ship."

Zack grinned at his two passengers.

"Who's never thought of changing his identity after the kind of crap I went through in the last few years?"

"Why?" Tran asked.

"Why not? I wanted to let go of the past and needed a job after we got home, one that would let me forget and more importantly let the folks who thought me dead forget. So far, it's worked. I even had you wondering whether your memory was playing tricks."

"And what's your story?" Steiger challenged Talyn.

"Crazy rich lady with a starship and an itch for adventure. I met Zack in a bar on Mykonos and the one night stand turned into a partnership. He was trying to get reacquainted with the bottle. I got him reacquainted with something he's superb at, cleaning up filth."

"And your name is really Pru Pasek. PP for short?"

"No, but I have enough money to make that identity stick. It'll do until I get tired of it."

"Tran tells me you're a heck of a military trainer and commanding officer, Sergeant – or is that Major – Decker."

"It's nothing at all. I'm retired from the Corps. Zack will do when there are no unfriendly ears around. I also answer to 'hey you' and the sound of a Shrehari ale popping open. For official purposes, Ser Whate will do even better. There are still plenty of folks in the galaxy who'd like to tan my hide and hang it on the wall."

"It sounds like you have a knack for making enemies."

Decker snorted.

"You have no idea, hence the change of appearance, name and career."

"What is it you folks say: once a Marine, always a Marine?"

"Yeah. So?" Zack glanced at his sensor, hoping he looked like he was fishing for an excuse to end this conversation.

"If Tran wasn't blowing smoke up my ass, we could use someone like you, and I'm willing to bet you wouldn't mind going back to your old line of business."

Steiger examined him with an almost frightening intensity, to gauge his reaction.

"I have no idea what Tran's been saying, which means the smoke you feel tickling your butt is pretty much your own business."

He took another glance at the sensor readout, but this time, he kept his eyes on the screen.

"I'm happy with my life these days, so you might as well put away whatever you were going to dangle in front of me."

"And here I thought you were a merc for hire." Steiger laughed derisively. "You should listen before making up your mind."

Talyn gave Zack a dirty look.

"It costs nothing to listen, buddy, and we've got a whole lot of sweet nothing going on anyway, so I'd like to hear Sera Steiger speak her piece."

"I thought you didn't like me."

"I don't, but I got rich by listening to propositions of the financial kind before tossing them away. My companion here isn't quite as motivated by profit as I am."

"Yeah." The mercenary smirked. "He's got other motivations."

"I'm right here, you know," Decker protested half-heartedly.

Steiger held up her hand, palm facing Zack.

"I'm negotiating with the organ grinder now, lover."

"As far as I can tell, we're not negotiating anything," Talyn replied, an amused smile playing on her lips.

"Not yet in any case," Steiger agreed. "My people aren't just in the market for weaponry, we're also in the market for trained soldiers. Again, going by what Tran said, your partner would be a heck of an asset, not just as a fighter but as an advisor."

"Are you preparing to invade the Empire?"

"No." She shook her head. "We're working on correcting a massive wrong done to some terrific folks. I hear Ser Decker has a thing about injustice."

"You mean doing what he can to avoid being the victim thereof? Yeah, he's good at it."

Decker caught Tran's eye and grinned briefly, to show he was amused and not at all put out by the mischaracterization.

"What's in it for us?" Talyn asked.

"A long-term contract. Action. The virtuous feeling of being on the side of the justice."

"Death?"

"Depends on how good you two are, especially the ex-Marine you sleep with."

"Oh, he's good. Take it from me."

"Though I'm sure Sera Pasek doesn't mean quite the same thing, I'll second that remark," Kidder said. "Zack Decker managed to turn around a screwed up company in no time flat and that, among his other virtues, saved two hundred lives when the mission went sideways."

Steiger held up her hands in surrender.

"Enough. I'm sure Ser Decker, or Ser Whate if he likes, doesn't need his ego inflated." She dropped her hands again. "First things first. We need to get the convoy together and reach our destination without interference. I'll hire you to ensure that we do. Once we're there, and you're still interested, we can make it worth your while if you'll lend us your skills."

"I prefer Ser Whate right now and where, exactly, is it that you're correcting a massive injustice?" Decker asked.

"Care to take a guess? A smart guy like you must be keeping tabs on what's happening along the Rim."

Zack locked eyes with Steiger.

"Garonne?"

The mercenary tapped the side of her nose with her index finger.

"Any problems with that?"

"Depends. Is our pay tied to the rebels winning, or are we getting paid no matter what?"

"You're getting paid. If you stick around long enough for Garonne to get its level three status, I'll see that you get a bonus."

"So our pay depends on the Senate doing what you consider the right thing? How stupid do we look?"

"The Senate will go along once we kick the Celeste administration off-planet, especially if the Fleet decides to step in."

"Maybe the Fleet will side with the colonial government."

"Perhaps. We'll take our chances."

"And you want us to take ours?"

"Got anything better to do right now?" Steiger smirked. "You're carrying ordnance for a rebel army. If the Navy stops this ship, maybe they'll take you in."

"Blackmail is such an ugly thing," Talyn said. "But well played nonetheless."

She put her hand on her holstered blaster.

"Of course, we could always space the two of you and sell your cargo for a profit."

Kidder looked distinctly pained, and he gave Decker a pleading look.

"Enough," Zack snarled. "If we're done with the posturing, why don't we agree that we'll give your convoy an armed escort to Garonne? Once we're there, we'll decide whether to stick around and extend our contract or leave, no harm, no foul.

You pay in installments. That's the best you're going to get until we figure out what the state of play looks like. Agreed?"

Steiger nodded once.

"Agreed."

The AI chimed softly, calling Zack's attention back to his screen.

"Two ships dropped out of FTL near the rendezvous coordinates," he said. "Their power curve is consistent with small freighters."

"That must be Verrill," Steiger said. "He was going for the mother lode."

"And this mother lode was where, exactly?"

"You have your secrets, Captain Pasek," she wagged her finger at Talyn, "we have ours."

"Fair enough," she replied. "Might I suggest that if we're being paid to protect your mother lode, we go 'up systems' and join them while we wait for number three?"

"By all means, Captain."

"I assume you have a recognition signal?" Decker asked. "It would be a shame if your man Verrill's ships jumped out on a scare or got stupid and opened fire."

"Of course," Steiger replied. She fished a data wafer from her jacket and tossed it at Zack, who snatched it out of the air with practiced ease. "Feed that through your commo array when we drop out of FTL. I'm assuming we're going to do a micro jump rather than join them at sublight speed, right?"

"Right." Talyn turned towards the helm console. "Be prepared for your coffee to try a bid at resurrection."

— SIXTEEN —

A bearded man of indistinct age appeared on the main screen moments after Decker had established a secure commlink to the freighters.

"Steiger," he said nodding at the mercenary and her companion, "Kidder."

"Verrill. You had success?"

"Of course. I see you brought some muscle along with your part of the ordnance."

"May I present Captain Pasek and her partner Ser Whate? Their ship, *Phoenix*, is an armed yacht with impressive firepower. I've witnessed them destroy two reiver needle ships shortly after lifting from Rakka. They've agreed to provide us with an armed escort us to our destination on top of carrying what I bought."

"Really?" Verrill stroked his chin while he examined Talyn and Decker through narrowed eyes. "How interestingly convenient. You're satisfied that we can trust them?"

"Tran has some history with Ser Whate and vouches for him unconditionally. Apparently, on top of turning reivers into dust, he's also something of a wizard at training troops and beating the crap out of anyone who desperately needs it."

"Even more interesting, isn't it, that they'd stumble across us at a time when we desperately need military experts." The doubt and mistrust in Verrill's face were plain for all to see. "I assume that by now you know who we are and what we're about, Captain Pasek, Ser Whate?"

"We do." Talyn nodded.

"And?"

"And what?   Are we uncomfortable with transporting weapons for a rebel movement?   Are we uncomfortable providing an armed escort for your clapped-out freighters and firing at anyone other than the Navy if need be? The answer to both is no. We're for hire, and provided you don't ask us to do something that'll put us on the Fleet's shit list, we'll deliver."

"I'm sure Miko dangled enough money in front of your eyes to take care of any scruples you might have had."

"She has," Talyn confirmed.

"That being said," he continued, "I'm more concerned about who else you talk to or work for. As you can probably figure out for yourselves, there are a few governments who'd dearly like to end our movement before we have a chance to shake off Celeste's yoke."

Decker shrugged.

"We talk to ourselves and our clients, meaning you fine people right now; no one else. If we don't cross the line, the Constabulary and the Navy leave us alone. The opinions of the various colonial administrations out on the Rim don't matter much. Half of them are corrupt, and the rest close an eye when we're around on the general principle that we could be useful in a pinch."

"Funny that we've never heard of you before," Verrill replied, unconvinced.

"Being too well known doesn't attract business. Our usual clients like things to stay nice and quiet, before, during and after a contract."

"Fair enough. I know you folks hold an ace in the form of your ship and the cargo it carries for us, which puts me in the position of having to graciously accept responsibility for the contract negotiated by Miko, whether I'm happy with it or not."

"As she mentioned, I can vouch for them," Tran said. "Bill Whate came out of the Coalsack with me after he saved our collective bacon on Garada. Two hundred people, me included, owe him our lives, first because he taught us how to fight and then because he led us out of the worst military disaster to befall our erstwhile employer."

"What about Captain Pasek?" Verrill asked. "You know her from your past adventures as well?"

"No, but Ser Whate trusts her unconditionally, and that's good enough for me."

"I see I'll have to swallow my reservations about this arrangement." Verrill nodded politely at Talyn and Decker.

"All that remains for me to say at this point is welcome to our little ragtag band of freedom fighters."

"Sera Steiger mentioned a third freighter," Talyn said. "Are you expecting it soon?"

The rebel leader gave a half shrug.

"We set a timeframe, not an exact time for the rendezvous. Once that period expires, whoever made it here heads home. Coordinating three missions isn't exactly easy when you don't have access to the Navy's subspace array. It's a miracle that you made it not long after our arrival, considering Tran had to look far and wide for extra transport. Few captains are willing to get involved with a colonial liberation movement, and many of those who do would sell us out at the drop of a cred."

"Hence your reservations."

"I believe that if it seems too good to be true, it is, Captain Pasek. You two seem too good to be true, but I have to remind myself that sometimes the stars do align, and we get a shot of good luck."

"Let me rephrase my question, then. How long do you expect to remain in this area if your third companion doesn't show up?"

"We've given ourselves a window of seven standard days."

"This deep in interstellar space and with reasonable emissions control, we should be reasonably safe from accidental discovery," Decker remarked.

"Glad that our arrangements meet with your approval, Ser Whate," Verrill replied.

Zack seemed unfazed by the man's cutting edge.

"If you're buying my services as an advisor, I'll advise. If you want me to shut up, just say the word."

"He generally stops speaking if you ask," Talyn chimed in, "though I find the best way is to stick a bottle of Shrehari ale in his hand."

Verrill's eyebrows shot up.

"Expensive tastes. Are you carrying any?"

"Why?" Zack's mouth curved into a broad smile. "Don't tell me you're an aficionado?"

"I've been known to take a nip when I can," he replied, a measure of ease loosening his tense features. "Perhaps you might be kind enough to invite me for a meal. Getting to know one's new allies around a good drink is rarely a bad idea."

"Consider yourself invited, Ser Verrill, now in fact, while we're waiting for your third ship."

**

The man who stepped out of the personnel pod seemed to match Zack in height if not quite in width. Though appearing older and more tired in person, he nonetheless exuded confidence with every spare gesture.

Decker stuck out his hand.

"Welcome aboard, Ser Verrill."

"Pleasure, and it's just plain Verrill. Ser Verrill is my father, as the joke goes."

The two men tested each other's grip for a moment, recognizing quickly that they were almost evenly matched.

"You said something about Shrehari Ale, Ser Whate."

"The name's actually Zack Decker — you can call me Zack. Bill Whate is what I go by publicly, but that's just between us. There are a lot of nasty people out there who want me dead, hence the cover identity."

"Aren't you afraid that I'll let it slip?" He asked, following Decker to the saloon.

"If you do, I'll just switch names and get a new face. Right now, we need to trust each other over more than the delight of a *T'klach* vintage."

"*T'klach* vintage?" Verrill whistled softly. "Nice. I may begin to like you, Zack Decker aka Bill Whate. You were a janissary with Tran Kidder?"

"I was his commanding officer in the Kashdushiya, the slave-soldier regiment."

"Interesting. Any regular military experience?"

"Twenty years in the Corps."

They reached the saloon door, and Zack stepped aside to let his guest enter first.

"Verrill, I'd like you to meet my captain and partner, Pru Pasek." He gestured towards Talyn, who'd risen from the bench, holding out her hand.

"Pleasure, Captain."

He tested her briefly and smiled when she winked at him. Turning to the other two he nodded.

"Miko, Tran. Well done. This looks like a hell of a good find. Zack gave me a tiny thumbnail sketch of his bona fides and based on that, I think we can actually use him."

"Did he tell you he used to be a Marine Pathfinder in a previous life?" Kidder asked.

"No, but somehow I'm not surprised after the stories you told me of your time in the Trans-Coalsack. Now," he rubbed his hands together, "I was lured here with the promise of fine alien hooch."

"And I always keep my promises," Zack held out a cold bottle. Verrill took it with near-reverence and scanned the label.

"You weren't kidding."

"I never joke when it comes to the good stuff." He passed out more of the potent brew then took one for himself, twisting off the stopper in a natural motion. "Mud in your eye, freedom fighters."

"Skoal." Verrill took a long sip, his face brightening with sheer delight at the taste. "You are a man of refinement and principles, Zack Decker aka Bill Whate."

"Live in close quarters with Zack for a while before complimenting him. His idea of elegance is not walking around the bridge in his birthday suit," Talyn said, smirking.

"Sure," Decker nodded, smiling pleasantly, "and if you don't like my principles, I can find others to suit."

Verrill chuckled.

"I'll take that under advisement."

"Sit." Zack pointed at the bench. "We're at least refined enough not to eat standing up."

"Glad to hear it." Verrill slid in beside Steiger. He gave her a quizzical glance, and she nodded.

"Tell me, Zack, if I run your real name through the net, what's going to come up?" He asked.

"Not much," Decker replied, busy at the autochef. "Service dates, my retirement a few years ago, membership in the merchant guild, that sort of stuff. Although," he turned his head to glance at Verrill with a crooked grin, "if you check the dark corners of the net, you might find that there's still a price on my head."

"And you, Captain Pasek?"

Talyn laughed.

"You'll find a lot less. I've haven't had a colorful life like my partner, thankfully. I'm not sure I'd survive what he's been through."

"So why is a retired Marine skirting the outer edge of the law."

"A man's got to make a living somehow, and this does just fine. I know what'll get the Fleet's attention, which means we can calibrate our contracts to stay out of sight." Decker distributed meal trays and then sat down in front of his own serving. "It's a good life if you have no anchors."

"Have you ever had dealings with the Avalon Corporation?" Verrill took a bit of his chicken and chewed thoughtfully, waiting for a reply.

"Here and there," Decker replied, noncommittally. "The grunts aren't bad, as corporate mercs go. The higher-ups in their shiny executive offices? Politically connected scum."

"Avalon's been contracted by Celeste to provide a naval blockade around Garonne and the government might even hire ground troops in the not too distant future."

Zack shrugged, cutting another slice off his meat.

"I said they weren't bad, and I meant that in the sense of respecting the Rules of War. As fighters, well, they're mercs and don't have the incentive to die for a cause. You folks, if you truly believe in Garonne independence, do. Advantage: freedom fighters."

"Pretty cynical view, isn't it?"

"Realistic."

Decker popped a chunk into his mouth and chewed slowly, meeting Verrill's eyes without embarrassment.

"See," he said after swallowing, "the Celeste government can't deploy its National Guard to Garonne, at least not as formed units and definitely no spacecraft. The laws laid down after the massacres of the Second Migration War pretty much bars any transport of planetary troops without Fleet authorization and no Grand Admiral is going to sign off on that. So if the colonial militia can't handle things, they hire mercs."

"I've taken the usual political science pap at university," Verrill replied. "What's your point?"

"You can kick Avalon Corporation ass from here to the galactic core, and all you'll get from Fleet HQ is a big fat yawn. So your governor hired Avalon. So what? Wallop 'em enough and they'll raise their rates until they break the bank. Then they walk away."

"And we're still sounding pretty cynical."

"Take it from me," Zack replied around a mouthful of steamed vegetables, "I've seen this story before. If you're ready to die, the mercs don't stand much of a chance. They didn't sign up to meet their maker. The Corps? That's another story. Once they land, you can kiss your rebellious butt goodbye. The trick is to become the colonial government that welcomes the dropships instead of remaining nasty rebel scum. You can do that, you're golden. Just make sure you don't execute the previous administration without a fair trial. These days, the Fleet never overturns the will of the people, even if it came out of the barrel of a gun. Hispaniola cured it of any nation-building delusions it might have had."

"I gather you were there?" Verrill sounded interested.

"Yep." Decker pushed his empty tray aside and sat back. "Damn near was the death of me. My buddy and I ended up in a mob show and no live ammo. I still have nightmares about it. Biggest body count the Corps saw since the last Shrehari war so it's not about to repeat the experience."

"Cogent thinking for a former command sergeant."

"Dummies don't get to wear the crossed swords on their stripes. Besides, the Corps runs on its command non-coms. Now about your real question concerning the Avalon rent-a-spacers: we have no problems putting them at the wrong end of our guns. They'll try to return the favor. Good luck to them."

"You're a very confident man."

Decker's mouth twitched.

"It's a curse, but so far, so good. Another one?"

"Are Shrehari ugly?" The rebel leader smiled when Zack reached over to the cooler and pulled out a few more bottles. "There's none to be had where we're going and what comforts we do get are pretty miserable. The militia might not be much on catching us, but they sure can make life hard for colonists who help out with supplies.”

“Have they done anything that crossed into war crimes territory yet?”

“None that would hold up in court, but how many settlements can you ruin before it stops being collateral damage and becomes a deliberate scorched earth policy?”

An evil grin twisted the Marine’s lips.

“I’ve seen that story before too. Perhaps the Garonne militia needs to experience some real pain.”

He ignored Talyn’s warning glance, knowing full well that she would be against any involvement unless it got them closer to finding the rebellion’s financial backers.

“And you’re the man to do it?” There was gentle mockery in Verrill’s tone.

“I’ll need a little bit of help from your fine young rebels.”

This time, Verrill laughed out loud at Decker’s disingenuous tone.

“I’m beginning to like you, Zack, and I’d be really chagrined to find out you’re not what you pretend to be.”

“He’s not pretending,” Talyn said. “My boy here has a ruthless streak when he puts his mind to it.”

“And you, Captain?”

“When we’re in space, he’s the first mate. On the ground, I’m his winger. Whatever needs to be done, I’ve got his back.”

“A wonderful non-answer,” Verrill replied, “but I’ll let it stand for now. Do you have any military background that might be useful?”

“Not even a whiff.”

“Meaning you have a military background and none of it is useful to us or you’ve never been in uniform?”

“Does it matter which one it is? I sail this ship where it needs to go. When we get there, I let the big guy run the show.”

“Another wonderful non-answer, Captain.” This time, Verrill’s tone was openly sarcastic. “Fair enough. Your ship, your rules.”

“And what’s your story, to coin a phrase?” Decker asked. “Verrill the rebel and all that?”

“It’s a long and complicated story, to coin another phrase,” he replied.

"I figure two bottles of my finest vintage pays for a long and complicated story, not a wonderful non-answer."

This time, Verrill's laugh sounded genuine. It reached his eyes and highlighted every wrinkle in his tired face.

"You know about the situation on Garonne?"

"Sure. Class one colony, bootstrapped its way to self-sufficiency, but it can't even get class two status, let alone class three independence, because Celeste, with help from its pals in the Senate, wants to keep a place where it can dump undesirables and appoint useless drones to profitable government sinecures."

"Succinct, to the point, and sadly true." Verrill sighed. "Though it's worse than you can imagine."

"Try me. I've been through a few colonial disturbances in my day, and they all suck in their own way. The ones with off-world political interference almost always have the most suckage."

"Our most excellent colonial administration has been hiring deportees into the militia, pushing out those who came from the original settler families. They've been promised free land and even tickets home to Celeste if they serve to the governor's satisfaction. Some of the deportees are politicals, and they're either on our side or keeping their heads down. Most, though, are criminals. How's that for being worse?"

Decker nodded.

"Sounds incredibly shitty. Let me guess. They have no problems burning down the homestead of an independence supporter and then claiming they were fired on while running a peaceful patrol in the countryside."

"Got it in one, with homesteaders often dying in the process. The properties then get handed over to government supporters."

"Why has evidence of this not been brought to the Senate?"

"We tried. Our envoys vanished and are presumed dead by now." Anger flashed across Verrill's eyes. "My eldest son was among them."

"And your cities, or make that your one major city is under the control of the militia, at least those parts not under direct control of deportee gangs, and independence supporters either flee, keep quiet or die."

"I guess you *have* seen it before." Verrill sighed. "Some days I don't know how we'll ever get out of this nightmare short of the Fleet risking direct intervention."

Talyn caught Decker's eye again, to remind him that he was not to play knight-errant. He ignored her.

"There are always ways, my friend." A slow, predatory smile spread across his broad face. "We..."

The AI suddenly chirped with alarming insistence.

"That would be the proximity warning. A ship dropped out of FTL within our security sphere," Zack said, rising to leave the saloon. "I hope it's your third freighter. If not, we might have a problem."

"May I join you?" Verrill asked.

"You can all come if you like. Just be ready to vacate the bridge the moment we say so. There's not much room, and if we have to fight, passengers get in the way."

When the others caught up with him, Decker was already at the gunnery console, scrolling through the sensor log.

"It's a freighter alright, looks like the other two, but it's pushing out an encrypted signal like crazy."

Verrill stepped closer and peered over the Marine's shoulder.

"That's our code. Can you open a link to *Marilan*?"

Moments later, a somber female face materialized on the main screen. She spoke before Verrill could open his mouth.

"It's Roste aboard *Clio*. He has some nasties on his tail. We need to get away quickly before they drop out of FTL and come at us."

— SEVENTEEN —

"Any idea who they are?" Talyn fingers danced on the navigation console, programming an emergency jump.

"Negative. Two ships, armed, unmarked and without an IFF beacon, but then, no one broadcasts an IFF out on the Rim unless the Navy's around." The woman looked at her leader with anxious eyes. "Are you coming back, Verrill?"

"Too late," Zack interjected. "I have emergence signatures one point five million klicks behind Roste's ship."

"Can you jump with my pod attached?"

Talyn thought about it for a moment and then nodded.

"It's small enough. The ship will treat it as part of its hull."

"Good. I'd hate to lose the thing. I guess I'm staying, Petra."

"Roger that. Any orders?"

"Might I suggest we jump in sync?" Talyn said. "I'll transmit the navigation data over to your ships and link them to my helm. If we jump in an uncoordinated fashion, we'll be scattered all over the place and make perfect victims for whoever just joined the party."

"Makes sense," Petra said before Verrill could speak. "Do it. I'll tell the others to expect your orders and spool up."

"Don't dawdle," Zack warned. "They'll be in missile range soon enough."

"I'm connected to *Marilan*, *Umberto* and *Clio*," Talyn announced moments later. "Transmitting navigation data."

"Folks," Decker glanced over his shoulder at the others, "find an empty seat and put your butts down. I don't want to mop blood off the deck."

Verrill seemed poised to protest, but thought better of it and obeyed Decker's order.

"*Marilan*, *Umberto* and *Clio*, this is *Phoenix* prepare to go FTL in thirty seconds. Acknowledge."

One by one, the captains of the three freighters responded, all sounding worried by the unexpected turn of events.

"Incoming from the unidentified ships," Decker said, chuckling. "Stand down and prepare to be boarded. Man, that never gets old around here, does it?"

Talyn held up her right hand in the rigid digit salute.

"You're authorized to transmit my response, but save the ammo."

Decker snarled into the audio pickup, his face distorted as he uttered the sounds.

"What in heaven's name was that?" Kidder asked when he was done.

"One of the few Shrehari expressions I've been able to memorize. I'm not sure their mothers would be impressed if they actually did what I told them to do."

"With your excruciatingly awful accent, it was probably wasted on them," Talyn said, finger hovering over the controls.

"Maybe," he shrugged, "but doing it entertained me and that's what really counts."

"Right. The universe exists for your enjoyment. Stand by everyone, five seconds."

"Doesn't it, though," Zack replied, but no one heard his words. Everything dissolved around them, and they became wholly preoccupied with keeping their stomachs from jumping out of their throats.

"Did everyone make it?" Verrill asked after a few moments spent swallowing convulsively.

"We'll find out when we drop out of FTL at the end of this jump," Talyn replied, turning in her seat to face the rebel leader. "The ships on our tail will need ten, maybe fifteen minutes to spool up again so we'll gain some distance but I doubt we're done with them yet. When we emerge, I'll put out fresh navigation orders that'll send us on a divergent course. It may take a few random jumps to shake them, so I hope you're not in a hurry to reach Garonne."

"Whatever needs to be done," Verrill replied, waving away any thoughts of objecting. "How long on this jump?"

"Ten hours. I suggest another round of whatever libation you like and then some shut-eye," she said. "There's nothing you can do while we're FTL other than fret, and you won't be doing that around me. There's bunk space in the cabin Miko and Tran have been using. Zack will get you some sundries from the purser's locker so you can brush your teeth. Any questions?"

Verrill seemed momentarily taken aback by her matter of fact orders, and then he gave a half-smile and nodded.

"You're very efficient, Captain Pasek. I'm beginning to think that I owe Tran for finding you."

"She's more of a force of nature," Zack said, rising from his seat and stretching. "Stand in her way and you'll feel like you're in the middle of an ion storm, but enough about my partner's friendly disposition. Is anyone interested in what the sensors picked up about our little friends in the fast ships?"

"Do we need to talk about it here or can we do it in the saloon? It's just that I think I've earned a nice gin and tonic for my masterful display of convoy captaincy."

"By all means." Zack swept his arm towards the door. "I'll even mix it myself. Lots of gin, a drop of tonic and half a lemon, right?"

"If you can find an actual lemon aboard, I'll be seriously impressed," she replied, leading the exodus from the bridge, "but please, reverse the proportions. Compared to some ex-Marines I know, I'm a smallish female whose capacity for booze is rather limited."

"And you're no fun drunk anyway." Decker winked at Kidder, whose slightly embarrassed smile seemed almost comical.

"So," Talyn said once the drinks had been passed out, "your sensors picked up something useful about our pursuers?"

She took a sip and nodded approvingly.

"Sure." Decker pulled up a chair and sat at the head of the table. "Those weren't your average, low-rent marauders. I'm about ninety percent sure they're our friendly neighborhood Confederacy of the Howling Stars."

"Jackals?" Talyn's eyebrows shot up. "Since when do they chase honest starships? As far as I know, there hasn't been a single instance of piracy ever traced back to the Confederacy. They're too smart to engage in the one activity that'll have the Navy come down on them like the Horsemen of the Apocalypse."

"How did you figure that out, Zack?" Steiger asked, sounding skeptical.

"They were a bit too hasty covering up their colors. I caught just enough of a marking to let the AI fill in the blanks."

"That makes it even more interesting," Talyn said. "The Jackals aren't known for their modesty. Covering up their colors isn't standard procedure."

"Neither is running down a freighter for shits and giggles."

"I'll have to speak with Roste when we drop out of FTL." Verrill's mouth was set in a hard line. "The most obvious motive is the ordnance he's carrying, which means our operational security might have been compromised."

"Perhaps it would help if we knew where Roste is coming from," Decker suggested.

The rebel leader bit his lower lip while he considered the proposal, then shook his head.

"Sorry. It's need to know and at this time, you don't."

"Fair enough." Decker drained his bottle and stood. "You can stay here if you want, but for us, it's bed time."

Once they were safely ensconced in their cabin and far from curious ears, Talyn sighed.

"This is getting increasingly messy. Is the Confederacy pursuing the Garonne rebels on orders of the *Sécurité Spéciale*? Or are they operating on their own behalf because they got wind of juicy weaponry and figure the Navy won't bother them if they take a few insurgents out of the picture?"

Decker stripped down to his birthday suit and grinned at Talyn.

"Maybe a game of hide the soap will loosen the old brain cells. C'mon."

"Why?"

"Because it relaxes me and when I'm relaxed, I can think more clearly."

"I suppose it's worth the aggravation of playing in a confined space just to see you get an original thought."

"That's my girl."

He put his arm around her waist and swept her into the shower stall.

**

Decker found Verrill, Steiger and Kidder speaking in low tones around a jug of fresh coffee a few hours later.

"Good morning or whatever time of the day it is." He reached over Kidder's shoulder to grab the carafe and poured himself a mug. "Telling tall tales to pass the time?"

"We were brainstorming why the Confederacy might have latched on to Roste's ship." Verrill didn't look like he'd had any restful sleep.

"Bad luck?" Zack took a sip and grimaced at the bitter taste. "Someone spoke too much in a place where the walls have ears? Usually, when the bad guys decide to focus their attention on a particular ship, it's because someone talked out of turn."

He scratched the side of his face and frowned.

"Of course, sometimes, the bad guys put a ringer on board who figures out the what, where and when for his buddies. Sometimes, they even..."

"You're a bucket of cheer, aren't you just?" Steiger said, shaking her head.

"Yep," he nodded, smiling, "and, as I was about to say, sometimes they even blackmail or buy off a senior officer to throw the game."

"Blackmail?" Talyn asked, entering the saloon with a smile to match Zack's. "What are we discussing? The reason why we have the Jackals on our collective asses?"

"You two look disgustingly cheerful, you know that, right?" Steiger made a face at them. "Obviously, your night was better than ours."

"A gentleman never tells." Zack winked at the mercenary.

"I can't see Roste either betraying us or being that lax with security," Verrill said. "I've known him for a long time. He's reliable, committed, and far from stupid. Besides, he'll have vetted the freighter's crew very carefully."

"Everyone has a weak spot," Decker replied. "Until you can see his face, you won't know whether someone's pushed hard on him or one of his folks, or whether it was just bad luck."

"We'll have to make the interval quick," Talyn reminded them. "Just long enough to re-sync navigation and retune the hyperdrives. I figure it'll be a few jumps before we can shake off any pursuit. If you want to speak with your man while we're sublight, sure, but the moment all ships are ready, we're off again."

"You seem to have taken control of my operation without much of a by your leave, Captain Pasek."

"You hired us to escort you safely to Garonne. I'm earning my pay, Ser Verrill. If you'd like to override me and thereby put us in jeopardy, it will nullify our contract. Your call."

"Speaking of blackmail..." Steiger's smile was more than a little sarcastic. "I know, I know – your ship, your rules."

"Your lives, actually, honey." Zack blew her a kiss.

Talyn poured herself a coffee, and then nudged Decker.

"If you're through flirting with the passengers, we have to get ready. The countdown clock is at thirty minutes. I'll need to know where the others are the moment you're done swallowing your stomach. They'll probably have drifted, even on a relatively short leg."

She paused for a moment and looked at the others.

"The three of you are welcome to join us with the usual caveats that you find a seat and stay there, and that you vacate instantly and without question the moment either of us says so."

"Most gracious of you, Captain." Verrill inclined his head. "Please believe that I'm grateful for the way you handled our swift departure from the rendezvous point."

She dismissed his thanks with a wave of the hand.

"All part of the service."

Then she vanished down the passageway, Decker in tow.

"Fascinating woman, that," Verrill commented to no one in particular before following the two operatives.

**

Decker swallowed convulsively when the FTL bubble dissolved around them and *Phoenix* returned to normal space. He focused on the sensor readout, eyes blurry for the few seconds it took his vision to clear.

"We're not in a tight formation if that's what you wanted to know," he reported, "but everyone's within reasonable distance except for *Clio*, Roste's ship. He's well behind us, further now than he was when we jumped. There's nothing else within sensor range."

"Transmit orders to *Clio*: accelerate and reduce the gap," Talyn replied, "remainder to maneuver in on us."

"Done," Zack said a few moments later.   "And no arguments."

He swiveled his chair to face Verrill.

"If you'd like to speak with Roste, now's the time."

"Could I take it in private?"

"Sorry, no. This is a matter concerning our collective safety. You'll take it here," Talyn said in a tone that dared him to argue. "You have twenty-five minutes."

"Perhaps I should be doing this in person rather than over the comnet." Verrill sounded less than enthusiastic.

"We don't have time to send you over to *Clio*, though we do have time for you to return to *Marilan* if you leave now. You can even take Steiger and Kidder with you, but keep in mind that if *Clio* does anything to jeopardize the rest of the convoy, I'll let Zack do a bit of target practice."

Verrill's face turned ashen when the implications of Talyn's statement sank in, but before he could speak, the AI chimed insistently for attention.

"Nope," Decker said after checking the sensor readout. "No one's shifting ship this time around. Our howling buddies just dropped out of FTL, or to be more precise, they dropped out of FTL almost a minute ago."

"How much time do we have?" Talyn asked, eyes darting to the hyperdrive status readout.

"Twenty minutes, tops. They're accelerating like stink."

"Let the others know. I'm pushing new navigation data through now."

"I wish we had some mines aboard," Decker remarked in a conversational tone. "Mind you, it would probably take me no more than fifteen minutes to rig a pair of missiles so they do pretty much the same thing. If the buggers don't scan carefully, we might just give them a headache or two."

"No." Talyn shook her head vehemently. "So far, no one has shot on anyone else. We'll keep it that way. I don't know what the Jackals want, but I do know that poking at them won't help the situation one single bit."

"Roger that," Zack replied. "I'll just ping them with the targeting sensor. No harm in that and it might get them to fire their braking thrusters."

"If it amuses you, be my guest. After all, the universe exists for your enjoyment."

Decker smiled at the three rebels.

"That's why I love the lady, folks. She's always thinking of my pleasure first."

His infectious grin suddenly vanished.

"*Clio* is warning of problems with the hyperdrives. It might take them a bit longer to spool up."

"What?" Talyn turned to look at him, incredulity writ large on her fine features. "Tell those idiots to sort it. We jump at the moment I tell them to jump. If they're not ready, they can invite the Jackals aboard for tea and crumpets."

"I'll do you one better," Zack replied. He touched his screen and re-opened the link. "*Clio* this is *Phoenix*, the convoy is jumping on schedule. If you're unable to follow, I will destroy you so that the material you're carrying doesn't fall into unfriendly hands. *Phoenix*, out."

He ended the transmission with a sharp gesture.

"There, that should motivate them to get going." He touched a control. "If someone's paying attention aboard *Clio*, they'll realize that I've just locked weapons on them."

Verrill was half out of his seat, face contorted with a mixture of fear and anger.

"Good God, man, you can't just destroy her and kill everyone aboard."

"Of course not." Decker held up a placating hand. "But it's a better motivator than being told they'd be left behind. How they respond is going to tell us a lot about what's going on."

Verrill dropped back into the chair, perplexed. Steiger was the first to catch on and laughed, at first softly and then with more gusto.

"You're a right bastard, Decker," she said after regaining control of her merriment.

"My parents were married, thank you very much," he replied in an aggrieved tone.

"Sure." Her face twisted into a smirk. "But not to each other, I'll bet."

Decker made an obscene gesture in her direction, but he was smiling broadly.

"What friend Miko seems to have figured out is that my motivator might result in a miraculously quick repair because there was nothing wrong with the engines, just our timing to get out of here."

"Still suspicious of Roste." Verrill shook his head. "I just can't see it, but maybe I'm too naïve."

"Alternately, if they really have problems but aren't screaming blue bloody murder, it might be because they know the Jackals won't do anything nasty to them. But don't mind me." The Marine shrugged and turned back to his console. "I have a very suspicious nature. It comes from associating too much with very shady characters, present company included."

"We've cycled through," Talyn announced, "but the others haven't yet. Did the gentle beings of the Confederacy bother to transmit anything yet?"

"Nope. They must figure that since we gave them the finger last time, it wasn't worth their while. They've begun decelerating, but I'm still not picking up anything to indicate they're targeting someone or preparing to unleash the awesome power of whatever crappy weaponry they crammed into those narrow hulls."

"If it's that crappy, why not just wipe them off the face of the galaxy?" Kidder asked.

"Because the boss said I couldn't. Plus I don't want to waste ammo on guys who aren't even threatening me, let alone shooting."

"And if we fire first," Talyn chimed in, "they'll be claiming they were navigating peacefully when some maniac in a ship with a dodgy registration number tried to blow them away. It might attract the kind of attention none of us wants."

With that, silence descended on the bridge while a countdown timer ticked away in the lower right corner of the main screen, the minutes passing sixty seconds at a time, as they usually do.

"*Clio* is signaling that they've solved their problems and should be spooled up in about ten minutes," Decker reported shortly after that.

He'd kept one eye on the approaching vessels and the other on their charges, ready to chivvy any slackers along. After a few pointed transmissions, even the captain of the slowest ship seemed at pains to cooperate.

"Cutting it very fine," Talyn replied, "but at least they're not forcing our hand."

"Note that it doesn't change my suspicions," Decker said to Verrill over his shoulder. "Dragging out our jump time gives the Jackals a chance to fully re-spool their drives as well, which means we won't be able to shake them on the next tack either. Maybe I should fire a few warning shots."

"I doubt it'll impress them. They're still well out of gun range."

"But not out of missile range. I think they've just decided that we were the biggest threat because both ships have locked on to us and are showing an energy spike that can only mean one thing."

"Four missiles," Decker announced, moments later, "and all headed for us."

"Time to strike?" Talyn asked, checking the readiness reports from the freighters.

"Five or six minutes. They're not expecting us to have close-in defense calliopes; otherwise, they wouldn't have given us so much time to watch the birds come in."

"Or they're trying to stampede us and don't expect to score any hits."

Decker groaned.

"Again? What is it with those clowns, thinking the tactic ever works out well for anyone?"

"Be thankful for the lack of imagination. It keeps our job simple." She briefly glanced at the helm readout. "*Marilan* and *Umberto* report ready. Tell *Clio* we're leaving in four minutes. If they want to come with us, they'll be ready. If not, they can go rot for all I care."

"Captain, please!" Verrill was half out of his seat again.

"The Jackals aren't the only ones who can use the stampede technique. Have no fear. We're all going to jump together. I get the feeling *Clio* will be..." her console chimed. "And she's ready, right on cue. Hang on to your stomachs folks; we're gone in thirty seconds."

— EIGHTEEN —

"Persistent buggers." Decker scowled at his sensor readout.

They were half-way through their third tack in so many days, and the Confederacy ships had once again shown up a few million kilometers behind them moments after the convoy began cycling hyperdrives.

He looked up at Talyn.

"The way I see it, either our navigational razzle-dazzle isn't razzly enough, or they have excellent detection gear or someone's broadcasting a subspace beacon that lets 'em know where we are every time. I know which one I'm voting for."

"I'm beginning to share your suspicions," she replied. "It wouldn't be the first time this happened to us. They also seem to time things well enough that we can't afford to investigate before we have to be off again."

"Yup. You were talking about them trying to stampede us the other day. I think you're probably right." He glanced at the status board. "At least *Clio* isn't buggering about anymore."

"There's no need to do so if she's carrying a subspace beacon. All they had to do the first time was make sure the Jackals latched on. Since then..." She shrugged.

"Time for an ambush, I think." He sat back and stared at the star field on the main screen. "Next tack, we drop out a bit earlier than the freighters, something that'll put us a few million kilometers behind them, and then we wait for the Wolves to join the party. When they do, I fire a few warning shots to stampede them into an emergency jump."

"Verrill might not agree," she warned.

"Bugger Verrill." He made a dismissive gesture with his hand. "I'd like to find out what their end-game is, though. They must have figured that we're headed for Garonne. I mean, if they know what we're carrying, then they have to know the destination, right?"

"A reasonable person would think so, yes." Talyn nodded. "Of course, no one has ever accused the Jackals of being reasonable."

"Not when there's profit at stake," he replied. "So what's the profit motive here?"

"Search me." She sighed. "Okay. We're just about ready to jump out again. Let's hope this one will shake them. Sound the warning so our passengers don't trip over their guts."

In the end, they didn't tell Verrill about the plan to ambush the Confederacy ships under the principle that it was easier to ask for forgiveness than permission. Not that they'd have bowed to the rebel leader's disapproval in any case.

They dropped out of FTL a fair distance behind the freighters after the next jump, prompting three anxious calls that Decker ignored in favor of finding the Jackals' hyperspace bubbles.

"There!" He crowed when he picked up the emergence signature. "Targeting on. They're out of effective engagement range, but having us on their butts should give them a fright."

Talyn fired the sublight drives, and *Phoenix* accelerated towards the new arrivals, now caught between the freighters and the Q-ship.

"Watch this." Decker flicked on the transmitter. "Unidentified ships, this is the Free Republic of Garonne frigate *Phoenix*. You are interfering with a duly constituted naval convoy; I therefore order you to decelerate and prepare to be boarded for inspection."

"Free Republic of Garonne frigate?" Talyn tried to restrain a sudden outburst of laughter. "Are you having delusions of adequacy?"

He grinned and shrugged.

"Why not? It'll give the bastards something to wonder about." He glanced at his screen. "Not that they'll reply after I called them by the name they hate. Maybe we should light up their tails."

He unmasked and deployed the ship's main guns, and fired a dozen times, sending streaks of plasma towards the Confederacy ships.

"It won't touch them, but they'll see it alright. I'm tempted to pump out a few missiles, but we might need them against ships that actually want to fight."

He switched the transmitter back on.

"Unidentified ships, this is the Free Republic of Garonne frigate *Phoenix*. Those were warning shots. Clear out and don't let yourselves be seen again. Piss me off and you'll be hitching a ride to the nearest star system."

"Still expecting an answer?"

"No, but it makes me feel like a big boy."

"Verrill should be here. He'd be thrilled to know his rebel movement has an imaginary frigate in its imaginary navy."

"Cynic." He paused, eyes widening. "They left. The bastards just jumped out without warning."

"I guess you scared them, big boy," Talyn smirked at her partner. "Good show. Let's catch up to our lost sheep and herd them to the promised land."

**

"Wasn't that risky?" Verrill asked, later that evening, after the convoy was FTL again.

Decker snorted.

"The Confederacy of the Howling Stars isn't in it to die but to make money. I showed them a big gun and scared them away."

"My wonderfully immodest ex-Marine." Talyn patted him on the arm, smiling. "Can't resist whipping out his weapon."

"Free Republic of Garonne, eh?" Steiger twirled her half-empty bottle on the tabletop. "That has a certain goofy ring to it. And calling this tub a frigate? Pure chutzpah. I like it."

"Mock all you want, folks," Decker smiled at his companions, "but it worked. I'm taking bets that we won't see their hairy asses when we drop out to tack next time."

"It does seem a bit too easy," Kidder remarked. "You really think they'd give up after all these light-years?"

"Who knows what the buggers were after?" Zack shrugged. "One thing's for sure: they didn't expect to find out *Phoenix* had some mean teeth to go with my bark."

"In any case, we do one more tack, and then I'll point us straight at the Garonne system." Talyn drained her glass and set it down. "Bedtime, Mister Big Guns."

Decker wiggled his eyebrows at the others, grinning.

"Have a great night, folks. I know I will."

Once they were in the privacy of their cabin, Talyn began to strip.

"You checked all the security measures?" She asked, tossing her trousers on the chair by the doublewide bunk.

He touched the terminal by the door.

"Our dear AI confirms everything's locked down. They can empty out the bar, play cards, or sleep on the deck for all I care. They won't be going anywhere."

"I'm not sure I like the way those howlers simply left." Talyn stepped out of her underwear and looked at him with raised eyebrows. "I thought you wanted a good night? It's not going to happen if you're still wearing your gun belt."

"Agreed – about the Jackals abandoning the chase, I mean." He quickly stripped down and then wrapped his arms around Talyn. "Enough shop talk. Live for the moment, I always say."

"You say a lot of things," she replied, moments before his mouth covered hers, ending any further conversation.

Later, much later, lying side by side, staring at the deck head, their bodies covered by a thin film of sweat, Decker turned to look at her.

"Off the wall analysis here, Commander Talyn," he said, any trace of banter absent from his tone. "What if the howlers were making sure the ordnance got to Garonne without any of the real filth trying to steal it? Shepherding, so to speak, not stampeding?"

"And once they saw that we were more than able to fight off trouble, they figured the job was done?" She nodded. "Plausible. We'll make a paranoid spook out of you yet, Chief Warrant Officer Decker."

"So riddle me this," he said after a few moments of silence. "If our analysts are right, and the *Sécurité Spéciale* uses the Confederacy as proxies for wet work, why would they want to make certain illicit weapons, a lot of it Shrehari at that, get safely to Garonne?"

"We're not on Garonne yet," she pointed out.

"True, but the question is valid. Why would they have an interest in helping the rebels? I'm sure the senior folks in the Celeste government are dues paying members of the Coalition and would rather not lose their grip on one of the last two colonies they still own."

"That's the conundrum, isn't it?" She turned onto her side to face Zack. "Of course, it could still be entirely possible that you startled them out of a planned piracy operation with your preposterous announcement and gunfire. There could very well be no *Sécurité Spéciale* strings pulling. Maybe Roste or someone else aboard *Clio* really is dirty."

"Sure. In that case, they'll regroup and try us out again, using a different approach. It's still just two against one, and they haven't seen my lovely missiles yet, let alone my calliopes."

"Why is it that speaking of weaponry lights up your eyes more than any invitation to play I've ever thrown your way?"

"A man's got to have his priorities, sweetheart, and I feel another priority coming on."

She reached down and grabbed him, a low, husky laugh rising from her throat.

"Funny that, I can feel it too."

**

"Why wait?" Verrill sounded impatient. He frowned at the tactical display on the main screen and said, "One more jump and we're home free."

The little convoy had emerged just beyond the Garonne system's outermost planet after two tacks without seeing any further evidence of pursuit, though Zack thought he'd picked up a sensor ghost both times.

"Before we run headlong into something we might not be able to control, wouldn't it be best to see what may be out there?"

Talyn sounded so calm and reasonable that the rebel leader felt foolish for a moment.

"You're the one who said Avalon had been contracted to blockade Garonne," she pointed out.

"Plus, you and your pals need time to shift over to one of your own ships," Zack added, "just in case we need to fight our way through. Remember, you also hired us as your escort, and that means our job is to cover you until you land."

Verrill exchanged glances with his two companions and then nodded.

"Tran and I will shift to *Marilan*. Miko will stay here with the cargo she bought."

Decker shrugged. "Suit yourself, though..."

The AI pinged, and he left the rest of his reply hanging.

"Our sensor ghost again, at the limit of our range, well out towards interstellar space."

"The Jackals?" Steiger asked.

"Possibly. It looks like the same contact we had during the last two tacks. It's almost like they're checking up on us."

"Why? To make sure we get where we're supposed to go?"

"That would be the most likely supposition," Talyn said. "The reason for such solicitude isn't apparent, however."

"Are you still thinking Roste or someone on *Clio* is in cahoots with them?" Verrill asked.

"One doesn't preclude the other. Provided we get you and your weaponry down in one piece, I suppose it doesn't matter."

"The ghost is gone again, like the last two times." Decker turned back towards the rebel commander.

"Not that I want to seem pushy, but you should head over to your ship now. We don't want to hang around here longer than necessary, especially if we're still being tracked for some reason."

"In that case, I'll thank you for your hospitality." Verrill stood and stuck out his hand. "You're sure you don't want to hang around after delivering the merchandise? We could really use a veteran of the Corps like you."

Talyn gave him a warning glance, and he briefly shook his head.

"The boss says no. We'll deliver and then it's off to whatever contract finds us next."

"Pity."

Tran Kidder shook Decker's hand next, disappointment writ large on his face.

"The Garonne colonists are good people, Zack, but the only way they'll get the freedom they've earned is through the barrel of a gun. There's a few more of us former silahdar in the movement, and they'd take a lot of heart from knowing you were helping out."

"Sorry, Tran." Zack pulled him in for a bear hug. "You take care now. There's nothing more I can teach you anyway, so I know you and the others will be all right."

Then, the two men were gone, leaving Miko Steiger as their sole passenger. The personnel transfer pod released its death grip on *Phoenix*'s airlock a few minutes later and sped off towards the lead freighter.

"If you'd like," Steiger suggested after they witnessed the pod's safe arrival, "I could help out with the system scan."

Decker stared at her for a few seconds, trying to decide whether or not she would be of any use. Steiger mistook his hesitation for a matter of trust, and a sardonic smile appeared.

"Guys, I already figure this ship is more than you make it out to be, for whatever reasons I'm not about to question. There's a lot of data to sift through that the AI won't be able to classify, and I've done this kind of work before, believe it or not."

Zack shook his head absently.

"It's not a question of trust, Miko. I'm just wondering whether doubling up on the job will make a difference."

He glanced at Talyn who shrugged as if to say it was his call.

"Okay. Take that station," he pointed to a console on the other side of the bridge. "I'll push the raw feed over, and you can look for anything that'll trigger a gut feel. While you do that, I'm going to sort through the AI's analysis. I know the wretched program well enough to understand its idiosyncrasies. You don't."

Steiger tossed off a mock salute and dropped into the designated seat.

"Ready."

**

"I'm drawing a blank," the mercenary said a few hours later. "If there's anything we need to worry about in this system, it's either running silent or in close orbit around Garonne."

"Concur," Decker replied pushing his seat away from the console and stretching his arms. "Time to get a little closer."

"Perhaps a brief moment to visit the facilities and maybe have a coffee?" Talyn suggested, rising from the helm seat.

"Our next jump will be short and who knows what we'll see then. Everyone's dialed in, so we're ready to go at any time."

Decker felt his bladder respond to the notion and smiled.

"Agreed. I'll make coffee. Neither of you has the right touch with the machine. Your brews always seem to come out tasting like sludge."

"Please, do impress us, O Master of the autochef," Talyn replied, waving her hand. "Remember, mine is pure, like my soul."

"I thought you said you had no soul."

"And thus, it must be pure." She laughed. "Something that doesn't exist cannot be corrupted."

"Your boss has a point," Steiger said, shaking her head. "I'll have mine like a proper human being, thank you very much."

"My job is to make the brew. What you two comedians do with it before it touches your soft, rosy lips isn't my problem."

"Is he always this touchy?" Steiger asked Talyn while the two women made their way aft to the heads.

"Must be his time of the month," the agent replied, in a voice loud enough for Decker to hear. She winked at the mercenary.

"Sludge from the environmental filters it is," Zack announced, following the two women down the passageway. "And I know just the right amount to draw from the septic tanks."

"As I said, touchy, isn't he?"

"Until I find better, he'll do." Talyn turned to blow a kiss at Zack over her shoulder.

**

Decker shook off the emergence disorientation and forced his eyes to focus on the sensor readout. Their little convoy had dropped out of FTL as close to Garonne as Talyn dared.

The AI began chiming with an insistence that drove away the last of the fog dulling his senses.

"We've got a clear view of Garonne's orbitals," he said after taking a deep breath, "and there's a pair of sloops broadcasting an Avalon PMC beacon."

"Got a visual?" Talyn asked.

"Coming."

A blue-green planet covered by streaks of torn white clouds grew at an alarming rate on the main screen as Decker zoomed in, hunting for tiny specks circling high above the atmosphere. Just when Garonne was about to fill the entire display, it slipped to one side while the camera locked onto a bright dot.

"There's one. It's in a polar orbit. The other is in an equatorial orbit."

Data about the ship appeared beside its image and Talyn frowned.

"Larger than us by about a third, though we might have parity when it comes to weapons. We are a little over gunned for our size."

"But they'll have autoloaders for the missile launchers, a feature that we conspicuously lack," Zack said, "so we'll get one chance only."

"Assuming we need to fight." Steiger sounded dubious.

"If your boss is right and these Avalon rent-a-spacers are here to enforce the colonial governor's will, they'll want to ensure your ships don't make it to the surface. Destroying a couple of small freighters isn't much of a stretch for them. Count on the buggers trying. After all, what good is a blockade if it doesn't block?"

"So you're saying we're basically screwed?"

A wide grin spread across Decker's face.

"Nope. Not in the least. They're seeing four freighters right now, ships that can't even scratch the paint job on those sloops. What they're about to realize is that one of us isn't an easy target. Remember, corporate types aren't in it to die for glory but to make a profit. Scratching the paint job costs money. Denting it costs even more. All we have to do is force them to pay attention to *Phoenix* while the actual freighters head for the ground."

He turned his grin on Hera Talyn.

"Permission to go to battle stations, Captain?"

"You look much too happy at the notion," she replied with a theatrical sigh, "though I suppose that your bloodthirstiness might be appropriate for once. I'll let Verrill know that we're splitting from the convoy with the intent to peel the blockade off Garonne for them."

"Don't forget to ask for landing coordinates," he reminded her. "We've got some of their stuff to off-load."

Then, Decker touched his screen, and a loud claxon went off while the lights dimmed.

"Battle stations, folks. I've hoisted the black flag so strap in because we're about to rock the galaxy."

— NINETEEN —

"Sir, four ships in a convoy formation dropped out of FTL just beyond lunar orbit and are inbound on a direct course."

The officer of the watch glanced over the sensor tech's shoulder and studied the readout.

"Small, clapped-out freighters? Could be the ones we were warned about, but the report said there would be three, not four." He turned towards the signals petty officer. "Petrov, warn *Merlin*. I'll get the captain."

"No need," a loud voice boomed behind him. "I have the bridge, Mister Keele."

"I stand relieved."

"We'll have no trouble intercepting those tubs."

Captain Gurik, commanding officer of the Avalon Private Military Corporation ship *Morgana,* rubbed his hands together in anticipation.

"Petrov, send out a warning on all frequencies that they're to enter orbit and await inspection. Any attempt to land without permission will be met with lethal force."

A few minutes passed, then the signals petty officer slowly shook his head and turned to face Gurik.

"We got a reply, sir. You're not going to believe this, but we've been told that any attempt to prevent the ships from landing would be met with lethal force."

Gurik guffawed loudly.

"I'd like to see them try. Sound battle stations, Mister Keele, though I doubt we'll raise a sweat."

**

"What do you mean you hoisted the black flag?" Talyn asked in a tone dripping with suspicion.

"If we're going to fight the Avalon buggers, we should do so under our own banner, no?"

"So you invented a flag for the Navy of the Free Republic of Garonne?" She kept her eyes on the countdown timer marking the moment *Phoenix* would change course and aim her bow at the nearest PMC sloop and didn't see Decker's mischievous smirk.

"Of course not. There is no such thing as the Garonne Navy. I made up our banner a few days ago, just in case we had to go into battle."

"Dare I ask?"

"Probably not. You've got a ship to sail."

"And you're afraid that I'll blow my top?"

"No. I'm afraid you're going to lecture me on the difference between appropriate and inappropriate again. We don't have time for that."

Talyn, eyes still on the helm, gave him the rigid digit salute, something Zack seemed to find so inordinately funny that he barely managed to swallow an outburst of laughter.

"Does he do inappropriate things often?" Steiger asked.

"You have no idea," Talyn replied. "There are days when I think he desperately needs adult supervision."

She touched her controls.

"We're changing course. You can turn us into a mercenary's worst nightmare now."

⁎⁎

"Sir, one of the ships has tacked and is headed for us."

"What?" Captain Gurik sat up in his command chair and stared at the tactical schematic. "Have they lost their ever-loving minds?"

"Its power curve just spiked."

"Put it on screen. I want to see what that idiot looks like."

The video feed zeroed in on *Phoenix*, just in time to see the camouflage plates move aside and reveal gun turret after gun turret. A dark opening, like the mouth of a shark, appeared on its underside, unmasking the missile launchers in its belly.

Gurik dropped back in his seat, eyes wide.

"What in heaven's name is that?"

"No beacon, but they've displayed some sort of identification." A clear visual of the Q-ship's flank filled the main screen.

Gurik's jaw dropped.

"Keele," he said in a quivering whisper, "tell me I didn't just have a stroke."

"No sir." The lieutenant fought hard to keep a straight face. He lost the battle within seconds and choked back a laugh. "We are indeed looking at a black rectangle with the representation of a raised middle finger in white upon it. Not quite a jolly roger, although..."

"Umm, sir..." the sensor tech raised his hand again, "they've locked on to us with what looks like naval grade targeting sensors."

Keele lost his amused expression and glanced at Gurik, whose face was quickly changing from its usual brick red to an alarming puce.

"May I suggest we break orbit and get some maneuvering room?"

"What?" The captain blinked several times before seeming to regain some of his composure. "By all means, yes, Keele. Warn *Merlin* and tell them to follow suit. We'll try to get that dumb bastard between us and teach him a lesson in courtesy. Giving me the finger indeed. I'll give him plasma indigestion."

**

"Really, Zack?" Talyn growled once she'd realized what he had done. "Isn't it a bit juvenile even for you?"

"Not really." He sounded completely at peace with himself. "It's the kind of thing that'll either have them rolling on the deck laughing or feeling insulted enough to seek satisfaction. Either way, I've just messed with their minds, and that gives us an advantage."

Steiger started laughing.

"He's got you there, Captain. I think it was a brilliant move."

"You would, Miko," Talyn said over her left shoulder, not bothering to restrain a brief chuckle.

"Okay, Zack," she continued, "I'll take your psychological warfare excuse at face value. It beats thinking my partner is still an overgrown adolescent."

"They're breaking orbit, both of them," he replied, ignoring her sarcasm. "I suggest you get on the ass of the nearest one.

Based on radio traffic, I think it's the lead ship anyway. With luck, we'll spook them long enough to let Verrill and his bunch land safely."

"You're not going to fight?" Steiger sounded surprised.

"Supreme excellence consists in breaking the enemy's resistance without fighting," Decker quoted, his right hand raised like an ancient orator. "Sun Tzu. Mind you, if they start shooting, I'll return the favor."

"Don't bet on self-preservation taking the upper hand with those Avalon folks." The mercenary replied. "Your jolly digit flag might have riled them enough that they're looking to count coup. Corporate prestige is a big thing with them, you know."

"As long as it gets the buggers away from Garonne long enough, I'm happy. Of course, we'll still have to land, but I'm counting on our smaller size and better maneuverability to help us evade them."

"What if they have missiles?"

"Then they have missiles, but nothing like ours and they'll definitely use them as a last resort - too expensive."

"And you don't have to worry about that?" Steiger asked, eyes sparkling with mischief.

"Ask Sera Moneybags when she's not busy trying to sail us up a sloop's skirts."

**

"He's turned to follow in our wake, and he's accelerating," an alarmed Lieutenant Keele reported. "We're now also being actively targeted by a missile controller. It could mean they're about to launch."

"Where's *Merlin*?"

"Still on the other side of the planet. He'll not be able to get this pirate in his sights for a little while yet."

Captain Gurik started gnawing on the drooping tip of his mustache, struggling with the question of whether or not to be the first to shoot and possibly face accusations of piracy or wait for the intruder to commit himself. There were still three freighters to consider. If he let the mystery Q-ship run wild for too long, they'd slip through the blockade. In the end, he decided to hedge his bets.

"Tell *Merlin* that they're to divert and intercept the others. We'll deal with this one ourselves. Guns, lock on and prepare to fire at my command."

**

"Crap."

"What?" Talyn asked, startled by the intensity of Decker's curse.

"He's run up his guns and has locked on to us. I guess it's time to drop Sun Tzu and go with the guy who said hit 'em hardest with the mostest. May I go weapons free?"

"You may. Try not to blow your entire load at once. There are two of them, and it seems like the other one is changing course to intercept our friends."

"I can help with that," he said, smiling. "Firing aft tubes at number two now. That ought to get their attention."

"Zack," Steiger asked, "do you want me to go down and reload?"

"If you think you can manage without blowing us up, that would be great. I'm about to fire the forward tubes as well, so knock yourself out."

"Was that wise?" Talyn asked once the mercenary had left.

"Does it matter?" Decker shrugged. "I may have mentioned that she seems to know her way around Navy ordnance, and besides, I get the feeling *Phoenix* might not make it out of this in one piece."

"Optimist."

"Nope. Realist. We're over gunned, but it's still two against one. They may be rentals, but we shouldn't assume that makes them stupid." He paused for a fraction of a second. "There. Let's see what our Avalon buddies do with four Mark Twenty-Threes."

**

"Fire."

Gurik's order seemed loud in the small bridge compartment, but the gunner's mate obeyed instantly.

"Sir, the intruder has launched six missiles, two in *Merlin*'s direction and four at us," Keele said, sounding more than a little alarmed. "If I didn't know that they weren't for civilian use, I'd swear we're looking at Mark Twenty-Threes."

"Or maybe it's a damned *Navy* Q-ship." The mercenary captain was suddenly horror-struck by the idea. "Don't tell me we just fired on a Navy ship. No wonder they gave us the finger."

A dozen plasma streams erupted from the intruder's impressive bank of guns, almost three times more than *Morgana* could fire aft, and Gurik's face lost its dark red shading in an instant, replaced by a greenish-white sheen that matched his pained expression.

The sensor tech made a quick gesture across his chest and murmured, "For what we are about to receive..."

"Engaging missiles," Keele announced when the gunner fired *Morgana*'s four close-in defense calliopes, each with eight tubes and capable of spitting plasma at a rate of three thousand rounds a minute.

But Decker had timed it well. His first gun salvos splashed against the sloop's shields almost at the same time as the fire control system opened gaps for the calliopes to shoot through. With the weight of plasma he'd thrown, a few rounds were bound to get through and hit the hull.

A few did.

First, they scratched the paint job, then they ate divots into the smooth hull, setting off damage control alarms on the bridge. Then, the first of the four missiles exploded, and the gunner's mate raised a cheer.

A second salvo bloomed from the intruder's guns, ready to take advantage of a weakened shield if one of the missiles managed to explode its warhead against it.

The calliopes took out a second missile.

The third one detonated within spitting distance, sending *Morgana*'s damage control warnings into overdrive while the shield generators fought against the energy released by the massive nuclear blast.

Missile number four's detonation sent such a huge feedback surge through the abused generators that they shut down moments before burning out.

Gurik stared at the status screen, mouth wide open, stunned by the unexpected reversal of fortune, unable to comprehend that a smaller ship had outfought him. The signalman's voice snapped him out of it.

"Sir, the intruder has just told us to bugger off before he shoots again."

"What?" The words didn't make sense.

"I said that the intruder told us, and I quote, bugger off before I shoot at you again, and make you swim home."

As if to emphasize the point, a single round streaked by *Morgana*, bare meters from her port nacelle. Then, as if it had already tired of the brief fight, the unknown ship began to turn away, giving them another good glimpse of the jolly digit ensign on its flank, the final insult to a captain who'd always thought himself equal to anyone in the regular navy.

Of course, he had no idea that the man who'd bested him was a lowly ground pounder, a species he personally looked down upon. That knowledge would have been enough to trigger a stroke.

"Should I fire again, Captain?" Keele asked in a tentative tone. "Perhaps use the missiles this time?"

Gurik shook his head, unable to speak. When he did finally find his voice, he ordered them to a safe distance so they could restart their shield generators. *Merlin* would have to take care of itself, but the enemy no longer enjoyed the element of surprise. The Avalon crews now knew exactly what they were up against. The intruder would be made to pay, with interest.

**

"One down, one to go." Decker sat back, beaming. "And Miko managed to reload the missile launchers.

"We surprised him. The other will be expecting your tricks. At this point, a head-to-head fight is going to cost," Talyn replied, "and he's turning away from the freighters to meet us. In fact, it looks like they're already entering the atmosphere."

"Mission accomplished." Decker gave her a thumbs up. "I propose to fire the entire missile load and then shoot like I'm the greatest practitioner of the old spray and pray method. There's no point in landing with a full ammo locker."

"You really do think we're not taking off again, don't you?"

"Call me prescient. We want to figure things out, we need to be down there."

"Figure what out?" Steiger asked from the doorway. She was slightly out of breath and covered in a sheen of sweat from the effort.

"Why we're in this line of business instead of making money at the poker tables." Zack shrugged. "Considering the success of my latest bluff..."

Steiger was smart enough to realize that was the only answer she'd get but still examined Decker with questioning eyes for a few heartbeats before sitting down again.

"He's locked on to us, and I imagine he won't stint on the missiles, this time, cost be damned," Decker said. "And since there's no point in hoarding ours..."

He touched the control screen and expelled his entire reserve into space.

"No need to head down to the hold again, Miko. We only had one reload."

"I noticed."

The missiles' drives were bright sparks on the main screen for a few seconds before they accelerated out of visual range, their warheads locked onto the second Avalon sloop. Moments later, the mercenaries launched a salvo in return.

"This ride is about to get bumpy," Decker warned, turning full control of the calliopes over to the AI so he could concentrate on the main guns.

"One pass, Zack," Talyn replied. "We're not turning back to duke it out."

"I got that. We'll not be landing with a dry ammo locker after all."

**

"Is he insane?"

Merlin's captain shook his head in wonder at the unidentified ship's wild rush.

Then, the intruder opened up with a stunning amount of firepower for its small size.

"With that much ordnance, I'd say his madness might be justified," the first officer replied, "but thanks to Gurik's stupidity, he's achieved his goal. The freighters slipped through the blockade without inspection."

"This one won't and his little joke of a battle ensign won't make me lose my temper either."

There was little love lost between *Merlin*'s commander and his colleague aboard *Morgana*, the former having privately voiced, on more than one occasion, his opinion that the latter was a blowhard.

"We're engaging his missiles now." A pause. "He's engaging ours."

"We'll shortly know which one of us gets to stitch the other's hull," the captain said, eyes locked on the tactical display.

It ended almost before it had begun. *Merlin* shuddered like a spastic eel when one of Decker's missiles got through the defensive fire, but the shields held. Barely.

The Q-ship's wasn't as lucky. Two mercenary missiles evaded the calliopes and collapsed the bow shield. In the seconds it took to turn the ship and put the keel shield between it and the oncoming salvos, a dozen direct hits ate away at the outer hull, damaging the forward thrusters and taking one of the calliopes out of action.

The two ships passed each other almost within visual range, connected by streams of plasma until the intruder entered the upper atmosphere and quickly vanished around the planet's curvature.

"Get us back into orbit," the captain ordered. "I want to see him land. With any luck it'll be somewhere we can strike without causing our paying customers any heartache."

"We'll likely be too late," the first officer warned.

"Then we'll be too late." He shrugged. "We're not responsible for what happens on the ground anyway. I just thought it might be a nice bonus. Their damned militia can find them for all I care."

**

"Told you we'd take a beating," Decker said, "the guys on that ship aren't as dumb as the others."

"You're a regular psychic. Well done. But it'll make landing just a bit hairy," Talyn replied, her attention focused on the

AI's damage control report. Then something caused her to look up.

"You're still firing?"

"Satellites. Why leave the opposition with eyes and ears?"

"Nasty, but effective," Steiger approved. "Verrill will like that."

"When you're done killing innocent electronics, get in touch with the folks on the ground and tell them we'll need a long runway to land. The damage we took will prevent us from making a vertical approach."

"How long?"

"Ten kilometers should do. If it can be free of stuff like sharp rocks or tall trees, so much the better. I'm not expecting a spaceport tarmac but trying to land on top of a jungle isn't going to work out well for anyone."

"I didn't think we were going to get back into space anytime soon either. Good thing there's work to do where we're going."

He activated the comlink, a pleased smile on his lips.

"A regular psychic," Talyn muttered, her attention back on the balky helm controls, "and a real pain in the ass too."

— TWENTY —

"You have got to be kidding me." Decker snorted loudly. "How good are you at water landings?"

"Why?" Talyn's tone held more than a mild edge of irritation, proof that she was feeling increasingly out of her depth flying the damaged starship.

"You've got your almost ten kilometers without big rocks or trees, though where I come from, we call it a river."

He touched his controls.

"The aerial view is on the port screen for your delectation. Note the sudden stop at the end of the rather narrow valley that holds our proposed landing strip. I would suggest we bleed off a lot of forward velocity well before kissing the water."

"Noted," she replied with dripping sarcasm.

"It's not as bad as you may think," Steiger interjected. "That sudden stop at the end is actually a broad and deep overhang carved out of the cliffside by the river eons ago. It's the closest thing we have to a secret lair big enough for small ships like *Phoenix* and the freighters."

"You mean there's room for all four ships under that rock?" Decker was incredulous. "How is it that the government forces haven't found something that large yet?"

"Not all four, Zack." Steiger shook her head, smiling. "Sorry about that. I meant it's big enough for a ship of this size. If you're not going to lift off for a while, it'll do just fine to hide *Phoenix*. The freighters will be leaving the moment they've offloaded."

"Good to hear. I'd hate to trigger the self-destruct on the old girl. I've rather gotten fond of her."

He patted the bulkhead by his console.

"Not to mention that you'd be turning something worth God knows how many millions into scrap. I haven't heard of any Sera Moneybags with that kind of funding," a knowing, almost ironic smile briefly crossed her lips, "and I doubt your underwriter would pay out if you did it yourself."

"Underwriter?" Decker put on a puzzled expression. "Damn. I knew I'd forgotten to do something before we left home. Honey, make sure you don't dent this thing any more than you already have. I forgot to buy insurance."

Talyn made a rude gesture over her shoulder.

"Now hear this," she said, "you two will shut up unless you have information vital to this ship's continuing survival to impart. A distracted helmswoman is a dangerous helmswoman."

"Aye, aye, *mon capitaine*." Decker tossed off a salute, then winked at Steiger.

**

"Did they say what kind of damage?" Verrill asked his deputy.

The two of them and Tran Kidder stood at the foot of *Marilan*'s ramp, a safe distance from the riverbank and five hundred meters short of the massive overhang hiding the channel.

"No. Only that they couldn't do a vertical landing and needed a lot of room," she replied with a shrug. "The river is it."

"I'm not sure I like this." He looked back to where the broad, lazy waterway vanished beneath millions of tons of rock, to reappear kilometers away in another valley. "If they overshoot, we'll have a massive catastrophe on our hands. I'd have been happier if they were coming in from the other direction, but there's no helping that now."

"I'm sure they'll be fine," Kidder said. "Zack's no fool, and he wouldn't be working with Captain Pasek if she didn't know how to fly a starship."

"From your lips to God's ear, Tran." Verrill clapped him on the shoulder. "I'll try to look at the upside for now — it being that your Mister Decker will be stuck here until they make repairs, and we'll use the time to good advantage."

"Verrill," the woman, binoculars glued to her eyes, nudged him, "I've got them. They're perfectly lined up, but they look like they're still going pretty fast."

"Right. Tran, light the beacons. Let's give them every bit of help we can."

He turned back to the woman and held out his right hand.

"Pass me those, Corde. If they're going to give me a heart attack, I'd rather see it coming from a distance."

******

"They've lit markers," Zack announced. "You should be able to see them."

"Yup," Talyn replied through clenched teeth. Beads of sweat had formed along her hairline and upper lip, and her usually pale skin was whiter than ever.

Bright red lights on both banks marched into the rapidly deepening valley where late afternoon mist rose from the leaden surface of the broad, slow river.

Zack felt his stomach clench when they dropped below the mountaintops, headed for the water at a shallow angle. Ochre and gray rocks formations, covered with sparse vegetation, whizzed by on either side of the ship at an alarming tempo.

"Come on," Talyn muttered to herself. "Let's get that airspeed down."

The far end of the valley was rapidly approaching, and suddenly those ten kilometers seemed much too short.

"Fuck it," Talyn shook her head, having concluded they weren't going to come to a halt in time. "Hang on folks. I'll have to do this the hard way."

The few remaining meters separating *Phoenix*'s keel from the river's surface vanished and her hull kissed the water. She immediately sprouted a massive rooster tail, sending droplets almost to the top of the surrounding mountains, but the additional friction was enough to drain her excess forward momentum.

Decker realized that he'd been holding his breath when the pressure in his chest became unbearable, and he forced himself to relax, knowing that whatever happened next, there was nothing he could do. At least, he consoled himself, the rebels had been smart enough to land the freighters far enough from the grassy embankments to give them extra room.

Their remaining thrusters whined loudly, fighting with the antigrav modules to keep the ship upright and stable. Talyn didn't dare deploy the landing gear until they'd come to a complete stop, lest the massive legs catch on a submerged rock and send them careening into a cliff wall, or worse, into one of the other starships.

"Zack, find out what the river's depth is, stat," she shouted over her shoulder once the realization that she'd forgotten to check hit her. "If it's too deep, we have other problems to deal with."

"No fear," he replied after glancing at his sensor readout, "three or four meters max, and I'd say solid bottom too, but that might be immaterial. I think we've got a couple of ground controllers waving us into the 'hangar'; they'll not want us to set down just yet."

Phoenix had slowed to a walking pace by the time the former yacht hovered past the rebels watching her arrival with bated breath.

Decker saw Verrill, accompanied by Tran and an unknown, middle-aged woman standing by *Marilan*. The rebel leader's applause seemed enthusiastic from a distance, though whether it celebrated Talyn's piloting skills or a landing that didn't break anything remained open to debate.

"We have a good twenty meters overhead clearance," he reported, anticipating Talyn's next concern, "more if you'd like to drown the lower hull a bit."

"Thanks." Although Zack and Steiger had begun to relax, Talyn wasn't quite done yet.

She steered the ship slowly beneath the overhang, mindful of the three rebels with light wands waving her forward.

Decker switched on the landing lights, revealing a broad, deep space left behind from a time when the river had been a raging demon rather than the placid waterway it was today.

Steiger hadn't been kidding. If necessary, they could fit one of the freighters in with them.

Four thuds resonated through the hull, announcing the release of the landing gear so that the moment the ground guides motioned them to stop, Talyn could set *Phoenix* down.

Finally, a few tense minutes later, the light wands stopped their slow come-hither movements and turned into red crosses above the men's heads.

Talyn gently decreased the power feed to the antigrav modules, and the yacht settled on dry ground with a tiny shudder. She slumped back in her seat and groaned.

"I do not want to do something like that ever again. As in never, ever, even if I live long enough to witness the end of the universe. I'm not even sure I want to try flying her out of here again anytime soon."

"I'd offer you a session at Zack's spa and massage parlor, but I think our clients will want our full attention until further notice."

He nonetheless walked over to stand behind the helm chair, placed his hands on her shoulders, and began kneading knotted muscles.

**

"That was some impressive flying, Captain Pasek." Verrill shook Talyn's hand enthusiastically. "Though I'll confess that when you touched the water's surface, I was afraid we were witnessing the start of a catastrophe."

"And I'm feeling amazingly drained," she replied with a wan smile.

"Understandably so. If you'd like to take a few hours to rest while we unload, please feel free to do so. We're in no hurry to move out, and I'm sure you'll want to secure your ship before we go."

"Security would be his thing." She pointed at Zack with her thumb. "And please call me Hera. Pru Pasek flies starships. Hera is my ground action *nom de guerre*. I'll be fine after a quick meal and some coffee. How far are we going?"

"Our group is heading down the river tunnel to the next valley where our main camp is hidden. It's just under fifteen kilometers."

"I can't help thinking," she said, "that maybe our shuttle could be of use."

"Perhaps," Verrill smiled. "But not for this. We've got everything planned and set up to move what you and the other ships have brought us. I'd rather keep your shuttle in reserve for something that might give the government severe heartburn."

He stopped speaking and looked at Decker and Talyn in turn searching for something in their eyes.

"Might I conclude," he finally said, "that you've decided to accept my offer to work for us as military experts for a while, until you decide what needs to be done for your ship?"

"You may." The Marine rubbed his hands together. "There's nothing I enjoy more than knocking dumb-ass colonial militia heads together."

Tran Kidder beamed at his former commanding officer.

"I'm really glad you're sticking around."

Decker put his arm around the man's shoulder and squeezed.

"We can relive some of our old glory days when we were the howling madmen of Decker's Demons and show these fine folks how it's done."

Talyn chuckled at her partner's tone.

"I wasn't intending to stay beyond unloading your cargo," she told Verrill, "but I can't risk flying through the Avalon blockade with the damage we've taken. Their captains will be looking for blood the moment they see us and Zack is fresh out of missiles, low on gun ammo and definitely out of ways to surprise them. Two sloops against a yacht doesn't end well once they're on to us."

"In that case, your misfortune is our luck. I'll see what I can do to help you with repairs, but I'm afraid that might take time."

"It might take you seizing a spaceport with maintenance facilities and spare parts, as a matter of fact," she replied with a tired shrug. "Either way, we have nothing better to do, so count us in."

"I will, thank you."

As Verrill turned to leave, Decker asked, "Did you speak with your friend Roste about the Jackals?"

"I did. He assured me that he and the crew of *Clio* took all necessary precautions."

"Mind if I speak to him? I've got some experience with the Confederacy?"

"I wouldn't mind, but he's already gone to rejoin his unit along with their share of the supplies."

"That was mighty fast."

"Their base is the most distant and so they need to cover as much ground as possible before nightfall."

"How convenient," Decker muttered when the rebel leader was out of earshot.

"Try not to take it personally." She motioned towards the ship. "Let's go sort ourselves out."

**

Talyn tore the lid off her food tray and sighed.

"I'm not sure that I'll miss this fine dining, but then, we have no idea what the rebels' catering is like."

"Provided it's not rat-bars three times a day, we'll live." Decker sat down across from her with his food and grinned. "Admit it; what you'll really miss is living in luxury on a ship you command."

"That too," she admitted, "but try not to gloat at getting your wish to help Tran and his mates."

"I never gloat." Decker put on a mock-wounded look. "I'm only pleased that we'll get a chance to weasel our way into the rebels' good graces and find out who's backing them, how they're doing it and more importantly why."

"And you get to fight the good fight while carrying out your intelligence gathering duties. I understand. You can't help it - you're a Marine."

"I'll tell you what else we'll be able to do," he replied before popping a piece of meat into his mouth and chewing slowly.

She raised her eyebrows in question, waiting for him to elaborate. Once he'd swallowed, the earlier grin returned.

"Maybe we can help sort this brush fire out before it turns into the kind of flaming inferno that gets the Senate's attention, followed shortly after that by a few thousand Marines doing a heavily armed tour of Garonne's sights. That never ends well for the locals."

"Pretty tall order for two intelligence agents, one of whom isn't a ground pounder and the other isn't a great strategist like Napoleon."

"Napoleon had his ass handed to him at the end. You can't be great if you end your life on a God forsaken island with no entertainment other than a bunch of sea birds. But I'll go with your lame attempt at a joke and give you this thought: when the man won, it was because his opponents were crap. When his opponents had their shit together, he lost, and usually ran away, leaving his troops in the lurch. I'm hoping the colonial government and its militia don't have their shit together. In fact, I'm counting on it."

"Just a small reminder, Chief Warrant Officer Decker, we're not here to carry out a regime change but to find answers to the questions the analysts have been asking. Once we have those answers, we're out. *Capisce?*"

Zack tossed off a salute.

"Aye, aye, Commander Talyn, sir."

She held his eyes for a few moments, to make sure he understood that her order was non-negotiable, but she saw just enough of a rebellious hint in his stare to know he wasn't going to go quietly.

"I mean it, Zack. Captain Ulrich will strangle us with our own guts in front of the entire special operations section if we go rogue."

"Only if we fail. We nail this before it becomes a big problem, and it'll be promotions for everyone."

When she didn't reply, he shrugged and got up to stow his empty tray.

"Time for one last taste of the good stuff." He took a bottle from the cooler, opened it, and downed half in a single gulp. "Ah. I'll miss that more than anything else. Speaking of which, you want to have a quick romp before I shut this thing down? I doubt the rebel camp is big on privacy."

"Beer and sex. Why does it always come down to beer and sex with you?"

"Because I know how to enjoy life. C'mon, I want to see my commanding officer in the buff one last time before we go where there are no showers."

**

Talyn dropped her heavy pack by the airlock and turned to Zack. Their grace period was over, the weaponry they and the freighters had carried was gone, and the latter had lifted, one at a time, to leave Garonne far behind. The time had come to leave *Phoenix* behind.

"Talk me through the security measures one last time, big boy."

"Right." Decker looked up at the deck head and ticked them off one by one. "The virus is set and will wipe the computer core beyond recovery if anyone other than us or someone sent by the boss tries to access anything without the proper codes. The weapons and ammo lockers might as well be welded shut for all the good it's going to do anyone without the right passcode. The navigation system is locked out, and the AI will not accept any orders unless it hears the magic word. All airlocks, outer hatches, and the ramp are locked; the gun turrets and launcher bays are covered up and locked down, and once we step out of this airlock, the AI will shut it behind us. This ship isn't getting out of here unless you or one of our naval colleagues is at the helm."

She nodded. "Good."

"My turn," he said, examining her from head to toe.

They both wore vaguely military-looking clothes that wouldn't seem out of place in a civilian environment but still provided the same protection as an issue battledress uniform. Each carried a holstered side arm, in Zack's case, his preferred Imperial Armaments fifteen-millimeter monster.

"What's in your pack?"

"Change of clothes, ammo for the blaster and the scatter gun, spare power packs, solar charger, first aid kit, ration bars, water, and water purification unit."

He nodded approvingly and checked that the scattergun strapped to her pack was secure. Then, he quickly listed the contents of his own pack, which mirrored Talyn's.

"No ale?" She asked, smiling mischievously.

"Not even a bottle of Scotch for medicinal purposes."

"You *are* taking this seriously. I'm impressed." She punched him lightly on the arm before picking up her pack and leading the way down to the cavern floor, where Tran Kidder waited.

The airlock slammed shut with finality when Decker's feet touched the ground. They heard one last chime from the AI, its own version of a farewell, and then *Phoenix* went dormant, waiting for someone with the right codes to wake her.

"Zack, I've meant to ask," Kidder said, "why doesn't your ship's AI speak with you?"

"Because someone programmed it to sound just like my commanding officer, and one of her aboard is more than enough."

"I love you too, Zack." Talyn blew him a kiss, then walked off to join the cluster of rebels heading deeper into the cavern.

— TWENTY-ONE —

For two long hours, they walked in a single file beside the river, on a narrow gravel bank that threatened to twist unwary ankles. A few hand-held lights, scattered throughout the column, provided just enough illumination to prevent anything worse than the occasional stumble.

Talyn and Decker, at the tail end of the group, save for a section of heavily armed rebel soldiers, wore night vision glasses, and were spared any near misses with unseen potholes.

The river's flow sped up when the tunnel narrowed and they were forced to wade through the cold water when the banks vanished beneath the surface. Then, moments before Zack was about to utter another pungent comment about the local tourist attractions, they caught their first glimpse of a faint glow ahead.

Soon after that, the column emerged into a verdant canyon and was met by a small detachment of men in camouflage uniforms. The newcomers led them down a barely discernible animal track for another hour until they came within sight of the canyon's mouth. There, another surprise awaited the two operatives.

"Is that what I think it is?" Decker asked, examining a worn façade carved into the reddish granite.

"If you think it's the remains of a L'Taung era fortress, you're probably right," Talyn replied. "It looks similar to other sites found in this part of the galaxy."

"That means it could be up to a hundred thousand years old. Our ancestors were barely homo sapiens back then." A note of awe crept into the Marine's voice. "To think modern Shrehari are such thick-skulled sons of bitches, yet their ancestors could build something that's lasted ten times longer than human civilization."

"We found it by accident about a year ago," Verrill said, joining them at the foot of the cliff. "It's not on anyone's records and from the air, it looks like just another worn-out section of the central range. The interior's not quite as impressive as the exterior, but there's plenty of space, and the surrounding rock is enough to block scans from overhead flights."

"A colonial rebellion's lair inside an ancient Shrehari fort. Only along the Rim..." Decker shook his head, laughing.

"Shall we?" Verrill waved towards an opening hidden by the shadows.

The moment they entered the ruins, a welcome wave of cooler air emanating from deep within the living stone washed over them. Once their eyes got used to the low lighting, Decker could make out corridors cut with such precision that all surfaces looked like polished granite, even after a hundred millennia of disuse.

A sentinel, well placed to cover the passageway, waved them by with a smile. They turned a corner and came face-to-face with a blank slab that shone softly under Verrill's lamp. He touched a spot on the wall beside it, and the pane of rock pivoted aside to reveal a brightly lit corridor with wires and conduits running along the ceiling.

"Welcome to Fort Independence," Verrill said.

**

"Impressive command post. All this must have cost a pretty penny." Decker could identify much of the gear assembled in this room, at the heart of the fortress, as military surplus, no more than a generation behind what the Corps currently used.

"Indeed." Verrill inclined his head briefly. "We have wealthy off-world friends who are concerned with the rights and freedoms of colonists, and who contribute handsomely to help us achieve independence."

"Handsomely indeed," Talyn agreed. "Do these friends also assist you with procurement? I seem to recognize one or two items that are on the Fleet's restricted technology list."

"Perhaps." Verrill sounded unconcerned by her comment. "But I'm sure you'll understand that while I'm grateful to have experienced folks like you rallying to our cause, there are things I can't discuss."

"Of course." Zack returned the man's smile. "I'd be concerned if you were to start blabbing your secrets to relative strangers, even if one of your guys vouches for me. I'm a big fan of need to know and what I need to know right now is where your facilities are. After that, we can discuss my need to know when the chow hall opens and what the passcode to the beer fridge is."

After a helpful soldier had guided Decker to the nearest latrines, Talyn walked over to a large map projection and searched for their location. Verrill joined her and pointed at a spot near the river they'd followed most of the day.

"We're right here, near the Yangtze River." His finger moved upwards and over the contour lines of the last mountain ridge before the coastal plain. "And this is the main settlement area, with Iskellian, the capital, just inland of where the river flows into the Gulf of Sorrows."

"Gulf of Sorrows?" Talyn's eyebrows shot up. "Interesting name. Is there a story behind it?"

"Yes, but I'm not sure how true it is. Apparently, when the first colonists set up shop on the location where Iskellian now stands, they had supply containers dropped from orbit, but the shipper who'd brought them at significant cost from Celeste wasn't terribly concerned about accuracy. One of the containers went off course and landed in the middle of the Gulf, never to be seen again. Legend has it that this particular one contained the colony's entire stock of booze for the year."

"You need to tell that story to Zack. He'll love it."

"What will I love?" A voice asked behind them.

"How the Gulf of Sorrows got its name."

"Someone lost a bottle of one-hundred-year-old single malt in it?"

"Close. The first colonists lost a whole container of the good stuff."

"Ouch." Decker winced. "That must have hurt."

"Fortunately, we have our own distilleries now."

"All of which are guarded by the militia, right?" The corners of Decker's mouth quirked up. "Speaking of which, can you show me their garrisons?"

Red squares materialized on the map like magic seconds after the words had left his mouth and he spent a few minutes in complete silence, studying the display.

"I won't ask you to project your own positions," Zack finally said, "but if you can show me where the hotbeds of support for independence are, I'd sure appreciate it."

When the technician had added those, in blue, to the map, Decker nodded.

"They've apparently read Mao Zedong."

"Pardon me?"

"Mao was a very successful revolutionary leader on pre-spaceflight Earth who waged a long guerrilla war and won it decisively enough that he died in bed, still revered as the Great Helmsman. One of his more famous dictums is to the effect that the guerrilla must move amongst the people as a fish swims in the sea. If you look at the overlap of militia posts and areas supporting independence, it's clear that they correlate to a very fine degree, and I'm sure that's at least in part aimed at preventing you from moving among your supporters."

"I wouldn't be surprised to hear that Colonel Harend has read your Mao's writing" Verrill replied. "He's the commander of the Garonne Militia, but he's also a former Celeste National Guard officer, a regular."

"A militia blowhard who doesn't call himself a general? I don't think your Colonel Harend is a *former* guard officer. More likely he was hand-picked for this job and is still drawing a paycheck from the guard."

"That's what we figured," Verrill replied, pleasantly surprised by the big ex-Marine's incisive analysis.

"Got a picture?"

"We have candid portraits of nearly the entire militia and colonial administration." Verrill made a motion at the technician and the map vanished, replaced by the image of a stocky, bald man in a close-fitted, rather drab uniform.

"Definitely active guard." Zack nodded at the photo. "A militia blowhard would wear a tin pot dictator's assortment of gewgaws. This guy just has a modest fruit salad, a colonel's oak leaves and stars, and nothing else."

"You almost sound like you approve of him?" Verrill's lips twitched in amusement.

"I approve of folks who stay professional, even if they're murderous sons of bitches. It makes killing them a simple business transaction and not a guilty pleasure of the kind that eats away at your soul. Ask Hera. She keeps saying she lost hers."

The rebel leader's faint smile became distinctly quizzical as if he couldn't decide whether Decker was serious or pulling his leg. A soft bell kept him from asking any further questions.

"That's the mess hall telling us the evening meal is ready."

"Excellent." Decker beamed. "Now all you have to do is point me at your beer fridge and my happiness will be complete."

**

"Mao? Really?" Talyn asked hours later when they had bedded down in a small cell carved out of the rock. "He was responsible for seventy million deaths. I don't think he's exactly the inspirational figure you want to emulate."

Decker laughed.

"Oh yeah, the man was a murderous tyrant for sure, but he ran a successful insurrection and didn't end his life contemplating bird poop on a small island, so there's something useful to learn from his guerrilla doctrine. Besides, like one of Chairman Mao's ideological soul mates once said, the death of one man is a tragedy; the death of millions is a statistic."

"Good thing I know you're not a psychopath, honey." She leaned over and kissed him on the cheek. "I don't like competition."

They fell silent, lost in thought, tired after a long and eventful day, but happy to be deep inside a secure fortress where they could relax for a while.

"Speaking of fish in the sea," Decker eventually said, "I wish we could take a little trip through the countryside and get a feel for the mood of the colonists. Unfortunately, I doubt Verrill would be thrilled by the idea of letting relative strangers who know about this place roam the outback without supervision."

"How very perceptive of you," she teased. "I'm sure we'll get the chance to accompany a patrol soon enough; or at least you will, considering you're the super-duper ex-Marine with decades of combat experience."

"At least the food around here is decent. I'd be curious to see what their supply system looks like, but that's another area where too many questions may not please our new friends."

"Might I suggest we find out if the sleep is decent as well?" Talyn yawned to underscore her request.

"Sure, but before I drift off to dreamland, I'd like to point out that you have many more decades of experience than I do when it comes to doing nefarious deeds."

"Are you saying I'm old?"

"I thought we already established that if you'd had a child shortly after reaching puberty, it would be my age by now, so technically, you are old enough to be my mother."

"Darling, you do know what that makes you, right?" She reached down to squeeze him.

"Of course and I thought you were too tired."

"I am." She made a face at him before turning on her side and promptly fell asleep.

**

"The governor will see you now, Colonel."

Harend rose from an uncomfortable chair, the only spare seat in an equally spartan antechamber, and pulled his tight-fitting uniform tunic down. Nodding his thanks at the aide, he entered Cedeno's office, came to a halt the regulation meter from the wooden desk, and saluted.

"Reporting as ordered, sir."

Cedeno motioned him to sit down. His bland face revealed nothing, though its hardness more than hinted at displeasure.

"I've heard the excuses and bafflegab from our Avalon contractors," he said by way of introduction, "but I find it hard to believe they'd be so inept. Avalon is one of the biggest private military corporations in the Commonwealth, and they didn't become that way by acting like incompetent dolts."

"From what we were able to piece together, sir, the rebels engaged the services of their own mercenaries in the form of a

Q-ship that thoroughly surprised the Avalon folks and gave them a bloody nose."

Harend's tone was deferential, cautious even; Cedeno didn't particularly like the colonel, and he had enough connections on the home world to warrant a respectful attitude.

"Fair enough.   But how did three of them subsequently escape Garonne and the fourth vanish?"

"The Q-ship did extensive damage to our satellite constellation, basically destroying our ability to monitor the surface from orbit. We've repositioned some of the surviving ones to restore communications, but large swathes of the planet aren't under constant surveillance anymore.   The escaping freighters managed to lift off and reach low orbit before anyone could detect them. They were pursued by one of the Avalon sloops, but it may have shown a bit too much caution in fear of meeting another Q-ship attack. As to the fourth, the one that attacked the sloops, we've been unable to find it."

"Surely an FTL-capable starship of that size can't just hide under a bush?"

"As I said, sir, with the destruction of the satellites, we had no way of tracking its course and subsequent landing. There are any number of places on this continent alone where it could hide, and those are only the ones we know about."

"I find the notion that Verrill's scum have an armed ship at their disposal to be rather alarming, Colonel. Don't you?"

"Avalon claims to have damaged it, sir. And believe me, the moment it lifts, we'll see it. The rebels aren't the only ones who've gone shopping for hardware. I've made a request to the home world for some surface-to-orbit missile launchers. Once I have those, their ship will become a target the moment it appears over the horizon."

"Let us hope that it remains hidden away until then, though I fear whatever it is that Verrill brought here will not remain hidden for long and your men will be the first to pay the price."

Cedeno's dry tone betrayed his irritation. But then, Harend thought, the governor was not a happy man and probably never had been. It was widely known that he had not volunteered for this assignment, though if he failed, he'd nonetheless pay a hefty price.

"There's plenty more who'll take the place of those killed by the rebels," Harend replied, shrugging, "especially if the home world continues deporting those deemed to be undesirable."

"You're rather free with your soldiers' lives, Colonel."

"I'd hardly call the latest recruits soldiers. Uniformed thugs would be more accurate, but they're good at putting the fear of God into those supporting independence. Admittedly, every now and then, I need to put the fear of God into my troops, but if there's one thing they understand, it's force."

"Just make sure things don't get out of hand to the point where the Senate has to take notice and send in the Marines. Your men don't stand a chance against regulars, and if the Fleet shows signs of intervening, Avalon will pull out what little they've provided so far, let alone agree to a contract for a few battalions of infantry."

A cruel smile appeared on Harend's square face.

"If the powers that be take notice, it'll stem from rebel atrocities, sir. You can count on that. When I'm done, no one in this galaxy will want to be associated with Verrill's bandits, not even Verrill himself."

"Just keep in mind that if I go down, you'll be coming with me."

**

"What were you thinking of doing with our new friends, Verrill?"

Corde looked intently at her commanding officer over the rim of a steaming cup of tea. Around them, the command post was quiet, with one technician monitoring communications and the perimeter sensors.

"I'd like to take Zack out on a raid and get his opinion on the way we operate. Tran can't stop singing his praises though I suspect part of the hero worship is due to Decker saving him from a life of slavery. Once we get to see the man in action, I'll decide how far to trust him and use him. His partner? I don't know. She's a blank slate and Tran's never met her before. I'm a lot less comfortable with her than I am with him."

"How about I use her as an analyst for a while?" Corde suggested. "She asked some penetrating questions over supper but was always careful not to pry into our business any more than she had to. I'd say there's a pretty sharp brain behind that disreputable haircut."

"Sure. Just be careful how much you reveal. Until they've been blooded, so to speak, we need to proceed with caution. Sometimes I get the feeling that Tran stumbling over his old CO, who just happens to be partners in a mercenary Q-ship, is a little too convenient. Especially when I consider that Decker's a former Marine Pathfinder. You know what they say, right?"

"Once a Marine, always a Marine. But we have ex-military types in the movement already, and they've been loyal to a fault."

"Most of them are loyal to the idea of Garonne getting out from under Celeste rule, at least those who were born here or who settled here after leaving the service. Mercenaries like Miko Steiger are loyal so long as we respect their contracts. Where does that leave Zack and Hera?"

"In the wait and see category," Corde replied with a wry smile. "Now off to bed with you. It's been a long, long day and we have some planning to do tomorrow. Your buying spree wiped out our last donation and we have to calculate how much we'll need to ask from our benefactors."

Verrill sighed, then stood and stretched out his tired arms.

"The voice of reason speaking. Good night, Corde."

"Good night, boss. Sleep well."

— TWENTY-TWO —

Decker, in the ghillie suit battledress worn by rebel soldiers and carrying one of their carbines in addition to his beloved Shrehari blaster, pushed aside the tarp covering the entrance to the briefing room.

Inside, two dozen rebels were chatting quietly while they waited for the appointed time for orders. One of them, a middle-aged man with a weathered face and iron gray hair, broke off from the group and greeted Zack with an outstretched hand.

"You must be our brand new ex-Marine."

They shook. He was stronger than his lanky frame would indicate, a strength reflected in dark eyes that measured Zack with frank openness.

"The name's Catlow. I used to have a first name somewhere, but it became too cumbersome for a simple soldier. I'm ex-army — infantry to be precise. I hear you used to be in the pathfinders. That means you'll enjoy our little walk around the countryside."

A grin accompanied his last few words, and he released Decker's hand. Turning back towards the others he called the room to attention.

"Folks, if you're done gossiping about the governor's sex life, we can start. This here's Zack Decker, former Marine, come to fight with us. If we have new guns and fresh ammo, it's because he and his partner flew it through the mercenary blockade. Seeing as how his basic branch was pathfinders, Verrill figured it might be good to send him out with us so he can see for himself what the militia scum are up to around Tianjin."

The others nodded politely at Zack, undisguised curiosity in their eyes as, one by one, they introduced themselves, usually with just one name. Whether it was first name, last name, or nickname, Decker didn't bother asking.

"Okay," Catlow said once they were done, "everyone grab a seat and pay attention."

A three-dimensional map projection appeared on the floor within the circle of chairs.

"Take a few moments to orient yourselves, folks."

A red light appeared by a rocky spur near the Yangtze River. Decker briefly followed the blue ribbon upstream to where they'd landed *Phoenix* a week earlier, and then looked back at the marker.

"This is where we are, of course, in case any of you had forgotten or developed selective amnesia."

That garnered a few chuckles. The red light shifted downriver and through a gap in the last ridge before coming to rest on a town surrounded by agricultural settlements.

"Tianjin, where the Yangtze River leaves the highlands for good."

"I wish I could leave the highlands for good," one of the troopers muttered, to the subdued laughter of his friends.

The light continued down the river and came to rest on a much larger town.

"And finally, Iskellian, home of Governor Cedeno, Colonel Harend and everyone else we'd like to ship back to Celeste."

"Preferably via a rogue wormhole that connects with the Andromeda galaxy," the same trooper added.

"As you can see, Decker," Catlow smiled, "Gareth is our platoon clown. He's also the heavy machine gunner so he's entitled to an extra ration of snark."

"Damn things were built for Shrehari marines, not civilized human beings," Gareth replied.

"Moving right along," the platoon leader said, "are there any questions about our orientation to the ground? Did anyone forget what planet we're on?"

"Sure, boss, I got a question," one of the women raised her hand, "I hear there's a new liquor store in Tianjin. Can you point it out on the map? I want to make sure I can find it."

Catlow snorted.

"You haven't been paid in months. How are you going to buy anything other than a good laugh from the sales clerk?" He shook his head, still smiling. "Okay. I hope you got all the funnies out of your system. Ladies and gents, orders."

For the next half hour, Catlow went through the reconnaissance mission in exacting detail. When he was done, he gave his troops a minute to think of any questions they might have.

"Okay," he said once the time was up and no one had raised a hand, "since none of you are giving me the lost puppy look, I'll assume you hoisted it all in, and that means it's time for the oral examination."

He quickly went around the circle, firing off questions at each soldier about various aspects of the orders they'd just received. When he came to Decker, a sly smile replaced the serious expression and without missing a beat, he tossed a few Zack's way, to show his platoon that the ex-Marine would be treated like anyone else.

Decker, who'd used the same reverse questioning technique every time he had issued operational orders, knew the score, and played along to Catlow's satisfaction.

The map projection faded away, signaling to the assembly that it was time to go. They stood up and stowed their chairs against the wall.

"Grab your kit and line up in the corridor for inspection in five minutes."

Zack obeyed along with the rest of them. This was Catlow's show; he was simply along for a familiarization tour. Since there was no dead weight on an operation, Chief Warrant Officer Decker, former troop leader in the 902nd Pathfinder Squadron and now undercover as a fighter for hire, would just be another private soldier in the patrol.

Precisely five minutes later, he was lined up with the others, pack at his feet, weapons visible and helmet on his head.

Catlow went down the line and made each trooper recite every item he or she carried, show some of the critical ones, and describe his role during the mission. It was the last check. They'd already had a thorough inspection in the barracks earlier.

When Catlow got to Decker, the Marine snapped to attention.

"Carbine, fifteen millimeter; blaster same caliber; fighting dagger; five hundred rounds, ten replacement power packs, ten grenades and my share of the heavy machine gun ammo; radio, set to receive only, first aid kit, rations for five days, three liters of water, purification kit, bivouac bag; night vision goggles."

"Job?"

"I'm your wingman throughout the mission. I keep you alive and in command."

The sly smile returned.

"No medicinals, especially of the distilled kind? I've heard of what Marines consider essential rations."

"Never on patrol, boss." Decker returned the smile with a knowing smirk.

"Surprised that we irregulars can find our asses with both hands?"

"I haven't seen you try to find your ass yet. Up to now, it's just been foreplay."

This time, Catlow laughed out loud. He clapped Zack on the shoulder.

"I think you just might fit in around here, Decker." He turned around to face the rest of the platoon. "Saddle up folks."

When they filed out of the ancient fortress, the last light of day had already vanished. Overhead, the long ribbon of the Milky Way dominated the night sky while unfamiliar constellations pulled distant stars into strange patterns.

Decker flipped down his goggles, turning the dark forest beyond the scree into a glowing green wonderland of outlandish shapes.

Then, the patrol disappeared beneath a thick canopy of trees, following a faint animal track towards the river and, beyond the pass, to Tianjin, a town that Colonel Harend liked to describe as a hive of separatist scum.

**

"Do you send out a lot of recon patrols?" Talyn asked Corde, after watching Decker and the others leave.

"Yup. From here and from the other operating bases. We always have a few going. It's the only way we can figure out what the enemy's doing, stay in touch with our supporters and collect enough information to plan our next strikes."

"Lose many of them?"

The woman shrugged.

"We get the occasional casualty when a patrol's unlucky enough to run head-long into the militia, but we're getting better at it. Back when we started, a couple of them vanished without a trace. I figure we'll eventually find a few mass graves near the place where they did their last radio check. Every time that happened, we had to shift one of our bases."

"How do you decide a patrol's been compromised?"

Corde pointed at the communications alcove.

"Every six hours, they send a status check via microburst. The message itself is nonsense if anyone ever manages to decrypt it, but there are a few variations that tell us whether they're fine, running, have taken casualties or are fighting the last stand. Miss one check and the patrol's parent battalion goes on high alert; miss two checks and the battalion sends out a security perimeter while the rest begin to pack up. If they see militia moving in their direction, the entire unit shifts to an alternate hide."

Talyn nodded.

"Makes sense. Is there any danger of the militia triangulating on the sender?"

"There was some, but after you and your partner turned most of the satellites into scrap metal, the chances are pretty slim. If we have to talk to the patrol, we use a laser communications relay to a burst transmitter a long distance from the base."

"Impressive."

"We have a few Fleet-trained commo techs in the ranks." Corde sounded pleased with the compliment. "And we've found some good suppliers who don't ask too many awkward questions when it comes to restricted gear."

When Talyn didn't rise to the bait, Corde waved towards a cluster of field desks in one corner of the command post.

"Do you want to spend some time looking over the intelligence digests of the last few months before going to bed? I'm afraid I can't offer you any other entertainment."

"Sure. My entertainment options left with Decker." She winked knowingly at Corde.

**

Anton Cedeno, reluctant governor of Garonne, looked up from his tablet when the door to the living room opened to admit a slim, tanned woman of indistinct age, wearing a long sundress and more gaudy jewelry than was decent on a Rim colony.

"Hello, hello, Lord and master of the planet," she blared in a nasal voice, making him wince. Shala meant well, but their marriage was dynastic and some days he felt like he'd gotten the short end of it.

"Darling." He tried to smile. "How was Zeli?"

"Dreary," she replied, dropping into an overstuffed chair. "We had rain most of the week and then those nasty rebels did something to the water supply so it was misery and the runs for everyone. Thankfully, I was sticking with the good stuff so it didn't take me, but most of the guests at the resort had a bad time of it."

She looked around for a servant and her face lit up with a smile when the maid appeared with a flute of bubbly wine.

"You're an angel, Mara." Shala Cedeno took an appreciative sip of the straw-colored liquid and sighed. "If the rebels are going to start targeting the Turquoise Coast, I don't know how we'll enjoy this place anymore. Perhaps Harend will come up with a way to flush them into the open before things get too bad. He's ruthless enough to get results once he finds the right lever."

Though she sounded flighty, Cedeno knew the outer shell of a bored socialite hid a shrewd and sometimes cunning mind, and isolated as they were on Garonne, he was more than happy to share matters of state with her. It was their marriage's biggest saving grace.

"The trick is to make sure his ruthlessness doesn't call down the wrath of the Senate, and through them, the Fleet, dear. There are days when I wonder whether he's not letting his enjoyment of the job override caution. By the way, the rebels may have received something of a boost while you were down south."

"Oh?" She sat up, a spark of interest in her eyes when he related the arrival of the freighters and the disappearance of the mysterious mercenary Q-ship.

When he told her about Harend's notion of turning the rebels into scapegoats for war crimes, she gasped.

"If that backfires, we're all going down."

"I know, Shala." A resigned sigh escaped his pinched face. "But some days I get the sense that Harend's agenda isn't the same as mine and that my authority over him is nothing more than a masquerade. His resistance to hiring off-world soldiers, for instance."

Her eyes narrowed while she contemplated the half-full glass of wine.

"He's afraid that their commanders will take orders only from you, which might marginalize his influence on the campaign against the rebels. After all, he took this assignment in the hopes of promotion on his return to Celeste."

"Incisively stated, my dear," Cedeno smiled at her.

"Thank you." She sketched a sitting curtsy. "Though I fear we shall have to take measures that will permit us to disavow Harend the moment he does something stupid."

He was pleased with her use of 'we' and 'us'. Dynastic marriages among his caste did have the advantage of interested loyalty when it came to social standing, power, and wealth, things neither had in sufficient quantity to escape censure, should the home world look for scapegoats.

"I suppose we will." He dropped his tablet on the sofa and touched a call screen. "I think I'll have one of those as well. It's been a long week."

**

"You're sure about this?" Verrill asked Miko Steiger.

They were alone in the room that housed all of the rebel leader's worldly goods: a cot, a desk, two folding chairs and a small holo depicting a smiling family.

"I'll be fine." She smiled reassuringly. "The militia is so starved for recruits who know the business end of a gun that they'll hire me on the spot. Besides, the entry controls on Garonne are crappy enough that no one will question my credentials. I just need to get to Iskellian without anyone seeing me leave the highlands. After that, I lose myself among the deportees."

Steiger had come up with the plan after the unplanned trip in *Phoenix* had left her at loose ends on Garonne. She'd expressed little desire to join one of the combat companies that formed the rebellion's backbone, preferring to work alone in a more meaningful way.

"We can send you back up the river on foot and have one of Tarri's folks waiting with a skimmer; after that, a little detour south before heading to Iskellian, as if you're a farmer coming to see the sights, and you should be good."

She nodded.

"That ought to do it."

He fished a small wafer from his tunic pocket and tossed it at her.

"That has instructions on how to get in touch with one of the cell leaders in Iskellian, should you ever need to get vital information back to us or you have to go in a hurry. You won't ever meet in person, for obvious security reasons. Once you've initiated contact, break the chip in half, and swallow it. You'll be given instructions on how to proceed."

"Swallow the wafer?" An amused smile creased Steiger's scarred face. "I hope it tastes like cherries."

"It tastes like crap, but your stomach acid will dissolve it quickly."

"Kinky." She picked the chip up and examined its surface carefully before tucking it inside her shirt. "Anything else?"

"No. I'll have the duty tech call Tarri and get an ETA for the skimmer."

Steiger stood to leave.

"I'd wish you good luck," Verrill said, "if I didn't know folks in your line of business consider it a jinx. Take care of yourself, Miko. Even though you're a mercenary, you've shown the heart and soul of a true believer in Garonne's freedom."

She shrugged off the compliment.

"I prefer to take contracts with folks who are on the side of what's right and not with those who only have might."

"A freelancer with a conscience." Verrill's smile took the sting out of his words. He stuck out his hand. "Good hunting. The faster we can push the government into a corner, the sooner we'll be able to end this."

**

The irritating chime of an incoming call broke through Colonel Harend's contemplation of a fine single malt whiskey, imported from halfway across the Commonwealth at significant cost. Very few people would dare disturb him short of a major crisis, so he had a good idea who it might be.

He carefully put his glass down and reached over to touch the dark screen. It immediately displayed the face of Captain Rika Kozlev, his intelligence officer and another member of the Celeste National Guard on loan to Garonne. A pleased smile creased her sharp, narrow features beneath a shock of black hair trimmed in an incongruously girlish pixie cut.

"Apologies for troubling you at this hour, sir, but Mathias finally gave up what he knew. We have the name of the rebel cell leader in the Tianjin district."

"With that kind of news, you're welcome to disturb me at any hour, Rika. In fact, why don't you join me in my quarters to celebrate? I've opened my latest acquisition and would be interested in your opinion."

"The Glen Arcturus?" A look of surprised pleasure replaced the smile. "How could I say no? Give me time to clean up, say ten minutes or so."

"Was it that messy?"

"By the time we were done, Mathias had permanently lost all of his higher brain functions, and it seemed unkind to leave him alive in that state. I took the occasion to practice my killing stroke."

"Always the practical one." Harend chuckled. "I hope you impressed the troopers assisting you."

"Actually, I hope I thoroughly cowed them. The only thing psychopaths understand is someone more dangerous than they are."

He laughed. "I think there's little doubt around here concerning you, my dear. Go get cleaned up. Then we can discuss how we'll deal with our rebellious friend in the Tianjin district."

"Will do."

Kozlev signed off, and the screen went dark.

Harend rose to get another crystal tumbler from the sideboard and placed it on the table beside the bottle of amber liquid. Taking Rika with him on the Garonne assignment had been one of the better decisions in a checkered career.

Command was glad to see her off Celeste, and he had someone he could trust at his side. Kozlev didn't give her loyalty easily, but after he'd saved her from a court-martial for an interrogation that had gone very wrong, she was his, completely and utterly.

—TWENTY-THREE—

"Beautiful countryside, very peaceful," Decker said, scanning the green, rolling fields below them.

"On the surface," Catlow replied. "The further from Iskellian, the greater the support for independence and that means more attention from the authorities. Besides, the number of deportees relocated to Tianjin is about to reach the point where they'll see the same crap that's been happening in the capital for the last two years."

Dawn had crept over the fertile plain less than an hour earlier, not long after the patrol had settled into a well-hidden position on one of the spurs overhanging the Yangtze River where it broke free of the last ridge in a welter of foam and rushing water.

The town seemed almost near enough to touch, and Zack could see tiny specks moving about in the morning light, colonists getting an early start on the day.

"The militia garrison is on the far side," Catlow said pointing roughly northwest of their position. "If you can make out the gray block of buildings behind the trees..."

"Got it," Zack replied moments later. "Strength?"

"The permanent garrison is a little over a hundred, working in three shifts, so no more than thirty-five or so on duty at any time, though we figure that'll be increased as they find more scum willing to do the government's bidding."

"I guess they're not doing constant patrols through the countryside with that kind of manpower."

"No." Catlow shook his head. "They'll show the flag a few times a week in their rural areas but most of their time is spent in town. Crime is on the rise and the governor knows that if the militia doesn't sort it, the colonists will and with a lot less concern for the letter of the law."

Decker grunted.

"Vigilantes become freedom fighters when the colonial government stops giving a damn?"

"Pretty much. Mind you, if they need reinforcements, Iskellian is just a hop and a skip by shuttle, a couple of hours by rail, longer by road. Lately, we've heard reports of a rapid reaction force, up to company size, coming from the capital to support local garrisons for specific operations. It hasn't happened here yet, but up north, where we have one of our units making trouble for the district magistrate."

"Where's our next destination?" Decker lowered his scanner and glanced at Catlow. "I'm assuming that we're not spending all of our time here watching in shifts. A good recon means getting a feel for the people as well as the ground."

"You're right." The rebel platoon leader nodded. "We aren't spending all of our time here. We got word that one of our guys working things in town - you know, regular job during the day, dastardly rebel at night – vanished on Monday."

"Militia?"

"Without a doubt. They'll have brought him to Iskellian for interrogation by the intelligence branch. Nasty people, that, worse than the uniformed thugs patrolling the streets. Anyways, we need to talk to the guy running things in this area. He owns a farm down there."

"Cell leader?" It was Decker's turn to grimace. "If your vanished man reported to the farmer in question, it's only a matter of time before a snatch team comes swooping in. Nobody can resist interrogation unless they've been conditioned and then we simply die when the bastards try."

"You've been conditioned?" Catlow sounded surprised.

"Fact. It's a requirement in my former line of business. When were you planning on having your little coffee klatch?"

"After dark. The militia doesn't go roaming at night, and most honest citizens are indoors. Fewer eyes on the countryside then."

"The snatch team will likely do the same when they figure everyone in the family is in one place, ready to be cuffed and dragged off to the dungeons. Better hope that it didn't go down while we were playing happy wanderers in the backwoods last night."

A worried look crossed Catlow's face.

"You think that might have happened?"

"He was taken three days ago. Assuming it was the locals who made the arrest, figure on twenty-four hours to get him to Iskellian and in the custody of militia intelligence. Few people last more than forty-eight hours, most not even that long, but some interrogators are sadists at heart and like to draw things out if there isn't an immediate operational need."

"So I heard."

"The Fleet gets rid of those the moment they're found out, but they tend to gravitate to national guards, private corporations, or militias. Chances are good you have that type here. Counter-insurgencies are like catnip for psychopaths. I think he's spilled his guts by now. The only question is whether or not the militia went for your cell leader immediately or they're playing it out slowly."

"What do you figure?"

"No idea. It's either over already, or it'll happen before tomorrow morning. Flip a coin. The only way to find out is to go there. Carefully. If they've done the deed, they'll leave a couple of troopers behind to see if anyone comes for a look."

"Not to be too nosy, Zack, but you seem to know a lot about this kind of stuff. A lot more than me in any case."

"That's because you and your buddies are new at the whole guerrilla war thing. I was on the Marine end of it often enough that I've learned the score, and the folks who met my little buddy here," he patted his blaster, "weren't always the ones called 'rebels.' May I suggest that a pair of your guys take over the observation duties so we can plan our next move?"

Catlow stared down at the plain again, clearly troubled. He raised his binoculars and aimed them at a particular cluster of buildings a few kilometers south of Tianjin proper.

"I can't see anything abnormal," he said after a long moment of silence, "but then I probably wouldn't if the militia's beaten us to the punch and are waiting for someone to show up."

He made sure Zack was able to zero in on the farm and waited.

"I don't know what it should normally look like," the Marine finally said, "but I can't see traces of a raid, which really means squat. We'll have to go down there. The question is when."

**

Rika Kozlev emerged from the bathroom suite and smiled at Harend, still in bed, head propped up by a muscular arm. He openly admired her lean body, fascinated as ever by the tattoo wrapped around her torso like a serpent of ancient myth.

"One more for the road, Cen?" She asked, sitting down beside him.

He ran his fingers along her jaw line and down her arm before briefly brushing her nipples.

"Still horny?"

He smiled lazily, recalling her intense craving a few hours earlier.

"You know what a good session with rebel trash does to my hormones." She let her hand stray under the bed sheet and grinned. "Your mouth says maybe, but the rest of you is saying something very different. We have plenty of time before briefing the snatch team. Larn Takan and his family aren't going anywhere. I've put eyes on his farm, remember? If we're lucky, we might pick up a few more independence sympathizers. Get enough of them under my care and I'll find the guerrillas' hideouts. Then, you can have fun sweeping them up."

The glow in her eyes when she spoke of taking prisoners into her care should have chilled Harend, but he'd gotten used to her particular tastes. Provided she got results, he was content to let her do as she pleased. Dealing with the Garonne situation was his last chance at promotion and the ability to indulge in his expensive tastes well into retirement.

Satisfying Rika Kozlev's voracious sexual appetite to keep her happy was a small sacrifice to make. After all, an indulgence like the Glen Arcturus was hard to come by on a colonel's pay, especially out here in the back end of the Commonwealth. And besides, she was fun in bed, something he couldn't say about the wife he'd left behind on Celeste.

**

"Who is this?" Talyn asked, turning her screen towards Corde.

After a quick breakfast in the mess hall, the two women had set themselves the task of reviewing all of the intelligence files the rebels had amassed, not just the digests but the raw data, to see if fresh eyes could find something new in old reports.

She pointed at a woman in militia uniform with a captain's rank insignia, smiling at whoever captured the image. She was standing close enough to Colonel Harend, who was scowling at something or someone, to suggest a degree of intimacy.

"As far as we know, her name is Rika Kozlev. We think she's Harend's adjutant or aide, though she keeps mostly out of sight. There's not much on her in our files, but she too is probably Celeste National Guard."

Talyn zoomed in on the narrow face framed by a pixie haircut and studied it in silence for several minutes.

"I doubt she's an administrative type." Her fingers briefly drummed against the tabletop. "Do you have any more pictures or information on this Captain Kozlev?"

"Probably." Corde tapped her screen to launch a database search. "Why the interest in an officer who seems to be barely there?"

"Because those are the ones who might be the most dangerous," Talyn replied, staring at Kozlev image.

What she couldn't tell Corde was that the dark eyes staring at her seemed chillingly familiar, that she recognized a kindred spirit in the shape of the militia officer. A kindred spirit that had crossed the line Talyn had carefully avoided all her life. She couldn't even explain to herself why this one picture seemed to reveal so much, but she'd learned to trust her instincts. They had rarely been wrong, particularly when fellow sociopaths were concerned.

If she was right about Kozlev, then anyone who fell into militia hands was doomed. And since the rebels weren't conditioned, one interrogation could unravel more than just a single rebel cell, no matter how well compartmentalized they were, dooming more of them to a bad end.

"Hera."

"Hmm?" Talyn snapped out of her trance and glanced at Corde, who was staring back with obvious concern.

"Are you alright? You look like someone just walked over your grave, as my grandmother used to say."

"Perhaps someone just did. Have you found more information on this Rika Kozlev? I have a hunch that she may be more dangerous to us than her boss."

Corde's expression betrayed both curiosity and disbelief, but she pushed the data over to Talyn's terminal nonetheless.

"As you can see, we don't have all that much."

"Indeed," the operative replied after scanning the files. "Maybe we can approach this from a different angle. Do you have records on independence supporters, whether they were involved in the rebellion or just politically vocal, who've disappeared since Kozlev came to Garonne?"

"Why is that important?" Corde asked.

"I'd rather build a dossier before committing myself, but do I think there will be a time when direct action against key members of the colonial administration becomes imperative, and who is and isn't key won't always be readily apparent."

Talyn's words sounded so matter of fact, her tone so business-like that Corde felt a chill run down her spine.

Decker, by virtue of his size, apparent strength, and calm aura of competence had seemed to be more dangerous than his partner. But now she realized that the woman so serenely discussing politically motivated assassination was, in fact, far more deadly.

"I'll pull up what we have."

******

Decker patiently chewed on a ration bar while he waited for Catlow to confer with his squad leaders. They were in the patrol hide, beneath the ridgeline, where those troopers not in the observation post or pulling sentry duty were sleeping soundly after the night's forced march.

The rebels seemed to come to a decision, and Catlow rose from his crouch to join Zack on a fallen log.

"Nolan and I are going to change into civilian clothes and take a walk down to Larn's place. We all agree that waiting until dark isn't going to cut it."

Zack nodded slowly while he swallowed a mouthful of the sweet-salty bar.

"Probably a good idea to not wait," he said. "If they've been and gone, we need to hightail it out of here anyway. If they haven't, then you can exfiltrate your man and his people."

He paused, eyes narrowing when a thought that had been nagging at his subconscious finally surfaced.

"Let me rephrase that. If the militia hasn't raided the farm yet but they've broken your vanished guy, I'd expect them to have eyes on the place, so we really need to make sure they get away without looking like they're getting away."

"You're a real bucket of cheer this morning, my friend." Catlow gave him a pained smile. "Would you care to go back to the OP and see if you can spot the surveillance?"

"Sure." Decker carefully rolled up the ration bar package and stuffed it in his pack, then wiped his hands before standing. "Though I doubt I'll see anything useful if whatever or whoever they have watching is properly deployed, and I never underestimate the opposition. The folks running grab and snatch operations on independence sympathizers won't be the average militia pukes you guys are used to."

"There's that cheer again." Catlow slapped him on the shoulder. "Tell you what; come down with Nolan and me. A pair of experienced pathfinder eyes will probably do us more good than having you sit around the hide scratching your balls. You did bring a change of duds, right?"

"Of course. I've been to this kind of dance before." He nudged his pack. "I've got all I need. But before we go, let's take a real good look at the Takan place. Just because they might have put a pro on the job doesn't mean we skip a step."

They spent a fruitless hour quartering the countryside with their sensors, but nothing and nobody stood out.

Decker slipped into the clothes he'd worn when they left *Phoenix* but switched over to a shoulder holster. On a Rim colony, walking around armed wasn't unusual, but an Imperial Armaments blaster might attract more attention on Garonne than he wanted.

Like Catlow and Nolan, he had transferred some water, rations, and ammo to a small pouch, leaving his pack with any overt military equipment behind. Unlike his two companions, he had also tucked a small hand-held sensor into a waterproof cargo pocket.

The three men, looking like hikers or maybe industrial prospectors, made their way to a gravel trail running along the river and emerged from the thick forest unseen by other human eyes.

It took less than an hour to reach the road leading to the Takan farm and the only local they met on the trail smiled and nodded politely at them as if he were an independence supporter who recognized men fighting for their collective freedom. It was momentarily unnerving for Zack, who was used to being on the other side of the equation.

Once they were on the main thoroughfare bisecting the district, a few simple farm skimmers whooshed past them, but it seemed like most people in the area, on this sunny, warm morning, were hard at work growing the food that supported the colony.

Decker's eyes never rested on one spot for more than a few seconds. He was looking for anything that seemed out of place or that struck him as odd and memorizing his surroundings, just in case they had to get out fast.

On either side of the road and right up to the foot of the nearby ridge, an ocean of golden grain, each stalk as high as Zack's shoulders, filled their immediate horizon. Trees, precisely lined up in long rows and topped with thick green foliage, marked breaks between vast fields and provided relief for eyes tired of the endless flat vista stretching out into the west.

They reached the trail leading off the highway to the Takan farm without spotting anything, but Zack hadn't expected them to. Surveillance would either be at long range or very close in. They couldn't do much about someone sitting kilometers away watching the feed from a camera sitting at the top of a transmission tower, but now that they were getting near, the risk of stumbling across one or more watchers grew.

"I'll take point," Catlow said. "The Takans know me, and they'll probably be edgy after Mathias' disappearance. I know they have a security system so there might be eyes on the access road. If we find someone who shouldn't be there, let's try to take them down quietly."

Zack and Nolan nodded their understanding, the former continuing to scan the environs with darting eyes while the latter glanced towards the distant farm outbuildings with visible trepidation.

Operating on sheer instinct, the Marine pulled out his sensor, taking care to keep it from being seen by unfriendly eyes and scanned the surroundings.

His pungent curse stopped the other men in their tracks, and they turned around to stare at him.

"What's wrong?" Catlow looked around with visible alarm.

"I think we've been made," Decker replied. "Keep your eyes on the road. Whatever I say, don't look up."

He paused to let his words sink in.

"There's a drone floating above us." He pointed upwards with his thumb. "We can't see it, and I would never have noticed if it hadn't gone live to transmit. Our crossing an invisible line on the road to the farm must have triggered something in its programming. I was lucky to have my sensor out when it happened, otherwise..."

"Militia?" Catlow realized how dumb that question sounded the moment it left his mouth and he shook his head. "What now?"

"Now? We continue with the plan, only a lot faster. They won't have bothered with a drone if they've already taken the place. What I'm worried about is whether they'll move up their timetable and whether or not the snatch team is already in the area. I doubt we can pass for mendicant priests of the Great Void, much less folks with valid business. Anyone legit going around in full daylight would be riding a skimmer."

Decker looked back at the main road, then down the lane towards the farm.

"We might not have long before we're in a firefight, and we'd best be under cover when it happens. Right now, the only cover in sight is over there."

Decker set off towards the buildings at a fast trot, one hand slipping into his jacket to make sure his blaster was ready to draw.

**

Kozlev stuck her head through the open office door, a cruel smile revealing small, white teeth.

"Three men on foot turned down the road to the Takan farm approximately ten minutes ago. We didn't get a good look at any of the faces, but at least two of them are armed and one of those triggered a possible match in the database – a man who we believe headed for the hills to join the rebel fighters."

Harend gently put his tablet down and breathed in deeply, letting a sense of satisfaction replace his irritation at Cedeno's increasing demands for detailed reports.

"Taking Mathias may have proven to be your best recommendation to date, Rika. I can only see one reason why three men would be headed for the Takan farm on foot on this particular morning, and it's not to sell the latest in food preservation technology. What do you propose?"

"The snatch team is already in Tianjin. We could have them hit the farm now instead of waiting for darkness. Even if we miss some members of the Takan family, taking three fighters who'll know where the rebel bases are will more than make up for it. We can always get the others later."

"And if those three aren't rebels?"

"Then I'll get some entertainment at no additional cost, but I'm convinced they are. There's a certain aura around all three that tells me they're fighters, not farmers, especially one of them, a big guy. He moves like a pro, and he's not visibly armed. That triggered all my bullshit detectors, especially once I saw the footage of him running moments after the drone started transmitting. We might have made them, but it's entirely possible that he made my little eye in the sky."

"Execute the raid, Captain."

— TWENTY-FOUR —

Catlow and a gray-haired man with thick arms embraced briefly before the latter waved them into the house.

"Larn, these are Zack and Nolan. Two of my guys. We don't have much time. Zack figures the militia are on their way here. They have a drone watching your place and what with Mathias disappearing the other day, it can only mean one thing."

"Shit." A look of pure disgust twisted the farmer's tanned face.

"Mister Takan," Zack said, "if the militia took this Mathias, they'd have discovered you're his cell leader in the Tianjin district, and they're going to want to make their way up the movement's ladder. Everyone eventually talks."

He waited until the man nodded before continuing.

"We need to get you and your family out of here now. They know we've shown up, thanks to that damned drone and they're smart enough to figure we're here to warn you."

"I suppose I should have figured this would happen when Jamie, that's Mathias' wife, called to tell me he hadn't come home even though when the guys at the Horse and Bull saw him leave, he was sober and walking upright."

Takan seemed to deflate under the realization that his quiet life had come to an abrupt end.

"Do you have a skimmer, sir, something that can carry you, your family, and us? We need to leave now." The urgency in Decker's voice seemed to revive him, and he nodded with some energy as if he'd come to a decision.

He turned towards the hallway and hollered a name. Moments later, a plump, pleasant-faced woman in working clothes appeared, wiping her hands.

"Marnie, it's happened. We need to go. Grab the bug-out bags and get the boys. I'll get the truck."

Takan then walked over to a cabinet and pulled the doors open.

"Might as well take these, just in case." He pointed at hunting weapons and boxes of ammunition. "Help yourselves."

"Sir, is your family all here?" Decker asked, taking a scattergun and checking the action.

"No." Takan shook his head. "My two sons and my wife are here. My daughter Kari is in Iskellian, staying with some friends."

"Shit." Zack slung the weapon over his shoulder and stuffed half a dozen ammunition packs in his pockets. "Can you get in touch with her and get her to go into hiding? Once the militia finds out that you've flown the coop, they'll be looking for her. Leverage to get you to surrender."

Takan suddenly looked like he was about to vomit.

"They wouldn't."

"They would. And once you surrender, she's dead." He checked his internal clock. "We have a few minutes. Call her, but make sure she doesn't tell anyone where she's going to hide. We'll figure out how to extract her later. Right now we need to extract our own butts."

The farmer pulled a standard civilian communicator from his pocket and ran a thumb over the screen, then held it up to his mouth.

"Honey, it's Larn. We're in trouble. When you hear this, get away, and hide, just like we talked about. Remember, we'll always be looking out for you, just like when you were a little girl and liked to visit."

He cut the transmission and grimaced.

"Voice mail. She'll understand the moment she listens to it."

"That wasn't smart," Decker replied. "If you had a pre-planned hideout, it wasn't necessary to remind her of when she was a little girl. A good investigator can track that down in a few days, a week, tops."

"You understood what I meant?" For the first time, panic crept into his voice.

"Yeah. I don't know where, but I know what. Like I told Catlow, this isn't my first dance, and I'm going to bet the militia has a few folks who've got some experience too if they tracked down Mathias and have you under surveillance."

Marnie reappeared, trailed by two teenaged boys, each with a pack and a hunting weapon. She carried two duffels, handing one to Takan before taking the last gun from the cabinet.

"I thought you were going to pull out the truck?"

"Kari."

The woman blanched. "Oh my God. Is she in danger?"

"I think she is, ma'am. But if we don't get out of here, we won't be able to help her." Decker waved towards the door. "And we're running out of time to do that."

Larn Takan took one last look around, to imprint the image of a vanished life deeply into his memory in the hopes of a return some day, then he flung the door open and raced towards a large outbuilding, duffle in one hand and weapon in the other.

"Shall we?" Decker asked.

Within moments, a transport skimmer with a spacious cab and a large bed with high sides emerged from the shed, driven by whining fans that left a cloud of dust in their wake.

"Ma'am, I'd like you and the boys to get in with your husband. Catlow, Nolan, and I will ride in the back, where we have a good field of fire when the militia bastards get on our tail, which they will."

Nobody even thought it strange that Decker, a newcomer to Garonne and to the cause, had taken charge. They could instinctively sense that he thought and moved like a professional rather than a colonist reluctantly drawn into the struggle for independence. They obeyed without a word.

"Where's the best place to get under some sort of cover, dump this thing and head for the hills?" Zack asked.

"The river," Catlow replied. "There's no other place. We'll go back in the way we came out."

He shouted a few instructions at Takan, then jumped into the truck's bed and wedged himself into a corner against the cab. Once Zack was on board, Catlow slammed his hand on the plasticized roof three times, the universal signal to get moving.

Dark specks in the distance caught Decker's eyes moments after the truck lurched forward and began to pick up speed. He nudged his companions, gesturing towards the horizon with his chin.

"I'm going to guess that's them, coming cross-country. If they haven't spotted us yet, it's probably just a matter of seconds before the damned drone relays some candid images of our escape."

The truck got to the end of the lane and turned left onto the main road.

Decker dropped into a crouch and rapped on the cab's rear window. One of the boys opened it, and he stuck his head inside.

"Are there any trails with a bit of cover you can take instead of staying on this road? You probably know the area better than the militia pukes. If we can drop out of sight, it'll slow them down, even though it'll take us longer to get to the river."

"There's an old track running along the edge of the Hartman spread just ahead. It goes right into his tree farm a few kilometers down. I think he's cut a few trails that run along the foot of the ridge."

"Do it."

He pulled his head out of the cab and rose to his feet, eyes automatically locking onto the rapidly growing black dots.

"They've changed course to follow us," Catlow said. "If they're riding standard militia skimmers, they'll be faster than we are."

Before Zack could reply, the truck slewed to the right and exchanged the broad road for a narrow track running between a row of windbreak trees on one side and head-high maize stalks on the other.

"The buggers want to take us alive," he said when they'd regained their balance. "They'll either try to cut us off..."

He looked over the cab at the fast approaching tree line, "...which won't happen quickly, or they'll try to disable our transport. The trick will be to make them keep their distance."

Something winked on the first militia skimmer and almost instantly, plasma streaked by the truck, incinerating a swath of maize stalks.

"That was a warning shot." He pulled out his blaster and steadied his arm on the tailgate. When he saw Catlow look at him as if he'd lost his mind, Zack grinned.

"I know I've got no chance of hitting them at this range, but at least they'll see us shooting back, which they won't expect."

He aimed slightly above the skimmer and pressed the trigger six times in rapid succession, sending a stream of plasma downrange. The effect was almost instantaneous. The vehicle's driver braked hard and slewed to one side, hoping to throw off his aim.

Decker fired again, still without a hope of hitting anything, but it was enough. Seconds later, low-hanging tree branches whipped over the truck's cab, forcing Catlow and Nolan down on their knees.

Zack holstered his blaster and turned around to sit with his back to the bed's high side.

"We're not out of the woods yet, to coin a phrase," he said, eyes twinkling with amusement at Catlow's theatrical groan, "but they can only come on one at a time and more importantly, right now they don't know where we're going."

"What about the drone?" Nolan asked.

"Crap." Decker slapped his forehead. "This is what I get for having too much fun with my gun."

He pulled out his sensor and turned it upwards.

"Yup." Zack nodded after a few moments. "It's up there. I can't tell whether it has a lock on us or not, but if it does and the militia have accurate maps, they'll eventually figure out where we're going to come out of the trees and wait for us there."

"I wish we had a way of warning the rest of the platoon without tipping our hand to the militia. We could have had them come down to meet us and add some firepower to the little we have," Catlow said, shaking his head with evident disappointment.

"Wouldn't help," Decker replied. "Right now, it's just a case of someone – us – tipping off the Takans. If they figure out that we're part of a platoon-sized patrol, they'll put everything they can into finding us and more importantly, finding out where our home base is."

"They're still on our tail," Nolan said, peering over the backboard. "I just got a quick glimpse of one of them before we turned the corner."

"If only we had some mines," Catlow muttered, "or even brought a grenade or two."

"Let me try something," Decker said, getting on his knees and peering back at the dark, earthen track running beneath a dense canopy. "Ask Takan to slow down."

He steadied his blaster on the tailgate again and picked a tree to the left of the trail. A thick stream of plasma stitched the trunk half a meter above the ground, eating through the wood. The tree came crashing down across the trail just as they turned out of sight.

"I doubt it'll stop the bastards for long, but let's get busy and put down some more," he told them. "Any little bit might make a difference."

The two rebels took up firing stances on either side of Zack and aimed their own blasters at the tree line.

"I hope this Hartman fellow is a firm independence supporter," Zack said after they stopped firing, "because I think we've just started a forest fire that'll torch a fair bit of his acreage."

"Is the drone still up there?" Nolan asked.

"Probably," Zack replied, pulling out his sensor. "It can't have missed our bit of target shooting." He paused. "Yep. It's there, still transmitting live telemetry, but it's off to the side, so maybe it still doesn't have a lock on us."

One of the boys poked his head through the rear window.

"Dad says to tell you we're about to run out of forest, and we're still about a kilometer from where the river comes out of the cut."

"Thanks." Decker nodded towards the cab. "Let's get set up to fire forward. If they don't know where we're going to come out by now, they're a lot dumber than any militia I've known."

"Damn drone. I wish I could shoot it down."

"Good luck. The thing might not be flying beyond weapons range, but with the stealthing it's got, we can't do much. Get ready."

The dark woodland trail quickly brightened and, moments later, they burst out into a field overrun by thick brambles and native giant ferns. Ahead of them, a militia skimmer blocked the way, its twin barrel plasma gun facing the onrushing truck.

Decker and the rebel soldiers opened fire, joined by Marnie and her two sons, hanging out the side windows. The militia troopers fired a warning burst over the truck, expecting Takan to slow down, but the farmer goosed his truck's fans and sped on.

Another militia skimmer appeared to their left and turned towards the tree line, intending to deny them any attempt at a withdrawal back into the forest.

The truck rose higher and began to sway when it lost some of the air cushion beneath its skirts. Unlike the sleek military vehicles trying to box them in, the agricultural truck lacked control vanes to concentrate the fans' output. Whether they'd clear the skimmer blocking the road ahead was questionable and even if they did, they'd expose the fans from beneath, giving the militia a chance to disable the truck.

Decker dropped down to yell a warning through the rear window when a stream of plasma connected with the car, at first creating smoking divots in the thin armor, then punching through the hull.

As soon as the last round vaporized what remained of the top hatch, Takan poured every available erg of power into his fans, clearing the top of the vehicle by millimeters. A heartbeat later, they were clear and headed towards the shadows at the base of the cliff where the Yangtze River spilled into the plains. The militia vehicle, its power plant damaged beyond repair, began to vomit thick black smoke.

Another burst of plasma came streaming down from the top of the cliff, targeting the second combat car, which prudently withdrew into the tree plantation.

Catlow began to laugh uncontrollably.

"That was Gareth. It had to be. No one can shoot that damn Shrehari gun like he can. They must have seen our escape from the farm and figured we'd need help."

Decker slapped the rebel platoon leader on the shoulder and grinned.

"Good troops, your people. Anyone who shows that kind of initiative when the boss is away will eventually beat the militia pukes."

They had little time to celebrate their narrow escape. Takan pulled the truck onto a rocky shelf overlooking the last bit of rapids and killed his fans.

"End of the line," he shouted, jumping from the cab with his bag and gun. "Everyone out."

Decker gave Catlow a nudge and winked.

"You're up, buddy. Time to rejoin the others and go home."

**

They met the rest of the platoon at the appointed rendezvous and simply kept walking. The militia would be trying to track down the machine gunner who was responsible for destroying a skimmer and killing its crew. After a four-hour hike, they stopped in a hollow beneath a rocky outcrop, invisible from above and impervious to sensors.

The farmers were used to hard labor and physical effort but were exhausted nonetheless by their narrow escape from imprisonment, interrogation, and almost certain death.

"I guess it's true then," Larn Takan said, accepting a mug of coffee from one of the troopers, "the militia have Mathias and got my name from him."

"More like *had* Mathias," Decker gently replied. "He probably didn't survive interrogation."

"Oh God. Kari." Marnie Takan hand flew to her mouth while her face dissolved into a mask of anguish. "If they capture her, she'll die."

Decker nodded slowly.

"Let's hope she got your message in time and took it seriously."

Marnie began to shake as she tried to hold back convulsive sobs. Larn put an arm around her shoulder and kissed the top of her head. He glanced at Zack with a pleading look that crystallized the idea the Marine had been nurturing for the last few hours.

He emptied his cup and got up to join Catlow and his squad leaders, who were discussing the next leg of their journey back to the ruined L'Taung fortress. They made room for him in their circle, and he squatted.

"I was just telling the guys how you saved our butts down there, Zack."

"It's nothing that anyone with good reflexes and a bit of common sense couldn't have done." He shrugged dismissively. "Can I have a word with you in private?"

"Sure." Catlow stood and took a few steps deeper into the shadows. "What's up?"

"The Takan daughter, Kari. After the militia fuck-up at the farm, they're going to analyze the video feed and realize she wasn't with us. They'll be trying to track her down, and it won't take long to find out she's in Iskellian. They find her, the girl will die, but not before spilling everything she knows, which is probably more than any of us figure. Sharp kids pick up a lot of stuff. I know I did when I was a teenager. That's not going to be good for anyone."

"Agreed." Catlow nodded. "May I assume that you've come up with an idea?"

Decker smiled.

"More than just an idea, actually. I've got a plan that'll kill a couple of birds at the same time, not least extracting the girl from under the militia's nose." He scratched his chin. "Though Verrill might not approve."

"Verrill's not here, and we can't risk using the radio at this point, so it's up to me. Remember your comment about showing initiative when the boss isn't available? It's one of those times," Catlow returned Zack's smile measure for measure. "So tell me."

**

"How?" Harend slumped back in his seat and sighed. "How did we manage to lose the best link we've ever had into the rebellion? How did they know we were about to close in on Takan?"

He squeezed the bridge of his nose with his thumb and forefinger. The daily meeting with Governor Cedeno had not gone well – again - and he didn't need another fiasco laid at his feet.

"Bad luck?" Kozlev shrugged. "Even if we have a leak somewhere, I doubt they'd have been able to mobilize an extraction force that quickly. This wasn't just another rebel cell taking care of its own; it was a full-fledged military operation. Rebel cells don't carry Shrehari-made machine guns around the countryside for shits and giggles. I'm sure this was a patrol sent to follow-up on news of Mathias' disappearance. Someone put two and two together, and figured out what was going to happen next, someone who's got a bit more background in this business than a bunch of farmers who headed for the hills with their hunting rifles.”

Harend nodded.

“Makes sense. We know they’ve been hiring specialists from off-world. Why not hire intelligence experts as well?”

“That’s what I think, but I’ll have my dogs sniff around to see if they find a rebel sympathizer in our ranks anyways. It’ll be good practice and who knows? But it’s not all bad news. The analysis of the drone’s telemetry did leave us one strand to pull on.” Kozlev’s cruel smile reappeared. “The Takan girl, Kari, wasn’t with them, which means she’s alone and vulnerable. I’ve made finding her the top priority for my people. We bring her in, she’ll give up enough to make it worth the effort.”

“Do we know where she might be?”

“Not yet, but I’ll find out soon enough. Takan called someone just before leaving the farm, almost certainly the daughter. He told her they’d be looking out for her, just like when she was a little girl, which could very well have been veiled instructions. All I have to do is dig into the family history and see if something correlates.”

“I’m sure you’ll enjoy doing that but try not to spend all of your time on her.”

“No.” She called up a still image from the video feed and tapped the screen with a perfectly manicured fingernail. “I also want to find out who that is.”

“Hmm?” Harend looked at her quizzically.

“One of these men is not like the others; the big one with the long hair. He seems to have been in charge of the extraction. Considering they all got away and we lost a squad of our best...”

“Another off-world specialist?”

“No doubt; he’s clearly a professional, not just an angry farmer. But from where?”

Kozlev stared at the indistinct image of Zack Decker taken by the drone.

“Who are you?” She whispered.

— TWENTY-FIVE —

"He what?" Verrill sounded incredulous. "How could you have let him go like that, Catlow?"

"If you'd seen how he handled things at Larn's farm, you'd have approved his plan too."

The platoon leader seemed unrepentant, and Talyn smiled. She knew how persuasive her partner could be when he set his mind on something.

"So not only is Kari Takan out in the wind, but we now have Zack Decker where he can be snatched by the militia and squeezed dry of everything he's learned about us since landing here." Verrill's face tightened into a mask of disgust. "Wonderful. Just bloody wonderful."

"Verrill?" Talyn stepped forward.

"What?" He snarled.

"Zack has been conditioned. He'll die in the interrogation chair before he says anything, so you don't have to worry on that account."

"So you say. And what do we know about you, eh? Diddly squat, just like your partner."

"I've been conditioned. There, now you know something about me you didn't a moment ago."

Her voice was soft, almost hypnotic and she smiled.

"Zack has a tendency to charge into situations sometimes, for the best of reasons, but I'll give the big boy his due: he always manages to walk out of the fire with a few trophies hanging from his gun belt. Hell, he brought two hundred former slave soldiers out of the Trans-Coalsack Sector on a starship he hijacked. If anyone can get the Takan girl out, he's your man."

"Fine, so Decker is our newest hero. What tells me you and he aren't plants for the government? Heck of a great excuse to high-tail it to Iskellian and give Harend the whole song and dance."

Verrill's anger seemed to be gaining steam.

"Fine." Talyn shrugged. "Believe what you will, but would the colonial government go to the extent of having its plants not only deliver four shiploads of weaponry to the rebellion but give some very expensive mercenaries a very expensive bloody nose? Not to speak of the damage they took during yesterday's little escapade? There are less costly ways of sneaking in a few spies, which I'll wager you know already since you've been doing it to them. Or at least I hope you've been doing it to them."

Corde chuckled.

"She's got you there. Governor Cedeno doesn't have the imagination to think of a double-blind scheme like that and Harend doesn't have access to the public purse at will; nor would he throw away some of his most elite troopers willy-nilly, by the way. He doesn't have enough depth in his organization to be wasteful, considering the quality of his current recruits."

The rebel leader took a deep breath and slowly released it.

"My apologies. I meant no offense."

"None was taken. I'd be wary of a man in your position who didn't have a healthy dose of paranoia."

"What now?"

"Now?" Talyn shrugged. "You carry on with whatever your campaign plan calls for. I'll keep helping Corde with the intelligence analysis, and Zack will do his thing. He'll succeed, in which case, we'll hear from him in due course, or fail, in which case we won't. There's nothing any of us can do, but as a favor to the Takans, I'd ask that you don't take it out on Catlow."

"I won't." Verrill shook his head ruefully, embarrassed by his outburst. "The commander on the ground needs to make his own decisions, absent direction from above, and Catlow did just that." He clapped the platoon leader on the shoulder and squeezed. "Go, get cleaned up, and have a beer. You did right, and none can fault your decisions."

"That sounded pretty cold-blooded," Corde said when the two women walked back to the control room. "If he fails, we won't," she quoted.

"Zack and I have an understanding," Talyn replied, "and mourning isn't part of it."

Corde shook her head while a burst of grim laughter escaped her throat.

"That sounded even more cold-blooded, but I get where you're coming from, though I'm not sure I understand where you're going."

"Some days, neither do I, honey, but it's a big universe, and anything can happen."

**

The burly man walking down Tianjin's main street towards the maglev station bore little resemblance to the one Rika Kozlev had fingered as an off-world professional. The long hair and beard were gone, and his clothes, though they retained a cut eerily similar to that seen on the video feed, were now the dull blue favored by laborers and farmers.

Evading militia pursuit had been easy for the former pathfinder. Most of them were city born and bred, and tramped through the bush like drunken Shrehari marines. He'd found a hiding spot well away from the rapids and watched the futile search while he transformed his appearance. After a shave and a trim, the quick application of his blaster's power pack to hidden electrodes on his garments had jolted the color pigments into a new alignment.

He walked with a deliberate slouch, to mask his bulk and avoid seeming like a man on a mission. It would take a sharp-eyed analyst to connect him with the events of the previous day, but they existed in every organization, and the Garonne militia wouldn't be much different, especially if there were a few key Celestan National Guard personnel seeded among them.

When he'd proposed going to Iskellian and retrieve Kari Takan, both her father and Catlow had initially been skeptical. He was new to the planet, didn't know anyone and wasn't in any database, something sure to get the authorities' attention if ever he were stopped. But all of those were advantages too, provided he didn't attract attention. Plus, as he'd reminded them, he had a lot of experience getting tough jobs done in unfamiliar places.

Marnie Takan had finally put down her foot and blessed Zack's offer. They'd given him all the information he'd need to track Kari down, what money they carried and their best wishes for success. He'd taken a few items that would be questionable at worst, innocuous at best, depending on who found them on his person or in his small pack, with the exception of his blaster and pathfinder blade, but there was no way he'd leave those behind. Anything else that might tie him to the rebellion was left with Catlow and his troopers.

After a night spent waiting for the militia to withdraw, he'd washed in the cold river and then walked down the trail like any local out for a spot of prospecting. No one he met along the way gave him so much as a second glance, though Decker suspected that for many it was because they knew that he wasn't a local, which could very well make him a member of the rebellion which so many of the colonists secretly supported.

When he turned the corner near the station, he almost bumped into a pair of troopers, a man, and a woman, wearing the dark green uniform and peaked caps of the militia. Both had holstered side arms, suspicious eyes, and a permanent sneer.

They stared at him briefly, as they did with every passer-by. Decker looked away, trying to seem fearful in their presence, something they'd likely enjoy and increased his pace. He thought he heard a soft snicker from the woman, but the call to stop and raise his hands over his head never came.

The maglev station was relatively new and built in a style evocative of a Celestan temple, no doubt to remind the locals of their colonial overlords. On the far side of the tracks, opposite the station, a more utilitarian building with broad loading docks dominated the horizon. It showed signs of heavy use, in contrast to the passenger side.

He stepped out of the bright morning sunshine and into the cool darkness of a vast hall that was almost devoid of life. Tianjin was by no means a village, but the station's interior decor was a bit much for an agricultural district capital.

Benches, strung together in seemingly random patterns, covered half of a shining granite floor. The almost antiseptic neatness was only broken here and there by the irregular shape of sleepers waiting for the next train, a pick up that would never come or a change in their fortunes that would lead to a more comfortable shelter.

A matte screen dominating the room announced the arrivals and departures for the day. The morning runs had already left and the first afternoon train was still hours away. Decker briefly debated going out again to find a tavern where he could while away the time with a meal and a cold drink, but decided to imitate the few people who had taken to a snooze instead of pacing.

He found the ticketing terminal, but when he touched the screen, it demanded that he place his identification chip against the reader. It was the first flaw in his plan.

Though he carried the Bill Whate credentials, he was pretty sure they'd be flagged as non-existent in the militia's database in a matter of seconds. After that, it would likely be a matter of moments before the two sneering specimens outside showed up.

He looked around for a human who might accept a few extra creds in exchange for ignoring the ID rules, but in vain.

Hitchhiking might be an alternative, but he didn't have time for such an unreliable mode of transport. Every hour that passed brought the militia closer to finding Kari.

A bright reflection through the bay windows trackside caught his attention, and he found himself staring at a string of shiny, windowless cubes, like a giant metallic caterpillar minus the legs, floating by on the single rail.

It was a freight consist arriving from Iskellian, and that meant another, possibly the same, would leave Tianjin within a few hours. If he could find a way aboard without being seen, he'd be able to bypass any identity check.

After a final look around the hall, to make sure no one was paying him attention, he left the station and retraced his steps to find the road that led to the freight terminal. The two militia troopers had left their corner to go sneer at passing colonists from another vantage point, and he quickly found himself looking at a closed gate behind which he could see the immense, low-roofed transfer shed. The only way in without triggering alarms would have to be on a vehicle entering to pick up whatever the incoming train had carried.

Another flaw in his plan. If he'd had local knowledge, which he didn't, as Takan and Catlow had pointed out, he might have found a sympathizer willing not only to let him into the freight compound but help him on the next train out of Tianjin.

"You alright, mate?"

He was startled by a gruff voice behind him and turned, his hand almost reaching for the hidden blaster. It was a bad sign that he hadn't heard the gray-bearded, stocky man in worn work clothes approach.

"Sure." Decker forced himself to relax.

The man chuckled.

"I bet you're wondering how to get in there," he nodded at the gate, "and hop a freight to Iskellian."

"What makes you think that?"

"No other reason for a stranger to come down this alley." When he saw Decker's face tighten, he raised a placating hand and smiled. "You wouldn't be the first looking to avoid the militia's security measures, mate, and I doubt you'll be the last. Plenty of folks hate the greenbottles and like nothing more than to tweak their bloody noses."

"And you're one of them."

"Aye. I'll not give you my name if you don't mind, and I won't ask for yours, but if you're looking to hitch a ride, I'll close my eyes and count to ten after you follow me through the gate. Fair enough?"

"You work at the terminal?" Decker asked, falling into step with the older man.

"Part-time, like when a consist comes in. One a day doesn't make for a full-time job. It takes an hour to unload, an hour to load and back it goes. And I go back to my other trade."

He touched a small panel to one side of the gate, and just like that, Zack was in.

"You might as well give me a hand while you're at it," the man said once they were inside the shed. "A big buck like you will look out of place sitting around grabbing his ass while I work.

"Sure," Decker grinned at his newfound co-conspirator. "Tell me what and where."

"Good man." He thumped the Marine's thick biceps with a closed fist.

It took just under an hour to off-load farming supplies and not much more than that to fill the cars up again. As he was about to guide the last pallet aboard, the old man stuck out his hand.

"This is where we part. You stay in the car when the loader comes back out. The trip shouldn't take more than three or four hours. Freight doesn't move as fast as the passenger runs, but it still moves faster than your legs can. When you feel it coming to a stop, crack the door open and make sure no greenbottles are pestering my friends at the Iskellian terminal. If it's clear, you just walk out with the load in your car as if you belonged there. The guys will see you out the gate and on your way. If you spot greenbottles, you'll have to escape on your own."

"Got it. Thanks."

"Good luck, mate." He dropped his voice and quickly glanced around. "I don't know what you're up to, but if it's to fuck with the governor and his pets, Godspeed to you. Garonne is owed its independence."

"I'll see what I can do to help that along."

Decker sketched a brief salute and vanished into the shining cube. The door slammed shut behind him, and he found a spot hidden behind a few pallets of produce to stretch out. Like every good infantryman, he knew how to take a nap anywhere, whenever he had the chance.

**

The militia recruiting sergeant looked up from his terminal and examined Steiger again, this time with a real interest in his eyes.

"Twenty years in the Commonwealth Army, eh? What brings you to the hind end of nothing?"

Steiger shrugged.

"After I finished my hitch, I got wanderlust. When I ran out of money, the pricks who were supposed to take me to Cimmeria kicked me off on Garonne without so much as a goodbye kiss. Saw the advert and here I am. I figure I can work my old trade for a while and rebuild the savings. Maybe I'll end up liking this place enough to stick around. I doubt it, but the universe is full of miracles."

He nodded, glad that she'd given him a reason he could understand, unlike the bullshit so many of them spewed when they walked through his doors. A former professional with a clean service record was worth her weight in rare metals these days, and she even had the kind of credentials that would attract the attention of that scary bitch Kozlev.

"You've come to the right place. We can always use people with time in one of the regular services. What we'll do now is go through the enlistment conditions and if you're okay with signing them, I'll have the training battalion check you out to make sure your service record isn't a load of excrement. Then the colonel will decide whether you're in or not and at what rank. We do give credit for folks who've worn stripes before."

"Sounds like a better plan than the one I had when I landed here with a change of panties and an old toothbrush."

She gave him a radiant smile.

"All right, then." He slipped a tablet across the desk. "Read this. If you have any questions at all, ask. I'll call the training sergeant major in the meantime and have him review your record so he can prepare."

**

"Sir?"

The rap of knuckles on the doorframe was loud in the hushed atmosphere of naval intelligence headquarters.

Captain Kos Ulrich, director of special operations, finished the paragraph he was reading and then looked up at his chief of staff.

"I assume you have news?"

Commander Manfred Yang knew better than to disturb his boss for trivialities, especially when he'd just begun digesting the latest report on growing Coalition interference in Fleet activities.

"Indeed. We intercepted a report to the Avalon head office from its Rim Sector division. A ship corresponding to the ex-*Syrah* broke through the blockade Avalon had been contracted to maintain around Garonne, after giving two of their sloops enough damage to trigger extra costs for the Celeste government. The three freighters that landed along with said ship took off again within hours and made a clean getaway, but the ex-*Syrah* has disappeared on the surface. Apparently they took out most of the satellites over the colony to stymie any attempt to search for them."

"Sounds like Talyn and Decker alright." A faint smile appeared on Ulrich's narrow lips. "I suppose that means they decided they'd find the answers on the rebellion end rather than going upstream."

"Or they had an unexpected opportunity and went with it."

Ulrich removed his reading glasses and considered his subordinate for a few seconds. He'd learned to recognize Yang's moods after so many years working together.

"Okay, Manny, what's bothering you?"

"I'm concerned that they might get directly involved instead of sticking to their proper intelligence gathering role, sir," Yang replied. "I've never hidden my opinion that Decker's a loose cannon with a savior complex and unsuited for our kind of work. This time, I'm afraid Hera might go along with his impulsiveness just for the heck of it. He's rubbing off on her, and I don't just mean in the biblical sense."

"Perhaps." Ulrich sat back and reflected on Yang's words. "But perhaps this is the kind of situation where the action part of our mandate might be appropriate as well. Hera's the commanding officer on the spot, and since I can't just send her orders from on high, I'll have to trust that she'll use her initiative for the greater good. Do we have any other assets nearby?"

"I'll have to double check the roster, but I don't think so."

"See if you can get another set of eyes on Garonne and warn Special Operations Command that we might need their help."

"For an extraction?"

"Or an intervention." Ulrich's faint smile returned. "Your loose cannon might need backup from his erstwhile comrades. If they have a ship available and can pre-position it near Garonne within the next few weeks, that would be helpful."

"Will do, sir."

Commander Yang vanished into his office, leaving the head of the Fleet's black ops group to stare at a blank wall, lost in thought. After a few minutes, he shook himself back to reality and picked up his tablet to resume reading the intelligence digest.

Whatever Talyn and Decker were planning, there was nothing he could do about it.

— TWENTY-SIX —

Garonne's sun had dropped low enough to kiss the horizon by the time the maglev from Tianjin slowed to a walking pace and entered the Iskellian docks area, a few kilometers upstream of where the Yangtze River widened before emptying into the Gulf of Sorrows.

Decker opened the door just a crack, as the bearded independence supporter had told him to do, and looked out at a scene of barely organized chaos seemingly frozen at the end of the working day.

Shiny, caterpillar-like consists sat motionless on various sidings while barges wallowed in the muddy water. A few figures moved about, but none of them wore the dark green of militia troopers.

A concrete loading dock attached to a shed even bigger than the one in Tianjin suddenly filled his narrow field of vision and the maglev came to a gentle halt.

There was a warning shout, and then the wagon doors slammed open in unison, letting in the scent of brackish water, lubricants, and honest sweat. He heard the rattle of automated loaders moving about and soon enough one of the machines entered his car to pick up a pallet. As the robotic stevedore backed out, he followed it onto the dock, trying to look like he belonged there.

A quick scan of the area showed he was the only carbon-based life from in sight, so he ambled towards the open sliding door and entered the shed.

Inside, he saw a man sitting at a control panel, similar to the one he'd seen in Tianjin and decided to take a chance that the stevedore was a kindred spirit to the one who'd smuggled him onto the maglev.

He was. The man pointed at a chair near his station, explicitly ordering him to sit. Zack obeyed and spent the next half hour or so watching a small army of automated loaders shift pallet after pallet of produce into various sections of the shed, ready for pick up.

When the dance finally ended, the little machines lined up to one side and fell silent. The man got up and stuck out his hand. He could have been a younger relative of his Tianjin colleague.

"Welcome, stranger. No names given and none taken, right?"

"Right." Decker nodded.

"You know where you're going?"

"Not really. I just need a place to eat and a bed for a few hours, preferably where the militia won't bother me."

"I can help you with that. Come on." He headed for the far side of the shed, opposite from the loading dock. "The bastards were through here earlier today so they won't be back until morning, though some of them get bored enough to harass honest folk on their way home after work, so I hope you have valid ID."

"I've got ID," Decker confirmed, deciding to omit the fact that it might not pass muster.

The man led him to a small personal skimmer and invited him to take a seat. When they were both strapped in, he switched the power cells on and gunned his fans, slewing the small car around and through the yard's main gate.

Iskellian had none of the charm its name might evoke. A collection of drab buildings, some rising high above their neighbors, clustered along the river and sprawled inland on both banks. They passed through an old section on the outskirts that seemed to date back to early days of the colony but still seemed inhabited.

The man didn't speak while he drove, but his face showed relief once they'd left the slums for a more respectable section of town.

"Nasty place?" Decker asked, nodding towards the rear of the vehicle.

"You have no idea, friend. The worst of what Celeste dumps on us lives in that area. And to think the damned militia recruits there too. When I was a boy, Iskellian was a beautiful place to live. Now? If I had the money to emigrate, I'd seriously consider it."

They crossed the core of the city and emerged on the other side, in a neighborhood that seemed just as old as the slum but had been maintained and nurtured with loving care.

The man pulled into a small lot beside a two-story building with a discreet sign advertising rooms for rent and home-cooked meals.

"The owner's a friend. She knows the score so you can trust her. Remember, no names given and none taken." He held out his hand. "Good luck in your endeavors, my friend. May we meet again when Garonne is free."

"Thanks for your help."

He waved Decker's gratitude away.

"I do what little I can."

Zack watched the little skimmer fade in the distance, then he opened the door of the inn, and a delicious aroma of roasting meat washed over him. His stomach, never one to stay quiet at the most inconvenient moments, growled loudly. A peal of delighted laughter came from the grandmotherly woman sitting behind a wooden counter.

"Come in, come in. I hear the sounds of a man who's just finished a long voyage. There's beefalo in the oven, a warm bed upstairs and no questions asked. I happen to know the gentleman who drove you here, so you're among friends."

An hour and a meal later, Decker was staring out his room's window at the soft lights of Iskellian. A gentle fog had risen the moment the sun vanished, fed by the waters of the gulf and the great central ocean beyond, and it blurred the outlines of everything in sight, even the harsh shapes of the gray high-rise buildings downtown.

He was still surprised that he'd stumbled into the informal network of independence supporters, or to be more accurate, he felt both surprised and gratified that the network had scooped him up so quickly after recognizing him as one of theirs.

In his experience, honed by putting down more than one colonial brush war, by the time ordinary colonists had developed such a fine discernment, they'd already traveled far down the road to violent rebellion. Eventually, a single spark would be enough to blow away the veneer of civilization.

The roast beefalo, accompanied by a generous helping of vegetables, had filled the vast, empty space left by a long day without a single bite to eat. He'd accepted a bottle of the local beer, which was tasty in its own way, but only one. He needed to rest, but by the time first light rolled around, the search for Kari Takan would be on.

It had been almost two days since they'd extracted the family from under the militia's nose, two days during which the enemy would have analyzed, investigated and hunted. The only advantage he had was in knowing where the girl might be hiding, with no guarantee that she'd ever gone there, or if she had that she'd stayed there.

**

"Okay, Steiger," Bleyd, the militia's training sergeant major, tossed her a towel, "you know your shit, and I'll gladly sign off on your application. Wipe down because we're done."

"Thanks."

"You got a place to stay tonight?"

"Sure. There's a nice bench in the park with my name on it."

"Bullshit." Bleyd laughed. "I'm recommending the colonel enlist you as a non-com, and that'll be enough to see you in a uniform by tomorrow, so you might as well take a bunk in the transient quarters and a meal in the chow hall."

He winked at her.

"We old pros need to stick together. There's not that many of us around."

"Oh?" She dropped the now damp towel in a bin set aside for that purpose.

"Sure, the colonel's a regular from the Celeste National Guard, so is Captain Kozlev and a couple of the other officers, but among the non-coms there aren't many of us with who've done a full hitch somewhere else, and I'm counting the mercs in that. It's why I figure you'll be offered a probationary sergeant's stripes at a minimum."

He shrugged his uniform tunic on and picked up his cap.

"Let's go eat."

The mess facilities weren't any different from those she'd seen all over the Commonwealth. They ate in the section reserved for non-coms after Bleyd had introduced her to his friends from the training and headquarters battalions.

She got the curious glances she'd expected, but the questions wouldn't start until she was wearing a uniform, their uniform. Before then, she was a tolerated guest and allowed among them only because Bleyd was near the top of the militia non-com food chain.

The training sergeant major spotted her a beer at the sergeant's mess after supper and gave her a high-level sketch of the militia's organization, equipment, and operations, seemingly confident that she'd be one of them within the next twenty-four hours.

He was right.

When she showed up at the mess hall early the next morning, she was intercepted by the recruiting sergeant who told her to report to the main headquarters building by oh-seven-hundred.

**

"Decker's in Iskellian," Corde announced over breakfast. "Our cell in the capital reported that the network helped a ghost, a man who doesn't exist in the militia database, down the pipeline from Tianjin yesterday."

"A ghost?" Talyn smiled. "You have people inside the militia then?"

"A few, mostly civilian clerical workers," Verrill replied. "They don't trust locals with anything more, but even the little bit we get is helpful."

He briefly considered mentioning Steiger's attempt to infiltrate the militia but then thought better of it. He was the only one to know, and it would have to stay that way for now.

"Why is it that I get the feeling support for independence among the average colonists has crossed the line from purely political to direct action?" Talyn asked.

"Because it has," Verrill replied around a mouthful of fruit. "More and more people are fed up with the daily indignities, the fear of semi-feral deportees, and the lack of a voice when it comes to Garonne's future – the usual reasons, so they try to fight back however they can. A few, those who manage to ensure their families' safety, join us, but most help in small ways, like getting your partner to Iskellian unnoticed, collecting intelligence, no matter how innocuous or seemingly unimportant. There are literally tens of thousands of active sympathizers out there on top of hundreds of thousands who lack the courage or the opportunity to become active."

"Is the government aware that it runs so deep?"

"Perhaps a few in the militia's top leadership and the governor's staff have begun to notice they're riding a tiger, but considering human nature, most are ignoring the warning signs."

"Too bad." Talyn drained her coffee mug. "There's still time to pull out of the death spiral, but from all I've seen so far, nothing short of allowing full independence without pre-conditions is going to do the trick. When a society is that angry with its government, it only takes one spark to trigger a civil war. Once that happens, it'll get ugly so fast that the Senate will have no choice but to send in the Marines."

"You seem well versed in these matters, Hera," Verrill remarked, an eyebrow raised in question.

"As Zack likes to say, this isn't my first dance, and I like to spend my spare time reading history, because where humans are concerned, there's nothing new under whatever sun they happen to live."

The rebel leader looked at her with undisguised curiosity.

"Who are you? I mean, really? You're not just some bored rich lady looking for adventure in her own starship. Corde tells me you've been invaluable in revisiting some of the intel we didn't know how to interpret."

"Believe what you want," she replied with a small smile, "but I am wealthy, eccentric and living the life of a hired gun, analyst, shipper and whatever else sounds like fun."

"Suit yourself," Verrill replied, smiling back. "I can't say I'm not happy Tran found you two, but you'll allow me some curiosity at why you've thrown your lot in with us."

"But of course. Though I warn you, I enjoy being a woman of mystery," her smile became overtly seductive, "which means I'll enjoy keeping you wondering."

**

Decker sat on a worn park bench and studied the government compound across the sluggish river. It was set well back from the water's edge and surrounded by a double defensive ring that tried to look innocuous and failed. Even in the bright morning sunshine, it exuded an oppressive atmosphere.

He picked out the various buildings based on the map he'd been shown by Catlow: the governor's mansion, the central administration blocks, the militia headquarters, and Iskellian garrison barracks, the prison, and the power plant.

He knew that security cameras were recording him, but so was everyone else using the park, be it the homeless, joggers, kids skipping school or deportees looking for an easy mark. A trio of them showed some interest in the lone man sitting apart from everyone else, but the moment he met the ringleader's eyes, they moved away with commendable speed.

Sitting here wasn't going to lead him to Kari, but spending some time eyeballing the opposition's strongpoint wouldn't be wasted in the long run, and he had to pass near it to get to the first place she might be hiding anyway.

Two militia troopers with slung carbines came down a gravel path winding its way through thick native vegetation, their eyes darting from person to person, but not in the way of cops looking for someone specific.

Although they were just a regular foot patrol, Decker took their arrival as the signal that it was time to move on. He stood up slowly, stretched, and swung his small pack over his shoulder.

He'd dropped a healthy heap of cred chips on the inn's counter after wolfing down a substantial breakfast, but the old woman running the place pushed most of them back at him with the remark that she only needed to cover the cost of groceries when it came to a 'friend.' She hadn't even blinked at his changed appearance – it wasn't dramatic, but enough to fool the casual eye.

The walk into town and towards the nearest bridge over the Yangtze River had taken him the better part of an hour. As he passed through downtown he had mentally recorded everything he saw, from the state of the buildings, the businesses, the roads and other public works to the mood of the population and the prevalence of loafers, many of whom wore what probably passed for gang colors on Celeste.

Iskellian was not a happy city. It didn't feel as bad as Port Premier on Hispaniola in the months leading up to the bloodiest outburst of colonial violence the Commonwealth had seen in over a hundred years, but Decker figured it was probably on the same trajectory.

He'd witnessed a militia patrol roughing up a civilian but had no idea what the man had done to offend the local law and order. Everyone in the general vicinity of the event did their best to scurry away, eyes avoiding all contact with anyone else.

Decker had to suppress his inclination to intervene, even if it was just in the name of fairness. Two armed cops taking on one unarmed civilian stank in his book, but he just walked on.

The militia troopers patrolling the riverside park examined him in the same way they examined everyone else while he headed towards the bridge looking like a man without a single care in the world. So far, so good. The authorities hadn't issued an all-points bulletin for a large man vaguely similar to his current appearance; otherwise, he'd have been stopped for an ID check.

He crossed the river a kilometer or so upstream of the government precinct and got a good view of it from another angle. Whoever had sited the small city within a city had made sure all approaches were open, flat, and difficult to cross under fire. As a professional, Decker approved; as a would-be insurgent, he began to look for ways of storming the place.

**

"Captain, the physiometric analysis has come up with a couple of possibles for the man that led the Takan extraction the other day."

Rika Kozlev crossed the room to stand behind her lead investigator, another Celeste National Guard transplant recruited by Colonel Harend to stiffen the militia.

Images of strongly built males aged thirty to sixty filled the large screen. They were culled from surveillance cameras all over the settlement area and compared to the few useful video captures they had of the burly, longhaired professional who cost them a snatch team and the chance to move up the rebels' chain of command.

Though the variation in hairstyle and color, facial features, and the degree of intelligence reflected in their eyes was vast, they all shared a similar physique and musculature, and to a lesser extent, posture and way of moving.

"Doesn't exactly narrow it down," the analyst said, by way of apology.

"Have you run repeats?"

"I'm doing that right now, but the number of variables is still very high."

"All right. There's no way around the limitations of the machine, is there?" Kozlev stared at the succession of stills parading across the screen when one attracted her attention.

"Stop," she ordered. "Enlarge number one-oh-five. Where was it taken?"

The analyst turned to a second console and entered a search string. The results came up almost immediately.

"The Tianjin station's ticket vending unit. He started the process to buy passage to Iskellian but then walked away when the machine asked for his ID."

"He's our man," she said, her voice husky with sudden excitement. "Look at his eyes. Those are the eyes of a pro. Have the program concentrate on this one. I'll wager he found a way to get here, which means we've got more of him somewhere in the database. If I'm right, he'll be a prize that will make our failure to take Larn Takan look like a mere trifle."

— TWENTY-SEVEN —

"Steiger, is it?" Colonel Cen Harend asked, examining the scar-faced woman standing at attention in front of his desk. She was wearing a crisp new militia uniform with a staff sergeant's stripes.

"Yes, sir. Miko Steiger."

"At ease, sergeant. I've read your service record, and Sergeant Major Bleyd confirms that you actually know what it says you know. As you might expect, the addition of a Commonwealth Armed Services veteran to our organization is very welcome."

Harend got up and rounded his desk, heading for a three-dimensional map projection floating over a large table. He motioned Steiger to join him.

"Do you have any counter-insurgency experience, sergeant?"

"A bit, sir. I was part of the division that reinforced the Marines on Hispaniola."

Harend grimaced.

"Then you've seen the worst kind. You have my sympathies. What do you know about the situation on Garonne?"

She shrugged.

"Not all that much. A bunch of farmers unhappy with the home world wanted level three status and independence, and when they didn't get it, they headed for the hills to play guerrilla."

"A good high-level summary," Harend smiled briefly. "But my people think the 'playing' part of the guerrilla operations is pretty much over. Off-world weapons have been flowing in, as have advisers and the rebels, the Garonne Independence Movement as they call themselves, have begun to step up their activities."

He pointed at the map.

"For example, just last night, a sizeable force, almost a full company's worth, struck one of our garrisons in Holback, two hundred kilometers north of here. We suffered almost thirty casualties, a third of them killed in action to an unknown number on their side. Our installations were expertly destroyed. This leaves a gap in our ability to police the Holback district until we can rebuild the surveillance apparatus and reinforce the garrison. The night before, the same thing happened in Oshin, three hundred fifty kilometers south of Iskellian."

Steiger nodded.

"That's definitely a step up from a couple of farmers annoying the odd patrol, sir."

"A few weeks ago, they managed to introduce something into the water supply of a Zeli resort favored by citizens supporting union with Celeste." He pointed out the oceanfront town on the map. "Several hundred got violently ill though thankfully no one died, but it was a clear warning that they have the ability to attack us through non-conventional means."

When she didn't react, he continued.

"Then, a few days ago, a group of rebels managed to rescue one of their cell leaders out from under the nose of a very highly trained and capable snatch team about to take him and his family into custody. We lost a half-dozen of our best troopers. I'd say play time is long gone, don't you sergeant?"

"Agreed, sir."

"I wanted you to understand what we're up against and the trajectory it seems to be taking. That's why I'm pleased to have a former regular non-com in my ranks. The troops aren't always of the best quality, but they're not afraid to knock heads or teach separatists an object lesson. They do need solid leadership to make sure the head knocking doesn't turn into something that may attract the kind of off-world attention the governor doesn't want."

"Understood, sir." Steiger nodded. She felt a presence behind her and was about to look back when Harend smiled at someone over her shoulder.

"Ah, Rika, join us and meet the newest recruit to our non-com cadre." He waved her into his office.

"So this is Miko Steiger, former Army command sergeant," Kozlev said after examining the mercenary from head to toe with eyes so cold Steiger had to repress a shiver. "Sergeant Major Bleyd helpfully provided me with a copy of her service record and his evaluation. A lucky find for the recruiting office, no? I understand you have field-level counter-intelligence experience, Steiger."

"Yes, sir. The mess on Hispaniola was big enough that they pulled a lot of us into special units to fight the insurgents on their own turf."

"Did you enjoy the work?" Kozlev asked, an icy smile briefly lighting up her narrow face.

Steiger lifted her shoulder in half shrug.

"It was a job that needed to be done, and the concept worked pretty well in our division's area of operations. Not without some issues, mind you, but the insurgents weren't exactly in a position to complain about real or imagined breaches of the Rules."

"Squeamish?" The smile returned for another brief visit.

"Not particularly, sir."

Kozlev turned to her superior.

"I'm not sure what you'd intended for our new recruit, but I'd like to see if she has skills I might find useful."

"By all means, Captain. She's yours until you decide otherwise."

He dismissed them with a wave that might have been a kind of salute and the two women left.

"So, Miko Steiger," Kozlev glanced up at the taller mercenary, "if I send your name, picture and vitals to the Armed Services personnel office for a background check, what do you think will come back?"

"A demand that you justify your request," Steiger replied without missing a beat. "They're not in the habit of doling that information out willy-nilly."

Kozlev's brief burst of laughter sounded eerily like a bark to Steiger's ears.

"Fair enough. Colonel Harend told you about the rebel cell leader slipping through our fingers the other day?"

"Yes."

"It was a professional job, run by a pro. The guerrilla wannabes hiding in the hills wouldn't have been able to pull it off, and that means an off-world pro. We're hunting for him right now. So tell me, Miko Steiger, what are the chances of two off-world pros, you and the man in question, showing up on Garonne almost at the same time?"

"Pretty good, actually," she replied without hesitation. "Word must be getting around that things are heating up around here, and that's bound to attract every freelancer along the Rim looking for a contract."

"And you're one of those freelancers."

"Sure. When I run out of funds. When I'm flush, I enjoy life."

"You're not much on using military courtesies, like 'sir' are you?"

"Seeing that you're not much on them either, such as calling me 'sergeant' I figured you weren't one of those chickenshit officers who infest most national guards." A slight pause. "Sir."

This time, Kozlev's laughter sounded genuine.

"I might actually begin to like you, *Sergeant* Steiger. Perhaps I should show you what we have on the man behind the extraction. Maybe you'll be able to identify a fellow freelancer you've run across at some point in your career."

**

Although he would have liked to see all four sides of the government precinct, Decker figured that the more their security system saw his face, the more they'd wonder why some backcountry hick was paying so much attention to something that should intimidate him. Therefore, without so much as a last glance over his shoulder, he walked away from the riverfront and eventually entered an area of shops and restaurants.

Since it wasn't quite midday yet, passers-by were relatively sparse, but all those in uniform carried a sidearm of some kind and even here, in the shadow of their own garrison, looked askance at any civilian, including him.

Decker could sense unease among them, even though he didn't know about the attacks on the Holback and Oshin garrisons, but he kept on walking and soon left them behind.

The stores and restaurants petered out the further he got from the rivers, replaced by tenements, then warehouses and then another of the ubiquitous slums.

Where he'd slouched before, to disguise his bulk and appear unthreatening to militia and civilians alike, he now squared his shoulders and walked with the easy gait of a natural-born killer. Most of the slum dwellers looked away when he tried to meet their eyes, unwilling to risk offending a man who probably could and would dispense violence at will.

A small group, three men and two women standing at the mouth of an alley, turned to watch his approach, calculating the risk-reward balance of mugging a lone pedestrian who looked like he wasn't much wealthier than they were.

As he got closer, Decker smiled and gave them a brief glimpse of his blaster, to discourage any notion that he was an easy mark. There was little doubt that he'd be able to kick them down the alley, and then some until they screamed for mercy, but that might attract attention he couldn't afford.

Thankfully, they were smart enough to look away once they'd seen the large weapon. Their postures now signaled a non-threatening disinterest, just like any semi-feral beings with enough cunning to understand danger when it manifests itself. One of the women, however, more curious than fearful, gave him a quick glance, and he winked at her. Soon, he passed the last of the run down squats beyond which he could see his destination.

Larn Takan had given him an address and some directions. He'd failed to describe what stood at that particular location and why it could serve as his daughter Kari's salvation, but one look at the intricate carving over a door cut into a high stone wall was enough to make him groan.

His last run-in with the Sisterhood of the Void hadn't ended well, and somehow he had the feeling this one wouldn't either, yet he still had to enter and politely enquire about Kari, with the full expectation that they would throw him out of their cloister the moment he started speaking.

The Sisters didn't have much truck with males and held fornication in very low regard. They liked weapons and soldiers even less. He knew from bitter experience that trying to hide who and what he was would only make things worse.

Decker walked around the block once, to steady his nerves and calm the churning in his stomach, then he lifted a latch on the gate leading to the only part of the cloister open to visitors and stepped onto hallowed ground, expecting lightning to strike him down at any moment.

**

"Take a look at these images," Rika Kozlev said after motioning Steiger to sit at an empty terminal, "and tell me if anyone strikes a chord."

"Yes, sir."

While the pictures slowly passed across the screen, Kozlev kept her eyes on Steiger's face. It unnerved the mercenary, not only because the captain exuded such a strong predatory aura but also because Steiger knew about the old interrogator's trick.

She doubted she'd be able to hide even the smallest sign of recognition, such as a tic, a flicker of the eyes or something else that would be subtle but very visible to someone who knew what she was looking for.

Then it struck her that this was really a loyalty test. Kozlev already had her suspect identified and wanted nothing more than a quick confirmation. But if Steiger failed to finger Decker, she'd be the next contestant in a game of probe the merc.

Sorry, Zack, she thought. *Captain She-Wolf will see something in my face the moment your ugly mug appears, so in the interests of my continued ability to infiltrate the militia, I'll have to give you up. I'm sure you can take care of yourself, big boy.*

And then it happened – the image from the Tianjin station popped up. He looked different from the last time she'd seen him, but it was unmistakably Decker.

"Him," she said nodding at the screen. "He's changed his looks, but I'm sure he's a freelancer I've met in the past."

"Name?"

"He called himself Mark Skeen at the time, but that wasn't his real name. He's the kind who coasts through life on a dozen different identities."

"Mark Skeen." Kozlev nodded. "Of course, he'll have ditched that name by now. Still, I'm glad you were able to help me confirm that the rebels have hired a pro. They're upping the stakes, but then we'd already figured that out. Any idea how expensive this guy is?"

"Not really, sir. We didn't compare pay rates, but I'd wager that he doesn't come cheap at all."

Kozlev put her hand on Steiger's shoulder and squeezed.

"How good are you at the ancient art of interrogation?"

"Why?"

"Why, *sir*? Let's not slip back into discourtesy, sergeant. And to answer your question, we have a recalcitrant customer in the basement who claims he knows nothing of the independence movement, but I don't believe him. Maybe you can show me how you'd do it."

**

"I'm impressed." Corde smiled at Talyn, and then pushed back her chair to stand and stretch. "You managed to squeeze stuff out of the raw data we'd all overlooked. It'll really help fine-tune our planning for the next couple of operations."

"Glad to be of service. While my partner is out chasing teenaged girls, it gives me something useful to do."

"Are you sure you've never worked in intelligence?"

Talyn laughed.

"Not even for a second. But getting rich enough to roam across the galaxy in your own pocket sloop requires pretty much the same mindset."

Corde considered her statement for a brief moment and then nodded.

"That does make sense."

"Of course," Talyn said with a slight smile, "I also get a kick out of digging through databases and coming up with linkages that no one else sees. It's a hobby that drives Zack crazy, but he can't argue with the fact that we remain gainfully employed nearly all the time. If you'd like to continue using me as a fresh set of eyes..."

"I'll talk to Verrill about how deep he'd want you to go. You understand that there are things we don't share with some of the Movement's inner circle, let alone outsiders, no matter how well intentioned."

"Of course. I'd expect nothing less." She inclined her head briefly before standing up and following Corde to the mess hall. "In the meantime, I think I'll accept a meal that I don't have to analyze before we continue. My stomach is threatening to shut my brain down. One of the bad habits I picked up from my partner, sadly."

Corde chuckled.

"I think the chef is trying a variation on the usual game stew for lunch. We might have to provide him with an after-action report."

"I'll let you deal with that. I've learned to never annoy a man who has access to sharp blades."

"Decker?"

"So he's shown you his dagger. Yeah, him too." Talyn smirked.

When they'd gone through the chow line, Verrill waved them over to join him and Larn Takan.

"How goes the analyzing?" He asked Talyn once she was seated.

"I've squeezed what I could out of the data Corde gave me. If there's anything else useful left, it would likely need Fleet intelligence's finest."

"Perhaps we can give Hera a few more chunks," the rebel army's second-in-command suggested. "Until Zack returns, she doesn't have much else to do, and she is willing to go through the mind-numbing stuff none of my folks want to tackle."

Verrill examined Talyn with eyes that seem to search for chinks in her cover and figure out whether she could be trusted.

"Sure," he finally said. "Everyone around here should be allowed to work for their keep. You know what I consider too sensitive for anyone but the inner circle, Corde, so go ahead, and have Hera delve into other areas. It may be some time before her partner's back."

"Speaking of which," Talyn said after savoring a mouthful of stew, "any news on my wayward boy?"

"Nothing." Verrill shook his head.

"By now he should have reached the Sisterhood of the Void," Larn Takan said. "If my daughter's taken refuge there, we might see them back soon."

At the mention of the Sisterhood, Talyn choked and then began coughing, her face turning a bright shade of red. By the time she'd recovered her composure, everyone in the hall was looking at her, Corde wondering whether she should have called the duty medic.

"Are you telling me you sent Zack to a Sisterhood of the Void cloister?" Talyn asked in a strangled voice.

"Yes." Takan frowned in puzzlement at the offworlder's reaction. "Is there a problem?"

"There might be." Her voice sounded strangled and she fought off another urge to cough. "You see, Zack is unafraid most of the time. Jumping out of a perfectly good shuttle in the upper atmosphere to land on some scumbag's head after spending an hour as a human kite requires a pretty defective sense of fear. But there is one thing that's guaranteed to send him into a spiral of dread, and that's the Sisterhood of the Void."

"Why?"

"I have no idea, Ser Takan. It's one of the things from his past that he refuses to discuss. All I know is that the Sisters terrify him."

"Will he not see if they have Kari then?" The farmer sounded deeply worried.

"You needn't be concerned; he'll carry out his mission," she replied without hesitation, "even if it leaves him gibbering in terror once it's over, but he'll hate every moment of it."

"Do you have issues with the Sisterhood, sera?" Takan asked.

An ironic smile lit up Talyn's face. "Of course not. I'm a woman."

— TWENTY-EIGHT —

A flagstone path, bordered on both sides by high, thorny bushes led to a small stone annex grafted onto the side of the cloister. Its interior felt bare, cold, and uninviting.

Though the Garonne colony was still young, its age not yet measured in centuries, the cloister bathed in the aura of permanence that comes from very long tenancy.

Decker knew the stones hid a door somewhere along one of the walls, but he also knew that to search for it would doom his quest before he even had the chance to speak.

After a brief survey of his surroundings, he took up a relaxed stance three paces from a shoulder-height grille covering an opening barely big enough for a human head. He crossed his hands in the small of his back and composed himself to wait, for hours if necessary. Through deep, mindful breathing he managed to push out most of the anxiety he felt at facing one of them again, but a small kernel of terror remained.

Visitors to the cloister had no way to summon the Sisters, no bell to ring or knocker to raise. They would become aware of his presence in their own good time, and if they decided to hear him out, the sister on duty might show a veiled face beyond the grille and demand that he state his purpose.

Decker would wait for as long as he had to. He'd promised Marnie Takan that he would make sure her daughter didn't fall in the militia's hands, and though he feared the Sisterhood, he would endure being in their presence so he could fulfill his pledge.

Outside, avian life forms chattered loudly, filling the late morning air with a discordant song never meant for human ears, but in the annex, only the sound of his own breathing troubled the deep silence. He struggled to keep it measured and calm, but the Sisters would know of his fear. Nevertheless, pride demanded that he present a stoic façade.

Decker's internal clock watched the minutes fly by without a change to his enforced isolation, yet he kept his posture upright and a facial expression that showed no emotions.

He'd endured many military ceremonies where the reviewing officer had taken his own sweet time, unconcerned by troops standing in the sweltering heat. In his experience, the Sisters were equally indifferent.

Eventually, he heard the whisper of slippers on smooth tile and a dark shape appeared behind the grille. His body tensed up into a bundle of strained muscles and taut nerves, and he struggled to keep his breathing steady, but the sister behind the wall would know.

A high, bright voice, evoking the peal of tiny silver bells rang out.

"What brings you to our solitude, sinner?"

"I was sent to find a young woman whose life is in peril from the militia."

And then that which he feared happened. A sensation akin to fingertips passing over his brain sent a shiver of disgust down his spine. Determined to keep a brave face, he successfully restrained himself from grimacing.

"You speak the truth, sinner," the sister said. "What is your name?"

"Zachary Decker, but everyone calls me Zack."

He knew that his real name would have eventually come out, even against his will, so there was no point in obfuscation.

"You are a man of violence, of war..."

"And of base physical needs," Decker added, to forestall the sister. "I make no excuses for who I am — a simple human trying to live as best he can in a chaotic universe. The Divine Power will judge me when my time comes and weigh the good I've tried to do against the evil I've done."

The fingertips on the surface of his brain turned into gentle strokes.

"Tell me, Zack Decker, if you cannot accomplish your quest to save this young woman, what is it that you choose to do?"

He thought about the question for a few moments, aware it was a trap and then replied with a depth of feeling that not only surprised him but also the sister because the hand sifting through his soul suddenly vanished.

"Absent anything else, all I can do is decide what it is I get done with the time God has given me."

"And if your time was to end now?"

"Then I can no longer devote what I have left to those whom I pledged my help. It would suck, but dead men can't be held to their promises."

He repressed the urge to make a face at the veiled woman but knew nonetheless that she'd have felt his unexpected surge of irritation at these word games. Instead, he concentrated on the image of Kari he'd been shown by her mother and projected it violently at the sister.

"That's who I'm looking for," he said. "If you have any mercy for her parents, help me."

The woman behind the veil gasped.

"You're aware!"

"Yeah. I'm one of the few men with the genetic mutation to sense when I'm being probed by an empath, so you can stop the metaphysical mumbo-jumbo." A pause. "Reach back into my mind and you'll know that the following is true: if Kari Takan falls into the hands of the militia, she will die after an interrogation that will leave her an empty shell. But before she dies, she will have revealed all she knows about her father's activities in the Garonne Independence Movement, and more people will die, dozens perhaps hundreds, thousands even. I know the Sisterhood doesn't give a flying damn about worldly affairs and recoils in horror at the casual violence of the secular galaxy, but if you truly believe in mercy, then help me."

"And yet if the independence movement is allowed to embark on an increasingly violent path, then thousands will die, perhaps tens of thousands. Perhaps it is best if the authorities find a way to end the rebellion now, even if it means a few lives lost, including that of Kari Takan and yours for that matter."

Decker snorted derisively.

"I know the Sisterhood doesn't see much in humanity that they consider redeemable, but I didn't know you were that cynical. The needs of the many outweigh the needs of the few, is that it? Trite bullshit. Your souls are no more immune from the darkness than mine is. At least I'm trying to do something about it. Reach back into my mind because I'm going to show you another truth."

When he felt the soft, feathery touch of the sister's probe return, a cruel smile twisted his lips.

"There's an evil force at play on Garonne, one that would turn the planet into a battleground for its own purposes. I have no evidence of what those purposes are, but I know that the end result will mean devastation under the weight of a military expedition the likes of which hasn't been seen in years. The only way to prevent this outcome is to give the colonists self-rule, and that means defeating the militia."

He felt the sister behind the grille recoil in horror at the images of death and devastation, culled from the memory of past wars. Decker laughed when he sensed her mental gasp of horror.

"The needs of the many indeed. When it comes to Kari Takan, the needs of the one will help take care of the needs of all, including your cloister. You do not have enough sisters here to influence the battalion that will overrun this little oasis of hypocrisy once the rebellion turns into all-out civil war."

"Yeah," he continued, "I'm a man of war, but that doesn't mean I enjoy taking lives. If the universe were to find total peace, I'd gladly hang up my gun belt and tend to my garden, but I'm realistic enough to know that it won't happen, not in my lifetime, not in yours, probably not in humanity's lifetime, so spare me your empty platitudes. I don't begrudge you a life of contemplation, but the real world won't stop doing the dumb things it's been doing since we hairless apes first took up a stick and beat up our neighbors. So what do you say, Sister? Will you help me?"

Decker had so warmed to his subject that he didn't realize the revulsion he'd felt at the woman sifting through his mind, tasting his emotions and judging his soul had been replaced by anger so pure it blazed with a white flame that burned away the sister's mental tendrils.

Her veiled face vanished to the sound of running feet.

Zack sighed but composed himself to wait again. Either she'd be back with reinforcements or they were going to leave him alone until he got get tired of waiting and walked out. The Sisterhood wasn't known for its social graces.

However, he heard footsteps only a few minutes later, heavier than those of the sister who'd played voyeur in his mind. A broader, yet equally veiled face filled the grille, and a deeper, older voice rang out.

"I'm this cloister's Sister Superior. The sister who spoke with you acquainted me with the substance of your request. She also said you're one of the few men aware of our abilities."

As there was no point in answering, Decker nodded once, waiting for the newcomer to run her fingers through his soul. To his surprise, nothing of the sort happened.

"You frightened her badly, Zack Decker," there was a hint of laughter in the Sister Superior's voice, "when you pushed her out of your mind. Few of the men who are aware have that ability."

"Until you told me just now, I didn't know I could do that," he replied, "but I'll take your word for it."

"It is true. If we were a breeding house, I'd ask for a sample of your gametes."

"To be collected in a natural way or in a laboratory?" He asked with a raised eyebrow.

The Sister Superior laughed.

"Since the matter is not one we wish to pursue, I'll leave that question unanswered."

"You're not probing me?" He asked, changing the subject.

"Unlike the sister who spoke with you first, I've gained enough wisdom to know when to use my particular ability and when to use my other senses. After looking into your eyes, I have all the answers I need."

"I still don't."

"Then you shall. Kari Takan spent one night with us after fleeing the home of the friend she was visiting, but felt that she would put us in danger should the militia track her down and therefore left yesterday."

Decker bit back a pungent curse.

"Would it have killed your sister to tell me that up front instead of going off on a debate about good and evil?"

He felt the Sister Superior shrug.

"Some of our younger brethren still feel the need to debate philosophy with outsiders. She is one of the more egregious examples, which is why she volunteers to take on more than her fair share as greeter. It will eventually lose its luster. Few who stand where you are will dare challenge one of us so openly."

"Yeah, well I've always been accused of having a thick skull along with a big mouth, so let the sister know that she shouldn't take it personally."

"I will. And now you'll ask me where Kari has gone. I'm afraid I can't answer that."

"Can't or won't?"

"I see that you're a man who analyses things very carefully and from a deeply skeptical angle."

"Hah." Zack snorted. "You're the first who's ever accused me of being careful. It's usually the other way around."

"And yet I sense depths that you keep carefully hidden, Zack Decker, even from those closest to you. I can't answer your question about Kari Takan because she did not tell us where she was going. All we know is that she headed down the road leading to Kaholo after leaving our grounds. Whether or not that was her destination is something you'll have to discover for yourself."

"Thank you, Sister Superior." He dipped his head briefly.

"My best wishes accompany you on your journey. We will pray that the outcome you've shown my young sister does not come to pass, though I fear we shall have to become hospitallers again before peace returns to Garonne. Goodbye, Zack Decker."

And then he was alone again in the annex grafted to the chapter house. Outside, the avian life forms had kept up their incessant chatter but only now was he hearing them again.

Though disappointed at the outcome of his query, he felt oddly elated by the notion that he'd developed the ability to shut empaths from his mind. How that had come about would likely remain a mystery, though Zack had the sneaking suspicion that his punishment in the Atabek's juluk pit might somehow be involved. He'd long suspected the insects' venom might rewire part of the human brain.

The sun was now almost directly overhead and heat shimmered over the empty road heading into the countryside. It just so happened that the second place Kari might flee to for refuge, according to her father, was in Kaholo.

**

"He's just a supporter," Steiger told Captain Kozlev after spending an hour with the prisoner. "I don't see any point in trying harsher methods. He might paint slogans on walls and attend meetings, but he's not the type to be trusted with inside information. We'd be better off letting him go and then watching who he talks to."

Kozlev's reptilian stare made the mercenary feel as if she were on the wrong end of a probe and she looked away rather than keep trying to find a soul in those dark eyes.

"You have my permission to use harsher methods," Kozlev said after an extended period of silence.

"If it's all the same to you, sir, I'll pass. I've never been that enamored with interrogation."

"Then perhaps I will." Kozlev stood up and adjusted her uniform tunic. "You're welcome to watch."

Steiger understood that the invitation was really an order and her heart sank.

On their way back to the cells, they were intercepted by the duty officer who, like his superior, was on loan from the Celeste National Guard.

"One of the patrol cars just reported a man whose description is with the parameters we've issued, walking on the Kaholo road a kilometer or so short of the village limits."

"Did they take video?"

"Yes, sir." The man nodded. "I've got it set up for you in the analysis center."

Kozlev turned to Steiger.

"Let the prisoner go and put a tail on him. We'll try it your way and save our energies for your freelance acquaintance. Once you're done, join me. I want your assessment on the man and how you'd go about taking him in."

"Yes, sir," she replied, fighting to hide her relief at the reprieve she'd been granted, even though it might come at Zack Decker's expense.

When Steiger had carried out her orders and reported to the analysis center, Kozlev pointed at a screen that showed a large, muscular man in faded work clothes walking on the side of a country road. He carried a small pack slung over his shoulder and had the gait of someone used to doing without transport.

"Is that your Mark Skeen?" The captain asked.

"The hair and shape of the face are different from the image you showed me earlier, but there are enough points of resemblance that I'd say it could very well be."

"That's what my analysts determined as well, except that they used three times more words." A quick smile passed over Kozlev's lips. "If brevity is the soul of wit, I'd say conciseness is at the heart of intelligence work, don't you agree, Sergeant Steiger?"

"Yes, sir."

"Why would this Skeen fellow be heading for a small farming community and not stay in Iskellian where he could lose himself among the teeming multitudes?"

Steiger thought about it for a few moments, and then replied.

"He's looking for something or someone perhaps. Do we have other views of the man, possibly from this morning? Perhaps if we can retrace his steps, we might get a hint of what he's doing. If he's the off-world professional you believe him to be, sir, he might lead us to something interesting."

"Those were my thoughts as well." Kozlev nodded with approval. "I've dispatched a team to shadow him. And..."

She glanced at the lead technician, "...I believe we're about to get a partial reconstruction of his morning."

"Yes, sir," the man said. "If you look at the left screen, we've picked up the same face in the riverfront park, then on the Jiang Bridge and after that at several places on the Harlo Road." A map came up on another screen with red dots appearing in a neat line from the river to Kaholo.

"Isn't it interesting that he seems to have taken his time to examine the south and east sides of the government precinct close-up," Kozlev remarked. She glanced at the map and then back at the images.

"What's that?"

"The Sisterhood of the Void has a house in that spot," the technician replied. "The time discrepancy between his appearance on the surveillance camera to the south of the cloister and when he was seen by the patrol might be explained by his having stopped there, assuming his walking speed was constant."

"There's a time discrepancy?" Kozlev went to stand behind the technician. "Show me."

When he had, she looked back at the map, tapping her chin with slender fingers.

"Why would an off-world pro, a man of war, visit the Sisterhood? There's something we're missing here."

"Perhaps he's trying to find someone who might have sought sanctuary at the cloister."

"A woman then," Kozlev nodded. "The sisters would never let a man step beyond the visitor's room."

She turned towards the lead intelligence analyst.

"Weren't you saying that Kari Takan might have been in Iskellian when we attempted to arrest her father?"

"Yes, sir, though we've yet to find someone who'll admit seeing her."

"Did we bring anyone in for a chat?"

"No, sir. Not yet."

"What if the pro was sent to find the Takan girl because she knows about her father's activities?" Kozlev began pacing, all the while tapping her chin. "And what if he had a list of places she might hole up, starting with the cloister, where he obviously didn't find her, hence the hike to Kaholo?"

"Would you like me to have the Sister Superior arrested?"

Kozlev shook her head.

"No point. If our man left the cloister by himself, then he didn't find what he was looking for. We need to keep eyes on him non-stop from now on, however."

"I've just about got a drone over Kaholo," the technician said. "Two or three more minutes and we'll have a live feed."

"How long until the team gets there?"

"Perhaps another ten minutes. They have to come in from the north to avoid alerting the target."

"This is it," Kozlev said in a husky voice that betrayed a deep, primal eagerness. "We'll get the man who queered the Takan arrest *and* the Takan girl. I can't wait to have both in my interrogation room."

She glanced at Steiger and winked.

"You and I might have some fun before the day is out, sergeant."

A sick feeling metastasized in the mercenary's stomach, and she struggled to control her urge to vomit.

Decker could take care of himself, but by fingering him to maintain her cover, she'd condemned a girl whose only sin was to have been born the daughter of a separatist leader.

— TWENTY-NINE —

An armored militia skimmer headed for Iskellian passed Decker just outside Kaholo. It didn't slow down, and he hoped that by hiding his face and size as best he could, they might not take an interest in him, but he knew that if they had their sensors running, they'd get a close-up of his dusty mug anyway.

He wondered what kind of place might be sheltering the girl in a small farming town that looked like it hadn't seen any new construction since the Shrehari War. As before, all he had was an address and a few directions. His destination could be anything: brothel, abbey, or sanatorium for that matter.

There were few people about, and even the main drag was more like that of a ghost town. The colonists he did meet didn't appear anxious to return his greeting nod, let alone his smile. It had become very warm, and he'd almost emptied his water bottle so he entered a food store to stock up. After paying for a bulb of cold juice, he stood by the shop window and took a long, satisfying sip while scanning the street for anything that might indicate someone was interested in the large, untidy stranger.

"Militia come through here often?" He asked the man busy doing nothing behind the counter.

"Yep." He didn't look up from his tablet.

"That why it looks like midnight in a graveyard out there?"

"Yep."

The man didn't sound interested in making conversation and Zack didn't insist.

"Cheers, mate."

He took another swig of juice and stepped back out into the sunshine, head swiveling around to make sure he hadn't missed anything that could bite him. There might have been folks watching him from behind polarized windows. In fact, he'd be stunned if there weren't, but he doubted the militia would be that low tech.

The thought nearly caused him to look up for an invisible drone, and he began to get a bad feeling about Kaholo. Not the town itself or the inhabitants, but the sense that he had left enough of a trail to bring the militia here, to a place that had a lot less by way of bolt holes than a city like Iskellian.

He felt an irrational longing to have Talyn or Steiger, or preferably both watching his back, but they were far away.

A small civilian skimmer came over a rise three blocks away, slowed, then turned left onto a side street. It was the first vehicle he'd seen moving about since the militia patrol car a kilometer from the town limits.

Decker tucked the half-empty bulb in his pocket. It was time to find the place where Kari might be hiding. He oriented himself and set off, senses alert; all of his training and experience told him that it was only a matter of time before the militia linked his two previous disguises to the man at the Takan farm.

His destination lay at the eastern edge of Kaholo, by a low mesa overgrown with native vegetation. It looked incongruous enough on the relatively flat river plain that he wondered whether it wasn't the remains of another L'Taung ruin, this one blending even further into its surroundings after a hundred millennia than the ruined fortress now sheltering the rebel movement's headquarters.

As he wound his way through alleys between increasingly dilapidated sheds and warehouses, his sixth sense began to itch. It was a bit like the feeling he got when the Sister of the Void touched his mind, but on another part of his anatomy. Whenever he had mentioned it to Talyn on previous occasions, he'd get one of her more pungently sarcastic replies.

He emerged from the shadow of a tall structure sitting precariously on the edge of a small plaza and stepped into a boarded-up doorway to examine his surroundings. The open space was overgrown by weeds and strangely shaped flowers with colors more appropriate to a house of horrors than a sunny day.

On the other side, hard up against the gloomy bulk of the mesa, there stood a large, two-story house with a discreet sign announcing its purpose. He knew then that he'd reached his destination.

The place wasn't a brothel or an abbey, or thank God, another cloister of the Sisterhood of the Void, but the inmates might have benefited from the latter's talents.

This part of town seemed quieter than the rest, with only an occasional cry from one of the native life forms who'd found a profitable niche among the alien invaders colonizing its habitat. A soft breeze occasionally stroked the tall ferns on the steep slopes behind the hospice, but it didn't reach Decker's improvised observation post, leaving him to swelter in the heat.

Though he wanted to get it over with, find out whether Kari Takan had taken refuge there and if she had, high-tail it for the mountains with her, something held him back, and until he figured out what that might be, he wasn't going to take another step.

A sound behind him, though faint, resonated loudly in ears turned hypersensitive by the tension he felt hanging over Kaholo. He slowly turned his head to look back the way he'd come and caught a brief spasm of movement near a shed with faded red walls.

Decker's right hand crept over his left wrist to loosen the dagger held against his forearm in a spring-loaded sheath. There were no further signs of life in the alley, but he could swear he heard muffled breathing not ten meters away.

Quietly, almost on tiptoes, his back against a wall turned leprous with age, he crept towards the shed. A soft scuffling sound confirmed his instinct. Someone was hiding just out of sight.

He flexed his left wrist, and the dagger's hilt emerged from his sleeve, landing in the palm of his right hand. He was going to look very foolish if it was one of the town's kids spying on the newcomer.

With a fluid movement that belied his apparent bulk, Zack turned the corner while keeping his body low, to make himself as small a target as possible. The man in nondescript civilian clothes who'd been hiding there seemed to blanch with a fright intense enough to make him forget the needler dangling from his hand.

Decker's fist lashed out, hilt first, catching him in the middle of the sternum. He collapsed soundlessly, like a deflating balloon. Another strike against the head put him out completely.

The Marine's eyes darted everywhere at once, searching for further threats while he rifled through the unconscious man's pockets. His fingers closed on a militia ID wafer, and he mentally swore in every language he knew.

There was no way this one had been alone, considering he wore plain clothes instead of a bottle green uniform. That kind of cop always worked in pairs. It had to be a snatch team sent to take him in once he'd found Kari Takan for them.

Unfortunately, the man's partner had better luck, and before Zack could turn to face the new threat, a hail of needles pierced the skin on the back of his hands and his scalp.

Then, all went dark.

**

"Sir, we've had to take the target down before he found the Takan girl," the team leader reported. "He made one of the men tailing him and counter-attacked. Sergeant Golin will be fine, but he might have suffered a concussion. Yavek, Golin's partner, had to use his needler."

"Is the target alive?" Kozlev asked, biting back her anger. Reaming the man out over the militia radio net wouldn't do anything for morale, and she knew from bitter experience that shit happened. It confirmed her notion that Skeen, or whatever he called himself today, was a pro.

"He'll have a heck of a headache when he comes to in a few hours, but he's breathing."

Kozlev bit her lip and stared at the tactical display.

"He was almost out of town at that point," she said. "There isn't much left before the mesa. Tell me what you see from where the target stood before he turned on Golin."

"Sir." The officer moved down the alley until he reached the edge of the plaza.

"I see one residential building, surrounded by a high wall, and a bunch of old warehouses."

"The map says it's a hospice." Kozlev nodded, her earlier rage replaced by a hard smile.

"Yes, sir, that's what the sign by the gate says."

"She's there. Takan is hiding in that hospice. Turn the place upside down, rip the walls open, do whatever you have to and no need to be gentle. Our man was headed there, no doubt about it."

Kozlev turned towards Steiger.

"Your freelancing buddy isn't all that good, is he? I can't wait to see if he's as tough as he looks. This will be so much fun."

**

"What is it, Colonel?" Governor Cedeno's pinched face betrayed his annoyance at Harend's interruption.

"Sir, I'm pleased to report that we've captured not only the man who prevented us from arresting Larn Takan but also Takan's daughter Kari. We'll soon have a hook into the armed wing of the independence movement."

Cedeno allowed himself a slight smile.

"Good news at last, Colonel. You'll keep me apprised of the smallest details, yes?"

"But of course, sir. Captain Kozlev is confident that she'll have something for us to chew on soon."

The governor barely repressed a shudder when he heard the intelligence officer's name.

"Make sure you do nothing that can attract the attention of the Senate or the Fleet. If either of them decides we've done something to warrant an investigation or God forbid, intervention, you and I will see our careers end most abruptly. The home world will not be forgiving."

"There will be no evidence, governor. Captain Kozlev will be most careful about that."

"I'm sure she will," he replied in a dry tone. "Was there anything else?"

"No, sir. I shall provide you with further bulletins as events warrant."

"Thank you, Colonel."

Harend's screen went black, leaving the Garonne militia's commander to contemplate his reflection on the matte surface.

Once they had sufficient details about the separatists' internal workings to flesh out the plan he'd been mulling over, any investigation by Commonwealth authorities would be directed at the independence movement. It would be enough to make the notion of a free Garonne wither on the vine.

If he accomplished that, he'd retire with a general's stars, Cedeno be damned.

**

A white-faced Verrill entered the small room Corde and Talyn had commandeered for the new all-sources intelligence center and dropped into a camp chair with the sound of a dying horse.

"News has come through one of our affiliates that the militia raided the Kaholo hospice. A young woman corresponding to Kari Takan's description was taken away, but not after several staff and patients at the facility were brutalized. Some are not expected to live. The same raid also picked up a man nearby described as large, muscular, and not recorded in the militia's database. I'm assuming it was Decker. Otherwise, the coincidence would be too much for belief."

The two women stared at Verrill for a few moments, aghast.

"Do we have any idea how they tracked them down?" Talyn asked.

The rebel commander shook his head.

"No, but my best guess is that your partner ran out of time. The militia's rank and file may not be much but their intelligence team is heavily seeded with Celeste regulars, and they're far from stupid. Since we have to assume they got a look at Decker during the escape from Takan's farm, it's a given that they would have eventually spotted him thanks to the surveillance cameras infesting Iskellian, whether or not he changed his appearance. Your partner isn't the kind to pass unnoticed for very long."

Corde, normally a very composed and gentle soul, began cursing to the point where the others looked at her in mild astonishment.

"Sorry," she said when she'd exhausted her fund of swear words, "I needed to get that out of my system."

"Of course. We all have those moments, honey." Talyn gently patted her shoulder, and then looked at Verrill. "What now?"

"There's not much we can do other than pray. We don't have the means to raid the government precinct and get them out."

"I supposed I should have figured as much." She slumped back in her seat. "No criticism intended, Verrill. But Zack's been conditioned, which means he'll die if they probe him. He may not look like much, but I've grown rather fond of him."

"Kari Takan hasn't been conditioned," he replied, "and though her father tells me she doesn't know a whole lot, any good interrogator can pull things from the unconscious mind we never suspected were there."

"And that will likely kill her." Talyn turned to the console and called up Kozlev's picture. "I've pretty much figured out that she's Colonel Harend's head of all things nasty: interrogation, torture, and execution. I don't think she'll care whether our people live or die, provided she gets everything they know."

"I'm going to send warning," Verrill said, rising up with a tired grimace on a face that seemed to have aged overnight. "We'll need to evacuate a number of folks and pull back some of the forward operating bases just to be sure. The cell system usually works well enough to contain damage, but we can't take too many chances. We're not resilient enough yet to absorb a major setback. It'll still hurt us. Damned militia."

"I don't think all is lost yet," Talyn replied, staring at Kozlev's dead eyes. "Zack's been given up for dead more times than I can remember and he's always turned up, usually after teaching the people who tried to kill him a fatal object lesson."

"And Kari?" Verrill asked, knowing his next stop was one level down where her parents and brothers had set up housekeeping.

"Zack won't leave without her, you can bank on that."

"I wish I had your confidence, Hera." Verrill shook his head wearily. "I really do. But I have to be realistic. I'll let the operations center know that they're to send any further information directly here. Maybe by some miracle we can figure out a way to get them back."

**

Steiger watched helplessly while two militia troopers strapped a naked and unconscious Zack Decker into one of the interrogation chairs. The antiseptic room in the basement of militia headquarters reminded her of an operating theater designed by a madwoman, and she fought to repress a shiver of fear.

"He'll be out for a little while yet," Kozlev said in a conversational tone, pointing at Decker's recumbent form on the other side of the one-way window, "and with any luck, he'll have a killer headache when he does. It'll help with disorientation, as you know from past experience."

"Sure." Steiger nodded, but before she could elaborate, the same troopers brought in a sedated woman, young with long auburn hair and an elfin face. They strapped her in a matching chair across from Zack.

"The girl should wake up any moment now. We'll leave her to stare at him until he comes around." A small giggle escaped Kozlev's thin lips. "Imagine how she'll react."

After a short pause, she turned away and motioned Steiger to follow her.

"We have plenty of time for a meal and a glass of wine, and we'll need to discuss technique. I'd like you to help me, but for that, we'll need a game plan so there are no slip-ups. The big boy in there is going to require a lot more than just a bit of a scare. The girl, perhaps not so much, but why waste the chance for a bit of practice."

**

A regiment of heavy artillery seemed to have taken up residence in Zack's skull and was practicing mass bombardment techniques when finally came to.

Nausea washed over him, and he retched dryly, coughing until his throat felt beset by a thousand fires. He dared not open his eyes yet. The glow coming through his closed lids was enough to send shards of glass through his optical nerves.

Zack's reaction to needlers had always been bad, much worse than most people's, but the tranquilizer the militia had used turned it into an ordeal that rivaled being impaled on a hot spit.

As he tried to reconstruct the last moments before he passed out, a growing sense of horror supplanted the pain.

Kari.

It didn't take a genius to figure out that the hospice might be one of her bolt holes. There was sweet bugger-all else around to attract his attention.

Which meant…

He forced his eyes open, only to snap them shut again when sheer agony burned through his retinas. Someone was panting like a dog that had been run over, and it took Decker a few moments to realize it was himself.

Unable to use his eyes, tied down hand and foot, he took a deep breath through his nose and tried to analyze the scents. Where he might have expected the bloody aroma of an abattoir, he only got a whiff of something vaguely medical.

That he'd landed in a militia interrogation room was not in doubt. Zack tried to relax and let his body flush out the last of the tranquilizer. He forced his breathing into a slow and steady rhythm, and that was when he realized he was not alone. Another person was breathing nearby.

This time, his lids remained open while his eyes attempted to focus on their surroundings. The chemically induced nausea was washed away the moment he caught sight of the girl strapped to a seat across from him. A sick feeling of failure filled him instead.

She was gagged, her eyes overflowing with the kind of unreasoning fear that reminded him of a trapped, badly injured animal he'd been forced to kill many years ago.

A door opened to his right, and the sound of two pairs of heels on a hard floor echoed across the white-walled room.

He couldn't turn his head, and so he waited until the first of the new arrivals came to stand in front of him. She wore a militia uniform with captain's stars and had a predatory expression on her face that seemed so natural she could only have been born with it. Her dark eyes seemed eerily familiar, and he felt a shiver of horror run down his spine when he made the connection.

A second woman, also in militia uniform joined her and this time, Decker struggled to contain his reaction.

"I trust you're feeling suitably miserable, Ser Skeen, or is it Whate today?" The captain held up his sheathed dagger. "Or is it something even more deliciously military?"

Then she laughed as if she'd just heard the funniest joke ever told and Decker felt his weakened bowels turn to water.

— THIRTY —

"But where are my manners? I'm Captain Rika Kozlev, the militia's intelligence officer, on loan from the Celeste National Guard." She inclined her head briefly. "And this is Staff Sergeant Miko Steiger, though I believe you two already know each other."

When Zack didn't respond, Kozlev seemed disappointed.

"I believe mere politeness requires that you introduce yourself in return, don't you? We know you're not Skeen, the name Sergeant Steiger knew you under, and I don't think the William Whate identification is genuine, but my compliments to whoever forged it."

"And this?" Kozlev held up the dagger again. "I believe it's issued only to Marine Corps pathfinders. Did you earn it honestly or did you buy it in some tawdry surplus store on Cimmeria? It certainly looks genuine."

Decker raised a scornful eyebrow but otherwise kept his mouth shut.

"I guess you're the silent type who prefers actions over words — *facta non verba*, which I believe is the motto of the Fleet's Special Operations Command. That's okay. We'll get to know each other quite intimately over the next few days; that is to say, I'll get to know every little thing about you."

"I doubt that," Zack said.

"It speaks!" A beatific smile creased Kozlev's pinched face. "Are you bragging or..."

She snapped her fingers and then pointed at him.

"You've been conditioned, haven't you? What fun. I haven't broken a conditioned prisoner yet, but you may well become the first."

She walked around Zack's chair to examine his naked body from all angles, leaving a hint of expensive perfume in her wake.

"I'm curious who you really are, big boy."

She ran slender fingers down his jaw line, triggering a surprisingly strong surge of revulsion in him.

"Your lovely muscles are almost a piece of abstract art, with all those old scars, the marks of a seasoned warrior. You claim to have been conditioned against interrogation, you carry an authentic pathfinder knife and, oh yes, I almost forgot, an equally authentic Shrehari Imperial Armaments blaster, re-chambered for standard issue Fleet ammunition and power packs. I get the feeling I should be hearing name, rank, and serial number."

She reappeared in his line of sight, and he gave her a sardonic smile.

"Hmm. Gone mute again, have you?" She pulled the dagger from its sheath and admired the tip of the blade. "I wonder how sharp this is. Shall we try?"

When Decker didn't react, she chuckled.

"Not on you, of course. There would be no sport in it. But the young Sera Takan on the other hand..."

Kozlev stepped over to Kari's side and examined her smooth face.

"It would be a shame to mar her at such a tender age. Perhaps restorative surgery might help if, of course, I get the answers I want from those rosy lips. Otherwise, life might be too short to worry about looks."

The terror in Kari Takan's face turned to shock, and she fainted.

"Not much of a challenge there," Kozlev mused, shoving the dagger back in its sheath. "I prefer to draw blood from prisoners who are awake to enjoy the experience."

"Now, how shall I start peeling away the layers of your conditioning, I wonder? Obviously, sitting there in your birthday suit isn't embarrassing you in any way. Bravo. I like a man who's comfortable in his own skin. Your kind is unfortunately all too rare."

She reached down to stroke the insides of his thighs, all the time watching Decker's eyes.

"Perhaps I should take you to my bed and see if I can loosen your tongue that way." A throaty chuckle punctuated her words. "I like loose tongues, you know."

Her hand ran up his stomach and over his chest.

"I bet you're trying really hard not to have a reaction right now." She glanced down. "And so far, it's working."

"No. You've probably had your share of dangerous lovers," she continued, "so I can't offer you any new sensations. Perhaps I should start off by gelding you?"

"Wouldn't help," Decker said, hiding his alarm at her matter of fact tone. "Being conditioned means even if I wanted to tell you something, I couldn't, no matter what you do. Push me far enough and I'll only die. It's not that I want to, but my conditioning will decide when my time's up."

"It can speak in complete sentences. I'm so pleased." Kozlev stepped back and considered him intently, her head tilted to one side like that of a curious bird. "I'm a firm believer that what humanity has wrought, a human can undo, conditioning included."

A soft moan escaped Kari Takan's gagged mouth as her eyes fluttered open. Kozlev glanced over her shoulder at the girl.

"Tell me, tall, dark, and handsome, if I try some of my more exotic techniques on this lovely, virginal lass and let you watch, would that help loosen your tongue?"

"Like I said," Decker tried to sound bored by the conversation, "even if I wanted to talk, I couldn't, so torturing her in front of me won't help."

It was perhaps not quite the truth, but it would have to do for now, provided Kozlev believed him.

"Yet it might entertain me, and I know she'll spill everything she can about the rebellion, but," Kozlev sighed, "a mind probe is more efficient. There's no chance she'll make up stories to please me and end the pain. It's just not as much fun. I've never been thrilled by mind rape. Of course, I'm sure a probe would kill you instantly, so I won't even try. It would be a shame to lose you too soon."

She turned to Kari and removed her gag.

"Do you know who this gentleman is?" She asked pointing towards Zack with her thumb.

The girl shook her head violently, and Kozlev reached out to caress a tear-streaked cheek.

"There, there. Relax child. I didn't expect you to know him, which makes me wonder how he'd have proved to you that he came on behalf of your parents to save you from the evil militia. Care to comment, big boy?"

"Considering that it's a moot point," he paused as if thinking about it, "the answer is no."

"I do believe it has something like a sense of humor. Good." Kozlev stroked Kari's face again. "Tell me, child do you know what a mind probe does?"

Violent head shake again.

"Do you?" She asked Decker. His eyes must have betrayed some sort of reaction because the predatory smile returned.

"Of course you do and through first-hand experience I'll wager, before you were conditioned. Would you like to describe the way it felt? The violation of everything personal, every memory; the rape of the soul? No?"

"You see," she continued looking at Kari again, "it's been described as the most horrible thing that could happen to you short of violent death. Of course, a fair percentage of those subjected to a probe end up as animated corpses, their minds irredeemably destroyed. Your father's friend Mathias – you remember him, right? He didn't make it. I slit his throat to end a hopelessly vegetative existence. But he gave me your father's name, and if it hadn't been for tall, dark, and handsome over there, Papa Takan would be in this chair instead of you so you can thank both of them for your fate."

Kozlev turned to Steiger.

"Have the guards take Takan to her cell. I feel like giving her the night to decide whether she'd rather have a friendly conversation with me or get the experience of a lifetime with my probe."

"Yes, sir."

"As for you, my warrior friend, I'll have to think some more. I wasn't expecting a freelancer to be conditioned, and that means I need to plan how I'll tackle your case. Since you don't need a quiet period to think things over..." she tapped her fingers on her chin for a few moments, "I'll just leave you here with an all-night sound and light show. Who knows, perhaps disorientation will blur the line between what your conditioning will let you say and what it won't. If you need to relieve yourself, go right ahead. The guards will hose this room out first thing in the morning, and if they're feeling charitable, they might even allow you a few sips of water and a bite of whatever rotting food the kitchen is about to throw out. Have a pleasant night. I know I will."

"You're a real queen among women, Kozlev." Decker blew her a kiss. This time, her laughter sounded both delighted and genuine.

**

"Conditioned?" Harend stared into his glass, swirling the amber liquid around. "Rare for a civilian, no?"

"He's likely ex-Commonwealth military," Kozlev replied. "Sometimes, it's impossible to remove conditioning at the time of retirement or discharge."

"And the weapons, especially the blade?" He reached over and picked up the sheathed dagger she'd dropped on his living room table.

"A souvenir from a happier time in his life?" Kozlev poured herself a glass of the Glen Arcturus and took a sip, smiling with pleasure at the smoky taste. "An active member of the Services playing spy wouldn't go around carrying something that obvious."

"Perhaps." He put the dagger down again. "But if he is from the Fleet or the Constabulary, then we have a very big problem."

"Not if he can't report back."

"Shoot, shovel, and shut up, you mean? The governor wouldn't be pleased."

"Bugger Cedeno." She shrugged. "He doesn't have the backbone for a proper counter-insurgency campaign."

"But he does have enough connections on the home world to make sure he can credibly claim his innocence when it comes to happenings on Garonne that cross the line."

"Would you like me to drum us up some insurance?"

"Unless it involves Cedeno being accused of something so unspeakably vile that even his closest friends wash their hands of him, it won't do much good. The man may not be the most charismatic politician in the galaxy, but he's got a good instinct for survival."

"Pity."

"Let's leave Cedeno to the side for now and get back to the man you have in your dungeon. What do you intend to do?

From all I've read, conditioning, especially if it was done by the Fleet, is damn near impossible to break. You'll have a corpse on your hands before you even get his real name."

"And if I do, he'll join Mathias in an unmarked grave, though it would be a pity. He's quite a specimen."

"Hormones acting up again?" Harend cocked a sardonic eyebrow at her. "Try to restrain your baser impulses when it comes to the prisoners."

"No fear, darling. I don't think I'm his type."

**

After the first hour of loud, often discordant music, including snippets of Shrehari opera, matched to flashing, multi-color lights, Decker finally managed to drop into a meditative trance that all but shut his awareness off from its surroundings. Though he hadn't been given much training in the spy business after he'd been forcibly recruited by Hera Talyn, one of the few useful items they did teach him was this little mind trick.

He wouldn't actually sleep through the night, but the guards would nonetheless find him relatively well rested and completely sane come morning, not that he'd let them know; quite the contrary, in fact. It would better serve his purpose if Kozlev thought she was weakening him. There had never been any question in his mind that he would try to escape and take Kari Takan with him, but he knew that he'd get one chance and one only.

At daybreak, the music abruptly stopped. One of the guards entered the interrogation room and immediately swore.

"The bastard's gone pissed and shat himself during the night. Get the hose, Otto. Her ladyship will want everything to be clean and smelling like roses when she shows up, and that could be any moment. I don't think she's the kind that sleeps much."

Moments later, a steady stream of cold water hit his bare skin. The guards, standing well away by the door, played the hose over him, his chair, and the floor, until he was numb and shivering like a leaf in a storm, now fully awake.

"That'll do, I think," the guard named Otto finally said, shutting off the water. "I hope he had his mouth open because I'm not in the mood to fetch him a drink."

"Should I turn the heat on?" The other man asked. "It'll help dry the place faster."

"Nah. He'd enjoy that too much. Her ladyship won't mind a bit of damp in a good cause. C'mon, time for some breakfast."

Just before shutting the door, Otto called out, "Have a painful day, asshole. Rennie and me lost a couple of buddies in Holback the other day to your stinking lot, so I hope her ladyship makes it long and hard."

Mercifully, the guards had forgotten to turn the sound and light show on again, and Decker promptly fell asleep once the shivers stopped.

He had no idea how long he'd been snoozing when a stinging blow across the face, delivered by an expert hand, woke him up with a start.

"Who said you could take your ease like an honest citizen?" Kozlev asked.

"Wh-what?" His eyes darted around the room as if he was disoriented by exhaustion.

"Rise and shine, big boy. Today we get better acquainted."

She removed her uniform tunic, exposing a white t-shirt that perfectly outlined her thin, wiry arms and hard-ribbed torso.

"Not interested," he mumbled.

"Oh but I'm very interested in you. My commanding officer has this notion that you might be Fleet, though I told him a proper spy wouldn't be advertising his affiliation by carrying a fine pathfinder blade and a re-chambered Shrehari gun."

"So? Maybe I used to be in the Service. What do you care? I was just minding my own business in Kaholo when your fucking thugs shot me."

She slapped him again, hard.

"Name, rank and serial number."

"Bite me," he muttered.

Slap.

"I'll find out eventually. We've sent your biometric data to Celeste where the National Guard will plug it into the various connections it has. If you've served in the Fleet, we'll find out. If you're still serving, we'll know."

Good luck with that, Decker thought. *They turned me into the man who doesn't exist before we left on this mission.*

He let his head drop against his chest and closed his eyes.

"Hey," she grabbed him by the chin, "it's not polite to fall asleep when you're talking to a lady."

"Sure, but you're no lady."

Slap.

"Maybe I should geld you after all." Kozlev walked over to the table where she'd carefully piled his weapons and clothes. "Your blade seems to be sharp enough for the task."

"Or," she continued after pulling the dagger from its sheath, "will the physical shock suffice to trigger your conditioning's suicide mechanism?"

"Try it and see," he replied with a tired grin. "I'm not getting out of here alive anyway, so now would be a good a time to go."

She locked eyes with him, looking for anything that might confirm the truth of his words. Whatever she saw must have been enough because she placed the dagger back on the table and dropped into the chair that Kari Takan had occupied the previous day. For what seemed like an eternity, Kozlev studied him.

"Somehow, you managed to make it through the night without looking like a wreck," she finally said. "I guess a man your size can take a lot of punishment before he starts crumbling. Mind you, everyone has his or her limits. I intend to find yours. If I can't practice my art on you in conventional ways, I'll have to find my entertainment through other means, but rest assured that I will savor every minute of it."

She got up and opened the door.

"I expect some fresh business later today, folks we know are associated with Larn Takan, so you'll be taken to a cell for another musical interlude. We'll talk again soon."

Kozlev gave him a little wave before leaving the interrogation room. He heard the click of her heels fade in the distance, and then Otto and his colleague entered and carefully released the seat restraints one by one before shackling his arms and legs together. Then, they escorted him down the corridor to a small, two-meter square cell with nothing but blank walls.

"I hope you enjoy your accommodations, asshole." Otto shoved him through the door. "Try to keep things clean this time."

He barely had time to lie down on the cold floor and prepare himself for another meditative trance before the discordant music and flashing lights started up again.

**

"Rise and shine, asshole. Her ladyship wants you back in the big room. I guess you two have a hot date tonight."

When Decker didn't move, Otto turned towards Rennie, who was waiting in the corridor.

"He's passed out."

"Shit."

The two guards entered the small cell and stared at him. Otto kicked Zack's leg, and when that got no reaction, he kicked him harder in the kidneys.

"Well, at least he's breathing, so there's that." Rennie knelt beside Decker's head and pulled up an eyelid with his thumb. "Totally out of it."

"Shrehari opera will do that to you I guess. But it doesn't excuse us from doing what Kozlev wants. She comes down, and he isn't sitting in his chair, we'll be lucky if we don't get to try it ourselves."

"Fucker's so big it'll be a bitch to carry him." Otto leaned down to grab Decker by the shoulders and lift. "Shit. It'll need both of us."

Rennie grabbed Zack by the feet, and they tried again, but his body sagged in the middle like a sack of mud and they let go.

"We're both going to have to lift him at this end and drag," Otto said, grimacing.

"Ain't going to work unless we take off the wrist restraints, and each grab an arm. I figure you and I are going to have to get in cozy with his armpits."

"I'm not sure that's a good idea." Otto's homely face twisted into a grimace of disgust.

"He'll still be shackled at the ankles. Where do you expect him to go with those? It's only for thirty seconds or so anyway, and he's not about to come out of his opera-induced coma."

Rennie chuckled. "Opera-induced coma, I got to remember that one."

"Okay."

Otto bent over to remove the wrist cuffs and hooked them to his belt. Then, he and Rennie heaved Decker up.

It was the moment Zack had been waiting for.

— THIRTY-ONE —

The moment Decker's feet were on solid ground, his limp body became a rock-hard mass of angry muscle. Before the guards could react to their prisoner's sudden awakening, he'd placed his right hand, fingers outstretched on the side of Otto's head and his left hand on Rennie's, and rammed both together in a bone-crunching collision.

The militia troopers dropped to the floor without uttering a sound.

Zack crouched beside Otto and put the man's thumb on his leg shackles' biometric reader. They clicked open and fell away. He briefly checked the guards. They were alive, barely and likely suffering from a severe concussion.

He poked his head out of the cell door, relieved to find the corridor empty. Any moment now, the lazy bastards manning the surveillance cameras in the operations center were going to realize something wasn't right in the basement; he had minutes, perhaps only seconds before the alarm went off. The moment that happened, he'd be forced to create utter havoc so he'd have a chance of escape.

After closing up his former cell, now holding the two unconscious men, he quickly found the interrogation room and his personal effects. Running naked through militia headquarters might make enough of the buggers hesitate just long enough, but he didn't relish the vulnerable feeling that came from letting it all hang out.

Decker pulled on his pants and tunic, stepped into his boots, and tucked the dagger into his waistband. He checked his blaster's magazine and power pack, then began searching for Kari Takan's cell.

The first one he opened held a man whose vacant look spoke of a mind probe that gone on for too long. His soul would likely never find its way back into his body and Decker couldn't afford to encumber himself with a zombie, even for the best of reasons. The next three cells were empty, but the fourth held a frightened, cringing young woman whose wide eyes spoke of a mind that still functioned.

They'd put Takan into prison coveralls and shaved her hair in preparation for a probe. But whether it was because she'd started to talk on her own or Kozlev simply hadn't gotten around to her yet, the girl's scalp was devoid of the small lesions Decker remembered seeing in a mirror a few years earlier, after his own brush with mind rape.

"We haven't been properly introduced," he said, holding out his hand to help her up, "but I'm a friend of your parents, and I was sent to get you away from the militia."

When she didn't move, he stepped into the cell, bent down and picked her up.

"Apologies for the familiarity, but we don't have long before someone comes down to check on us. This is our one chance of escape."

The sound of booted feet hurrying down the stairs told him time was up. With Kari slung over his left shoulder and the blaster held in his right fist, he waited, partially hidden inside the cell.

A green-uniformed shaped appeared at the far end of the corridor and Decker's weapon coughed twice, the first shot drilling a smoking hole in the man's face where his nose had been and the second through the left eye. He crumbled to the ground, dead.

Zack sprinted towards the stairs, the girl feeling light as a feather to his adrenaline-fueled senses, and took the steps two at a time.

An alarm siren began blaring and behind him, a steel door cut the basement off from the rest of the building. A few seconds slower and they'd have been trapped, likely gassed and then he'd have been a dead man walking. Sociopaths like Kozlev were unforgiving when someone dared to thwart their will.

He burst onto the ground floor in the midst of scurrying militia troopers driven to action by the siren, most of them not very effectively if the aura of chaos was any indication. They looked like they hadn't practiced the escaped prisoner drill very often, if at all, and had no muscle memory to take over when the shit hit the fan.

Though it felt like shooting hatchlings in a nest, he began firing as he ran towards the door leading to the outside. Green uniforms collapsed to a cacophony of alarmed shouts and agonized screams; the odor of burnt flesh, blood, and voided bowels quickly filled the air, turning a quiet office building into an abattoir.

Decker stopped counting after the first four, shooting through open office doors to add to the pandemonium. His eyes found Steiger, prone under a desk and he hesitated.

Because she hadn't given Kozlev his real identity, he held his fire, to her evident relief. Then, she mouthed the word 'skimmer' and pointed to a door on the other side the squad room. He nodded once, shot her office mates twice, then ripped the door open and stepped out into the early evening twilight.

There, parked for the night, was an armed militia combat car. Its side hatch opened smoothly at his touch, and he dropped Kari in the back before jumping into the operator's seat.

Militia troopers began streaming out of the building he'd just left and from the ones forming the other three sides of the hollow square. He shot a few who'd made the mistake of approaching without covering fire before he closed the hatch.

The skimmer's reactor came online instantly at his command, and he sent the fans spinning when he goosed their motors, creating enough lift to get the heavy vehicle off the ground.

Small arms fire began splashing against the lightly armored hull, and he caught a glimpse of someone setting up a heavy machine gun at the far edge of the square.

Skimmers weren't flyers. Though equipped with anti-gravity modules, they relied on fans to create the air cushion upon which they rode. However, they could jump over low obstacles if the driver was willing to redline the motors. Since he didn't much care about the vehicle's lifespan beyond the next few minutes, Decker did just that.

He aimed them at a two-story office block directly ahead and pushed the revolutions per second to the limit. Screeching and shaking as if it were about to fall apart the combat car left its comfortable air cushion and rose on a shallow arc towards the building's roof.

Then, he was over the peak and down the other side, leaving a gaggle of militia troopers firing at an empty, rapidly darkening sky.

Decker turned hard towards the nearby river. Their only hope was to get upstream well ahead of any pursuit and ditch the vehicle by the rapids east of Tianjin before vanishing into the thick forest.

At first, the skimmer was too low over the water and left a giant rooster tail in its wake, and then Decker adjusted their altitude and set the autopilot to follow every meander, treating it like a dry highway. The bridges upstream of Iskellian should have enough clearance to let the low-slung vehicle pass.

He activated the remote weapons station and slewed it aft, looking for any indication of pursuit on its targeting sensor.

He found it.

They hadn't made it quite far enough to lose the city lights in the distance when six bogeys appeared on the horizon. Two settled over the waters of the Yangtze River while the remainder split up along both banks.

Given that the pursuing skimmers were identical to the one Zack had stolen but had more experienced drivers at the controls, it was just a matter of time before the militia ran them down and it turned into a firefight.

At six to one odds, Decker would quickly discover whether or not the Takan girl knew how to swim.

He examined the controls more closely, looking for something, anything that could give him an edge when the time came. His ammunition locker was full, but then so were the ones in the six pursuers, who likely also had troopers with a lot of trigger time on the guns.

Zack's eyes lingered over the commo unit for a few moments. He shrugged. "Won't know if it works until I've tried, right?"

He glanced over his shoulder at Kari and grinned, then quickly tuned the radio to the frequency Catlow had told him the rebels monitored day and night. Decker hoped that someone would think of handing Talyn a microphone instead of ignoring a guy whose voice no one recognized and who didn't have the proper codes. If he made it sound outlandish enough, the duty tech in the ruined fortress might twig.

"To anyone on the freedom road, this is Rookie Trooper wanting a chin wag with Phoenix. I'm headed upriver in a stolen militia car and have six more of them on my tail looking to score. I've got a lovely young lady with me who wants to see her momma and poppa. Over."

Then, he set the message to repeat in an endless loop and waited, watching small dots grow imperceptibly larger on his screen while they ate up the kilometers separating them from Tianjin and the highlands.

**

"Sir," the radio operator held up his hand to catch the duty officer's attention, "I'm getting a strange message on the emergency channel."

"Let me listen."

"To anyone on the freedom road," the loudspeaker blared, "this is Rookie Trooper wanting a chin wag with Phoenix. I'm headed upriver in a stolen militia car and have six more of them on my tail looking to score. I've got a lovely young lady with me who wants to see her momma and poppa. Over."

"Don't answer."

The duty officer went off in search of Verrill. Standing orders meant the boss had to be notified of anything unusual, and this qualified in spades.

He found Verrill sitting with Corde and Talyn in the all-sources intelligence center next door.

"Sir, there's a looped transmission on the emergency channel from some joker calling himself Rookie Trooper, wanting to speak with a Phoenix. Says he's running from the militia in a stolen skimmer and has a girl with him."

Talyn sprang to her feet the moment she heard Decker's nickname, excitement wiping away the weariness she'd felt after twelve hours of digging through the rebel database.

"It's Zack. He escaped with the Takan daughter. I need to speak with him."

"Rookie Trooper?" Verrill looked openly skeptical.

"A joke nickname he gave himself with the idea that no one in his right mind would want that sort of tag."

"And Phoenix is obviously you, correct?" He asked as they headed for the command post.

"Yup."

Without asking for permission, she joined the operator and demanded that he hand over a microphone.

"Rookie Trooper, this is Phoenix. What's your status?"

"I'm ten klicks upriver from Iskellian in a militia combat car, headed for Tianjin and using the water for my highway. They've put six of them on my butt and might have called up more from outlying garrisons, so it's a foregone conclusion that they'll eventually get me. If there's anything anyone can do to give us a hand, it'll improve our chances of survival. I have the one I went for with me, and she's okay. They haven't sucked her soul out yet, but if they recapture us, it'll be the first thing that happens after a charming psychopath called Rika Kozlev slices through my carotid artery, probably after cutting my balls off."

Talyn glanced up at the name and turned to Verrill.

"If you have anyone close to Zack's route who's capable of shooting down militia skimmers, now's the time to activate them. My partner doesn't know of any better way than the river to get to Tianjin and the trailhead that leads back here. He'll skip the odd meander but he can't afford to get disoriented, and that's easy to do at night, in unfamiliar territory when you're going full speed, even for a pathfinder."

When Verrill didn't answer, Talyn let herself get livid with rage.

"Zack just saved all of your butts by getting Kari out of militia hands before they mind probed her. You owe him enough to take the risk of using assets you've been keeping in reserve."

Something in her expression must have broken through the rebel leader's hesitation. If it was fear at the Fury who had replaced the calm, emotionless woman previously standing before him, so much the better.

He nodded and then spoke to the duty officer.

"Activate Case Green Three." He turned back to Hera when a thought struck him. "My people will need something to differentiate your man's skimmer from the others. You know how it is, at night, going full speed..."

"Touché," Talyn smiled, her earlier anger gone as swiftly as it had appeared. She took the microphone again. "Rookie Trooper, you need to fly the flag. Blue on blue sucks when it happens."

There was a lengthy pause, then, "I'll be the one who's shipshape by the figurehead."

"What does that mean?" Verrill asked.

"Tell your folks that the skimmer with a red light to port, a green to starboard and a white on top when seen head-on is the one they *don't* want to shoot down."

He stared blankly at her.

"If you're looking head-on at Zack's machine, you should see a triangle with a red light on your right, a green on your left, and white on top."

"Wouldn't the militia cars show the same thing?"

"And make themselves easier targets for Zack's guns?"

The rebel leader nodded. "Makes sense."

He glanced at the duty officer. "You got that, Terry?"

"Sure." The man smiled. "I used to be in the Navy."

"Anything else?" Zack's voice asked. "Because I need to focus on flying this thing now."

Verrill took the mic from Talyn.

"If you see the hillside winking, it's not for you."

"Got it. I won't wink back. Rookie Trooper, out."

"Do you have anyone who can meet them by the rapids?" Talyn asked. "Because that's where he'll be headed. He doesn't know of any other spot to get into the highlands and hide."

The duty officer looked at a computer screen and nodded.

"There's a platoon-sized patrol in the area. I'll have them divert to intercept our man. They should be there in about three hours, which might be cutting it close, but it's the best I can offer."

"That's plenty, thanks," Talyn said. "Provided he gets there in one piece, I'm sure he'll find the patrol if it doesn't find him first."

**

Decker knew there was a good chance the militia might have intercepted the transmission – it was their radio gear after all

– but hopefully, they were too busy running after him to wonder what the nonsense language was all about.

A quick look at the sensor readout proved that they'd gained a little more ground but were still out of range for his weapons, which meant he was out of range for theirs.

Rolling hills rose from the starlit prairie and the river began to meander, forcing the autopilot to slow them down lest they skip over the embankment, and Decker switched it off, preferring to fly by the seat of his own pants instead of losing ground to militia drivers who knew the terrain better than he did.

It was just as well that Kari still lay curled up in a ball in the crew compartment. Had she looked out through one of the thick viewports or at Zack's navigation screen, she might have asked that he drop her off immediately so she could take her chances with the militia on foot instead of risking a sudden stop caused by running into a large rock at two hundred kilometers an hour.

He eventually caught sight of the maglev line's steel ribbon, a bright slice in the velvety texture of the darkened fields that filled his horizon.

Suddenly, a bright flare zipped by his port side, like a shooting star that had lost its way. He looked at the targeting sensor and swore. A seventh skimmer, come from who knew where, had joined the hunt and it was half the distance from the others, which meant he was in range. But then, so was the militia vehicle.

Turning control back to the autopilot, he focused his attention on the weapons station. It was simple, almost elegantly so, geared for colonial troops and reservists who had little time or inclination to learn how to use more complex ordnance.

The targeting pip quickly centered on his pursuer, and he smiled. They had no doubt been ordered to bring them down in a manner that left at least Kari alive. He had no such limitations and selected the thirty-millimeter gun. One touch of the firing stud and it vomited three fiery rounds in rapid succession.

The first one splashed across the skimmer's front skirt while the other two missed and sped on into the night.

Decker fed minute adjustments to the computer and touched the firing stud again. This time, all three rounds hit, and the combat car slewed violently to the left, either trying to escape his next salvo or out of control thanks to battle damage. Either way, it lost ground and Zack took the controls back from the autopilot to push his fans into the red.

When the newcomer didn't reappear on his sensor, he smiled. It had been a clean hit after all. One down, the original six to go.

**

"I sure hope the next issue we get isn't going to be as damned heavy as Mathilda." Piers Jung, a farmer by day, rebel fighter by night, heaved the antiquated plasma gun off the farm truck's open bed.

He and his companion, Udo Koba, both dressed in black, with black caps and blackened faces, were two-thirds of the independence cell hailing from the farming hamlet of Odaran, two kilometers up one of the Yangtze River's tributaries.

"Never happy when you don't have anything to complain about, are you?" The older man replied. "Luck of the draw that we have to set up here."

"I think it's just a bit strange we get Case Green Three without warning like that. Tell me again what the orders said."

Jung waited until Koba had swung the tripod and his share of the ammo over his broad shoulders before heading towards a cluster of trees at the top of the bluff. It and its counterpart on the other side of the river were the best firing positions for kilometers around, and he briefly wondered whether another cell, just a stone's throw away, was doing the same.

"Ambush a flight of militia skimmers coming from Iskellian but make sure we don't touch the first one that'll come by. That's our folks in it, and they have to reach Tianjin. It should have three lights on its nose, a red on the right, a green on the left and a white on top, like a triangle."

"The green on our left or the skimmer's, because on a starship, green is on the right, starboard?" Jung bulled his way through the dense scrub towards the firing position they'd marked out weeks ago when they first got the new set of contingency orders.

"If we're facing the car, that makes it our left, right?" Koba chuckled.

"Everyone's a friggin' comedian."

They eventually came to a small depression at the edge of the bluff, well covered by vegetation on all but the side facing downriver and Koba, who was huffing like a primitive steam engine, put the tripod down.

"Set her here, kiddo. I'll go make sure we got a clear line of fire. The speed they're likely to go, we're going to get a minute, tops."

"You realize that humping Mathilda out of here if the militia decides to change targets and come after us is going to be a bitch."

"The plans for Case Green Three say that if we can't take her back, we turn her into a booby trap and run. Word is we got newer stuff coming down the line anyway."

"A sad end to a fine piece." Jung attached a large magazine to the side of the receiver, switched on the power pack, and then patted the ungainly weapon. "But if she can take out a few more of the scum as an IED, it'll be a good way to go."

Koba rejoined the younger man by the gun and handed him a set of binoculars.

"Here, you get first watch. When your eyes start seeing stuff that doesn't exist, I'll take over."

"You think we have company over there?" He nodded towards the south bank of the river.

"Why don't you go stand on the edge of the cliff and wave?" Koba nudged his friend in the ribs. "Maybe someone will wave back."

"Perhaps the next time," Jung replied, binos glued to his eyes, "there's something just popped up on the horizon. It's still too far away to see, but at this hour, who else could it be?"

"Lock and load, little buddy. It's time to shoot us some militia scum."

A broad smile appeared on Koba's wrinkled face as if he expected this to be the most fun he'd ever have.

— THIRTY-TWO —

"How did this happen?"

Harend tried to keep his voice calm, but there was no mistaking the intense anger behind it.

"A prisoner from your dungeon, Captain Kozlev, escapes with one of the best leads we've had up to now and leaves us with almost twenty casualties, six of them killed outright. How? The moment this gets around – and it will – the rebels will gain at least ten thousand more active supporters."

The other officers, standing at attention around the conference room table, carefully avoided meeting their colonel's eyes, and those closest to Kozlev tried to edge away, lest they become collateral damage.

"He can't have been just an ordinary pro, sir," she replied, her basilisk stare defiant. "I've reviewed the security camera recordings, and I estimate that he's a veteran of the Fleet's Special Forces at the very least, or maybe even naval intelligence. That would explain how he managed it."

"Or maybe he's a damned regular on a mission to fuck with us," Harend shouted, striking the table with his fist. "Not a veteran, Captain Kozlev, but a Fleet operative. Did you think of that when you decided to play games with him? Obviously not."

He fought to regain his composure in the face of this disaster.

"Sir," Major Alegre, the militia's operations officer ventured, "as of the latest report, the pursuit squadron is gaining. They'll be able to splash him well before he reaches Tianjin."

"They'd better make damn sure both of them survive. If the Fleet's already here, we need to move up the timetable."

Harend waved his hand at them.

"Dismissed, except for Captain Kozlev. I want updates every fifteen minutes."

The assembled officers snapped to attention in unison and saluted before filing out of the room. When the door shut behind the last one, Harend turned his stare on Kozlev.

"You fucked up, Rika, and you're going to fix it, or I'll make sure you stand in front of a firing squad when we return to Celeste. This escape makes us look like a laughing stock. In the space of a single evening, your dungeon of doom has become nothing more than a basement with a revolving door where anyone can leave whenever they want. That's the spin the separatists will use to win over more of the undecided."

"Ridicule kills," she replied, nodding, not in the least put out by his rage, "and right now we look ridiculous. Agreed, but that'll be sorted the moment the pursuit shoots them down and brings their carcasses back, dead or alive."

"I wish I had your confidence, Captain, but after that escape, I fear your off-world pro is going to be laughing at us all the way back into the highlands where we'll never find him."

"Perhaps." She shrugged. "If that's the case, a bit of clean-up with extreme prejudice around Tianjin might incline the colonists to opt for healthy fear instead of ridicule, especially if we can make it look like the rebellion lost its way in the wake of this little contretemps."

"I'd rather we bring both your man and the Takan girl back. It'll send the message that no one, not even the best off-world pros can escape us."

"And we will," Kozlev smiled. "I still have a date with a dagger and some tender flesh."

Harend stared at her for a few seconds, wondering again, as he'd had so many times before, how she lived with herself.

"Dismissed, Captain. We'll discuss the matter in greater depth once this is over."

She came to attention and saluted him with what seemed almost like a hint of mockery. Then she turned on her heel and left him to mentally compose his report to Governor Cedeno.

**

The mathematics of time and distance weren't open to bribery nor did they respond to Decker's creative curses.

Ahead, he saw dark shapes materialize on either side of the river where the central plateau separating the Tianjin district from the capital pushed bluffs right up to the water's edge. He'd be funneled down a narrow pass with no ability to evade his pursuers other than by going forward, and they were catching up fast.

A burst of plasma bracketed his skimmer, fire from the lead militia car. It was a warning salvo, telling him to land, but he knew the next one, should he not obey, would be aimed at his rear fans. He flicked on the remote weapons station and fired back, targeting the vehicle's center of mass. As before, the first round splashed on target, digging a divot in the metal glacis and the remainder lost themselves in the night. He was about to adjust and shoot again when bright blooms of plasma erupted from the top of the cliffs on either side of the riverbed.

They streaked over his skimmer and struck the nearest militia car, destroying part of its bow and sending it into an uncontrolled spin over the water's surface until it hit a large rock broadside on and came to a jarring halt.

Decker barely had time to see a second militia skimmer take a bad hit while the remainder broke left and right to avoid sharing the same fate before he was swallowed by the narrow river canyon.

"I don't know who you guys are," he shouted, relief flooding his nervous system like an euphoric drug, "but BOOYAH!"

He glanced over his shoulder at Kari and grinned maniacally.

"Looks like your dad's buddies got themselves a piece of our action, kid. We're not alone in this anymore."

They were half-way to Tianjin by now which meant it was quickly becoming bandit country for the militia. He was going to make it after all.

**

"I guess we did have company," Jung shouted, running through the woods a few steps behind Koba. "Did you see them nail one of the fuckers? A thing of beauty. Too bad about Mathilda, but she'll go out like a champ after scoring a most beautiful hit."

They reached the farm truck hidden under a clump of native giant ferns and climbed in.

The older man switched on the reactor and lit his fans. Moments later, they were careening down a dirt track in absolute darkness, and only the farmer's instinct and knowledge of the area kept them from crashing into trees that were hard enough to dent armor.

A dull thump suddenly reverberated and a brief, bright glow outlined the crest where they'd left the booby-trapped gun.

"Yes!" Jung pumped his fist. "Nailed more of the bastards."

"I'll be happy if the remainder don't take it into their minds to come looking for us just now. I've no wish to end up singing for my life in their damned dungeons."

**

Major Alegre, face drained of all color, stood rigidly at attention in front of Colonel Harend's desk. His lips trembled while he tried to find a way of reporting the newest disaster that wouldn't result in a thorough reaming out. In the end, he decided there was no way to sugarcoat bad news

"The pursuit squadron reports two cars out of commission from enemy fire and two more damaged by rebel IEDs on the Odaran bluffs. Five dead, nine injured. We haven't heard from the Holback garrison skimmer who joined the chase an hour before this incident, so I'm presuming it went down as well. That leaves two cars still in pursuit of the escapees."

Harend didn't immediately react, though a vein began throbbing on the side of his bald skull while his jaw muscles worked their way through an indigestible piece of news.

"Have you scrambled the Tianjin garrison?" He asked in a voice so soft that Alegre had to lean forward.

"Yes, sir. They sent two cars downriver to intercept and a patrol upriver as a backstop by the rapids."

"You warned the garrison commander that if the escapees make it into the highlands, his next posting will be to the southern polar weather station?"

"I did."

"Then you may go."

Alegre escaped Harend's office with a sigh of relief, astonished at his CO's uncharacteristic restraint. Provided he could bring some good news before this was over...

Alone once more, his fingers drumming impatiently on the desk's polished surface, Harend wondered how he could spin this latest loss of face. Cedeno's disgust would be the least of his worries if more farmers volunteered to take up arms.

His forces weren't strong enough to keep control over the entire colony in the absence of fear. He could lower standards to increase the number of recruits of course; but that would mean reducing the militia's fighting ability as a whole, at least for a while.

Given enough time, it would be a viable solution, yet there was a bigger problem when it came to enlisting less desirable volunteers from among the deportee population. He just didn't have enough regular or ex-regular non-coms in the ranks to keep reprisals against colonists from getting out of hand.

Already, there had been too many incidents for comfort, and if they became too well known, it would only be a matter of time before a Marine landing force dropped down on the government precinct and started dictating the law. Once that happened, he could say farewell to any chance of finally getting his general's stars.

If he lost the ability to strike fear into the colonists' hearts, their minds would soon be looking for more inventive ways of thwarting the government. No, he had to catch the bastard who thumbed his nose at them and execute him in public. It would undoubtedly send the right message: fuck with us and die.

There was a soft knock at the door, and Harend glanced up to see Alegre again. The major looked like death warmed over.

"Sir," he began, evidently unwilling to step inside, "the two Tianjin cars were shot down with short-range missiles shortly after leaving town. There were no survivors."

Harend stared at the operations officer as if he was having difficulties deciphering his words.

"Have the Tianjin folks determined where those missiles were fired from?" He finally asked.

Alegre nodded nervously.

"From the heights over the Yangtze River rapids."

Harend tilted his head back and sighed.

"God give me strength. Isn't that where the backstop patrol was supposed to go?"

Alegre nodded again.

"Did someone warn them that they might be running smack dab into the rebels?"

This time, the operations officer shook his head.

"And why not, pray tell?" Harend asked even though he suspected that he knew the answer.

"No one has been able to raise the patrol since their transport dropped them off at the trailhead."

"So we can presume the worst, I gather." He closed his eyes and breathed in deeply. "That doesn't leave Tianjin enough troops to send out anyone else without seriously compromising our hold on the town itself."

"The two remaining Iskellian cars are still on the escapees' trail, sir."

"Yes, and we've seen how well that worked for the others, haven't we?"

**

"Rookie Trooper, his is Phoenix," Hera Talyn's voice startled Zack. He'd been staring at Tianjin's lights, now glowing on the horizon, wondering whether the militia would seize them this close to freedom.

"Rookie Trooper here," he replied.

"DZ's clear, I repeat, DZ's clear. No bogeys circling. Watch for the markers."

"Roger. Be advised I still have two of them stuck to my ass and closing in."

A streak of plasma glanced off his side armor, and the car shuddered but remained on course.

"Amendment to my last. I have two of them stuck on my ass *and* delivering effective fire."

The skimmer shuddered again when a further salvo skipped off the protected aft fan housing.

"I might not make it to the DZ," he added, aiming his own main gun on the lead militia car. He might as well empty out the ammo locker at this point.

"Hang on just a little longer," Talyn replied. "Help is almost within range."

No sooner had she uttered the word 'range' that a twin streak of plasma erupted from the ground, two kilometers ahead, where the open fields gave way to dense native vegetation.

Caught between Decker's gun and the rebels shooting from their prepared positions on either side of the river, the last two militia cars veered sharply away, unwilling to risk their comrades' fate.

"Phoenix, this is Rookie Trooper, tell the nice folks who just gave me some covering fire I'd like to buy them a beer someday, and tell the DZ master that I'm inbound."

This late at night, few people wandered through Tianjin's streets, but those who did were treated to the spectacle of a militia car skimming the river's surface at high speed, ducking under bridges and firing back at militia squads attempting to bring it down.

Within a few short minutes, Decker had left the town's bright lights behind and was fast approaching the dark mountain range where the highlands began, and no militia soldier dared go.

"Rookie Trooper," a familiar voice came over the radio, "this is Silahdar One-Four, we've got your red-green-white in sight. Watch your front for the markers."

Tran Kidder. Only he would use that call sign. Decker smiled. Old comrades indeed. A man he'd trained to become a first class platoon leader in the most screwed-up army he'd ever served.

Zack cut his speed, lest they run up the first of the rapids without due care. It would be the height of stupidity to ground himself so close to the finish line after all the effort Verrill's troops had put into covering their wild run.

Faint red lights suddenly appeared, and he slowed down to a walking pace when he realized they led away from the churning waters to a flat piece of ground covered by an overhang dripping with riotous vegetation.

He crept under the drooping ferns with caution and then when the soldier who'd guided him in held his glow sticks up in a diagonal cross, he cut the fans and let the skimmer settle to the ground.

A bead of perspiration ran down the side of his face, skirting his left eye, and he suddenly noticed that he was soaked with sweat.

The sound of a hand knocking on the skimmer's side reminded Decker that they had to get away fast. Rebel fire might have made the last two militia cars keep their distance, but they weren't out of the fight yet and would have picked up his trail again when the rebel ground gunners had melted back into the night.

He unlocked the hatch and stepped out, stretching muscles that had come within a hair's breadth of cramping up most painfully.

"Zack?"

"Yup." Decker's teeth were a brilliant white in the faint light. "I never thought I'd say this about an ugly mug like yours, Tran, but you're a sight for some very sore eyes, even if I can barely see you."

"You've got Kari Takan?"

"Alive and scared out of her wits. She's in the rear."

Kidder waved at a pair of soldiers who then climbed aboard to retrieve the girl.

"She's our problem now, buddy. We'll take care of her on the march. Are you set for a long hike yourself?"

"Not particularly. I had to get dressed in a hurry after I knocked some heads together."

He briefly related the conditions under which he'd been imprisoned.

"We'll rustle up something for you at the rendezvous point while we regroup."

Kidder was about to turn away when a muffled shout came through the curtain of moss and ferns.

"Bogeys inbound. They might have spotted the markers before we shut them off."

"The last of my escort, no doubt," Decker said. "They won't want to face their CO empty-handed so you can count on them trying to kill us with whatever they have left."

"That's what I figured," Kidder replied with a nod at his patrol sergeant, who began chivvying the troops towards a narrow path that wound its way along the foaming rapids.

"We shot both of our missiles at the Tianjin skimmers the moment we figured they were headed your way, but my machine gunner's got himself a good position up top. He'll keep them away until we're on the other side of the ridge where they can't follow us."

The thumping of large-bore plasma fire reached their ears over the rushing water, and Kidder grinned at Zack, who responded with raised thumb. The weapon fired a few more times and then fell silent. All that remained was the sound of the Yangtze River tumbling down from the highlands as it had for untold millennia before the first humans set foot on Garonne.

**

"Your Rookie Trooper and Kari Takan have been recovered by Kidder's patrol," Verrill said, dropping on the bench beside Talyn. He looked and sounded worn out. "They're unharmed. We should see them around mid-morning. The patrol is going to march all night."

A smile of relief touched her lips, and she reached out to lay a hand on the rebel leader's arm.

"Thank you. I know what it might cost to have activated your folks for this, but it had to be done."

Verrill nodded.

"Agreed."

"If nothing else," she continued, "the display of strength and the casualties we inflicted on the militia will give independence supporters heart and make the enemy look and feel weak. That alone is worth its weight in antimatter."

He gave her a tight grin.

"From the handbook of counter-insurgency, is it?" Then before she could answer, he nodded towards her cup of coffee. "If you haven't caffeinated yourself into oblivion, might I suggest you grab some shut-eye? There's nothing left that won't wait until daylight. Maybe thinking about the turmoil your partner's caused among the enemy will give you sweet dreams."

She drained her cup and rose.

"One of the useful things Zack's taught me is to fall asleep anywhere when I had the chance to get a bit of rest. I think I'll go exercise that little nugget of wisdom."

Talyn touched Verrill again and then left him alone in the empty mess hall to contemplate the consequences of the day's events.

His mind's eye tried to imagine Colonel Harend's rage and a tired smile slowly creased his craggy features. It may have been chaotic at best, but this was the first real defeat they'd inflicted on the colonial government and it felt good.

— THIRTY-THREE —

Decker tossed a flat rock at the clear mountain tarn, grunting with satisfaction when it skipped five times before sinking. Two days had passed since his frantic run up the Yangtze River, and Talyn had taken him out on a walk in the woods behind the ruined L'Taung fortress. They needed a place to speak where none of Verrill's people could overhear them.

Though alien, the Garonne forest had an eerie beauty that soothed the eye and gave the two operatives a rare moment of peace. Small creatures skittered in the undergrowth, some poking triangular heads through the tall grass to briefly examine the intruders before deciding they were neither prey nor predator.

A faint scent of herbs, both sweet and savory wafted on the sunny morning air, and there was nothing within sight or earshot to indicate they weren't the only humans on the planet.

Zack wiped his hands on his trousers and sat on the fallen tree trunk beside his partner who was enjoying the warmth of the sun on her face after days stuck inside the cold rebel lair.

"Did you find anything interesting while I was gone?" He pulled a coffee bulb from his pack, opened it, and took a tentative sip. "Not bad. Not the real stuff, but not bad."

She reached for the bulb and tasted it herself.

"It's what I was putting down my gullet twenty hours a day during your little jaunt to Iskellian. It may not taste like much, but it works." She handed the bulb back to Decker.

"I haven't been able to drill down into the more heavily encrypted parts of their database, but what I found proves that there's a lot of money flowing into the rebellion's coffers. A heck of a lot. More than they could ever raise through contributions from the colonists or even the gaggle of off-world supporters who'll feed the kitty of any organization trying to stick it to a home world."

"So they have a couple of rich uncles in the Senate." Decker finished his coffee and tucked the empty container back into his pack.

"No uncles are that rich, Zack. Whoever is funding the independence movement has to be expecting a quid pro quo at some point."

"Evidently." He opened a small package containing pastries freshly baked that morning. "Croissant?"

"Sure." She took the proffered confection and nibbled on one end. "Very nice."

"From what I saw of the militia, compared to other shitholes on the rim, they're not suffering for lack of funds either. The skimmer I stole was almost brand new, not some clapped out piece sold down the line by the Constabulary after they rode it into the ground. Ditto for the interrogation gear and the weaponry. The colonial government has some rich uncles too."

"They've got Celeste funding them, remember?"

"Normal pattern is militias get the hand-me-downs from the guard. They're not playing with big brother's old toys. I'll bet if I took stock of their armory, I'd find stuff that goes for top price. That got me to thinking about why Celeste is so keen to hold on to a place that can support itself but doesn't produce all that much to earn hard export currency. It doesn't seem worth the hassle, especially once the Senate gets off its duff and takes a hard look at Garonne's development status."

Decker fell silent, staring at the pond while he slowly chewed.

"You heard that the militia has been running rampant through the Tianjin district for the last day or so?" He asked after a while.

"Yup. You embarrassed them and made the buggers look ridiculous so they're working hard to get fear back into the colonists."

"That's going to backfire. It always backfires. Harend can't be much of a strategist if he figures it'll do them any good in the long run."

"We all have our blind spots," Talyn pointed out, "and most people lose their objectivity when they're made to look foolish."

"It won't end well for anyone." He shook his head. "I'm getting that sweet, sweet sensation of déjà vu all over again. Pour a lot of money into a place where both sides have drawn bloody battle lines, and you *will* get civil war. Verrill's generous funding allows him to buy massive amounts of modern weaponry and the militia's getting new toys. The math isn't hard to do, Hera."

"Why all the money?" She pulled out her water bottle and washed down the last of the croissant.

"That's the question, isn't it?" He watched a couple of small critters cautiously approach the far side of the pond. "You'd think if Celeste wanted to hold on to Garonne they'd do something smarter than letting the likes of Rika Kozlev satisfy her perversions on the backs of civilians."

"Nasty customer?"

"She's what you might have become if you'd given into the ugly side of your nature. She crossed the line you didn't and at high speed too. I'm usually not that choosy when it comes to playing, but just one glance into her eyes shriveled me up."

"Coming from you, that says something." She smirked at her partner.

"I'll bet her dungeon is filling up with suspects right now and by the laws of probability, they'll haul in someone who knows enough to give the militia a thread to pull on."

"And then things start getting out of hand."

"That's the typical pattern when it comes to colonial wars. They start off small and then some get too big to contain," he replied.

"When that happens, in come the Marines, up goes the system blockade..."

"And the Fleet gets sucked into a quagmire that distracts it for years and earns it new enemies from among the independence-minded systems. Shit." Decker swore. "That has to be it."

They contemplated the shimmering surface of the tarn in silence until Talyn spoke again.

"I can think of another possibility."

"And what would that be?"

"There's at least one L'Taung site on Garonne – we're living in it right now – which means that there are probably a lot more that haven't been found yet."

"So someone's trying to fight a proxy war to secure control over those sites? Why?"

Talyn picked a blade of grass and rolled it between her slender fingers.

"Seventy-odd years ago, so the top secret, never to be declassified report says, the Fleet set up shop on a L'Taung site in the Arietis system where they found artifacts, some of which apparently were still in working condition. Imagine if the same exists here on Garonne. The value to whoever took possession would be incalculable."

"Bullshit." Decker laughed. "Nothing could stay in working condition after a hundred thousand years."

"What if the proto-Shrehari developed a form of stasis that did just that? Most of the scientists who've been studying the sites found in the last few decades figure they were more advanced than we or their descendants, the modern Shrehari, are."

"What happened to the Arietis site?"

"It was destroyed in a reiver attack and abandoned. As a matter of fact, Admiral Dunmoore was there, according to the report I read."

"Really?" He looked at his partner, eyebrows raised. "And why is the report top secret never to be declassified if we've found other remains since then?"

"Politics, what else?" Talyn stood and stretched. "There was a movement afoot to overthrow the government because of its mishandling of the war and some senior officers were deeply involved, including the admiral responsible for the Arietis site."

"Oh." He frowned for a moment. "Say, I forgot to mention this, but I think there's a site right beside the town of Kaholo, where Kari Takan and I got taken by the militia." He went on to describe the overgrown mesa. "Considering that it's the only pimple in an otherwise flat area and has a top flat enough to land a starship..."

"So you're saying my theory has validity." She smiled down at him.

"I'm saying it has some merit, but I still can't see how ancient piles of rock warrant feeding massive amounts of off-world

money to both sides of what'll quickly turn into a nasty war."
He rose and wiped debris from the seat of his pants.

"So you're sticking to your theory?" She teased.

"I prefer to let the big brains in the analysis section figure that one out. In the meantime, I'm more worried about things spiraling out of control around here. Once the militia decides that they have to crack down the hardest with the mostest and Verrill's rebels decide to strike back just as hard, the colonists in the middle are going to die in job lots."

"No arguments from me."

"So far, neither side has pushed real hard. Verrill's still hoping to put enough pressure on the government to come to a negotiated solution, and Cedeno doesn't want to risk outside intervention because things went sideways and out of his control. My gut tells me they're both about to lose control of their respective forces and then..."

He let is voice drift off before continuing.

"As the saying goes, if you make peaceful change impossible then violent change becomes inevitable."

"Don't let your nightmares of other times and other planets influence your judgment, Zack." She gently touched his arm.

"Those other times and other planets all ended up with piles of innocents bleeding out their last on the farms they'd carved from an alien landscape, not to speak of all those good Marines ending up in body bags because they tried to stop the killing. If there's the slightest chance we can help avoid it by short-circuiting the long, deadly spiral into full-out war, then we have to act."

Talyn shook her head.

"We're hunter-gatherers, Zack, not knights in powered armor speeding to the rescue. Our job is to hunt for bad guys and gather intelligence so that the knights can do their jobs."

"By the time the Senate authorizes Fleet intervention, especially if the rich uncles throwing money at both sides like drunken spacers are political, it'll be too late."

"We cannot get involved in this fight without authorization, Chief Warrant Officer Decker."

"Tell me this, Commander Talyn," he replied, a sly smile slowly spreading across his square face, "who's the senior Commonwealth Ground Forces officer on Garonne?"

She stared at him momentarily, and then shook her head.

"Oh no. You don't get to play barracks lawyer with me, mister. If you're the senior ground forces officer, then I'm the senior naval officer for the entire Garonne system and still your superior."

"So use your initiative, senior naval person. We're out of contact with HQ and have a unique opportunity to make sure the mistakes of the past don't infest this lovely place."

"If I order you not to, you're going to do it anyway, right?" Talyn sighed. "And one of the first lessons they teach at the Academy is never give an order you know isn't going to be obeyed."

"What if I told you I think the Coalition is behind the growing mess here? Would that be incentive enough?"

She was brought up short by his words and went back through all the intelligence she'd gathered. After almost a minute, Talyn met her partner's eyes and nodded.

"Plausible. What prompted that leap of logic? Fomenting rebellion on the colony of a planet whose government plays nice with the Coalition, based on all of the intelligence reports I've read, is a departure from their usual modus operandi."

"Cui bono?" He raised his arms, palms facing upwards and cocked an eyebrow. "Who, of any group we know, would profit from ensnaring the Fleet in a nasty colonial war on the Rim? Who would profit from laying the blame for war crimes on the Fleet? Heck, who would profit from distracting our admirals and generals for a few years?"

"The Shrehari?' She asked, just for devilment's sake. "Some of them are still smarting from the armistice we forced on the Empire seventy years ago."

"Possible, but my instincts tell me this is homebrewed. The Shrehari never got a good understanding of how the human brain works, or doesn't work, as they case may be, and this smells of basic mass psychology. I'm telling you, it's our Coalition friends."

"And distracting the Fleet by setting the Rim on fire gives them room to advance their schemes." Talyn nodded. "Sadly, your theory is probably the right one."

"It is, and I don't want to end up serving a human empire controlled by the likes of the late Harmon Amali and his buddies. For all its imperfections, the Commonwealth is still a damn sight better. The way to stop them is to stop this war, here and now."

Talyn glanced at the smooth surface of the pond, wondering how her rough and tumble Marine partner had become a perceptive intelligence officer without her noticing.

"I suppose you have a plan, otherwise proposing to put this planet under your remit as senior ground forces officer rings kind of hollow."

"But of course." The grin widened. "Decapitation. Swift, hard and, compared to any other alternative, clean. I've seen how their HQ folks react when things suddenly go to hell. Lay it on them hard and fast, right in their safe space and they'll crumble."

When he finished outlining his idea, Talyn was forced to admit that decapitation had a chance of succeeding. And if it did, it would bring the Garonne rebellion to a swift end in favor of the independence movement without sucking in a Marine division or two along with a few naval battle groups who'd be better employed keeping the star lanes safe from marauders.

Selling the idea to Verrill and the rest of the rebellion's leadership would be another issue altogether.

"We'll propose it," she said, "but if they reject the plan, we stick to our hunter-gatherer job and collect enough proof to give our bosses back home leverage to force a resolution."

She waited until he nodded his acceptance of her terms, but she wasn't finished.

"If Verrill agrees, we'll help with the planning, but we will not get involved in the fighting. The optimum outcome is the independence movement succeeding in such a way that the Fleet can never be accused of aiding them, much less be seen fighting on their side. If the Coalition is behind this and can accuse the Armed Services of favoring rebellion in the colonies, the damage could be just as severe as a full intervention."

"I doubt that. The bastards wouldn't creep out from whatever swamp they own and point a finger at the Grand Admiral. Not after you and I have proved to them the Fleet can and will sic its hunters on their leadership if they go too far. I bet there's still a bunch of people called Amali who look over their shoulders every few seconds in fear that they might share the fate of the last two heads of the family.”

“Perhaps, but we will not get involved in the fighting, understood. You may be the de facto senior grunt on Garonne, but that doesn’t mean HQ will endorse exceeding the limits of our mission parameters by actively shooting at government forces.”

“Too late for that, remember?” Decker picked up his pack and headed towards the trail leading back to the base. “There are a dozen militia corpses that say I’ve already begun fighting.”

“As a freelancer called Bill Whate.” She caught up with his long stride. “And that’s how it’ll stay.”

When he didn’t answer she said, “The expected response is aye, aye, sir.”

“Yes, sir. I understand, sir. I will adapt and overcome as the situation warrants, sir.” He made a face at Talyn, proving that even though he’d matured as an intelligence officer, the warrior with a volatile temper still lurked below the surface.

“This Captain Kozlev character really got to you, didn’t she?”

“Not to the extent she did with those who suffered through her interrogation techniques, or the ones who will until we put an end to this garbage. Maybe I’ll stay out of the fight, but if I get my hands on Kozlev...”

**

“I’m very troubled by the recent events, Colonel Harend.” Governor Cedeno looked up from the report with a frown on his pinched face. “I fail to understand how a rebellion that was supposedly weak and uncoordinated could carry out such a coup.”

“The individual who escaped with the Takan girl, variously known as Skeen or Whate, seems to be a highly trained operative, possibly even Fleet, sir. It’s the only explanation.”

Harend stood in the parade rest position in front of the governor’s desk like a junior officer about to be read the riot act.

“Perhaps.” Cedeno sat back and studied Harend’s face. “But that’s not what troubles me, Colonel. Nor are the casualties the man caused when he broke out, or the fact that he rescued the daughter of the first real lead into the independence movement's leadership that we've ever had. No, what troubles me is how the rebellion was able to organize a well-equipped force to cover the escape and do so in the space of a few hours. Weak and uncoordinated? I doubt the assessment still holds true if it ever did. Five combat cars totaled. They were almost new and cost a fortune. The home world won't be happy when I ask for more money to buy replacements."

"We know from radio intercepts that this Whate character got in touch with the rebellion shortly after he escaped. That gave their leadership plenty of time to activate armed cells throughout the countryside, cells we didn't suspect existed."

"Obviously." Cedeno's irritation, never far from the surface, rang out clearly in that single, dismissive word.

Harend's face tightened.

"It won't happen again, sir. We're searching everything and everyone along the escape route. I can assure you that we will find those who shot down our cars and bring them in. My intelligence officer is confident that we'll be able to make a serious dent in the rebel infrastructure along the Yangtze River and in the Tianjin district in particular."

"Take care that they don't make another dent in *your* infrastructure, Colonel. If they can afford to abandon their weapons after turning them into IEDs for your troops to find, they must feel quite confident about their supply lines. And do try to keep Captain Kozlev on a tight leash. I'm well aware that her methods sometimes border on the illegal. A few questionable actions might pass. Too many of them and someone will take notice. Neither of us wants that. Nor do we want a growing population in your stockade, so make sure those you do arrest can actually be connected to the rebellion."

"Yes, sir," Harend replied, suppressing his growing anger at the governor's didactic tone. "I can guarantee that they'll be connected to the rebellion once we're done with them."

"I'm not sure I like your tone, Colonel."

The two men stared at each other, neither willing to be the first to break eye contact.

"And I don't appreciate your innuendo concerning one of my subordinates, sir."

"It's not innuendo when there have been at least three cases in the last month where a detainee vanished into your headquarters, never to re-appear." Cedeno waved towards the door. "You're dismissed."

Biting back a sudden flare of rage, Harend saluted then turned on his heels with parade ground precision and marched out of the large office.

If it weren't for Cedeno's orders restricting his prosecution of independence movement supporters, the damned off-world pro might never have had the ground support that saved his worthless ass. They would have recovered Kari Takan, which would have made the current raids against suspected rebel cells that much more precise, less bloody and with less collateral damage.

On the other hand, blooding his troops might just provide additional motivation and draw in new recruits. It was an ill wind that brought no one any good.

He walked out of the governor's residence just in time to see a freighter land at the spaceport south of Iskellian. It reminded him that there was still an armed starship in the service of the rebellion hidden somewhere in the highlands. If it weren't for the need to deal with recent events, they might have found it by now and really hurt the bastards, perhaps even crewed it with their own people so he didn't have to rely on mercenaries who ran the moment someone shot a few missiles up their skirts.

The idea that control of events might begin to slip from his grasp never occurred to Harend. For him, the rebellion was still a nuisance force made up of farmers, failures, and off-world adventurers, notwithstanding their propensity for good marksmanship and grasp of effective IED construction.

His militia, though its faults were many, was still a force with professionals at the helm, and it would get better at counter-insurgency faster than the insurgents got better at fighting back. He had staked his hopes of promotion on it and he would see it through, Cedeno's delicate sensibilities notwithstanding.

His eyes were drawn to the arrival of a combat car across the square. It stopped by the side door of the main headquarters building and disgorged a trio of green-clad troopers who then pulled two struggling civilians from the crew compartment.

He knew Kozlev would let them marinate for a while before introducing herself. Perhaps he'd join her later today. His anger at Cedeno had woken a nasty streak within him that might only be assuaged by the sight of some rebel sympathizers laid low under Rika's tender mercies.

— THIRTY-FOUR —

"You can lead a horse's ass to facts, but you can't make him think," Decker grumbled after he and Talyn left the conference room after a particularly acrimonious discussion.

"I've never seen a bunch of people who were more frightened of their own shadows. If Verrill hadn't shut that idiot Roste up, I swear I'd have reached across the table and throttled him myself."

"That's a tad harsh, Zack," she chided. "You're asking them to risk everything on a single gamble. And don't tell me it's a sure thing. You're the one who keeps saying that no plan survives contact with the enemy."

"Granted," he said, trying to shake off his anger at the cold reception they'd been given by the rebellion's command group. "But the longer they wait, the harder and bloodier it'll get, something Ser Roste, for all his high and mightiness within the independence movement, seems singularly determined not to understand, no matter what I do."

"I'll remind you of something a Marine I sometimes sleep with likes to say." She smiled at him, mischief dancing in her eyes. "You shouldn't argue with a moron; he'll just beat you down with experience."

It was enough to break down the last bits of anger that still poisoned his mood and Zack put an arm around Talyn, hugging her.

"Trust you to use my words against me, sweetheart. I think if it hadn't been for Roste, I might have swayed enough of them that we'd still be in there, looking more closely at the details. Maybe I should waylay the bastard tonight and take him out for a long hike in the woods that'll see me come back by my lonesome."

"No."

"Just like that: no? So what do we do instead?"

"Focus on our mission. Remember, hunting and gathering? And once we have what our bosses need, we bugger off."

He suddenly stopped and turned to face her, placing a hand on each of her shoulders.

"Want to try a bit of threat analysis, since we're gatherers of disconnected facts that often merge into a coherent picture?"

"Dazzle me with your brilliance, big boy."

"Not here. Let's go visit the great outdoors."

She gave Zack a surprised look but followed him to the back entrance, where a trail led to the mountain tarn they'd admired a few days earlier before.

When Decker figured they were far enough from indiscrete ears, he found a large rock and sat down, indicating with a nod that Talyn should join him.

"So?" She asked.

"Roste. He had the Jackals on his trail when we joined the other ships for the run to Garonne. They stuck with us until they were sure the weapons shipment would make it. Our analysts figure the bastards sometimes do wet work for the *Sécurité Spéciale,* and those buggers have been known to do the Coalition's bidding. Now, he's the one arguing the loudest against a decapitation strike that has a good chance of working and ending this before it sinks into an all-out, drag-down war. Do you see what I saying here?"

"To use another one of your favorite expressions in vain, once is happenstance, twice is a coincidence. I don't see the third item that'll convince me it's all due to enemy action. Correlation does not imply causation. Rule number one for any good intelligence officer."

He shook his head, frowning while he replayed the discussion with the rebel leadership in his mind.

"Sorry. With all due deference to your greater experience, my instinct tells me there's fire under that smoke. It may not be what I think, but my gut is willing to bet on Roste having reasons of his own to shoot down the plan; reasons that aren't related to tactical difficulties."

Talyn analyzed Zack's suspicions in silence before speaking again.

"Okay. For some reason I still can't identify, I'm willing to humor you for now. I'll have a quiet chat with Corde. She strikes me as a sensible sort, and we've bonded over long hours of sifting through data while you were playing tourist with a gun. But for now, you *will* leave it be, Chief Warrant Officer Decker. Maybe Verrill will think some more once he's away from all the noise of a full council meeting. He was interested when you first broached the idea."

"Someone needs to remind him that a military organization isn't a democracy. The commanding officer makes the final decision."

She chuckled at his vehemence.

"That's pretty rich. As your commanding officer, I spend way more time arguing with you than I should."

"Yeah," he grinned back at her, "but as my commanding officer, you shouldn't be having sex with me either and you don't hear me complain."

**

"Sorry about how the discussion went, Zack." Verrill held out a mug of coffee. "As a former military man, you'll appreciate how hard it is to bring together a bunch of folks with little to no experience of working in a command-driven environment. Be thankful I managed to squash the idea of putting orders to a vote in the early days of the rebellion."

"Thanks." He took a sip, and then helped himself to more sweetener. "No offense but this stuff tastes like burning camelot dung."

"What the heck is a camelot?" The rebel leader raised a hand. "No. Never mind. I don't think I want to know."

"I noticed that Roste was the most vocal in there," Decker remarked, stirring in a glob of the syrupy stuff the mess hall had on offer.

"Yeah. He's one of the more opinionated members of the inner council."

"More opinionated?" Zack raised a skeptical eyebrow. "He's got a stubborn streak and a mouth that would put the camelot I mentioned just now to shame. What's his story?"

Verrill shrugged.

"Same as anyone's. He came here from Celeste a long time ago to settle. The militia shut down his business on suspicion of spreading sedition when the independence movement started getting vocal. He lost nearly everything he worked for, and when I canvassed those in the movement willing to go beyond slogans and pamphlets, he was among the first to volunteer."

"Military background?"

Verrill hesitated before answering.

"Yes. He and I served together in the Celeste National Guard before immigrating to Garonne at the end of our hitch."

"Any chance either of you knows Colonel Harend personally from those days?"

Again, the hesitation, then Verrill nodded.

"We both do, but it was a long time ago when we were junior non-coms in the same regiment. He stayed in and went for a commission while Roste and I left the uniform and Celeste behind."

"Neither of you was cut out for a military career?"

"Not in the National Guard at any rate." Verrill grimaced. "But that's all long in the past, well before Garonne turned into the latest case of home world oppression. Why the interest in Roste's past?"

Zack stared down into his coffee for a few seconds.

"I'm trying to figure out why he was working so hard to shut down any discussion of the plan Hera and I presented. Most of the others seemed willing to explore the idea and see if it offered us a chance of ending the conflict before it got too bloody."

"I'll grant you that he was unusually aggressive, but he's a bit of a hothead to begin with, and when a notion enters his mind, he takes it far more to heart than other people." Verrill paused when he noticed Decker's sardonic expression. "I'm sure that if he believed your idea had some merit, he'd have muted his opposition. None of us wants this to go on forever. We want our old lives back."

Zack stared at the rebel leader with a raised eyebrow.

"Really? None of you want this to go on forever?"

"What are you trying to insinuate?"

"Insinuate? Verrill, doesn't Roste's vehemence sound suspicious, especially before we even discussed the details? We're talking about the guy whose ship was trailed by the Confederacy of the Howling Stars all the way to the rendezvous and then to the edge of this system for all we know. I seem to recall you never got a satisfactory answer to that little incident. And now he's afire to toss out something that just might short-circuit the militia's idea of a small colonial war. I get that he doesn't like me, and the feeling is mutual, but really?"

"Roste can't be held responsible for the Confederacy and like I said, he's quick with his temper."

Verrill seemed to shrug the Marine's words off, but there now was a spark of doubt in his eyes, and Zack figured it was time to change the subject to something more immediate: the on-going militia raids in every settlement within twenty kilometers of the Yangtze River and what the rebels could do about them.

It proved to be safer ground for both men.

**

Hera found Corde in the all-sources center, staring listlessly at a computer screen.

"Cred for your thoughts?" She asked, sitting across from the other woman.

"If it buys me something I can use to shut people up when they get thoroughly annoying, sure."

"Roste?"

"Yeah. I can't recall seeing him try to shoot down an idea with such vigor before and that's saying something. He likes to think of himself as the conscience of the Movement's armed wing. A lot of us think he's more of a horse's ass, but there you have it."

Talyn related Decker's earlier quip and Corde laughed.

"That just about sums him up when he puts his mind to it. Pity we can't just write him off as a moron. IIe's actually pretty smart in many respects."

"Then why does he think, right off the bat, that the decapitation option has no redeeming qualities that might merit closer scrutiny?"

Corde shrugged.

"Beats me. My best guess is fear of failure and the consequences if we put everything we have in a single operation."

"But you wouldn't be doing that."

"Sure, and I understand what you were getting at, but Roste and some of the others aren't buying what you're selling. It's the whole recent arrivals telling us old-timers what to do syndrome."

"Even though Zack's a twenty year Marine command sergeant with more combat experience than any ten veterans you have in your ranks put together?"

"Human nature." She met Talyn's eyes. "I'm sure you know all about that."

"So what do we do about it?"

"*We?*"

"You're the number two in this outfit. Your voice should count for more with Verrill than any of the others, no matter how close they were before picking up a gun in the name of freedom."

"And you?"

A faint smile appeared on Corde's lips.

"I'm Zack Decker's keeper. My job is to make sure his enthusiasm for a good fight doesn't take us places we'd rather avoid and Iskellian isn't one of them. In fact, it's the only place we can't avoid, either now or in the future. Only, the longer we wait, the harder it'll get and the harder it gets, the bloodier it'll be."

"And the bloodier it is, the harder it'll be to build a sane, free society afterward." Corde nodded. "I've read the analyses of the Migration Wars and nearly every colonial conflict since the last one."

"So why don't you encourage Verrill to override the inner council and use his power as commanding officer?"

"If I thought it would do any good, I'd be nagging him until his ears fell off. It won't. He respects the senior leadership and their opinions, and figures overriding them won't be good for the Movement's continued health."

"A drawn-out war of attrition won't be either. What's going on right now is the first harbinger of the coming bitterness between factions. It hasn't touched anyone beyond the river valley and the Tianjin district yet, but it'll spread inexorably as the militia's ranks and confidence grow."

"What is the quaint expression I've heard so often from my late father? You're preaching to the choir?"

"So? Let's go out and convert some heathens, you and me." Talyn grinned. "It beats sitting here, reading the latest depressing reports from the front lines."

**

"Sergeant Steiger reporting to the Captain as ordered."

"At ease." Rika Kozlev waved towards the sole chair in front of her desk. "Sit."

When Steiger had obeyed, Kozlev examined her in silence, head tilted to one side.

"You seem to have come through the mess of Ser Whate's murderous rampage better than any of the others in my section."

"I've been shot at often enough that the experience has lost some of its punch, sir."

"Glad to hear it, because I'm about to send you into the closest thing we have to bandit country on Garonne outside of the highlands. The garrison commander in Tianjin has requested a qualified field interrogator so he can process more suspects on site rather than send them all the way to Iskellian under escort. With your counter-insurgency experience, it should be a good fit. I've noticed that you're less than enthusiastic about the deeper kind of interrogation we practice here at HQ, and I hate wasting talent in a job that isn't a good fit."

"Yes, sir. Thank you, sir."

Though she kept a straight face and an even voice, she felt deeply relieved by the change in duties. She'd begun to fear that participating in Captain Kozlev's treatment of civilian detainees was pushing her into a dark place from which she could never escape.

"You'll be supporting Tianjin, but you will still be part of my unit and report to me. Any detainees you think need my personal attention, you will ship them here, and the garrison commander will have no choice but to assist."

"Understood, sir. When do I leave?"

"On the next train headed east which would be," she glanced at her tablet, "in two hours. Get packed and hand your open files to Mikkels. The duty driver will take you to the station."

Steiger stood up, came to attention, and saluted. Then, when she was about to leave, Kozlev said, "Don't disappoint me with this task, Miko. I thought you had more stomach for what needs to be done. You know things aren't going to get easier any time soon."

"Yes, sir."

As she left the headquarters ng to collect her belongings, Steiger couldn't help thinking that she might well be more useful to the rebellion in Tianjin.

The most direct route from Iskellian to the highlands ran right through it, as Decker had proven with his wild escape. One day, the rebels would have to strike in the other direction, hopefully in full force, and she intended to provide all the help she could from inside the enemy's walls.

When she climbed aboard the passenger pod a few hours later, it occurred to her that the rebellion had so far left the train line along the Yangtze River undamaged, unlike that which led from Iskellian south to Zeli. It had been hit hard by a raid two nights ago and would likely be out of commission for a while, cutting the capital off from quick access to its favorite resort and more importantly, the planet's second-largest spaceport.

Come to think of it, none of the lines leading to the other eastern districts had been hit either. Miko Steiger smiled at her reflection in the window as the train began moving. Now there was a thought she didn't intend to share with Rika Kozlev or anyone else.

**

Decker found Roste sitting on a rock not far from the back entrance to the fortress, staring at the carpet of stars stretching from horizon to horizon. He sat beside the man without bothering to ask for permission.

"Do your colleagues know you're taking money to make sure this little disagreement on Garonne's future turns into a bloody civil war?"

Though Zack's tone was conversational, it was a stab in the dark designed to unnerve the other man.

Talyn would likely have his balls if she found out about this little talk, but if got Roste to shut up and let them discuss the decapitation option at length, it would be worthwhile.

The rebel turned to stare at Decker, unsure that he'd heard right.

"What are you on about, asshole?"

"I've got a theory, see," Zack grinned at him. "There are folks out there, in the big, wide galaxy, going to a lot of expense, time and trouble to build up both sides of this family spat. At this rate, they'll make sure the lot of you can tear the planet apart to the point where it'll take three Marine divisions to sort out and an Army division or two to sit on Garonne for a generation. And I won't even mention the number of starships that'll be necessary to blockade the system."

"That's a big, stinky load of manure, Decker. How a clueless bugger like you ever became a pathfinder is beyond me."

Roste looked up at the stars again.

"Hear me out," the Marine continued. "This decapitation option, if it works, will end the war before it gets bloody enough for outside intervention. So I have to ask myself why a smart guy like you, with time in a soldier suit, won't even listen to it. Know what I answered myself?"

Roste shrugged. "Do I look like I care?"

"Of course you do. You want to know how much I figured out and with whom I've shared my thoughts."

He held up his hand and ticked off his fingers one by one.

"Going with the second item first, there's my partner Hera, of course; I share everything with her, including a lot of good times. There's Verrill and Corde because they hired me as a military advisor, so I advise, but I haven't yet brought this up with any of the others, out of respect for Verrill."

"And what did you tell them?"

A hint of fear had crept into Roste's voice. Zack smiled, knowing now that his stab in the dark had come dangerously close to the mark.

"My theory that says there's a possibility you and others on Garonne no doubt, might have been handsomely paid — or blackmailed — to make sure a small rebellion turns into a re-enactment of the last Migration War. Now, what do you think of that, eh?"

He gave Roste a comradely pat on the shoulder.

"I think you're full of it, Decker."

"Perhaps. I've been known to bark up the wrong tree pretty often, but my gut instinct is telling me you're the right tree this time. The question you have to ask yourself is what you're willing to risk as one of the guiding lights of the independence movement. Even if it turns out to be nothing more than a lot of hot air, your colleagues won't ever look at you the same way again once I speculate out loud. Your big mouth this morning has made sure of that."

He paused to let his words sink in.

"Now about the decapitation option, are you going to shut your yap and let the leadership think it over, or do I share my theory with everyone?"

"You're a right bastard."

"For your general fund of knowledge, you should be aware that my parents were married." Decker stood and looked down at the man. "Take the night to think about it. I'd like to resume the discussion after breakfast tomorrow."

Then, whistling an off-key tune, he returned to the ruins and the hunt for a cold beer. He had the feeling that he'd deserved one tonight. All he had to do until morning was make sure Hera didn't find out about his gross breach of protocol, orders and nearly everything the intelligence world held dear.

By noon the next day, with Roste still the sole, albeit muted dissenter, the inner council authorized detailed operational planning, to be completed within fourteen days. If they liked what they saw, preparations would be allowed to proceed.

**

That evening, when they were alone in their quarters, Talyn gave her partner the evil eye.

"Out with it," she ordered. "What did you do to Roste last night? He didn't change his attitude just because it's Tuesday. I checked the security recordings, and they show the two of you sitting by the back door having a fine old chat."

Decker's smile was a hair away from turning into a satisfied smirk.

"We talked about this and that. I shared a theory or two with him. All very companionable. He's actually a reasonable guy once you get to know him."

"Bullshit."

He shrugged. "Believe what you will."

"I could order you."

"To do what? Remove my clothes and await your pleasure? To quote a commander of my acquaintance: aye, aye, sir."

He pulled her against him and lowered his head to meet her lips.

— THIRTY-FIVE —

"What happened to us not taking an active part in the fighting?" Decker asked Talyn in a quiet voice. "You were pretty adamant that we remain hunter-gatherers. And anyway, it's not accounted for in the plan."

"You've read the same reports and seen the same videos as I have. Congratulations, I've finally come around to your point of view. I'm using my initiative as senior Commonwealth officer in the Garonne system on the premise that I can help bring about an outcome in the Fleet's best interests and not coincidentally limit the long-term damage to the colony."

"Besides," she smiled mischievously, "maybe my little surprise will make a difference when the almighty plan fails to survive contact with the enemy."

The two agents were alone in their quarters, packing what few belongings they owned before leaving, hopefully for good. The operations plan for the decapitation option had been ready in just over a week, and it had taken the inner council less than half a day to bless it, with some minor modifications.

In the four weeks since, they'd been forced to watch the situation across the colony deteriorate while the militia became more aggressive. Many moving parts had to be prepared, briefed, in some cases trained on new weapons and then pre-positioned.

Once the word was given, speed would be of the essence. Shock and awe, as Decker liked to remind everyone within earshot.

"Are you sure you can manage by yourself? I have to see this through with Verrill and the rest of them."

Talyn smiled at her partner.

"Your concern for me would be touching if I actually had a soul, big boy. But I won't be alone. Corde's got experience, and she volunteered, with Verrill's approval."

"So I'm the last to know? Nice."

He made a disgusted face.

"I figured you'd find reasons to object so I left it until now. And since futile arguments just before triggering an operation of this size don't help anyone, all you have left to do is give me a kiss, pat me on the ass if you feel generous and then join the command group. A long hike is staring me in the eyes and the sooner Corde and I get going, the longer I'll have to sort things out. I'll see you when it's over, one way or the other."

"Take care of yourself, commander, sir. If something happens to you, my universe is going to be a lot less interesting."

Talyn snorted.

"Maudlin's not your style, Zack. Besides, Captain Ulrich is capable of reaching beyond the grave and making my eternity thoroughly miserable for the sin of letting you loose on an unsuspecting galaxy without adult supervision. That's the one thing I really don't want to face, so I'll be extra careful."

She kissed Decker with a passion that surprised both of them, then she stepped back and inspected him one last time.

"Remember, Marine Boy, there's a big difference between 'duck' and 'fuck'; try not to confuse those two when the plasma's flying."

Zack came to attention and raised his hand to his eyebrow with military precision.

"Aye, aye, sir; see you on the other side. I'll be the one sitting on a throne of skulls waiting for you to serve me some cold Shrehari ale."

His last sight of Hera Talyn was her retreating back and a finger raised high in the rigid digit salute.

**

"You've made sure that your people understand what they're supposed to achieve, Captain?" Harend's eyes remained on the map projection, trying to find any last minute flaws in the planned operation.

"Very plainly, sir," Rika Kozlev replied. "I personally inspected them to make sure they could not be identified as militia members and Sergeant Major Bleyd personally checked them off on the captured mortars and guns. There's no chance it will be traced back to us."

"I'm not sure I share your confidence, Captain." Harend turned to look at Kozlev and Major Alegre, both standing in the parade rest position, hands joined in the small of the back. "Your people have been racking up a lot of failures lately. If I didn't know any better, I'd almost think we've been infiltrated by independence supporters."

"We almost certainly have," she replied smoothly. "Every insurgency spreads its tentacles into the security forces, but I'm sure of the people involved in this operation. It's fully compartmentalized. Not even Bleyd is aware of why we had him train the team on rebel weapons. By the time we're done, the rebellion will look like a bunch of yahoos with a talent for carelessly causing collateral damage."

"The propaganda feeds are ready?"

"Yes, sir," Alegre replied. "I've had the news releases prepared, the combat camera crew is standing by, and my proposal for the governor's statement is on your desk."

"Very well." Harend nodded. "You may launch the operation. By the time this is done, I hope a lot of colonists are going to rethink their support for an independence movement so inept it mortars the Holback children's hospital instead of the militia garrison down the block. If that goes off as planned, then we can target the Tianjin train terminal, this time making it look intentional."

"Have you told the governor yet?" Kozlev asked.

"He'll find out about the 'rebel' attacks at the same time as everyone else, and I'm sure he'll be the first to deplore civilian deaths in Holback. He may even shed a tear or two for the children."

**

"Every column has reported ready," Verrill said when Decker joined the command group at the foot of the ruined fortress. "Our lead elements are almost half-way to Tianjin. We'll soon see if our friends in the transport commission have lined up everything we need."

"Have we heard from Steiger?"

"Not directly, but she sent word via one of the sympathizers that everything is in place."

"Let's hope she and the diversion force deliver enough chaos to cover our loading the trains."

"I'm confident," Verrill replied, sounding anything but. Nervousness, now that the operation had been launched, was to be expected. Only a fool didn't worry about the outcome of an all-in strategy.

"Tran's company is already in position to strike once Miko gives the signal. Apparently the combat car you stole is still sitting where we left it."

"Really?" Decker's eyebrows shot up. "I didn't know the militia was so well armed they could afford to let one go."

"Perhaps they believe we took it deep into the highlands and didn't bother searching. In any case, Tran's men checked, and it still runs fine."

"Did they inspect for booby traps?"

"Yes, and they disabled the transponder. The ammo stocks aren't great, but we didn't plan on it still being there, so I consider that a bonus, just like Hera's little addition to the overall scheme."

"I'd hardly call that one little, but yeah. We'll use it to escort the lead train. If nothing else, it might throw off any curious official long enough to get by. But first we need to get to the station without the Tianjin garrison noticing, or at the very least sounding the alarm in Iskellian."

"Any last piece of advice?" Verrill asked before the command group stepped off and headed down a trail slowly turning blood red from the setting sun.

"If it moves, shoot it," Decker replied. "If it screams in Shrehari, shoot it again."

The joke drew appreciative chuckles from those who heard it, and Zack sensed a slight lightening of the mood. It almost made him feel like whistling an old fighting song, but he held back out of deference to the musical sensibilities of the others. He had never been able to carry a tune.

⁎⁎

As she had for several weeks, Steiger volunteered to take an extra turn as shift sergeant in the garrison operations center that night, claiming the quiet pace helped her work through the interrogation analyses she owed Captain Kozlev.

Her devotion to duty surprised no one, nor did the garrison commander question her wide-ranging authority. Kozlev's reputation had made sure of that.

Being pleasant and cheerful with the rank-and-file troopers did the rest. Some of them were decent folk who believed in colonial rule and opposed the rebellion on moral grounds. She'd be sorry to see them pay the price for wearing the dark green uniform.

Many, however, were in it for themselves, be it because of money, power or other venal inducements. She wouldn't be sorry to see those go. Working the field interrogator job had exposed her to the nastier side of the militia, and she'd had to use her rank and influence to limit the suffering inflicted on colonists, whether innocent or active guerrilla. But, she consoled herself, it would only be for a few more hours.

Steiger looked up from her console at the duty trooper, busily fighting off sleep with an immersive game he technically shouldn't be playing but for her indulgence.

Of course, it meant he wouldn't see any reports coming in from outlying patrols. They'd go straight to her, and the first of those might start flowing in any moment now.

**

Decker gently backed the combat car out of its hiding spot and set down on a flat piece of ground at the foot of the rapids. It now bore the symbol of the Garonne Independence Movement, a broken chain lying at the foot of a native silver fern. With any luck, colonists taking part in the armed uprising would recognize it as a sign that the combat car was manned by rebels and not use the roundel for an aiming point.

The heavy mortar battery, key to Operation Decapitation, was already loading at the freight terminal while Tran Kidder's company had effectively taken control of Tianjin proper after sweeping up any militia patrols they found, with the help of armed rebel sympathizers.

So far, thanks to Steiger, neither the local commander nor HQ in Iskellian was aware that they'd lost the town. It only had to remain that way for another eight hours, perhaps even less.

If they hadn't decapitated the Garonne colonial government by daybreak, the gamble would quickly turn into a protracted fight neither side could win.

Verrill climbed into the commander's seat beside Zack while a squad of heavily armed soldiers, the rebel commander's escort, filled the crew compartment.

"Nice of Steiger to assume the town commandant's job," Decker said grinning, his bared teeth white in the glow of the instrument panel. "It'll be even nicer once Tran overruns the garrison and links up with her. If one word gets to Iskellian about us coming out of the woodwork, so to speak, the buggers will have plenty of time to prepare."

"The attacks north and south of the capital in battalion strength should focus their interest," Verrill glanced at his timepiece, "starting in about three hours."

"Only if they don't realize they're diversions. At some point, the radio silence from Tianjin is bound to trigger some bright analyst's bullshit detectors."

An impish smile appeared on Verrill's face.

"If Tran can secure the entire garrison, he'll ask Steiger to simulate a panic that mirrors what'll come from Holback, Oshin, and the other targets."

"What is it today that people don't bother telling me about these changes to the plan," Decker grumbled.

"A last minute idea that Tran brought up just before he set out. He said it was something you'd do, given the chance."

"Hah." The Marine laughed. "That's what I get for having pulled the same crap on my superiors back in the day. Good luck to them, in that case."

He banked the combat car around a sharp curve, and then crossed the Yangtze River on a stone bridge that led straight into Tianjin.

Though the streets seemed quiet, Decker saw plenty of armed men and women standing in the shadows, watching and waiting.

They pulled into the freight yard through the open gate just as the last of the troops detailed to protect the mortar battery were climbing aboard personnel pods interspersed between the larger cargo pods from which the large caliber tubes would fire at their target.

When he'd ridden the rail weeks earlier, Decker had noticed that the pods could be opened not only on either side to make loading and unloading easier but also on top, and that's what had given him the first spark of an idea.

Bringing twelve of the heavy Shrehari artillery pieces within effective range of the government precinct, unseen, hidden inside a freight train turned mobile gun platform, lay at the heart of the plan. A passenger train would follow immediately behind, carrying a large assault force, while all over the settlement area, including within Iskellian itself, small groups of sympathizers, stiffened by guerilla detachments, answered the call to arms.

Decker landed the combat car on the roof of a passenger pod immediately behind the power unit and locked it in place with magnetic grapples.

Moments later, the long string of metallic pods began moving west along the single rail shimmering faintly under the light of the stars. After the requisite safety interval, the second train followed. Soon, both were traveling at maximum speed towards Iskellian and what would either be a new beginning for Garonne or the end of the independence movement.

**

A soft but insistent chime jerked Colonel Harend out of a dream that involved his taking command of the Celeste National Guard in a ceremony dripping with bizarrely barbarian splendor. He tapped the screen by his bed with a fingertip, glad that Kozlev had opted to sleep in her own quarters once they'd sated each other's appetite.

"What?"

"Sir, it's Major Alegre. I'm in the ops center. We've been receiving contact reports from all over the place. Patrols catching sight of colonists up and about in the middle of the night, traveling in groups and in some cases appearing armed."

Harend was instantly awake.

"From all garrisons?"

"Yes, sir."

He jumped out of bed and got dressed.

"Alegre, put everyone on alert. It may be nothing, and if it is, we'll call it a training exercise. I want a full report from each commanding officer."

"Do you think the rebels are preparing to attack, sir?"

"No, dammit they're just rehearsing for the next colony-wide half-marathon." He stared into the video pickup and snarled. "Of course the bastards are up to something. Wake the command group and call them together, then institute a radio check with each garrison every fifteen minutes."

"Acknowledged."

The screen went dark.

"Shit, shit, shit." Harend cursed while he fastened his tunic. "It's just my damn luck that the rebels are launching something at the same time as my first false flag operation."

When he entered the ops center, Major Alegre looked up, his face ashen.

"The Holback garrison just came under effective mortar attack, and some of their street patrols have been ambushed by armed rebel groups. They're screaming for assistance."

"Are we sure it's not our people who somehow forgot to dial in the right target?"

"The local CO says it feels heavy like it's not a hit and run but a sustained effort to knock them out, so I'd say no."

Harend went over to the map projection. Small red icons were rapidly popping up to mark the increasing number of spots where enemy contact had been and still was being reported. So far, it seemed localized in Holback, but it was bound to spread. Coordinating attacks over wide distances could be difficult even with the best commo gear, which the rebels didn't yet have.

He opened his mouth to ask for more details when Alegre, standing behind one of the duty operators' shoulder, spoke.

"Oshin now reports that it's under effective mortar attack as well, with patrols getting ambushed in the streets."

Kozlev stormed into the ops center and joined Harend by the map.

"What the heck is going on, sir? I'm getting screams from my operatives, warning that the rebels have triggered a general revolt."

"I thought you'd assured me no later than yesterday that all of the intelligence you've collected so far indicates the rebels don't have the numbers or the weight of weapons to risk throwing everything away on a premature rising."

He nodded at the map.

"So far, two district headquarters report coming under heavy fire. I expect to hear the same from Tianjin momentarily. In fact, I'm surprised it wasn't the first to be attacked, seeing as it's on the edge of bandit country."

Kozlev stared at her CO for a few seconds, and then shook her head.

"I'm willing to bet they seized Tianjin before the garrison could call for help. It's the one place at which they can throw the better part of their force." She turned to the operations officer. "When did Tianjin last report?"

"Fifteen minutes ago. Why?"

"Who was on the other end?"

"The duty sergeant, Steiger. One of yours I believe."

"And she reported nothing unusual? No rebel activity?"

"None."

Harend glanced at her with a grim expression.

"If you're about to tell me one of your specialists has gone over to the rebels or was one of them all along, spare me. Instead, figure out what the rebels' game is."

"Sir."

"What is it, Major?"

"The maglev line to Zeli's been cut again, this time very close to the terminus."

Kozlev's eyes roved over the map projection while she worked feverishly to put the pieces together.

"There can only be one answer," she finally said. "I don't know how they intend to do it, but we — Iskellian - are the actual target."

"What?" Harend sounded incredulous. "How is that even possible?"

"A famous intelligence officer from the time before spaceflight once said that if you remove the impossible, whatever's left, no matter how improbable, has got to be the answer." She pointed at red icons marking reported enemy activity. "See how..."

Her voice faded when red icons appeared in and around Tianjin.

"Fresh contact reports are now streaming in from Sergeant Steiger. Tianjin is under attack as well."

Alegre paused when a fresh red mark appeared along the Yangtze River.

"The transport commission reports that the eastern maglev line has been cut at the height of Odaran, where we had rebel activity a few weeks back during the escape."

"You were about to say, Captain?"

Anger was beginning to creep into Harend's tone.

"It can't be." Kozlev shook her head. "If Tianjin is now also under attack, it makes no sense, especially if they've cut the line."

"Pretend you didn't just hear about the new contact reports and spit it out."

"I was about to say," she sounded shaken, "that a rebel force seized Tianjin and is using its railhead to send a strong force downriver to attack us. Here. Everything else is just a diversion."

She whirled towards Alegre.

"Get patrols out into Iskellian. I need to know whether or not the locals are stirring."

"If that's actually the case, then why?"

"Decapitation," she whispered. "I don't know how they intend to do it with the forces they have, but that was the only answer before the latest reports came in."

"They've cut the maglev line," Alegre protested. "Why do that if you're aiming a significant force from the highlands straight at Iskellian?"

"Because," she said, "the report is either false, which means the transport commission has already passed over to the rebels, or they've well beyond Odaran. In fact, they could already be here. Do we have video from the yards?"

"Yes," Alegre said after checking with the duty technician. "It shows an unscheduled freight arriving."

He tried to call up a live feed.

"It's dead now."

"I guess that's our answer about the commission," Kozlev smirked. "Colonel, I believe Iskellian is under rebel attack."

"Get the rapid reaction company out to the train yards, now!" Harend's voice rose to a shout when the intelligence officer's words finally sank in.

"And sound the general stand-to."

"Sir," Alegre's voice had dropped to a whisper, "the entire sensor network is dead. We can't see what's happening anywhere."

— THIRTY-SIX —

"Ready?" Talyn smiled at Corde, now occupying Decker's old weapons station aboard *Phoenix*.

"As I'll ever be." She nodded nervously. "It's been a while since I touched one of these."

"Don't worry, gunnery isn't something you forget in a hurry, and the AI can help you."

A chime rang out as if the ship agreed.

"Doesn't your AI speak?"

Talyn laughed.

"It does, but Zack shut the vocal functions off."

"Why?"

Instead of answering, Talyn entered a string of commands, and a clear alto voice rang out.

"All systems ready, Captain."

"That's you, Hera!"

"Yup. Some wag programmed it with my voice and locked out any attempt to make changes. Zack said that one of me aboard was already one too many."

"The cheek of the man." Corde smiled, her earlier uneasiness gone.

"Meh." Talyn shrugged, smiling. "He's like fungus – he grows on you to the point where you not only can't get rid of him, you end up not wanting to try."

She turned on the main screen and then *Phoenix*'s landing lights to illuminate the cavern. A pair of rebel troopers, part of their escort from the base, raised light wands and waited. She briefly flicked the position lights on and off twice, the agreed-upon signal, and then fed power to the thrusters and antigrav units.

Though she'd vowed never to go through the ordeal of piloting an FTL-capable starship in such a tight space again, Talyn bit her lower lip and gently followed the ground guides until *Phoenix* was above the riverbed, where the opening was at its largest. From there, some gentle maneuvering brought them out into the open night air.

She set the ship down on the flat, broad riverbank once occupied by the now long gone freighters they'd escorted to Garonne and breathed in deeply.

"That, believe or not, was the hardest part of our mission. Now, we wait."

"You think it'll work?"

"If it starts going off the rail, so to speak, I can guarantee Zack will do everything he can. Other than that?"

She shrugged.

"He's good guy to have beside you in a fight, but a one-man army, he's not. A lot depends on how badly we surprise the militia."

**

Moments after the train came to a halt, pods disgorged armed rebel soldiers while, one after the other, roof hatches were flung aside to give the mortars hidden within a clear field of fire.

After making sure no militia soldiers lurked nearby, ready to pounce before the rebels had established a secure perimeter, Decker released the magnetic clamps and flew his combat car off the lead pod and down onto a wide gravel road running along the tracks.

The second train was due to stop several kilometers away in an area of warehouses fronting the river, not far from the government precinct, and that's where they needed to be for the assault.

"The forward observers are in place," Verrill said after listening to a muted radio transmission, "and the battery is ready to fire."

"Crap," he said a moment later, "a column of cars just emerged from the compound – estimated to be at company strength."

"This is where the plan starts fighting for survival," Decker replied, gunning his fans when they came out of a sharp curve and onto the main road cutting through town.

"I'll bet they picked up on the mortar train. Our friends in the commission may have waited too long before cutting the yard's security sensors."

"I've warned them," Verrill said moments later.

"All fine and dandy, but combat cars against dismounted troops isn't what you'd call an even fight. Our best bet is to launch the attack now and make chaos our friend."

They reached the spot where the assault battalion had disembarked only to find a small rear party waiting for them.

"Alfa and Charlie companies are across the river on the upstream bridge and advancing to the target," the battalion executive officer reported, "Bravo and Delta companies are beginning to cross downstream. The locals have taken down any militia patrols they came across, so I don't think the alarm's been sounded yet."

"It'll sound any second now," Decker replied. "They know we're here. A rapid reaction force is heading for the yards. They just haven't figured out yet how we'll do it to them. Where do you want us?"

"I'd suggest the downstream crossing."

"Works for me," Decker replied. "Works for you, Verrill?"

The rebel leader nodded.

"I guess we leave our car here?"

"Not much use to us at this point." He touched the XO's arm. "The thing's yours. Feel free to deploy it as you see fit. I'd suggest the park right across the river from the precinct. Clearest field of fire you could want; though I'd advise you to rig the weapons station for remote firing. No sense in risking one of your guys inside the damned tin can."

At that moment, heavy gunfire erupted to their left, and all hell broke out over the radio.

"Sounds like the militia combat cars ran right into Bravo and Delta," Decker said. "If Alfa and Charlie are within range of the target, I suggest the mortar battery open up now."

**

"Time." Talyn checked her seat harness. "Make sure you're strapped in tight. Flying this close to the surface is going to make things rocky."

"Already done," Corde replied.

The captain and sole pilot of the smallest Q-ship in the Navy flicked on her thrusters, sending shivers through the hull. *Phoenix* immediately broke contact with the ground and rose slowly above the shallow riverbed. Talyn retracted the landing struts and then sent power to the aft thrusters, flying them upwards and out of the narrow valley. Almost immediately, the radio came to life with frantic messages on the government frequencies.

"Sounds like the party's started," she said, banking the small starship to starboard and Iskellian. "You can spool up the calliopes, but keep the main guns at weapons tight. I don't want to increase the risk of collateral damage, especially since my partner is going to be somewhere below us, no doubt leading the charge."

**

"We're getting reports of armed groups moving through Iskellian." Alegre paused to regain some of his composure. "And we've lost contact with a lot of the regular patrols."

Suddenly, the radio erupted with a string of shouts punctuated by the sound of gunfire and the screams of men who'd been shot.

"HQ, this is RRC," the rapid reaction company commander sounded as scared as Alegre looked, "we've run into a large hostile force blocking the downstream bridge and are taking heavy fire. We can't get across."

"Estimated strength?" Alegre asked.

"A battalion, maybe a bit less," came the reply.

"How did they get a battalion so close without anyone noticing?" Harend turned on Kozlev. "It can't have come from the train yards. There wouldn't have been enough time."

The intelligence officer stared at the map projection while chewing on the inside of her cheek.

"A second train from Tianjin. It can only have been a second train, one which stopped around here." She pointed at a spot near the center of Iskellian, between both main bridges. "Thanks to the traitors at the transport commission, we never saw it arrive. If they have a couple of companies trying to force their way across the downstream bridge, there has to be something crossing upstream. Not using the easier route when you're ready to throw a major force at the most densely built-up spot in the downtown area just wouldn't make sense."

"Why haven't we picked anything up yet?"

"Because you haven't been looking, Major," Kozlev snarled. "With the surveillance network down, you need to get eyes on our east flank, and I mean actual eyes, not a fresh batch of sensors – they've been singularly unreliable tonight."

"What actually came in on that first train, I wonder?" She tapped her chin with extended fingers.

Chaos, Decker's best friend for the night, was spreading his dark wings over Garonne's capital. Things were about to get much worse, and only Rika Kozlev had an inkling of what was coming.

"Crap." Her eyes widened in shock when she made the final connection. "Colonel, the unscheduled train that we saw entering the yards carries their indirect fire support. It has to. There's no other reason to send it there instead of..."

Harend held up a hand to silence her when he heard a sound he knew only too well.

Moments later they heard another pair of muted crumps, the second ranging salvo.

"There's your answer, Captain," he whispered, mentally ticking down the seconds before impact. "The freight train carried a heavy mortar battery."

Then, the center of the government precinct erupted in gouts of flame, earth, and stone.

**

Decker, Verrill, and their escort joined up with the commander of Bravo Company on the south side of the river, at a spot where they could see both the near battle for control of the bridge and the brooding mass of dark buildings that marked their target. No sooner had they arrived that the first rounds landed, lighting up the night.

"Perfect," Decker smiled like a proud father. After all, he'd overseen gunnery training. "When your first shots are on target, the fight is almost over."

As if the forward observers had heard him, a voice on the radio ordered the mortar battery to fire for effect seconds later.

Within moments, twelve one-hundred-and-twenty millimeter rounds fell less than a thousand meters away, turning night into day.

The troopers of the rapid reaction company, caught between two conflagrations and already staggering under the sustained fire of two dozen rebel machine guns, wavered for a few seconds, then the combat cars furthest away from the engagement, turned tail and sped west along the riverbank, away from the main action. It was enough to cause a general rout.

Bravo and Delta companies surged across, Decker hot on their heels, carbine held at the high port as he ran. A second salvo came thundering in, and the earth shook beneath his feet. Then a third.

The moment he stepped onto the north bank of the Yangtze River, now bright with the reflection of bursting shells, Zack heard a familiar voice on the special radio channel.

"Rookie Trooper, this is *Phoenix*. We're inbound and can see the center of the target. No need to mark, just have the assault force hold in place and suspend the mortar fire."

"Roger. Wait, out." He nudged Verrill and passed on the news that their air support was almost here to help deliver the deathblow.

Then, when the orders had been duly transmitted and acknowledged, Decker called Talyn.

"You're weapons free over the target. The last mortar salvo is about to...there it is. Have fun."

He looked towards the east, squinting until he could detect an approaching shape, dark against the night sky and no more than five hundred meters above the ground. It grew larger at an alarming rate, to the sound of a deep roar that threatened to overwhelm the noise of battle.

"There she is." He pointed at the sudden eruption of small-bore plasma rounds stitching a wide swath of super-heated ruin across the heart of the government precinct.

"Oo-RAH!" Decker shouted when a combat car, parked near the governor's mansion, exploded in a fireball of molten alloy, adding to the damage already inflicted on the building's facade.

Then, with an ear-splitting rumble, the starship's bulk passed over them and momentarily blotted out the sky. The keel calliope slewed all the way back, kept up a steady stream of fire while *Phoenix* withdrew towards the western horizon.

A new mortar salvo whistled in, though, at this point, Zack figured they were mostly bouncing the rubble.

Verrill must have had the same thought because he gave the order to advance over the now shredded security perimeter and seize what was left of the Garonne colonial government and its militia.

With the artillery storm over, Decker gave into his urges and sprang forward with the lead company. A wolfish grin spread across his face when he heard the wail of pipes to his right, where Alfa and Charlie companies had overrun weak militia resistance.

He saw a shadow move behind a ruined second-floor window and snap-fired two rounds. A militia light machine gun began to chatter on the left, and a few rebel troopers went down, screaming.

Decker's eyes tracked the flash of the weapon's muzzle, and he shot back, pumping a dozen rounds into the dark recess where the militia soldiers had holed up. He heard them die noisily before he clambered over the debris of a wall blown down by a direct hit.

Once past the outer row of buildings, he saw a sight that made him smile so broadly it almost went from ear to ear. The center of the government precinct was no more than a burning ruin.

Chaos had indeed done good business in Iskellian this night.

Verrill finally caught up with him and laid a restraining hand on his shoulder.

"My people can take care of the rest without you, Zack. It would be a shame to catch the last militia round of the mopping-up operation. Hera would have my guts for garters if that happened and I'm a lot more scared of her than I am of you."

**

Landing at the Iskellian spaceport had turned out to be a lot easier than taking off, once Talyn had talked down an indignant controller with a brief demonstration of firepower.

Finding a ground car to take her and Corde into town to rejoin the rebel forces proved to be a lot more difficult, though, in the end, they commandeered the personal vehicle of the self-same controller, leaving him to examine *Phoenix* in wonderment.

Their trek took them through the streets filled with throngs of civilians, both curious and jubilant, some exacting vengeance for years of insults from the colonial administration by setting fire to deportee slums, abandoned militia posts, and government offices.

The far horizon began to show a line of increasingly pale pink, heralding the start to a day of reckoning, while by the river, in the gray city within a city, the independence movement's rage burned itself out.

They passed through the rebel cordon sealing off the area and were directed to the remains of the governor's mansion where Verrill had set up his headquarters.

Talyn found Zack sitting on a step partially shredded by the exploding combat car, chewing thoughtfully on a ration bar. Around him, Verrill and the rebel officers dealt with the aftershock of the decapitation operation: rounding up prisoners, seizing intelligence, taking care of the wounded, stacking up the dead and sending orders to rebel units still battling the militia in outlying districts.

His face was creased with fatigue, his battledress was covered in dust, and the charred mark of a near miss creased one arm, but he smiled when he saw her and patted the stone beside him.

"How's my air support?" He asked, leaning over to kiss her.

"Apparently getting a good whiff of your goat smell, mister," she replied after coming up for air, "although I suppose I'm no better."

"I like you down and dirty, don't forget." Decker held out a second ration bar. "I know you get as horny and hungry as me after a fight, but this will have to do for now."

She bit off a chunk and examined the plaza separating the mansion from militia headquarters in the growing light of dawn.

"I think we may have gone at it harder than we needed to," she remarked.

"Restraint in war is the ultimate perversion."

"Is that a Deckerism?" She asked, accepting his water bottle.

"Probably, but it's been proven right more often than not. The Celeste government won't say boo when the matter of Garonne independence is put before the Senate, not after they see pictures of what the supposedly weak and uncoordinated rebel movement did to its lackeys." He jerked his chin at the ruins.

"A few love taps, just enough to take control, wouldn't have had the same effect. I think we did well, all things considered."

"True," she nodded after considering his words. "Mind you, we still don't have any evidence who was pouring in all that money to trigger a bloody civil war."

"Also true." He shrugged. "We'll share our pet theories with the analysts when we get home, and they can think it through. At least we made sure the bastards weren't able to ruin Garonne, and I figure that's called a successful mission."

"Captain Ulrich might disagree."

"So what? I told him I'd give this gig a year. The year's up. He decides to kick my ass out of the section for going rogue, he's welcome. I can find myself a good billet in a lot of units where I don't have to be the man of many faces, none of them mine."

She was about to reply when the commo unit linking her to *Phoenix* beeped.

"Who knows your number around here?" Decker asked.

Talyn slipped an earpiece on and opened the link, listening for almost a minute before shutting it off.

"*Mikado*'s arrived in-system with your parakiting buddies. She'll call again when she's about to slip into orbit."

"That should give the Avalon sloops a few nervous hiccups."

"I think by now they know there's been a change in ownership, so they'll no doubt be very careful."

"Why would Ulrich send in the Marines?" Decker mused before biting into an apple he'd pulled out of his pack. "I'm already here, sorting things out properly."

She chuckled.

"The boss may be freakily good when it comes to our business, but he doesn't have precognition that I know of. He'll have asked SOCOM to dispatch someone a few weeks ago, and SOCOM, in turn, sent folks who are used to your little explosions of creativity."

"As long as I can welcome Ryent and Vanleith in proper style, I'm happy."

"No doubt." She playfully jabbed an elbow in his ribs. "Just make sure it doesn't offend each and every morals law on the planet, will you? I don't want to be summarily run off before we have a chance to sift through whatever Verrill's men have captured."

"Speaking of running, how's *Phoenix*? Can we ride her home as she is?"

"Probably, but I'd still like to have a proper engineer look her over. She took more damage than we thought from the Avalon ships."

"I'm sure your buddy running *Mikado* will lend you his."

"Actually," she stood and wiped the dust from her buttocks. "I'd be even happier if he sent a few of his people to crew *Phoenix* while we take the long way home. Sailing a starship single-handed loses its charm after a while."

"The way I remember things, you weren't single-handed. I was doing most of the stuff not involving the arcane and ancient mysteries of astrogation."

Decker stood as well after tucking his water bottle away.

"You know what I mean, big boy." A weary, yet fond smile softened her features. "Flying that little monster in and out of places not designed as hangars gets old fast."

One of Verrill's troopers jogged up to them.

"The boss wonders whether you'd like to join him in inspecting the prisoners."

He waved towards an open area in the northwest corner of the precinct that had been largely spared by both mortar and starship.

A cruel grin twisted Decker's lips.

"Oh, would I ever. There's a certain militia captain I'd like to nominate for summary execution on a charge of war crimes."

— THIRTY-SEVEN —

The rebels had erected a makeshift stockade using the precincts own fences. Row upon row of men and women in green militia uniforms to one side, and in civilian clothes to the other, sat on the damp grass under the watchful eye of machine gunners set at each corner.

Verrill met them by the entrance, looking like he'd aged fifty years overnight.

"We've got the top leadership that survived, thank God. My folks haven't started processing them yet, but I'm hoping I can convince someone with sufficient rank, military or civilian, to convince the rest of them in the outlying districts it's time to surrender."

"The fighting's still going on?"

"Pretty much everywhere except Tianjin, thanks to Miko, though the government's utter defeat should be obvious even to the dumbest militia trooper. I just want to stop the killing."

"Maybe some are fighting on because they figure your people will string them up the moment they put down their guns."

"A not unreasonable fear, considering recent history." The rebel leader shrugged.

Decker gripped Verrill's shoulder.

"I don't know if it's sunk in yet, but absent any other claimant, you're the interim president of the provisional Republic of Garonne now. You need to set the tone for this planet's future, and if it's to be one built on a foundation of law, you need to make sure all prisoners are treated in accordance with the Rules of War, tried fairly by a court and if found guilty, punished accordingly. And if your own people don't want to obey, you also need to deal with them for violations of the Rules."

"The surest way to get Fleet intervention on Garonne and years of martial law," Talyn added, "is by going rogue. The surest way to get Fleet backing against those still wanting to deny your claim for independence is by being better and cleaner than the colonial government you just replaced."

Verrill nodded.

"I know. I just feel a bit overwhelmed right now."

"Then delegate until you have enough time on your hands for a day at the beach," Decker replied, grinning. "Cleaning up after a successful decapitation and setting up a new government is going to be a lot harder than anything you've done up to now."

He nodded towards the stockade.

"If you're open to another piece of advice, find some of the colonial administration's better people, the ones who haven't bloodied their hands, and hire them. I wouldn't be surprised if a lot don't want to go back to Celeste and face the music. Hell, hire Cedeno as your advisor, if you can stomach it. There's a guy who knows how to run this place and who probably doesn't have any appetite to go home."

"None of my inner council would stand for it," Verrill objected.

"Bugger them. You're the president now, not first among peers. If Garonne goes to crap after today, it'll be on you, not them."

A small sigh escaped Verrill's lips.

"I'll think about it." He waved towards the stockade. "Do you wish to examine the prisoners?"

Zack nodded. "There are a few people I need to sort out."

The rebel leader looked at him curiously, then motioned his men to open the makeshift gate.

Decker ignored the civilians after glancing at a bedraggled ex-Governor Cedeno, looking more composed than one would expect and the still elegant woman by his side.

He had no problems identifying ex-Colonel Cen Harend or ex-Captain Rika Kozlev.

The former commanding officer of the Garonne militia sneered at the Marine when Zack stopped to examine him.

"You have no idea what's going to happen to you, rebel scum." Harend's voice was raspy, damaged by the fumes and smoke of battle. "Celeste is going to petition the Senate to send in the Fleet and restore the rightful government. You'll find Marines don't mess around with the likes of you. When that happens, I'll gladly see you hang."

Decker smiled and leaned down to whisper in Harend's ear.

"I'm Chief Warrant Officer Zachary Decker, Commonwealth Marine Corps, senior ground forces officer on Garonne. The Marines have been here all along and approve of this change in government so there won't be any hangings unless President Verrill decides to institute the death penalty, in which case, you'll be at the head of the list."

He stepped back to watch Harend's reaction to his startling announcement and, as expected, the man turned a lovely shade of puce, struggling to speak.

Decker leaned down again.

"The lady over there, standing with Verrill – she's the senior naval officer in the Garonne system and my CO. Between the two of us, I'm the nice one. My advice to you is don't piss her off."

Laughing, he walked down the row of prisoners until he was level with Kozlev.

She looked at him with such disinterest that he shook his head, snorting.

"Remember me? The guy you wanted to geld just to see if my conditioning would take that as a reason to initiate cardiac arrest?"

Decker pulled his dagger from its forearm sheath.

"For all the crimes you've committed, no one would blame me if I executed you here and now."

The blade flashed in the morning sun, and Talyn tensed. After Decker's speech about rules and due process, killing even a psychopath like Kozlev would make his words ring hollow.

Zack grabbed Kozlev's hair and yanked her head back, exposing her pale throat. Then his blade came down, and a collective gasp rose from the watching soldiers.

Kozlev screamed, but when Decker let go of her head, instead of a carotid artery spurting blood, all they could see was a thin red line under her jaw. He flicked a crimson droplet from the tip of his blade and then wiped it on her shoulder before sheathing the dagger.

"I claim coup."

With that, he walked away from a sobbing Kozlev, to Talyn and Verrill's relief.

**

"Are you sure you have to leave now?"

"We are, Mister President."

Decker finished the last of Harend's Glen Arcturus whiskey, recovered from the ex- colonel's quarters, and smacked his lips.

"If you have a case of this stuff stashed away somewhere, I might try to convince Hera we need a holiday on Garonne, but not here. The air is still too thick."

Even after three days, the smell of smoke hung heavily over Iskellian, a reminder of the violent night that had ended colonial rule.

To the surprise of everyone but Decker, ex-Governor Cedeno had been able, at Verrill's behest, to talk the last militia holdouts into surrendering a few hours earlier. The Garonne insurrection was officially over.

"Sorry," Verrill smiled. "But if you're ever in these parts again, I'll be sure to have some on hand."

Talyn's commo link beeped for attention, and she raised her hand briefly.

"I think that's our business associates, telling us they're in orbit, which means we should get to the spaceport."

She listened to the message via her earpiece and nodded.

"Time to go."

"In that case, the only thing left for me to do is thank you on behalf of all colonists no matter what side they were on. We'll always be in your debt."

Decker waved away his thanks.

"Just make sure we don't have to come back and pull your ears, buddy."

"Count on it." Mischief appeared in the interim president's eyes. "I'd introduce you to my new advisor, but he's busy recruiting some capable administrators from the bunch in the stockade. Apparently, the Celeste government isn't known for its mercy towards those who fail, especially governors."

"What about Harend and Kozlev?" Talyn asked.

The mischief turned to merriment.

"I'm sending all of the Celeste National Guard folks home on the next freighter, securely shackled in a cargo hold. Cedeno tells me the punishment they'll get from their own is going to be worse than anything we can do. Those who were recruited here will get a chance to clear out new settlement areas to expiate their crimes, along with any deportees unwilling to take the jobs on offer. Their free money from Celeste is gone, and we're not about to replace it with free Garonne money."

"Good plan." Decker held out his hand. "Take care, Verrill. Give Miko Steiger a kiss for me. I know she's doing good work up in Tianjin right now, but she'll get bored and when she does, let her know she can look us up."

"Will do."

"Always keep in mind that we'll be back to check up on you some day, so make sure you do it right. Maybe you'll see us, maybe you won't, depending on Hera's mood, but if she's unhappy with you..."

Zack's grin finished the sentence for him.

"Understood." Verrill nodded soberly. "Godspeed to both of you."

**

"What's the deal?" Decker asked once they were standing alone on the tarmac beside *Phoenix*'s imposing bulk, staring at the darkening sky for a hint of *Mikado*'s shuttle.

"Tom's sending down a crew to fix whatever ails our old girl and sail her home. We're taking a cruise on *Mikado* where I'm sure your buddy and mine, Kal Ryent, will debrief us extensively. HQ won't want to wait until we're on Caledonia for that."

"Provided the bar's well stocked, I'm up for a few days of intercourse and intoxication."

"You would be." She nudged him in the ribs with her elbow.

"It's a shame we couldn't arrange for a few quiet hours with Harend or Kozlev and see what they know about rich uncles who enjoy a good civil war."

"It would have been a waste of time. I doubt they know anything more than Roste did."

"I guess." Decker nodded. "Do you think they'll ever find his body?"

"Buddy, when I make someone disappear, they stay that way. Notice how even Verrill has stopped wondering?"

"Remind me to never piss you off. I'd rather not have an 'accident' on my way home."

Talyn touched his arm and smiled.

"You piss me off every day without fail. There must be something wrong with me that I've tolerated you for so long."

"That would be the fault of the old Decker charm, baby."

"No. It's probably got more do with the fact that I have a weakness for strays."

Zack bared his teeth and mimed biting her.

"Later, honey." She blew him a kiss. "We don't want to scandalize the locals. Besides, I think that's our ride."

She pointed at a boxy, unmarked shuttle on final approach.

"It looks like one of *Mikado*'s."

And it was.

The dull little craft landed beside *Phoenix* and disgorged a half dozen spacers in civilian clothes. One of them walked over to the agents while the others hauled crates out onto the tarmac.

"I'm Fong, the guy who'll be taking this little beauty back to where it belongs. I've read the status report, but is there anything else I should know?"

"Yeah. The Shrehari ale in the cooler is mine, but you can have it. Just ignore the heel marks on the ceiling of the master cabin."

Fong laughed and then waved towards the shuttle.

"If that was all, your chariot is ready to spirit you up into the heavens. The skipper and Kal Ryent are eagerly waiting. Apparently, overstepping mission parameters to the extent you've done is a bit of a novelty for our lords and masters, and they're impatient to hear the full story. Whether it's because they'd like to distill the essence and replicate it on other planets or as evidence for your upcoming court-martial, I don't know."

"You're a funny guy, Fong; I like that," Decker clapped him on the shoulder, "but a word of advice. My partner's sense of humor tends to the painful rather than the cheerful."

"Noted." He sketched a mock salute and joined his crew at the foot of the small starship's belly ramp.

When they climbed aboard the shuttle, a youthful face peered out from the cockpit.

"Welcome aboard, Commander Talyn, Major Decker. I'll have you aboard *Mikado* in no time. Just grab a seat and strap in."

Zack's head swiveled slowly to the left so he could lock eyes with Talyn.

"*Major* Decker?" He growled. "Is it because that young pup up front can't tell a working Marine from a bloody officer or did you do something to ruin my reputation?"

"It's a well-deserved promotion, Zack." Talyn managed to look both solemn and naughty at the same time. "I found out just before we left Verrill's temporary palace that my recommendation had been rammed through by the Chief of Naval Intelligence in person. Apparently, the Marine Corps had some hesitation when the request for an out of sequence promotion was first submitted to the Commandant's office."

"What the hell did I ever do to piss off the CNI, eh? It's a fine way to repay a guy from getting damn near killed every time he leaves Caledonia for the big, wide galaxy on the Fleet's business."

"Oh quit grousing. You have more experience leading troops in combat than many majors in the Corps. Anyway, somewhere, deep inside, I know you're pleased as punch you'll finally be able to flip the bird at the human toothaches who kicked you when you were down. Who knows, you might even run across that moronic captain you smacked for being stupid, and he'd be forced to salute you."

"Oh crap," Decker replied after a few moments. A look of pure anguish came over his face, and he didn't speak while the shuttle lifted off and raced towards orbit. "I'm going to kill that bastard."

"Who?"

"Kal Ryent. I'll bet my next paycheck he engineered it so I'd have to pay the promotion round to *Mikado*'s saloon and senior enlisted mess. It'll cost me a bloody fortune."

"Don't bet your next paycheck; just use it to buy the round. I'd have thought a field grade officer could do simple logic problems. Maybe I should tell the CNI that I was wrong and have them rescind your commission.”

“Would you, pretty please?” A puppy-like look filled his eyes.

“Not even on a dare.” She stuck her tongue out at him. “Now shut up and enjoy the ride, *Major* Decker. Only lieutenants are allowed to whine.”

“Hey wait a minute,” he said when her quip about logic finally registered. “If I bet that Kal did it, and he didn’t I lose the paycheck. If I just go ahead and buy the round without betting, I lose the paycheck anyway. If Kal did it, I win the bet but still have to buy the round. That’s not logic, it’s bloody robbery.”

“Now you’re thinking like a senior officer.” She patted his arm. “Captain Ulrich will be so proud of you – after he tears you a new one for not only failing to complete the mission he gave us but also for providing Fleet support to a bunch of rebels.”

“You’ll be getting reamed out right along with me. But if we get a week or two in the section’s beach house to relax...”

“Don’t count on it. He doesn’t like his agents to go on leave with unfinished business hanging over them. Enjoy the time we have during our transit home.”

“After I get most of the 251st Pathfinder Squadron drunk on my coin. They’re capable of ruining even the bit of downtime we’ll get if they think I’ve stiffed them. Pathfinders are a nasty bunch.”

“Don’t I know it?” Her peal of laughter echoed through the small compartment. Zack winked at his partner and then sat back with an expression of immense satisfaction softening his features.

“You know,” he said, “all things considered, it’s been a successful mission, except for the minor matter of not figuring out who tried to stir up a small colonial war.”

“True.” She patted his hand. “But I wouldn’t worry. I’m sure the Coalition will give us a reason to go after them again soon enough.”

“That’s what I’m afraid of.”

“Why?”

"Because I'll be stuck with intelligence until the day I die. You guys can't organize a piss-up in a brewery, let alone stop a conspiracy in its tracks."

"Perhaps, but the universe wouldn't survive your return to a regular Marine unit, Major Decker, so you'll just have to grin and bear it."

"Aye, aye, Commander, sir, and on that note, may I ask if you've ever kissed a commissioned Marine before?"

"I have, but never by a major pain in the butt like you."

"Then it's time to rectify that little oversight."

He leaned over and took her chin between his thumb and forefinger.

"You'd never survive without me, honey."

About the Author

Eric Thomson is the pen name of a retired Canadian soldier with thirty-one years of service, both in the Regular Army and the Army Reserve. He spent his Regular Army career in the Infantry and his Reserve service in the Armoured Corps. He currently works as an Information Technology specialist.

Eric has been a voracious reader of science fiction, military fiction, and history all his life. Several years ago, he put fingers to keyboard and started writing his own military sci-fi, with a definite space opera slant, using many of his own experiences as a soldier for inspiration.

When he's not writing fiction, Eric indulges in his other passions: photography, hiking, and scuba diving, all of which he shares with his wife.

Join Eric Thomson at:

http://www.thomsonfiction.ca/

where you'll find news about upcoming books and more information about the universe in which his heroes fight for humanity's survival.

Read his blog at:

https://ericthomsonblog.wordpress.com

If you enjoyed this book, consider leaving a review on Goodreads or with your favorite retailer to help others discover it.

Also by Eric Thomson

Siobhan Dunmoore
No Honor in Death (Siobhan Dunmoore Book 1)
The Path of Duty (Siobhan Dunmoore Book 2)
Like Stars in Heaven (Siobhan Dunmoore Book 3)
Victory's Bright Dawn (Siobhan Dunmoore Book 4)
Without Mercy (Siobhan Dunmoore Book 5)

Decker's War
Death Comes But Once (Decker's War Book 1)
Cold Comfort (Decker's War Book 2)
Fatal Blade (Decker's War Book 3)
Howling Stars (Decker's War Book 4)
Black Sword (Decker's War Book 5)
No Remorse (Decker's War Book 6)
Hard Strike (Decker's War Book 7)

Quis Custodiet
The Warrior's Knife (Quis Custodiet N° 1)

Ashes of Empire
Imperial Sunset (Ashes of Empire #1)